THE LADY AND HER SECRET

THE LADY OF BOHEMIA, BOOK 4

SARA R. TURNQUIST

MOUNTAIN
SUMMIT PRESS

If you would like to stay up-to-date on this and all other series from Sara:

https://saraturnquist.com/list

For my History teachers,
who inspired me more than even I realized.

PROLOGUE

The year is 1421. The future of the Kingdom of Bohemia is in question. It has been six years since Jan Hus was burned at the stake for his objections to practices in the Catholic Church, sparking the Hussite Wars. The Royalist Catholic army is commanded by Holy Roman Emperor Sigismund, who has a voracious desire after the Czech crown. This army of mercenaries and foreigners faces off with a cobbled together Hussite army. Despite overwhelming odds against them, the Hussites have seen a series of victories. Surely the Lord is with them.

During these dark days, Pavel, Zdenek, and Radek find the women to whom they pledged their lives. Though these brave men fight on the side of the Hussites, their friend Stepan has sworn his services to the Royalist army.

Pavel and Karin have found a lasting love. However, that has not meant all is well. Having lost their first child to miscarriage, they found joy in the birth of their second child. In the midst of these challenges, Karin's wellbeing remains uncertain after a difficult labor. This comes on the heels of Pavel's father's death at the hands of a vicious Royalist. While Pavel has returned to the front, but concern for the safety of his wife and child, as well as his mother, follow him into battle. The Krejiks' castle, lost to a fire, is now being returned to its former glory.

Zdenek and Eva continue to fight on the side of the Hussites, though his father scorns the very idea. Still, they seek to do the Lord's will for their lives. Even if that means his father will disown him. And so, after a failed attempt to right his relationship with his father, Zdenek and his wife Eva rejoin the Hussite effort.

Radek and Hana have been through much. Though he initially struggled with the happenings at war—questioning the great Hussite general, Jan Zizka, and some of his tactics—Radek found he could not support the Royalists either. After rescuing Hana from certain death as a prisoner in the Royalist camp, the two hope for their happily ever after. Only one thing stands in the way—Radek's uncertain relationship with his father. Leaving Hana in the care of her father, Baron Novak, he trudges to Horice in hopes of making peace at home.

Stepan struggles with the numerous horrendous things he has witnessed and experienced at war. So much death weighs on his conscience. And even more so, the memory of those who fell by his hand. But he is determined to push forward. Perhaps his father, Viscount Dvorak, will finally grant his son the favor he so desperately seeks.

Patricie has found her purpose in utilizing the knowledge of herbs and healing taught by her departed mother. She now serves as an apprentice to the Hussite army healer. And she couldn't be happier for her sister, Eva, who has found happiness at last. But there is the dream and hope for her own happily ever after.

And now, the continuation...

THE KINGDOM OF BOHEMIA DURING THE HUSSITE WARS

CHAPTER 1
KARIN & PAVEL

Singing greeted Karin as she awoke—a soothing lullaby. Bright light filled her vision, a harsh contrast to the gentleness of the melody. Where was she? What time of day was it?

Her eyes adjusted to the sunlight in the room, and she remembered. She had been settled in chambers within Duke Novak's castle. This room in which she labored and nearly died became her only refuge. Her return to health had been taxing and long. So long.

She turned in the direction of the voice. A maidservant sat, rocking a baby. Karin's vision cleared as she blinked. It was *her* baby. Hers and Pavel's.

A weak smile spread Karin's lips but slightly. God was good. She had been to the very brink of death. And survived. As had her son. It was a long-fought victory, due in no small part to many prayers lifted on her behalf.

The nursemaid continued to sway and bounce the small bundle. After several seconds, her gaze drifted to Karin. And the older woman startled. Was she so surprised to see that Karin had awakened?

"My lady," the woman said as she stood and drew near. "How do you fare?"

Karin closed her eyes and made an inventory of her body, taking care as she shifted her limbs to assess their state. A sharp pang stole her breath when her movements reached her abdomen. Beyond that, a dull ache seemed to pervade her whole being. Despite this, she found only gratitude. "All is well. There is some discomfort, but I cannot complain."

The woman's brow furrowed.

Just then, the babe cried, distracting them both from any further discussion.

The servant's warm brown eyes met Karin's above the babe's blue ones that squeezed shut. "I think he is hungry."

Karin nodded. "Help me sit." She maneuvered her arms to pull herself upward.

"My lady," the woman protested as she took another step toward Karin. "I can fetch the wet nurse, I—"

"No." The word was not gentle. They had been through this. It was a kindness to be sure, but Karin wished to care for her child in this way.

The nursemaid frowned.

"I assure you; I am well enough." Karin grimaced against renewed pains, due in no small part to her movements. "Just help me."

The older woman set the babe on the bed—several inches from the side—and turned to assist her mistress.

But the infant's wails intensified.

With features drawn, the nursemaid stepped back toward the infant. Then to Karin. Only to turn back to the child.

"Please," Karin seethed. "Make haste!" She had not the time nor the patience in the moment for the woman's well meaning but confused intentions.

Proving herself capable, the woman helped Karin raise herself into a seated position. Then propped a pillow behind Karin's back.

"Now, my son." Karin motioned for the babe.

"Aye, my lady." The servant scooped up the infant and brought him over.

Though Karin's arms felt weak and useless when she lifted them, she downplayed the pain as the nursemaid laid the child in them.

Moments later, and with a bit of maneuvering, the babe nursed and was content once more.

Karin sighed and let her head fall back. Why must everything be so challenging? She parted her lips to ask that Pavel be summoned. But she stopped herself before the words formed. Her husband had returned to the heightened conflict with the Royalist army. The war hadn't stopped because of her delivery and subsequent difficult recovery.

Sigismund still grasped for control over the Czech lands. And the power he had lost in their forfeit. And so, a month past, he marched back into Bohemia in an attempt to retake ground previously lost. Even now, General Zizka—completely blinded in his last battle—led the Hussites to intercept the would-be king and his army. Zizka's men—a cobbled together contingency of peasants, farmers, merchants, and warriors—would make every attempt to push the invading force out. If Zizka's successes up to now were any indication, it would be done. And quickly.

Pavel had needed some convincing that Karin was well enough for him to resume his stand with General Zizka. After all, Duke and Duchess Novak would see to her comfort and safety. She had been loathed for him to depart, yet it was she who insisted he go. Knowing her husband, he would never forgive himself if the conflict at the front turned for the worse in his absence. However, all she could think now was that she would never forgive herself if Pavel were to be injured or...she couldn't even piece the words together in her mind.

She put a stop to the errant thoughts that would lead to naught but worry. God was with Pavel...and with the Hussites. Had He not proven faithful already?

The nursemaid bustled about the room, straightening this and that. Perhaps only attempting to give Karin and her child some space.

She lifted Karin's psalter from a nearby table. "Shall I have someone read to you?"

Karin looked at her briefly and then back down to her son. "I do not wish to disturb Father Dominik."

The servant woman nodded but ventured further. "If only there were others who could read Latin."

Karin's gaze caught the woman's before her attention returned to her work. The nursemaid spoke the truth. Precious few were educated enough to read the Holy Writ. Karin's parents had seen to that in her tutelage, for which she was grateful.

The thought struck her. What would it mean if her son—if all—could read the precious words of the Holy Writ for themselves? To no longer rely on priests and bishops to impart the Scriptures to them? The idea spread wings within her as if preparing to take flight.

But she suppressed even this. It was forbidden to transcribe the sacred writings. Only...

The Catholic Church no longer held authority in these lands. Would there, then, be a chance...a hope that someone could ink these ancient words into Czech?

Karin watched her son. The babe had fallen asleep nuzzled against her body. She covered herself and held him close. With the lightest touch, she traced a finger down one side of his face, admiring the chubby features. Angelic. Her chest expanded as it always did when she held her son—a piece of Pavel and of her, evidence of their love.

She marveled anew at the life in her arms that had not an inkling of the conflict around them. Such innocence. Would he ever know these things that created distance and hardship for his parents? Would he know *why* they sacrificed? Would he understand? Perhaps...in time. Would that be best? Or dare she hope to preserve his ignorance of these hard things?

She sighed, considering the name that seemed big for the small child—Jaromir.

Her fervent wish had been to name their child after Pavel's father. A deeper pain surged through her at the memory of he who had accepted her as his own flesh and blood. He was gone and would never see his grandson. Pavel, however, had determined that Alexander would be the boy's second name. He wanted for his son to represent the peace they fought so fervently for. And so, they chose Jaromir for 'fierce peace.'

It was fitting, she decided. The name suited him.

Karin only then realized she hummed—the same tune the nurse-maid had just earlier sung to the babe. And though Karin's arms had since tired, she could not make herself relinquish her son.

A knock on the door broke her reverie.

Her gaze darted to the nursemaid, now across the chamber.

The woman, likewise, looked at Karin.

"I am able to receive," Karin said, nodding as she permitted a smile to touch her features.

The nursemaid strode across the room as Karin readjusted the top of her gown for better coverage.

"Yes?" The gruff voice of the nursemaid spilled into the hall. Was she so put out that someone would disturb her charges? Karin found comfort in the woman's concern for them.

Craning her neck, Karin spotted a younger woman who worked to find her voice. The words seemed to crowd her mouth as her tongue shifted within and her lips twisted.

Karin sensed the growing frustration of the nursemaid. The older woman's body fairly radiated her ire.

After several moments, the servant in the hall managed to state her purpose. "I have a missive. For the Lady Krejikova."

The nursemaid jerked her head and moved aside, permitting the servant girl entrance.

Karin maneuvered Jaromir so she could receive the letter. But as she struggled, the nursemaid again intervened and plucked the rolled paper from the girl's fingers.

The nursemaid then shuffled the young servant back into the hall, dismissing her with the flick of her hands, and closing the door. She turned and moved toward her mistress. "Shall I take him, my lady?"

Karin hesitated. She did not wish to end this moment with her son, but her heart ached to see what news the missive bore. Even from this distance, Pavel's seal was visible.

The letter must hold information about his wellbeing. Now desperate for whatever the papers contained; she motioned the woman over.

Time slowed as the nursemaid set the missive on a side table and collected Jaromir.

His face scrunched and, for a moment, it seemed he might wake. However, his features soon smoothed as the older woman commenced her swaying.

It was all too much. Even distracted by Jaromir, her heart raced to discover the contents of the letter. Now that the babe had settled, she stretched to the very extent of her ability to reach for the message. Indeed, her muscles protested the action.

Ignoring it, she tore at the seal. Her eagerness for word of her beloved almost led to ripped parchment. Soon enough, the stamped wax gave way.

She searched the pages, her first fears quelled as she recognized Pavel's writing. He was well enough if he could write, wasn't he? Calming herself, she forced her gaze to still and focus.

Pavel first offered words of love and of hope that her health continued to improve. They were a balm to her heart. Then he spoke of the soldiers and their preparations for battle. Zizka had marched on the town of Zatec to push out the Royalists, who had a tenuous hold on the town. The enemy had halted their barrage and pulled back.

Karin paused. Would the Royalists turn tail and flee? After all their efforts, they would pack up and retreat so quickly? Perhaps Sigismund's fear of Zizka's abilities was greater than anticipated.

She glanced at the date. Some time had passed since Pavel pored over these words. Had the Hussites overcome? Or been defeated?

Karin prayed for the former and hoped that her husband would not have known combat in the days that followed. Oh, how she prayed.

Death. Destruction. Battle. These things—and their imagery—filled Pavel's mind as he pressed onward, trying to make sense of all that surrounded him. But was there sense to be made? The clash of metal and the smell of sweat and horses assaulted him. Yet, in some measure, they invigorated him. His gaze dropped to the horse beneath him. Would the animal be able to continue? For how long? The destrier had been his valiant companion these last weeks...and for the torrent of the day. But in the press of battle, Pavel had pushed the massive horse hard.

The day had seen more than its share of bloodshed, but there was much to be grateful for. Pavel had survived the massacre at Kutna Hora. The Hussite army was betrayed by some villagers who had opened a gate for the opposing mercenary army. They then cut off Hussite forces from their war wagons. And disaster ensued.

Many of Pavel's comrades-in-arms had been cut down. Indeed, all would have been lost—and should have been—were it not for General Zizka and his tactical skill. The man continued to prove just as capable despite having completely lost his ability to see. Their hand cannons had driven the Royalist forces back and freed the remaining Hussites from complete loss.

And now, days later, they pursued the enemy army southward. Was Sigismund so afraid of the great general and his army? Had Sigismund assumed they would be weaker without their general's vision? If that was the case, the would-be king had been terribly mistaken. For they were as strong as ever. And ever as determined. Their efforts to defend life, limb, and freedom had soon seen the crusading army's retreat.

Pavel now led his troops into Habry. Sigismund's attempt to maintain control of the village had been pitiful at best. Again, the Royalists fled. And so, Pavel pushed his troops in pursuit of the enemy.

Even with all he had seen these last days, it did not prepare him for what he found when he reached the bridge. A few feet away, a horde of Royalist soldiers jammed the bridge as they sought escape.

Pavel called for his men to hold.

The entirety of the bridge's surface teemed with fleeing men. And they seemed to no longer have a care for fellow soldiers. Pushing and butting others, the mercenaries fought for release from the crowded mass. There were some who, pressed by the approaching Hussites, attempted to find their freedom by crossing the frozen river. Surely, such was madness! Were they so desperate?

"What say you?" a voice called out to General Zizka.

"Forward," the large man bellowed.

Pavel maneuvered his horse alongside Zizka's. "General, the Royalists are fleeing. And the bridge clogs with the sheer number of them fighting to get across. Many have taken to the ice-covered water to claim safety on the other side."

Zizka's features remained hard. "We shall overtake them."

Was this not a time for mercy? Pavel was equally irate about the brethren lost in the massacre only days ago. His sword hand weighed heavy, eager for vengeance. But this? This did not suit him—picking off men as they ran for their lives.

Crack.

The splintering sounds drew his attention to the turmoil upon the bridge and the men desperate to save themselves. And also to the river.

Pavel paused. Had that noise come from the bridge? Or the ice? Far too many men tried to cross the hardened surface of the water.

The frozen expanse would not hold. Even then, it crunched under their weight.

A loud crash and a *whoosh* filled the air as the ice gave way in several places.

Before Pavel could utter a word, openings to the watery darkness spread across the entire wintery covering of the river. Men slipped into the chilled depths. They would not survive this. Not with their armor, not with the freezing temperatures.

He turned back to Zizka. The man's firm expression betrayed that he, too, heard the sound and knew what went.

"Onward," Zizka cried.

The men around Pavel advanced as commanded. How could Pavel not join them? Though with much resistance within himself, he pushed forward.

A mass of utter chaos in the thick of bodies ensued. Who was friend and who was foe in the tight confines? Pavel fought against Royalists who had paused to take on the coming Hussite soldiers.

Despite the efforts of the mercenaries, all movement ceased before long. Pavel stopped and breathed for a moment—just one— to survey the damage and try to find reason. He took in what remained. The bridge and surrounding area—both river and ground —were littered with fallen men.

The Hussites cheered as the last vestiges of the retreating army— at least those able to escape their doom—faded. Yes, they had dealt a serious blow to the Royalists today. But at what cost?

Pavel slowed his horse as yells and shouts of celebration drowned out all else. Yet he did not cheer. Rather, he absorbed the scene and the devastation it contained. His gaze pulled to the forms of those who had lost their lives—from both sides. Directing his horse along the side of the path, he dismounted and walked the riverbank. So many warriors' lives had been snuffed out here...too many.

Pavel firmly believed in the Hussite cause; however, this was trying—the reality of the sheer number who would not return home. On both sides.

They weren't just mercenaries, though they had been his enemy and sought his death. Still, each was someone's brother, son, cousin, maybe even a husband and father. It weighed on him. He said a prayer of thanks that his own wife and son were tucked safely away. His shoulders tightened as images of their faces filled his mind. What if it were Karin who would receive news her husband had fallen in battle? The cavern in his chest expanded and then contracted painfully as a wave of emotion overcame him.

Lord, may it never be.

Pavel walked beside the river, praying for the men, their families, and their souls. Regardless of which side they had fought on. As he moved toward the outskirts of the remaining bodies, his breathing became labored. And his body reminded him of how he had pushed it.

Relenting, he shifted to return to his men. Something—perhaps a movement—at the water's edge caught his eye. He scanned the embankment and the bodies scattered there, having crossed only to breathe their last on this side. Tragic.

But there was nothing of note. He must have imagined it. Mayhap nothing more than hopefulness born of desperation. As he turned once more, he closed his eyes, prepared to leave this nightmare behind. As much as possible.

But when he lifted his lids, there it was again—definite motion.

An arm flailed.

Pavel halted and focused.

A man, dirtied and damaged, struggled for life.

Even at this distance, Pavel took in the figure. The man bled, most profusely from a leg badly wounded. By a blade? Or perhaps crushed by fleeing soldiers? Taking a step closer, confusion cleared. And what was once hope became dismay. With so much blood loss, it was doubtful any intervention could save this man.

Still, Pavel could not simply dismiss the enemy soldier. Though...

what could he do? What should he do? He thought to offer what comfort he could for the man's last moments. That thought was followed by a warning—what if the man were more aware than he seemed? Would the man take up his sword or a dagger and strike at the one lending aid?

Pavel frowned as he considered his options. And, despite the danger presented, he could not walk away and leave this man alone in his final minutes of agony. Drawing near, Pavel knelt beside the now-stilled man and prayed. He spoke the words aloud, hoping it might bring some measure of peace to the one who breathed his last.

The man's torso convulsed and lifted, his movements slight. He groaned as his eyes opened. Did he seek the source of the prayer?

Dirt marred and scarred the man's face. His features all but lost. As his eyes became visible in mere slits, Pavel lost his words. This was his long-lost friend—Stepan Dvorak.

CHAPTER 2
PATRICIE & STEPAN

Patricie crept into the room of her next charge, mindful to keep her footfalls light. The day had worn long, and she had become weary. Yet her work served to reinvigorate her. Perhaps the part that made her happiest was the opportunity to hone what skill she had gleaned from her mother. As much as Patricie relied on the knowledge passed on to her, the memory of it stung. It had been too long since she sat with her mother poring over various plant life. The woman had been known for her ability to heal with herbs. Patricie prayed for but a piece of that respect.

The room had been darkened, but not completely. Beams of light filtered in and warmed the space. She wished to throw the drapes back and bask in it. Her charge's need of recovery stilled her hand. Yes, the dimness assisted his rest.

"Dobry den," she said as she drew closer.

There was no answer. Not that she had expected any. The man had yet to regain consciousness since being brought to the healer.

She set her supplies—bandages and a bowl of herbs—upon a stand, one of the few pieces in the room. The inn had been a godsend in the midst of great loss, even if it was sparsely furnished. But as Ludek said, they would celebrate the victories as they could and make do with the accommodations.

Patricie smiled at the still form. "How are you today? Still abed, I see."

It helped her to make conversation, even if it was with herself. How else was she to pass the time? Besides, it made her feel closer to the men she cared for.

"Why don't I take a look at that leg?" She settled onto the edge of the bed, pulling back the blanket from the man's lower limbs. It was important to retain as much modesty as possible for the soldiers. And for her purposes, she need not venture beyond baring wound sites.

"This might hurt a bit, but I promise I'll be gentle."

She peeled back the bandages and peered at his injury. And grimaced. It was bad.

Ludek had tended and sutured as best he could. And then tasked her with keeping it cleaned, dressed, and the proper herbs applied as needed.

While she enjoyed her work with Ludek, she had never quite become accustomed to the damage done a body. This man's leg had been terribly battered. So much so that she knew not how he still breathed. But he did. And she would give the whole of her effort and skill to preserve him.

"How did this happen?" she asked, not for the first time. "What did you get yourself into?"

This, she knew the answer to. He had fought in the recent battle and quite nearly died at the bridge.

Pushing her long dark braid over her shoulder, she leaned closer to the marred limb. She worked as quickly as possible while maintaining some level of gentleness about her movements. Just because he was unconscious didn't mean she shouldn't take care.

"It is a wonder. But I don't have to tell you, do I?"

The stitching held and the heat radiating off his body had lessened. Mayhap he improved, then. The danger of the wound becoming putrid still existed, but perhaps the worst had passed.

"It is fearful cold outside today. I had the hardest time making my fingers work when I went to the stream."

She glanced at his face.

Nothing. His strong, square jaw was still, and his mouth remained set.

Once more she considered, with gratitude, the refuge the inn provided from the frigid temperatures. True the rooms might be small, but they were not at the mercy of the winter chill. Except for her trips to gather water.

"There now." She straightened her back. "All done."

She tugged the thin blanket back over his extremities and stole a long look at his face. His features gave the appearance of youth. But Lord Krejik had said something of this man having been a former friend. That being so, the soldier must have more years than it seemed.

"Not so bad today, was it?" Her words were soft as she watched him.

His mouth twisted.

She did wish he could be more at peace. Did he sense what went on around him? Did he know what his body had been through? Or did he simply fight to maintain his hold on life?

Not for the first time, she lingered and thought on this man who would be her enemy. What was he like? Why had a Czech chosen to fight with the Royalists?

Perhaps she could take heart in Lord Krejik's mention of friendship with the man. Might that be reason to hope? As one of the most admired Hussite warriors in the camp, Lord Krejik's good opinion held weight. So, this man—had Lord Krejik called him Stepan?—couldn't be all bad. It was possible he would change his allegiance when he awoke to find himself in this Hussite-controlled town. If he ever did regain consciousness.

The healer still wasn't certain of the man's recovery. This only made her more determined, her work all the more vital. Her ability to maintain the repair to his leg and tend him may very well determine his fate. Not so long ago, that thought would have weighed heavy. But after working alongside Ludek for some time, she knew what she was capable of. She would not lose this man to the depths. No, she would fight it every day. And she would win.

He had come so far in such a short time. After all, the fever had abated. Surely his wounds would heal. Maybe not completely, but enough for him to live a full life yet.

"I am hopeful," she said more to herself than him.

Patricie plucked a cooled wet cloth from the basin that she would have to refill soon. She rubbed it over his face, shoulders, and to the opening in his tunic.

He was solid. Well built. But such was the case for many of the soldiers she tended.

Still, there was something different about him. Perhaps it was only the thrill and curiosity of working on one from the Royalist side of this conflict. It seemed dangerous.

"Not that you would ever hurt anyone."

Wishful thinking. It was likely this man had snuffed out the lives of many of her people. Yet she couldn't find it in herself to hate him. Not when she worked so diligently to see him healed.

Might he be thankful for their efforts such that he would renounce the Royalists? Anything was possible.

"I'm letting my thoughts run away with me again." She bemoaned that tendency within herself.

The truth was that she knew precious little about him. Nothing more than the scant details Lord Krejik had supplied. Stepan was noble, the son of a viscount. How would he have held himself? She could imagine his broad shoulders raised, strong and proud. Was his presence overbearing? Or might he be more genial?

That must be the case. For certain, he would be kind. And

concerned about all the happenings in Bohemia. Yet did that fit with his choice to fight his own brethren?

She rubbed the cloth down his arms. Her mind had indeed strayed far and did so quickly.

"Enough daydreaming," she admonished herself.

It was time to finish and move to her next charge. She pulled the cloth back, dragging her arm the length of his.

A hand shot out and grabbed her wrist.

Holding back a scream, she tugged against the iron grip. But it wouldn't give.

And she knew. She just knew.

Peering down, she found dark eyes watching her. The intensity of his gaze bore into her, stealing her breath.

She opened her mouth to call for help but could not push the words out.

"Who are you?" his hoarse words demanded.

She tried to pull free again. His hold was firmer than she would have imagined, especially in his weakened state.

Drawing in a breath she hoped would still her shaking, she attempted words again. "My name is Patricie. I but tend your wound."

He grimaced. Did the very mention of the injury pain him? For certain, his body must ache.

"Please," she said as she worked to free her arm again, pressing down her rising dread. "Turn me loose."

His steely glare pinned her. Still, he did not slacken his grip. If anything, his hand tightened.

"Where...?" His voice caught. No doubt, he found speaking diffi-cult with a dry mouth. "Where am I?"

"You are in the Hussite camp near Kolin."

His eyes widened. "The Hussites?"

She did not miss the hardness in his voice. But all she could do was nod.

He thrust her arm away.

The abrupt movement surprised her and almost caused her to lose her balance. But she managed to remain upright. She wished for something to say that would calm him, but she wasn't even able to draw in a grateful breath before more venom spewed from his mouth.

"Don't touch me."

She stared at him. He couldn't mean that. Not the man she had tended these last few days. The man she had been certain was not as he seemed...perhaps only misunderstood.

Rubbing her wrist, she soothed the skin there.

He afforded her another brief glance before staring at the ceiling. "I will speak with someone of authority."

Emotion clogged her throat, but she pushed past it. "I assure you, my lord, I—"

"I do not wish to say it again." His features became stony, and he would not look at her. As if she were beneath him. If he had slapped her across the face, she would not have felt more stung. Never...never had she been treated in such a manner.

She tossed the cloth into the basin and rose. "I don't know how I thought you anything but—"

"What?" His eyes—accusing and stern—were on her again.

Had she spoken aloud? Though she had not intended to do so, she would not shrink away. "I only mean to say, my *lord*, that I dared believe—err, hope—you had a real heart beating within your chest despite your allegiance to that brood of vipers. I was wrong. You are just like the rest of *them*."

His eyes widened before narrowing. "I care not to speak with you further."

Just as well. Patricie had no more words and lacked the ability to form them anyway. She gathered her remaining things and fled the room in a huff.

After closing the door, she leaned back against it lest her legs give out completely. What a pitiable woman she was! A fanciful girl indeed. Why had she allowed her imaginings to create such a fairytale? This Stepan—Lord Dvorak—was as rotten within as a Royalist soldier should be. And though she must continue to see to his care, she need not interact with him. Or have any kind regard for him.

She wiped at the moisture collecting in her eyes.

She could not. She would not.

The door slammed. Or at least Stepan imagined it was the door. Whatever that noise, it had jarred his every sense. An accompanying squeal left him surprised that the door remained on its hinges. Was this place so decrepit?

With the Hussite woman now gone, he scanned his surroundings. He lay abed in a simple room—small and somewhat quaint. What manner of place was this?

The relative size of the space along with the presence of wooden walls and ceiling gave the impression he was within an inn or other simple dwelling. And in Kolin? He gritted his teeth. Hussite-controlled territory. Was there any hope for him?

Stepan's thoughts remained somewhat hazy...perhaps from his languid sleep. And his vision blurred in intervals. How long had he been here? Been unconscious?

With the increased awareness of his body, sharp pains pounded and throbbed through his being. More and more so every second. He attempted to assess the state of his body. Indeed, he ached...deeply. Nothing hurt so much as his right leg. Bracing himself, he shifted his arms to press up into a sitting position. How else would he take stock of the damage? His body screamed at even the slight movement. Releasing the burning muscles, he surrendered his weight to the thin mattress once more.

For some time, he had been returning to himself. Little by little. For the last several hours...maybe even days. He had been all too aware of the woman's ministrations—both the tearing pain in his leg as she worked and the tenderness of her touch. How often had she been at work about his person?

Closing his eyes, he tried to push through the pain and put his thoughts together. Yes, images of her—perhaps only glimpses—came to him. Her long dark hair framed her face in his limited recollection. And that gentle voice. True, his memories were but snatches. However, it was the fitful dreams of *her* that he found most disturbing.

Now that he was more aware, he found her not to be the angel he'd supposed, but a Hussite wench. How did she even think she had the right to touch him?

He was surprised at the ache that blossomed in his chest at these thoughts.

Enough!

This would get him no closer to wholeness. He must turn his mind to more productive things. What *was* his condition? What were his options for escape? He could not let these Hussite dogs keep him here. Did they mind his wounds only to execute him once he was whole? There had been talk in the Royalist camp of what these Hussites were capable of. And he had no delusions that he would be treated any better than those he had heard tales off.

The door creaked. Did the villainess wish to try again? He wouldn't have it.

He gathered what strength he could and prepared to send her away. At least as much as he could in his state. He could do nothing beyond his words to enforce the desire to expel her from the room.

But the figure drawing closer was masculine.

Stepan met the man's gaze. Who was *this*? Was he the one who held control over Stepan's future?

Calming his thoughts, Stepan attempted to take in any and all information he could. The man was simply dressed. Nothing about him spoke of refinement. He couldn't be in charge here. Then again, these Hussites had not a care for station. Mayhap a mere commoner was, in fact, the authority here.

As the man came closer, Stepan tightened the muscles in his arms, steeling himself to defend his person in any way possible. But as he opened his mouth to naysay this intruder's advance, the man spoke.

"You should consider your state before sending away the hands that have kept you alive these last days."

Did this man dare condescend? He appeared more peasant than anything else. And while he may have some position with the Hussites, he did not speak for Stepan. Why should he, then, let this man continue?

Stepan opened his mouth and, again, the man cut him off.

"It is nothing short of a miracle that your bone was not broken. And, considering the extent and depth of the damage done to your flesh, it is only because of God's will and *her* efforts that you still take in breath. And *that*," he said as he pointed toward the door, "is how you show your gratitude?"

Stepan swallowed. Part of him tugged toward softening. Though...why did this man think he had any right to chastise someone so far above his station? He drew in a breath and spat, "I believe I will no longer require *that woman's* assistance."

"Oh, you will." The man's tone was even and cool. "Unless you'd prefer to face down the Lord God Himself. For that will be your end —and soon—if we cannot keep this wound from becoming putrid."

Stepan bit back a rising retort. All things considered; he did not want to die. Not even for the momentary pleasure of throwing insults in this man's direction. Or toward the woman.

"Yes, I should think you might reconsider." The man's slender face settled into a thin-lipped expression.

Stepan pressed a breath through clenched teeth, preparing to respond. But again, fought within himself.

The peasant spoke again. "I have done what I can. And now your fate depends on *that* woman's ability to maintain your wound."

Stepan looked away, setting his gaze on the ceiling once more. "What if I do not wish it?"

"That cannot be so." Another, more familiar voice spoke from the doorway.

Stepan strained to catch a look at the newcomer, but his body would not angle in such a way. Still, he had to know if his ears but played tricks. For it could not be who his mind told.

Footfalls on the wooden floor betrayed that the man in question came closer. And soon enough, Stepan's vision homed in on the face. His eyes clashed with those of his old friend—Pavel Krejik.

CHAPTER 3
KARIN & PAVEL

The final words of mass came to a close. Karin had waited for this moment. But now that it was here, she struggled to make herself stand. It was not her weakened physical condition that made it so. As much as she wished it wasn't true, there was a hesitation in her spirit. What she sought, what she intended in her heart to ask, went against the mandates laid out by the church.

Still, she could not deny the growing urgency within, driving her to move forward with her plan. At some length, she did rise and make her way to the front of the chapel. Little by little, hesitant step by hesitant step she went. Until she stood but a few feet from Father Dominik. An uneasiness within belied her trepidation. How would she push forward? But she must.

Father Dominik had always been an understanding man. Perhaps her worries were for naught. But her considerations were rather unorthodox. How would he respond? The reality of her situation begged that she seek approval. And his aid. For the task was great and her heart already pulled in more than one direction.

She closed her eyes and said a quick prayer to the God Who Sees.

He would know best how to guide her, how to go before her and prepare the way as He had for the Israelites at the Red Sea. Indeed, they had been at an impasse, unable to move forward without God's hand of provision. As was she.

She finished her simple plea, and a calm flooded her being. A calm that went beyond herself. As if the very presence of the Lord rested on her, giving her the courage and strength needed to step forward. She could do this. She had to. With her renewed sense of purpose, she moved closer to the priest.

One of Duke Novak's knights spoke with Father Dominik. She did not wish to intrude. So, she paused to allow space for them to finish their conversation in privacy. An awareness of this thing she asked threatened to undo the peace within. This was not about her, but about her people. That thought held the tide of self-doubt at bay.

After a few moments, the knight spotted her. In truth, he would have known she neared the second she scooted closer. Perhaps he now brought his petition to conclusion.

The priest shifted, looking to where the knight's gaze had set. A slight smile tugged at Father Dominik's mouth, and he motioned for her to draw near.

She complied, though not without a measure of apprehension. It had not been her intention to interrupt. However, as she took tentative steps toward the pair, the words she could discern were of polite regard. Mayhap the knight had shared what he wished or had not anything of a private nature to speak about.

Heeding the priest's behest, she closed the distance. The knight nodded to Father Dominik and then tipped his head in Karin's direction before moving off.

The priest opened his arms and curled one hand inward. "Come, my child. What might I do for you this day?"

Karin pressed a smile onto her features—a smile she didn't feel but hoped to. "I beg your pardon, Father, but I must speak with you. Alone."

He glanced about the chapel. As did Karin. The small gathering dwindled. The few that remained were close to the doors.

She turned her focus to the priest and found his gaze set on her once more.

"What is the nature of your need?"

She looked about her, ensuring that those still in attendance were farther away as she believed. No one was close enough to overhear.

"Father, I confess that my need is rather…singular. And I must put it forth directly."

His face remained stoic, but he nodded. "Please." Taking her elbow, he then drew her a few steps farther away still from the lingering few.

Content that no one might hear, she began. "I have been…thinking. About many things."

"Oh?" His kind eyes were intent on her. It gave her a hope she had not dared claim.

"I have…concerns…about the limited access to the Holy Writ."

His brows furrowed for a moment, then settled back into their position on his placid expression. "Yes?"

She took in a deep breath; grateful he gave her leave to speak her mind. So many men of the cloth were far more concerned with expressing their own thoughts and not enough, in her opinion, on listening.

Karin fought the urge to wring her hands, forcing them to remain at her sides. "There are not many who have God's Word within reach. And fewer who are able to read Latin."

His features scrunched. Did he surmise what she sought?

A part of her thought to back down and rescind her words. Or make them seem more neutral. But the fire in her soul would not allow her. She must press on.

"What if…*all* Czechs could read these holy passages in their own language?"

His face smoothed and became an unreadable mask. How did he

do that? Disguise his reaction so completely? Though he shook his head as he spoke. "My child, why do they have need when God's servants are ready and willing to shepherd them in the manner God intended?"

Karin chewed on her lip. This was not the response she'd desired, but it was as she anticipated. Though Father Dominik may align himself with the Hussites, old ways of thinking were not easily dismissed.

"Lady Karin, you have much on your mind these days—your son, your husband, your recovery." He paused. Did he think to impress something on her? Then he continued, "Your thoughts for the people are generous. But I fear they are misguided."

She watched him even as her heart sank. There would be no support and no help here.

His warm voice soothed, even as it chastised. "Perhaps it would be best to focus on your child and your health at this time. Your thoughts seem scattered and, if I may, your concern misplaced. There are greater battles to fight today...more pressing battles."

Karin nodded and dropped her regard to the floor. What else could she do? Though kind and tender, he had dismissed her entreaty. With finality.

"Now, my child, is there anything else you wish to speak with me about?"

She shook her head as she lifted her gaze to meet his.

"Then let's hear no more of this dangerous inclination. You well know the consequences should anyone attempt what you suggest."

Fighting to keep her features as much a mask as his, she gathered what courage remained. "I understand, Father. And I thank you for your counsel."

He studied her as if he wasn't certain she understood the weight of his words. "May God bless you. And your child." Then, with one more meaningful look—one brow lifted and his mouth set—he moved off.

Karin's heart squeezed. It was only wisdom to follow his advice.

An image of dear Tomas flitted across her mind. The consequences for his defiance to the church had been dire. After being found supporting Jan Hus's teachings...and spreading that message...the young nobleman's life had been forfeit. Would she share that fate?

Yes, she should heed Father Dominik. Yet something in her was not at peace with that. What was God asking of her?

Pavel watched his reflection in the passing stream. Hunched over, he had finally found a moment to scrub the battle from his skin. If only he could wash away the memories as easily.

Water dripped from his hands, making small ripples that did nothing to disturb the rushing flow on its way to places unknown. A cold wind cut through him, causing his wet skin to sting. But he didn't care. Rather, he was grateful. For it awakened his senses and testified that he still breathed.

Something remained after the washing took away the outer signs of his struggle for life. A pondering of sorts. How did one live with the images? The pain, the destruction, the death...it plagued him. Would he ever be free? He doubted these waters would provide deep enough cleansing to absolve his spirit.

Perhaps after he returned to Karin... Could her love bring healing? Now that was a fanciful thought indeed. He could not—and would not—weigh her with these things. Or with expectations that she could not live up to. Mayhap it was only time he needed. That in the following days, months, years, he would find his memories covered with a haze. Would that dull his anguish? He could but hope.

The chill of the air tormented his exposed, wet skin. He rubbed his hands together to bring feeling back to his fingers. But he allowed the frigid wind to torture him. Why did he linger so? As if he didn't know. What the remainder of the day held did not appeal.

It was necessary for him to inquire after Stepan. As much as his stomach churned at the thought of facing his former friend, he must. Pavel owed as much to that friendship—tattered though it was.

Regardless of how they had last parted, he cared too much for Stepan's wellbeing. Perhaps more than he should. Though their last interaction had been a clash of swords, there remained hope that Stepan might soften to their cause. Radek's telling of Stepan's aid in his and Lady Hana's escape indicated as much. Perhaps Stepan no longer felt at home in the Royalist army.

Pavel closed his eyes and let the breeze wage its assault on his flesh.

Karin.

What would she say? Would she wish him to face his now-enemy? But he knew the answer...she would. As long as Stepan retained breath in his body, there was the chance for goodness to win. And Pavel must embrace every opportunity, no matter how small, to foster any hint of tenderness toward their cause.

Pavel rose, his decision made. He turned toward the small village beyond the forest line. Now. He had to go now. For every moment he delayed, the real possibility grew that Pavel would find cause to discourage the action.

It had to be now.

CHAPTER 4
HANA & RADEK

The metal of Radek's horse's shoes clomped on the stone walkway as he urged the animal forward. A solemn sound if he'd ever heard one. His journey had been easy. More so than he'd hoped. Against all sense, he'd wanted for something to delay his arrival. But here he was, the castle's drawbridge rising behind him and cutting off any thoughts to turn back.

Midday's sunlight streamed into the inner bailey he had been certain he would never see again. Perhaps he had, at one time, even wished as much. He scanned the area. Guards stared him down from all sides. Did they suppose he came to bring harm to their lord? Had he the intention to storm the castle, his plan would for certain not be so lacking. As if he wished to be a lamb to the slaughter. Still, he would not begrudge their concern. For it was their purpose.

The mood shifted—a stirring rippled through all present. It seemed as if all were inclined toward the donjon, the air thick with expectation.

Someone approached.

Across the bailey, a man strode forth. His short, wavy brown hair had grayed in patches—evidence of the years that had passed. But his beard had the same slight red tint to it that Radek had always found curious. And the lines of the older man's face were deeper.

Radek took in every detail, for he had long since feared he would never again lay eyes on this man—his father, Margrave Artur Miklas.

After the way their previous encounter ended, there was no certainty as to how his father would receive him. But he had reason to hope. For his father was ever the gentle caretaker, ever the first one to show mercy. Even to his own detriment.

The margrave moved closer with set features. His eyebrows drew together as he gazed on the intruder to his lands.

Radek held his breath. How would his father receive the long-lost son who had, with painful clarity, laid out his grievances before leaving this place?

As the distance between them dwindled, Radek dropped from his horse. He would face his father's disappointment no matter how it might sting. Yes, he would bear the man's anger...and more, if necessary. After all, that was why he had come.

The margrave continued forward. Would he go so far as to strike at Radek? That seemed doubtful. But if not, why did he not slow his advance?

Father drew nearer still.

Radek sucked in a breath. He would bear it. He would.

The margrave didn't slow but opened his arms as he closed the gap and embraced Radek. "My son has returned."

As much as Radek hated such a display, he could not deny that his breaths came easier, and he settled into the moment. Briefly.

Father leaned back, shifting his steps yet keeping his hands on Radek's shoulders.

"I feared..." His voice faded and he coughed. "I believed I would not see you again."

Radek dipped his head. "As did I."

Miklas's eyebrows lifted, but he did not speak further. As if he but gave Radek space to sort out whatever he intended to say.

Radek glanced at the knights and guards gathered around them.

Father's man-at-arms stood some yards away as the closest onlooker, holding back from the exchange. The man averted his gaze to the side, away from the interaction.

Why should Radek care what these men thought? He had come for this—to see his father and attempt to heal the rift between them. Yet a part of him did wonder at the audience and their thoughts.

Radek pressed out a breath, attempting to push such musings out of mind. They would only distract him. Too long had he feared others' perceptions. Too long had he allowed that to keep him from moving forward when he should.

No more.

He regarded his father again. The man's eyes were wider than expected. Did his father, too, consider the cost to his pride?

It mattered not.

"I was wrong." The words did not have the strength Radek wished they would. But it was what he had to offer.

The margrave's mouth tightened, and he drew a long breath in. "Come, my son. Your mother will be anxious to see you."

Then his father turned, bidding Radek follow.

Radek's every muscle held its tension. Nothing he said to himself would allow them release. Why was he still so concerned? His father had welcomed him with arms wide. What could keep him from full relief?

Nothing.

They moved through the castle and into the Great Hall. He was eager to see his mother. The woman had always been his champion, his most eager support. Why had he let the challenges with his father keep him away?

It took a few moments to adjust to the dimmer interior. But as he did so, he spotted a woman by the hearth—Mother. The second her eyes met his, a strange sensation coursed through him. He had missed her.

Mother set her stitching to the side and rose. She faltered. It almost seemed as if her legs wouldn't quite hold her.

"My ladywife," Father announced, his voice warm and bold. "Come. See our son has returned!"

She blinked as if afraid Radek would disappear. But why then did she appear disappointed?

He did not intend to let the years of separation prevent reconciliation.

As she stepped toward them, Radek decided that her blinking was more likely to staunch tears that threatened. Had he hurt his mother with his absence? That had never been his intention.

"Mother—" he started, but she silenced him with a shake of her head.

Did she not wish to hear his reasons? Or did they not matter to a mother approaching her son thought gone for good?

Her lips pinched.

His chest tightened as he watched her fight with her emotions.

She paused when she was but an arm's length away, staring into his eyes. The stirring within the hazel there squeezed at his heart.

She lifted a trembling hand.

His eyes slid closed as he prepared for the touch of her fingertips.

Then she slapped him.

Hana Novakova stood at the back of the chapel, scanning those that remained. What kept so many in place? Conversations with others? A desire to seek an audience with the priest? Indeed, Hana herself waited, looking for Lady Karin Krejikova.

The lady stood near the altar across the room. Not only did Hana's gaze single her out, she found herself admiring the woman. Lady Karin held herself gracefully despite all she had been through. Why must bringing a child into the world be so dangerous? The woman had nearly lost her own life trying to give life to her son.

Though now she had a wonderful treasure—a son—a living

promise. The child was a piece of Lord Krejik with her always. No matter what lay before her. No matter how uncertain the future.

A shiver disrupted Hana's concentration. This dreadful cold! She had never been fond of the winter, but even less so now. How could she not after experiencing the warmth of what it was to be so deeply loved, cherished, and cared for? Only it seemed even that had been ripped away.

Perhaps that was a bit much...though she felt every bit of it in her mind and heart. Radek left for his father's lands a full week ago. And for a good reason, a noble reason. But he had not wished to bring her along.

He said it was to do with the state of things in Bohemia. Dangerous times, he believed. His concern over the civil unrest may be well-founded...perhaps. Or was it only an excuse to put her off?

Either way, she knew not what she would do in his absence.

Hana returned her focus to the lady who was now situated beyond the altar, conversing with Father Dominick. Would Hana ever be able to hold herself with such poise? Such restraint?

But as Hana watched the pair, Lady Karin finished her entreaty, and Father Dominick shook his head. The kindly face of the priest drooped. It appeared as if her request was not received well. He seemed rather set against whatever they discussed. What had she asked? Hana wondered about Lady Karin's purpose in seeking the holy man. And whether the lady was likewise disturbed by the priest's reaction?

Chiding herself, Hana averted her gaze. Such was not for her to concern herself with. What went between a man of the cloth and one of his parishioners was for them alone. And God. A young woman passed close to Hana, nodding in her direction. What was her name? Hana could not recall. Rather than admit as much, she simply dipped her head and smiled.

That seemed sufficient for the woman, for she moved off and out of the sanctuary. The exchange was but mere moments, but as Hana glanced toward Lady Karin's position once more, she found that the lady had turned from the priest and now walked toward the chapel's exit.

Hana side stepped to intercept her. As she neared, Lady Karin's gaze met hers. The baroness seemed upset. It gave Hana reason to pause. What exactly had transpired with the priest? Dare she interrupt the woman's deep thoughts?

Yet, the stirring within Hana was too great. As was her reason for seeking out Lady Krejikova. Hana just had to find release for her burden. Perhaps she should consider speaking with Father Dominik herself. He had always been a capable listener, not as quick to point out where she erred. Still, Hana craved a sense of understanding. And it was unlikely she would get such from the priest.

"Baroness Krejikova," Hana said as the woman moved closer. She hoped against hope that she wouldn't be a bother. Perhaps she might even offer some camaraderie for the lady as well.

"Good day, Lady Hana." Lady Karin nodded and came to stop just short of Hana's position. "How do you fare today?"

Hana dipped her head. "I am well. Though I should ask the same of you. Are you well?"

Lady Karin's lips thinned, but only for a second.

If Hana had not been so intent on the woman, she would have missed it.

"I am as well as can be expected, I suppose. And I continue to grow stronger by the day."

"And your son? How is he?" Hana cringed at her inability to push past the pleasantries. Did she only imagine she might be able to befriend the woman?

Though at the mention of the child, Lady Karin's features seemed to lighten. "He is wonderful."

Hana smiled. What must it be like? To have a babe to care for and dote on must fill long days and lonely nights. So much about these early days of being a mother remained foreign to her. But dare she venture questions in such a sensitive area?

Only then did Hana realize that they stood, all but facing off, in silence. She must broach the subject that pained her else detaining the lady would be for naught. A quick glance about the area portended that, while the chapel emptied, there remained too many ears for her comfort.

"I do not wish to keep you from him one moment longer than necessary. Shall we walk?"

Lady Karin considered her. Did she think Hana intended to invade the sanctum of her private chamber?

Hana opened her mouth to clarify.

However, Lady Karin spoke into the moment before she could. "Please."

They turned once more toward the back of the chapel, picking up step in that direction.

Though they moved farther from those still gathered, Hana found herself reluctant to delve into something that weighed so heavily on her heart. And opted for simple chatter. "What a fine day it is." She breathed deeply. "Even if it is a bit too cold for my comfort."

Lady Karin nodded but did not seem ready to engage with her on that topic. In truth, it was a distraction from Hana's real purpose.

"I do wonder what is planned for our nooning meal. I under-stand that there is some fine venison in the kitchen." Hana bit at the inside of her mouth. Why would she continue to banter about?

Lady Krejikova murmured an agreeing sound but did not contribute further to the conversation.

What else might Hana speak to? Her father often said she could cross words with a post. Why, then, was this so difficult? As if she didn't know.

Hana noticed a tremor in her hands. She gripped them to still the shaking. And plodded on as if nothing of consequence pressed on her.

"If it weren't so chilled, I might seek out a ride this afternoon. But I despise being on horseback with so many layers about me. It takes something from it, don't you think?"

When Lady Karin did not answer, Hana glanced at her. From all appearances, the woman was deep in thought. Maybe this was a mistake. Perhaps the lady had more than her share of troubles. She didn't want to hear Hana's.

Clearing her throat, Hana prepared what words may be needed to politely end the strained interaction.

"Hmmm? Oh, yes...horseback can be difficult in the winter." Baroness Krejikova's voice surprised Hana.

But it shook Hana's thoughts. If she were to speak with the lady in a way that mattered, she'd best do so now. Swallowing, she pushed forth. "Lady Karin, I—"

The lady halted abruptly. So much so that it took Hana a moment to stop. She glanced back over her shoulder to where the lady stood.

"I apologize, Lady Hana, for my distraction." Lady Karin's words were just as abrupt, devoid of emotion. "But I must speak plainly."

Hana drew in a breath.

The lady's eyes pierced Hana, yet there was a soft sorrow about them. "I am grateful for your family's hospitality, and I do not wish to be rude."

Hana bit at her lower lip, fighting the urge to respond. It was best to give the baroness room to speak.

Lady Karin's gaze clouded, and moisture filled her eyes. "I do wish to avail myself to your need, but I must ask you to tell me what you seek. My mind is much on other things."

Hana swallowed; she felt every bit the intruder. But as she considered sharing final polite words and letting the woman be, she found she could not. Perhaps it would be best for her to be as direct.

Stilling her wringing hands, Hana said, "I...do not wish to overstep, Baroness. Still, I find I am much in need of your counsel."

The lady's eyes widened. What did she think Hana sought? It would be best if she came to it.

Averting her gaze, Hana continued, "I have been rather...put out... since Radek's departure. I find I cannot...manage myself with him so far away."

When Hana's eyes met Baroness Krejikova's once more, she found a tenderness about the woman's features. Though she did not speak.

So, Hana mustered what courage she could. "I...wondered...that is, I hoped...you might advise me."

Lady Karin's eyebrows lifted.

Hana scanned the corridor around them. From all appearances, they were alone. Still, she lowered her voice. "I have given thought to...journeying to Horice to join him."

Lady Karin sucked in a breath. "Joining him?"

Hana watched the lady and nodded.

"That is very bold indeed, Lady Hana." Karin spoke slowly, as if considering every word. "Have you thought of how Radek would receive you?"

Hana drew in a long breath, allowing the pause to fill the space between her and Lady Krejikova. "I have."

"And?"

"I do not think it will please him." Hana's heart dropped a little at the confession.

Lady Karin's features eased. "I think you are right."

The tightness in Hana's core that had become her constant companion moved into her throat. Would she be able to speak with it as such?

Even as she spoke, Lady Karin's soft words attempted to soothe. "Radek does what he must. And he may not wish the distraction you would bring."

Hana struggled for a response. This was not as she had hoped. "I...know you are right. But I fear my heart cannot resist the impulse to do so."

The lady frowned. "Have you spoken with Duke Novak?"

Hana shook her head. "I do not believe my father would be any more open to the idea."

Lady Karin's mouth became a thin line for a moment. "Even should you decide Radek is in need of you, the duke must give you leave."

The baroness was not wrong. Perhaps Hana would be able to convince her father, perhaps not. She had not tried out such a prospect even in her thoughts.

A small smile touched Lady Karin's lips. "I see that these are not the words you expected."

Goodness, the woman was outright with her thoughts. Though instead of being put off, Hana found it refreshing.

There may be hope for a friendship here. Mayhap Hana could push just a bit farther. "How do you manage it? With Lord Krejik so far away at war?"

Lady Karin's eyes softened, and she blinked away the pools that gathered in them. "It is not easy. However...he does what he must...as do I." The woman appeared more thoughtful in that moment. Was she even speaking to Hana anymore?

Regardless, something in her conviction, within the words she spoke, gave Hana reason to believe.

He does what he must...as do I.

Despite the difficulty she might face trying to convince her father, despite her fear that Radek may very well be ill at her arrival, she must do what she must as well. It was doubtful she could maintain her heart and her sanity with him so far away. Perhaps he might need her as well. She could bring compassion and understanding into his situation. She would.

Remembering Lady Karin, Hana looked to her again. "I thank you...for your frankness and your words." Hana watched the baroness, but the woman no longer seemed to attend the conversation. Was she, too, deep in thought?

"Baroness?"

The lady set her eyes on Hana once more. "My apologies, Lady Hana. I believe I am rather tired."

"Please allow me to take my leave so you might find your rest." In truth, Hana needed the space to think, to plan.

Lady Karin moved toward her chamber, leaving Hana looking after her.

Hana held her breath and counted to three. Yes, this just might work. Pressing down the thrill that expanded her chest, she then picked up step herself. There was much to do.

CHAPTER 5
PATRICIE & STEPAN

Stepan wanted to look away from the intense gaze of his former friend, but he couldn't. Something within the piercing blue goaded him to maintain eye contact and, if possible, issue an unspoken challenge in return. Only...it didn't settle into him well. Still, he did his best to press what animosity he could onto his face. He would not let Pavel make him feel less than he was.

"You cannot wish death upon yourself. No matter how obstinate you can be." Pavel's words shook Stepan but did not have the bite he would have expected.

And this, Stepan could not abide—his one-time friend showing mercy. Or worse, pitying him. That would not do. His lips curled into a snarl. "As if you care."

The healer stepped to the side, allowing Pavel to move closer. "You know better."

"Do I?" Stepan challenged. He let the fire stirring in him consume any goodwill he might yet harbor. "Or do you not remember that when last we met, our swords clashed over the woman who became your wife? The woman you *stole* from me." Looking away, Stepan attempted to hide any pain that may leech onto his features. He silently cursed such weakness.

Pavel did not move, nor did he speak. For several moments. Why would he not? Couldn't he say something to get more of a rise out of Stepan?

But Stepan knew. That was not Pavel's way. How could the man possibly have a care for Stepan after all that had happened?

The door shut, drawing Stepan's gaze. Had his mind become so clouded he missed Pavel taking his leave?

But that was not so—his old friend stood as he had been. The healer, however, was no longer attending to their conversation. Perhaps now Pavel might speak his piece and make known his true intentions.

"I cannot imagine what you hope to gain here," Stepan spat out, wishing it were more than words he threw in Pavel's direction.

"I but try to ensure you are well cared for. And thriving." Pavel's words were simple. And convincing. Did he still wish Stepan well?

Stepan turned away once more. He could not bear the weight of Pavel's kind regard. "The healer has assured me that death may yet be a possibility. Mayhap that should satisfy you."

"Why would that satisfy me?" Pavel's words were pained. Did he struggle as much as it seemed? Why, then, would he not just walk away? He didn't owe Stepan anything. Much less his concern.

Stepan stared at the wall opposite. "How can you care? After all that I...that happened." He had almost said too much. There would be no recovery if the ever-forgiving Pavel knew about Stepan's nightmares...those that revisited the day he had nearly ended Karin's life. But Stepan wouldn't take the blame. Not then, not now, not ever. Pavel had betrayed him. *She* had betrayed him.

Pavel frowned but did not move closer nor back away. "Your memory, it seems, has holes about it."

Stepan grimaced. What might he do to escape this? "My memory is fine."

"Do you not remember that you helped us escape your father's wrath? That—"

"Do *not* speak of my father, coward. It is unfit for your lips." Intense ire seeped into Stepan's voice. But he did not regret it.

Pavel held up his hands as if in surrender. Then he sidestepped to the wall and leaned on it, crossing his arms. "You seem to have also forgotten that you brought Karin a wedding present. And that you and I nearly met at blades during the Battle of Vitkov Hill."

Why would Pavel invent such lies? What had he to gain from...

An image of Pavel, horseback, with sword drawn, appeared in his mind's eye. And just as quickly, Stepan saw that the man who had been his dearest friend moved his horse to the side and let Stepan escape into anonymity. And again, the weight of the grace bestowed by this man fell heavy upon him.

"It is no matter," Stepan lied, tightening his mouth. "None of it matters."

Pavel drew in a breath. "I confess, I had hoped to find you more receptive."

Stepan dared peer at his friend and found in Pavel's eyes more consideration than he deserved. It pained him. So much that it dulled the ache coming from his injury.

"What...?" Stepan stopped the entreaty as it formed. Dare he ask Pavel for a recounting of the recent battle—the one that left him marred, perhaps crippled?

As if Stepan had voiced it, Pavel's lowered voice spoke of it. "The Hussite army pushed the Royalists across the bridge, and all is as it should be. Though..." Pavel swallowed hard. A crack in his armor? "Many were lost in the river."

"More of your Hussite heretics?" Stepan grumbled. Despite his stand on the war, he could not make himself revel in the death of any Czech, no matter their cause. Not now. Not after all he had seen.

"No." Pavel's gaze seemed to deepen in that moment, his affect sullen. "Royalists."

It was Stepan's turn to swallow his words. If only he had been counted among the dead. Would his father find a hero's death worthy enough? Or would the Viscount Dvorak have looked upon his son's inability to survive with disdain?

"Do you not wonder how you came to be here?" Pavel's entreaty sounded innocent enough.

What, if anything, did Pavel know of it? Dread crept into Stepan's awareness. But he found reason to deny it. "Some Hussite soldier must have thought there was gain in seeing me suffer."

Pavel's gaze was placid. "It was I who found you."

A great heaviness fell upon Stepan's chest. This, too, he could not excuse. Couldn't Pavel have left Stepan to his final moments? It wasn't as if anyone had need of Stepan's continued existence. Least of all should he be permanently maimed.

"Stepan." Pavel stepped toward the cot again. "I do not expect the sort of restoration I wish were possible between us. Still, I find reason for a miracle, a hope that you will see the light."

Stepan glared at him, a hardness building under his regard. It was unimaginable that Pavel would seek good here. None existed. Not anymore. "You hope in vain."

The room quieted, except for the breaths the two men took in and expelled.

"Please..." Pavel spoke into the silence. "Do not let this eat you alive."

Stepan closed his eyes and focused on deepening his breaths. He meant only to feign sleep so that Pavel might leave him be. But a shroud of darkness surrounded him, pulling him down, down, down...

Patricie moved through the hallway of the inn as her thoughts dwelt where they had of late—on the Royalist prisoner. Of all the insufferable, intolerable...that man had nerve. He had no right...*no* right. She could not escape this mental space whenever she paused for a moment between patients or at mealtimes. Why must this...mercenary of a soldier...invade her thoughts? Insufferable. Yes, that's what he was. Patricie had long since levied her verdict on Lord Dvorak.

Yet, something in her gave her pause. What could bring the man so low that he would strike out at the hands that sought only to heal? To bring him comfort and sustenance?

It was no matter. She was determined that there would be no more kind thoughts for him. Not from her. Not after what he had said.

Though his indictment rang in her ears, she pressed the matter from her mind. Moving down the stairs and out of the small structure, she began a search for her sister. Eva had been more difficult to find of late. Perhaps her distraction was to blame—she had much on her mind, and on her heart.

At one time, Patricie had thought nothing would alter their closeness. But the love of a good man had indeed changed their relationship. For Eva had less time for her sister. Even when they did have a moment together, Eva was ever thinking of Zdenek.

Though...how could Patricie begrudge her sister's happiness? Patricie was filled with joy to see that her dear sister had found lasting love. Wasn't she?

Yes, she told herself firmly, she was.

Patricie brushed her thoughts to the side and made her way farther into the town. The members of the Hussite camp still reveled in their hard-earned jovial spirits. They had overcome. Against great odds. Surely the hand of the Lord was with them. And would remain so. For they fought on the side of righteousness.

Weaving among the celebrating soldiers, Patricie searched out the darker hair of her sister. To no avail. Was Eva even here?

Patricie frowned. The longer she looked, the more unlikely the hunt would prove fruitful. She accepted that her desire to see her sister would go unmet.

The men and women around her were all smiles and excitement. Although, instead of becoming caught up in the merriment, Patricie's mind drifted yet again to Stepan Dvorak. This recent battle, the one that gave cause for Hussite dancing and feasting, was the very one that nearly saw Lord Dvorak's life forfeit. Perhaps should have. Yet for whatever reason, the Lord saw fit to pluck him from the abyss and spare his life. For what possible reason? It was beyond her.

But she wasn't Almighty God. And His ways, as the Holy Writ said, were higher and better. She believed that to be true. That did not mean it was always easy to accept.

Lord Dvorak had likely seen the deaths of many Hussites by his own hand. One might believe he deserved such himself as retribution. Though he had not met his end. Could it be that the Lord had bigger plans for him? More to task him with on this earth? And more, would such a man rise to that occasion?

If the Almighty did have intentions for him, Patricie's labors were not in vain. And she could not slight her duty. Nor sidestep it. There was reason to assume that, just as God had spared Lord Dvorak, that He had also placed him under her care.

She frowned and wrapped her arms around herself. Could she hold up under the man's hurtful words and hard opinion? It may require that she endure even more insult in the course of Lord Dvorak's healing. Could she?

With God at her side, she believed it was possible. And more so, it became imperative that she do so.

"Mother," she whispered. "If only I had your compassion."

The woman had been tireless as she worked with Patricie, teaching her how to find medicinal plants and herbs, as well as apply their properties to various ailments. It was those very qualities she now longed for—patience and perseverance. Truly, Mother had been a saint in her dealings with all manner of people. If only Mother could be here now to guide her.

Patricie rubbed at her eyes and found moisture there. Mother's passing, no matter how many years lapsed, stung the same. Patricie should have been there for her. Should have been able to help her. Shaking her head, she tried to dissipate the memories. It would not serve her. She refused to be enveloped by the pain.

Turning her mind back to her patients and shifting her body in the direction of the inn, she firmed her features and strode back to her mission.

CHAPTER 6
KARIN & PAVEL

Pavel glanced once more over the bridge and at the waters below. The dark river had claimed many lives. Too many. By the last count, they had pulled over 500 Royalists from the depths. It wasn't right. It was senseless.

True, many were hired soldiers bent on taking *his* life. But they had also been men, likely with a father and mother who would miss them, perhaps with wives and children who would mourn them.

The ache in his chest gave way to a tightening. It became too much to bear.

Stepan Dvorak had quite nearly been among them, so close to that precipice. Did he mean what he said—that he wished himself counted among the dead? And that even now, he longed for his own end?

Stepan was but a shadow of the former friend Pavel had spent so much time with. How could he have known what darkness dwelt within Stepan, under the surface? Perhaps Pavel had seen glimpses and dismissed them. It was in his nature to see the best in others. But was that a failing?

This trait only became harder to exercise as the war continued. He had seen too much death, too much destruction. Could he ever go back? Would he be able to make his life with Karin and their child in peace? He prayed so.

Moving away from the river, Pavel walked toward the field beyond the village. He passed the last of the houses and as far as he could see, his brethren celebrated their hard-fought victory. A man and woman passed close to him, hand-in-hand, as they ran toward the melee. The woman waved and smiled at him.

He pressed a slight smile onto his features. It was the most he could offer her. But as she passed on and moved into the crowd, he found he could not hold it there. No, too much about this had been wrong. And so, he could not find it in himself to join in.

"There you are," a voice sounded from his far right. A voice he knew too well.

Pavel turned to see his comrade Zdenek drawing closer with his wife trailing behind, gripping his hand. Her features were alight, exuding her joy in this moment.

That gave Pavel the strength to put his smile on once more.

"You have not been easy to find." Zdenek halted a couple of arm-lengths away.

"I...had things to attend to." Could he not just tell Zdenek of how he struggled within himself to find right amongst the wrong?

Zdenek's gaze grew serious, his brows came together, and his mouth tightened into a thin line. "Stepan?"

"Yes, I did see him." Pavel's words were measured.

Zdenek watched him in silence for a moment. It almost seemed as if he wished to read Pavel's thoughts. Something Pavel prayed was not possible.

"And...how is he?" Zdenek's question seemed uneven. As if it were difficult to put the words out.

Did the man feel as torn as Pavel? Their former friend even now fought to sustain his own life. But should they wish for his recovery...

only for him to again seek the death of Hussites? Killing Czechs? Or perhaps to be used as a pawn in this conflict? What should they—should *he*—want for Stepan? What *did* he want? Even that was unclear.

Pavel then realized he had not responded to Zdenek's question. Licking his lips, he pressed forth, "He heals. But he is not pleased with it."

Zdenek grimaced and looked to Eva, whose gaze fairly glowed as she peered up at her husband, yet Pavel saw evidence of concern amid her features, in the tightening about her mouth.

When Zdenek's bright green eyes turned back to Pavel, his friend said, "Perhaps it is all we can hope for."

Pavel nodded. That it was. Still...Pavel wanted more. Expected more. Wished for more. In vain.

Eva moved closer to Zdenek as she turned her regard toward the dancing merrymakers beyond.

Zdenek put an arm around her and drew her closer to himself.

Pavel swallowed as his heart pained anew. How did Karin fare? And their son? He did not doubt Duke Novak's ability to keep his family safe. But even the duke had little say over Karin's return to health. That belonged to the Sovereign God alone.

Zdenek pressed a kiss to Eva's forehead and whispered something for her ears alone.

The movement pulled Pavel from his musings.

Eva nodded and stepped toward the gathering throng.

"You do not seem as if you intend to join in," Zdenek said to Pavel, though he watched his wife moving off.

"I...yes." What was the point in denying his friend the truth?

"For certain, your heart is back in Tabor." Zdenek settled into his stance as he scanned the group filling the small field. Then he turned to Pavel. "But you deserve this moment. We all do."

Pavel grunted. What could he say?

"You do not agree?" Zdenek folded arms across his chest and set his gaze on Pavel.

"I cannot." Pavel trained his eyes on the horizon.

Silence met his statement.

Still Pavel pressed on, "Not this victory. Not this way." He turned and watched his friend's reaction.

Zdenek's forehead scrunched as his brows furrowed.

Why use veiled speech? There was nothing about this situation Zdenek did not know. But would he find Pavel's judgment too harsh? Either way, Pavel could not keep his thoughts trapped within. He looked across the field at his fellow soldiers, a number among those celebrating had been under his command. And he had not stopped them from bringing destruction upon the Royalist army.

"I have never moved against a white flag," Pavel admitted.

Zdenek's breath did not alter. Did he not care for these things Pavel alluded to? At length, however, Zdenek's words cut through the tension. "It happened as it was meant to."

Pavel took in a breath, weighing his response. "I cannot justify such action."

Zdenek released a long sigh. "It was due to the behavior of a few who pushed in when they ought not. What had we to do but defend our men, our brothers at arms? Lest you forget, *they* attacked us."

Pavel kept his tone as even as possible. "Because our men breached the walls whilst General Zizka was distracted with negotiations for a laying down of arms. It could have ended differently. It should have." What more could he say? This victory...what was it worth if they lost their honor in gaining it?

Zdenek shook his head. "I am sorry you feel that way."

How could Pavel not think such? How could Zdenek not?

The surrounded Royalist army had indeed raised a white flag and initiated talk of a peace. But a few of the Hussite soldiers found a break in the wall and entered. They were met with resistance, which fed an outright conflict. The general had moved to protect his own, but not without some measure of regret.

"I won't stand here and question things that cannot be changed." Zdenek's tone was devoid of hostility. But his words were delivered flatly. He stepped toward the crowd. Perhaps to find his wife and join her.

"Zdenek," Pavel spoke out.

His friend, only a few paces away, turned.

"I am thankful in spite of all. You fought well. And we are graced with another day."

Zdenek nodded. "Praise be to God."

Pavel found a genuine smile for Zdenek. "Enjoy the moment with your wife. For tomorrow is...another day. Perhaps another fight."

Zdenek offered a slight bow of his head before moving off.

As Pavel watched his friend disappear into the movement of the fading day, he lifted a prayer of gratitude once again for their survival. For there were many—on both sides—who did not. Lord willing, the Hussite army would not linger, but return to Tabor soon. And he, to his beloved.

It was no use. Karin shoved the papers away from herself. Her head ached and her eyes felt as if they crossed. This wasn't quite what she had pictured. The little work she had done on transcribing the Scriptures thus far had been tedious. And the force within that drove her to return to the work dulled as the memory of her conversation with Father Dominik drifted to the forefront of her mind.

What if she were discovered? The Church would excommunicate her for certain. If she were fortunate, that would be all. That gave her pause. Was her very life at risk? She recoiled from such thoughts. In Hussite-controlled Bohemia, surely that was not likely.

Or was it?

Father Dominik had certainly been put off by the idea. To say the least. In their exchange, he went so far as to withdraw from her as if he wished she had not even asked. That wasn't the reaction of someone who believed the Church and its oversight a distant memory.

Was it not?

She pulled back from the pages that had spread out on the tabletop and gazed out the window. Midmorning had come and gone already. And she had yet to show her face belowstairs. Would others worry after her? Did she care?

The Church could be a powerful adversary. Those in authority had a reach which exceeded any other. And the political games often played by those devoted were subject to the whim of the Pope. Or so it seemed.

No one—not the nobility, nor even the Holy Roman Emperor Sigismund—were above the Church's influence and overarching power. Hadn't Sigismund been beholden to seek permission for the moves he made against Czech lands?

As if she hadn't learned this well enough. One took on great personal risk when defying the Church. How she wished this lesson had not been visited upon her. Some years ago, her dearest friend, Tomas, was lost after a perceived insubordination. An image of her childhood playmate came to mind, unbidden, and her breath caught. The young man had been important to her. If not for the turn of events which took him, she would have wished to join her life with his. But that was not to be. Tomas's allegiance to Hus and his teachings had been discovered. And then he was gone.

What would have been if his disappearance had happened just one month prior? Before she had become convinced herself through Tomas's efforts that Jan Hus spoke truth. For it had been Tomas who showed her the writings and told her of the man's work and challenges with the Catholic Church.

Would she still live in ignorance? Perhaps she would have even married Stepan Dvorak as her father intended. And without regret. That would have put her on the opposite side of this war.

She closed her eyes and whispered a prayer of gratitude for God's hand on her life. Then...and now. For He was at work, was He not?

A stirring nearby drew her gaze to Jaromir, who but moved in his peaceful slumber. What would life be without him? Already he had become a rather substantial part of her days, of who she was. And she found reason aplenty to delight in him.

As she studied him in sleep, she noted that he had pulled his arms free of the swaddle. Such had become his habit of late. Though it did not disrupt his rest.

She smiled. Yes, she was thankful her story had been woven this way—by the divine hand of God. He had brought her to this time and place. For a reason. Was it to do this work? To aid in making the Scriptures more accessible?

Her heart tugged. For certain, she would not feel so strongly if, like Queen Esther, she had not been fit for such a time as this.

Father, I ask for Your direction in this. Help me. Show me.

The door behind her creaked as it opened.

"My lady!"

Karin turned, laying a hand across her work. Would that keep any prying eyes away?

A servant girl stood just beyond the wooden barrier to the room, though it now swung wide.

"Pardon, my lady. I did not wish to disturb you."

"It's all right." Karin let the corners of her mouth lift slightly.

"I have a missive." The girl extended her arm, a sealed envelope in hand.

Karin rose and crossed the room to retrieve the letter.

The girl curtsied, but as Karin turned, something felt odd. She looked over her shoulder in the direction of the servant. And noted that the girl's gaze drifted to the desk. Would she see the papers and know what they were?

Karin sidestepped, moving directly between the younger woman and the table.

The girl's cheeks reddened. "I beg your pardon, my lady. I did not mean to—"

Karin shook her head. How would she make it seem as though it were nothing? "Do not concern yourself. Nothing is amiss." She attempted to play off her nervousness with a light tone. Though perhaps she made it worse in guarding the contents of the papers. Would the servant find that curious?

"You may go." Karin gave her a meaningful look. One she hoped would dissuade further prying.

The girl gave another quick dipped curtsy and quit the room with such speed it did give Karin reason to wonder. She watched after the servant for a few moments. The young woman had left without closing the door.

Striding to the opening, Karin pushed the door back into its frame. Her heart beat hard. She couldn't deny that she'd behaved as if she had something to hide. But did she? Perhaps it was only that she became more uneasy about the work she attended to.

Karin released her weight against the door, leaning on it. And she knew, therein lay her answer—the danger was too great.

Turning toward the table, her papers littering the surface, she sighed. Why must she be so concerned? In all likelihood, the girl was not able to read. Even should she possess such skill beyond her station, did Karin expect malice from the girl? That was, likewise, improbable.

Pushing her worry to the side, she calmed. Only then did she remember the missive. Jerking it upward that she might peer closer, she spotted Pavel's seal.

Sliding a finger between the papers near the seal, she snapped it and let them fall open. She settled into the chair earlier vacated and pored over the words within.

Pavel wrote of the Hussite army's recent battle. And told that he had rescued Lord Stepan Dvorak.

A gasp caught her breath.

Stepan?

She had not heard much of the man she was once intended for since Pavel nearly came to blows with him at the Battle of Vitkov Hill.

How did their former friend fare?

She glanced over the words once more. Pavel mentioned a rescue. Was Stepan injured? If so, how badly?

Her pulse raced as memories flooded her awareness. She had nearly married the man. Had even believed she could love him. Only to find herself a breath away from him running her through.

No, she did not relish these things. Or wish to dwell on them. However, that didn't mean she had no care for Stepan's wellbeing. She let her gaze fall back to Pavel's words.

Stepan indeed healed, and his survival became more secure. But keeping the injured leg was less certain. There was the ever-present danger it may still become putrid. Knowing Stepan as she did, she wagered that he would not tolerate life without his limb.

Her hand covered her heart. No, she did not wish ill upon the man who had, at one time, intended her great harm. She had hoped he could move on and forgive her any trespass against him. Had he been able to find life beyond their shattered betrothal?

More, should he heal, would he continue his mercenary efforts with the Royalist army and their crusade to obliterate the Hussite movement? Or might he be persuaded to join their cause? The harsh anti-Hussite sentiments he had expressed those years ago echoed in her mind. Yes, she had reason to doubt that would be possible.

But she could pray for a miracle. Perhaps Stepan could look beyond his father's beliefs and his own desperation to please the Viscount. Could he, then, be able to discern the truth? That would change so much. Then he might learn to live better with himself and build a legacy worth leaving on this earth.

What of her? Was her own legacy worthy? Her life, her place in this war...all came into sharp focus. Perhaps she had been put here for this task, regardless of the risk, that she might affect her kinsmen for God's eternal kingdom.

She released a long breath and set her hand upon the tabletop. Her fingers grazed the papers she had earlier rejected, and the course texture called to her.

Dare she?

Dare she not?

She set Pavel's letter to the side and combed through the parchments. Could she do this? Was there reason enough to abandon it?

Jaromir's shuffling once more drew her regard. And she couldn't help but venture a thought as to whether her work would endanger him as well. Or maybe, just maybe, it would offer him freedom.

CHAPTER 7
HANA & RADEK

The walls of the castle, dark and gray, offered little solace. But was that what Radek wanted? He moved up the stairway and into his father's solar, unsure of which feeling to take hold of. Was the side of his face still red—a mar to testify to his mother's anger of days past? Her reprimand still stung even if his cheek no longer did. What had happened to the woman? To her kind thought of him? No matter how he rolled over these questions, he could find no answer.

Father looked up from the book that held his attention. As his gaze landed on Radek, a smile crossed his features. "Come in. I planned just now to seek you out and inquire after your desire to join me for a jaunt about the lands to the eastern side of the demesnes."

"Oh?" Radek hoped his response sounded more intrigued and did not smack of the surprise it truly was. Did Father seek to speak more privately with him about what had happened with Mother? Or did it not seem at all odd to the man?

"Yes." Father shut the ledger and stood.

Radek fought within himself to find calm. So that his entreaty would find the right place and time. But he could no longer hold back his emotions...or his concern.

"How is Mother today?" The words were out before Radek could halt them.

Artur Miklas lifted a brow. "She is well." His words came slowly, measured.

Radek swallowed. He did not believe that was all. How could she be well and yet receive him thusly?

Father stepped closer, setting a hand on Radek's shoulder. "Give her time, son. It was..." The man looked to the side as if he could not meet Radek's eyes. Was he truly such a coward? "...difficult for her when you left."

Something like an anchor settled low in Radek's being, but he refused to let it show in his affect. He held himself tautly, determined to remain so. As if he had nothing to betray.

"Come now, let us make the most of the day." Father moved around Radek and toward the door.

Still, Radek remained as he was. Dare he prove as complacent as his father? Simply forget the exchange with Mother? Perhaps Father hoped his wife would soften, and all would go back to the way it had been. Could Radek do that?

"Are you coming?" the margrave asked from the threshold. "We have but a couple of hours before the nooning meal."

After a brief pause to reconsider, Radek nodded and followed.

They moved back through the castle almost tracing Radek's earlier steps. Father neither stopped nor spoke again until they arrived at the stables. From somewhere, father's man-at-arms appeared upon horseback alongside two saddled horses.

How did the man know Radek would comply if he himself questioned it? Radek dismissed the concern. It did not mean that his father knew him better. Perhaps Ondrej prepared both horses in hopes that Radek would be well with it. Yes, that must be it.

Without anything further, Father mounted his destrier. The dark colored horse seemed more intimidating than the man upon it. How was that possible? But as the animal snorted and shifted, its presence looming over Radek, he noted that it was so.

Pushing that thought to the side, Radek lifted himself into the saddle of the waiting horse. Then he offered a nod to his father and Ondrej, even as his gaze wandered about the stables. Where were the others? Would not more of Father's knights accompany them? Such a vulnerable man surely needed more protection.

But Radek dismissed this easily as well. He did not doubt his own abilities. Or Ondrej's. Yes, he had seen the man-at-arms in action far too many times to think otherwise.

Now settled, Radek nodded to the margrave again as he directed the horse toward the east.

Father jerked his heels into the horse's flank, and they were off.

Riding had always been one of Father's favorite ways to spend an afternoon. The man loved little more than the oneness with the horse's movements. And so, riding had been one of Radek's first pastimes. Certainly, the first skill he mastered. Long before he held a blade. That had come far too late for his liking. But his father was not, after all, a man of war but of words. Though what good were they in moments of arms and swords?

They continued moving eastward for some time until they came upon a wooded area.

Radek paused, but Father pushed his horse onward. If possible, urging more speed from the animal. Ondrej followed, as did Radek, reducing their speed only slightly as they avoided the thickness of trees and brush. Father and Ondrej seemed more adept on their horses than Radek. Still, he pushed on, only falling behind for a short time.

The forest opened to a hillside just there on the edge of their visual range. Radek kicked his heels to the horse, affecting more speed. In a few moments, he passed the two older men, a smile breaking his features at the small victory when he cut between them.

Tree coverage in Radek's path gave way and he looked back, intent on his father.

The man offered a slight smile before bending over the mighty destrier's neck and encouraging the animal to go faster. It mattered not. Radek would not let up, would not let him gain.

He discerned a sharp *whoosh* before something struck his shoulder. The impact had enough force that Radek lost his balance and landed on his backside. The world spun as he blinked. What had happened?

There was little time to register the hot pain in his shoulder before a strange man stood over him, sunlight gleaming off the blade at his side.

The sword came down just as Radek rolled to the side and out of the way. A thud on the ground behind told of what would have happened to his heart.

Searing heat tore at him from his shoulder. The roll had only made matters worse. Warmth poured from what could only be a flesh wound. But he could not afford it even a glance. Not if he wished to survive.

Radek struggled to his feet as he pulled out his own sword. His balance was unsteady, and his vision wavered.

The blade came toward him again, but he raised his own weapon. Metal clashed as he successfully defended his person.

"Go," he yelled in Father's direction. He would not let these brigands have their prize.

Again and again, Radek deflected slashes this way and that. His opponent wore the garments of a peasant. A dirty peasant at that. Grime and muck covered every stitch of clothing. But there was little of the stuff on the man's face. How was that possible?

Radek had not adequate time to consider this if he was to preserve his life.

The man launched at him again.

Radek sidestepped, but the man only stumbled, not falling as anticipated.

Scanning the immediate area, Radek noted two things: his father had not fled and another, yet larger man fast approached. The intensity of the pain in his shoulder drew Radek to distraction, but he could not allow it. He had to focus.

Hoofbeats pounded. Radek glanced in that direction.

Ondrej was upon the larger man in a moment.

This gave Radek a brief reprieve. The sword of his opponent came again. And as they engaged once more, Radek's head cleared. His every awareness sharpened. He embraced the exchange. What should perhaps be an easy thwarting became much more difficult.

These men were skilled. Something about that nagged.

Radek's vision blurred again. How long could he maintain his footing? Blood seeped from his wound...which for certain was made by a bolt. A couple of times, he tried to loosen it. Without success.

One moment he fought for his life and the next the brigands were on the run.

"Do not let them escape! Ondrej, after them," he called.

"Do not," came Father's command. "We must see to Radek."

"No, I..." Radek sank to the ground, frustration burning hotter than his torn flesh. "We have to..."

Ondrej was beside him, clasping his shoulders. "Be still, my lord. All will be well."

Would it? How could he be in such pain and survive?

With the knight's aid, he lay. But as he met Ondrej's gaze, he set his jaw. "How bad is it?"

Ondrej frowned. "It is nothing."

The man had never been a capable liar.

In the next moment, Father's shadow fell across him. "We must get it out and stop the bleeding."

Radek's senses were overcome with the pain. It mattered not to him that they intended to pull the bolt from where it had lodged. Though perhaps it should.

Ondrej put a hand to Radek's chest and gripped the bolt with the other. "This will hurt."

Radek almost laughed at that.

But as Ondrej pulled, all went black.

Hana startled awake, pulling in air as if it were her last. The bedclothes clung to her as did her chemise. She brought a shaky hand to her forehead and pressed it. Where was she?

Looking about the room, she placed herself in her own chambers in her father's castle. She was safe. She was well. Then why did she tremble so?

As her mind calmed, she remembered...she had dreamed. The fitful sleep was born of hard memories raised from her subconscious. She had seen the events of her and Radek's flight in the night again. And experienced anew the stream that had attempted to steal her breath and her soul.

On nights such as these, she would wake gasping and clawing against invisible water. Until she found her way to herself again. Such as now. Pushing a hand through her hair, she heaved. She let her hands drop into her lap as she stared into the night. It was too much.

Collapsing back against the pillow, she counted her breaths—in and out—as her heartbeat found its natural rhythm once again. Still, even as she settled into what comfort the bed offered, she could not shake the uneasiness within.

She turned to her side, and her hand stretched over the vacant part of the bed as if of its own accord. Though she had never known anything but emptiness beside her as she slept, still she ached for something that wasn't there. How long would it be until Radek filled this space? During their time in the wilderness evading the Royalist soldiers, she had become accustomed to waking and finding him nearby.

But it would not be proper were he to be here now, the two of them yet to wed. Would it be months before they were joined in matrimony? How she hoped not! Could she live with this ache? This loneliness that stemmed from his absence?

Closing her eyes, she attempted to reclaim her fitful sleep. She conjured an image of her beloved. Great emotion, even distress was evident upon his features—and it bothered her. Apprehension ebbed from his being, almost foreboding. Was it a sign? Was he in danger? Hurting?

She opened her eyes, refusing to give way to the pull inward and found some comfort in the fading darkness. At least this did not stir her heart so but gave her a measure of ease. Still, she could not shake the image of Radek and the depth of sorrow seen in his imagined gaze. He needed her. She was certain of it.

Sitting up once more, she looked about the chamber. The day approached—her room was not as black as it had been when she was first awakened. Yet it chilled, causing her to draw the covers about her. Was it the coolness of the room that made her shiver? Or her worry for Radek?

She rose and stepped to the window. Dare she open it—and herself—to the colder exterior? Almost without thinking, she pushed at the panes separating her from the outside world. A breeze cut through her. But she welcomed the sting. It distracted her from her thoughts—for at least a moment. Would this day offer a chance to gain Father's permission to join Radek? Her heart dropped as she feared the likely outcome, but she forbade herself to give in. Wasn't there reason to hope?

As she peered across her Father's lands, the weight abated somewhat as she noted that, on the horizon, light foretold of the sun's arrival. The day must bring with it promise. And possibilities. That thought only drew her mind back to the more immediate source of her anguish. Would she find herself at her father's door in the coming hours, begging him to release her to journey to Horice?

The larger part of her knew this was nonsense. Why would her father give her leave? For such an ill-advised, dangerous pursuit—traveling in this weather, and for such a distance. For certain if she sought Father's concession it would be to no avail.

A deep pain shot through her, straight from her heart. Dare she *not* make her request? And have to live with this burden? This despair...not knowing how Radek fared?

Chirping from just outside dispelled the silence of the coming day. The sound was louder than she would have thought. And obtrusive. She scanned about her. A favorite tree, just beyond her window, must be where it originated. Sliding her gaze over the branches, she did at some length locate a blue bird. It seemed an oddity. Why had it not abandoned these frigid lands for warmer weather? The bitter cold could not be easy on the creature.

As Hana listened, she reflected on the bird's call—almost mournful. Did it bemoan its situation? Was it unable to fly farther south? Or did it express sadness?

Perhaps the creature, too, longed for its faithful companion.

Now that was a fanciful thought indeed. Surely, her mind had become too clouded. This proved it must be so. Yet the throb within Hana's heart as she thought of Radek remained. Could she bear it? Or would it, bit by bit, eat her alive?

Yes, she had no choice but to seek out Father as soon as possible and make her request. After all, she wouldn't know his answer until she tried.

Then again, if she did make such a request and he denied her, she would be trapped. For this glimmer of hope, albeit small, wound no longer remain. As long as she delayed, she could nurse the possibility and find some warmth in it.

Radek would not be pleased even should she gain father's approval and aid. He would be vexed. This she knew full well. But did that mean he had no need of her? She couldn't think this true.

What if he did have need of her and she remained in Tabor, bemoaning as the feathered creature outside the window did? Her courage hoisted, she decided that all sense provided that she make the journey.

Determined, she dressed. All the while, she watched the coming day. Would Father be awake at this hour? Would the disruption of his rest hinder her efforts? And the outcome?

Her heart thudded, almost painfully. She could no more wait than she could force the beating to slow. No, she was bound by her decision and could no longer tarry.

The sky had continued to brighten, and she basked in the sunbeams for a moment before moving beyond her chamber and into the hall. Her timid steps gave her pause as she passed through the keep. She must dismiss this nervousness if at all possible. It would be best to present a confident plan to Father. If she didn't believe, how would he?

As she neared Duke Novak's solar, Hana prayed he would be up and about. But how would she know unless she knocked? Steeling herself, she raised a hand to do so.

"What?" Her father's words echoed in the hall even though heavy oak separated them. Had something angered him? Or did he ascertain that she slinked about?

She held her breath and listened, unmoving.

"One man rule all of Bohemia? Such would thwart our very purpose in this war...and everything we are fighting for. If that priest wishes to rule on his own power, he must be stopped. Can he not see the challenge this presents?"

She picked out another voice, lower—perhaps a trusted servant—discernable through the door, though not as well as Father's. Should she keep her presence secret and listen to the conversation her father believed private?

"It will not happen!" It was her Father again. "The man over-reaches. Does he truly seek to make himself a king? Bohemia's over-seers must be numbered. At least until Poland answers. If King Wladyslaw ever will."

Was there trouble in the Czech lands? Hana had become largely ignorant of the political maneuverings in Prague, whereas once she followed them quite well. Should she remain so? She leaned closer to the small space—a mere crack—between the door and the stone wall.

The servant spoke again, so quietly that she was not able to make any of it out.

"Yes," came Father's response to whatever was said. "Poland will answer. We have hope there. While General Zizka does succeed time and again to keep Bohemia free of Sigismund's clutches, our kingdom must be under the protection of a powerful king if it is to have any future."

Was that true? The Hussites in Tabor desired a self-governed way of life, to retain the freedoms they had found in the absence of a monarch. At least that was how it seemed to her. Would they lay down what autonomy they had acquired if the Polish king rode in to claim the crown? She doubted such would be achieved in peace. Could the Czechs not be led by the city councils? Without a king?

Hana shook her head. Such was not done. A country needed a ruler. And she prayed Bohemia would find a worthy king...hopefully soon.

The door creaked. There wasn't time for her to hide or disguise her intrusion before it swung wide, revealing her crouched position.

She jerked her gaze upward. One of Father's man-at-arms stood in the threshold, surprise written on his features. Chiding herself, she pushed out a ragged breath. Could she not have been more careful?

"Hana?" Father's deep voice sliced through the thick moment. "What are you doing?"

She rose to her full height, side-stepping the large guard to catch her father's eyes. And found herself under the intensity of his sharp glare.

He was not happy. This was not the start she had hoped for. If anything, she may have just forfeited any chance of his approval. Should she ever have had a prayer to begin with.

CHAPTER 8
PATRICIE & STEPAN

Despite Patricie's best intentions to face the difficult charge with dignity and grace, she had avoided the viscount's son with determination. But she would have to see him in a few moments—it was time to check his wound and refresh the bandage. As much as she wanted for an excuse to send the healer instead, she would not. That might affect Ludek's opinion of her. His good opinion. And that was not something she would sacrifice. Not for that Royalist soldier.

She stood in front of the medicinals shelf and gathered the things she needed for Lord Dvorak's treatment. Her mind drifted to the forthcoming interaction and the possibilities therein. Would he ignore her? Would he attempt to insult her again? She paused, breathing in, and then pressing the air out. She could do this. She would.

It would not be necessary, after all, to actually speak with him... or to him. Or let any words he spit in her direction bother her.

A hand fell on her shoulder.

She jumped, biting back a scream.

"Patricie?" It was the healer's voice.

She turned, a hand over her heart, pressing against the tightness there.

"Are you well?" Ludek's eyes widened. His concern was evident.

"I am." She offered the best smile she could muster. "That does not mean I am able to tolerate someone startling me." Her words were bold, but she had never known him to creep up like that.

His brows furrowed. "I have been here for several moments. And I called to you more than once."

Her face warmed. Had she been so distracted? By Lord Dvorak?

Ludek's warm brown eyes searched her features. Was he attempting to discern if she were ill?

"My apologies." Patricie let out a breath. "I...my thoughts were elsewhere."

He took a step back. Had they been so close? If his creating distance was necessary and yet he still stood an arm's length away, they must have been. Now her features heated for an entirely different reason.

"I hope it wasn't something I did." A smirk made its way across his face.

"No." She dipped her head and looked to her supplies. "It is nothing."

Part of her wanted him to pursue the issue. That was the part of her that wanted him to be someone she could share such things with. Perhaps to be able to tell him about the viscount's son and the things the man had said. And how it still bothered.

She peered up at Ludek again and studied the attractive curves of his face.

Ludek cleared his throat.

She jerked her regard to the floor. What had he seen? Perhaps she could dismiss her attention as something else. But as she opened her mouth to take such a chance, Ludek's words cut her off.

"Is Lord Dvorak your next charge?"

She nodded, lifting her gaze to his once more, trying to put on her healer's apprentice role as much as possible.

"Good," he said, his eyes on her softened, a display of his kind concern. "I pray his manner has improved."

So, he did know about her challenging interaction previously? Somehow, he knew. Did he care so for her feelings? That thought stirred something in her. Something pleasant.

"Thank you." Her cheeks burned all the more, and she spun toward the cabinet, hoping he hadn't noticed. Everything within the row of shelves was neatly lined up, evenly spaced, where it could be accessed when needed. If only life could be so easy. So orderly.

If only Patricie could know her own mind—and heart—so well.

Silence fell between them, and his gaze moved to the cabinet. Perhaps he was finished with her and needed to move to his next patient.

Patricie offered him a small smile of gratitude and stepped around him.

His hand connected with her upper arm. His hold was gentle, but sure. "Patricie?"

She could not avoid his eyes in that moment. Intent on her, the golden brown seemed to dance. So little distance separated their bodies and, even though they stood shoulder to shoulder, it was difficult to control her reaction. "Yes?"

"I..." His voice was smooth and deep—more so than she had known from him.

She resisted the urge to shudder. This was a moment to maintain a calm, collected exterior.

He did not speak further, but let the unfinished sentence linger between them.

"Yes?" she repeated her entreaty, wanting so much for him to continue.

He looked away and ran a hand through his hair. "If you find Lord Dvorak difficult, let me know."

She nodded. Was that what he truly had wanted to say? If so, why did she doubt it? Her own wishful thinking? Either way, she couldn't decide how best to respond.

His gaze remained set on her, examining her features once more. Was there something he still needed to ask?

It was a moment before she realized she had not responded. "Thank you."

He released her and grabbed for a container of witch hazel.

She watched, hating the loss of contact.

He peered over and, nodding, moved past her and down the narrow hall with nothing further.

She stared at his back as he walked away. What had he been thinking? Were his thoughts inclined toward her? Or just for the safety and wellbeing of a valued assistant?

What of her own thoughts? The viscount's son had filled them most of the day, remembering his words as if they repeated in her mind. But that was nonsense, she cared not for his opinion. Or had it bothered so because they stung more than she'd thought?

She shook her head. Perhaps she should not put such weight in the turning of her mind. After all, the Scriptures told that the heart was deceitful. Might she not, then, let it inform her actions? Closing the cabinet, she moved toward Lord Dvorak's room. And, though she had fresh determination about her, she braced herself.

Stepan stirred and opened his eyes. However, it was not Pavel's visage before him in reality, but that of the Hussite woman. The one that assisted the healer.

At first, he thought himself still asleep. For often she had visited his dreams.

But the scowl on her features betrayed that this was not a flight of fantasy, unwanted as those thoughts were.

"Why are you here?" he asked, pressing disdain into his tone.

Her gaze clashed with his. What was that within the flash of blue? For there seemed a great mystery about her. One that pulled at him to untangle it.

He opened his mouth, tempted to retract his harsh words. But closed it again and looked to the wall opposite her. Yes, keeping his guard up was best.

"I am to tend your wound."

In his periphery, he noted movement. Yanking his regard back to her, he saw that she reached for the blanket covering him.

He jerked away, causing pain to slice through him. "I do not wish it."

Her wide eyes and downturned mouth betrayed that he had dealt injury with success. But he refused to let it affect him. Her feelings were not his concern.

She turned away. Why? Did she fight her own emotions? Did she actually care what happened to him?

"I wish to be left alone," he pushed out through gritted teeth, praying his pain was not evident. Directing his attention to the ceiling, he then closed his eyes and prepared for her to withdraw from the room.

Instead, he felt her gaze upon him. Why would she care? Because of her desire to please the healer?

When she spoke, her voice was firm, but gentle. "That's not possible."

He scoffed. Was she so stubborn? He would have to try harder.

Turning a glare with all the rage he could muster, he prepared to spit out something...anything that would make her leave him be. But her gentle affect stopped him. She *did* seem to have a care. But why would she? He had been part of bringing death to her fellow Hussites. So much death...too much.

"I will not leave you. I will not let you push me away. Your life is... valuable. If not to you, then to your Creator. And He will not give me leave until I have done what I can." Her words were simple, but there was a thickness to her voice...and to the emotion surrounding them.

Where did that fire come from? For a blaze had ignited in her eyes. A determination to help him perhaps?

He wanted to naysay her. And continue to refuse her aid. Yet when she reached for the blanket and exposed his bandaged leg, he did not stop her.

She focused her gaze on his injury as she relieved the limb of its wrappings.

He seethed when the exposure to air hit it.

She frowned.

If only he could push her away. Make her hate him as much as he hated himself.

Pain assaulted him as she applied salve to his wound. He gripped the mattress and tried to place his thoughts elsewhere.

Her gaze flicked to his face.

His eyes caught hers. He should look away. But he would not, nor would he further betray the effects of her work. Wasn't it enough that he permitted it?

Not long after, she had dressed his wound and shifted away.

He was both relieved and oddly regretful. Because of his treatment of her? Swallowing against that thought, he pulled from deep within and dragged every foul emotion to the surface. Surely, he could find some venom to direct her way.

She stood but then paused. "You can fight me every step of the way if you choose." She surprised him by speaking. "But my decision to tend you and fight for your survival has nothing to do with you."

Did she seek the healer's favor? That must be it. The pang he felt surprised. Because she didn't care for his life? Or because she cared more for the healer?

He must better attend his imaginings. His dreams of her had crossed into the realm of conscious reality. All because of a fair face and fine form. Surely, he was most ridiculous. "So, I should care that you seek to gain more from the healer because of your good work?"

Her shock was displayed all over her features rather plainly. She must be a terrible liar when the need arose.

"As I thought," he grunted. "Your praises will not come to his ear from my lips."

The lines of her face softened and eased. But she did not react to his taunt.

"Oh, what a most helpful assistant you have," he mocked, feigning a conversation with the healer. "Wherever did you find such capable help?"

She jerked away from him, her chest heaving. Had he hit his mark? Why, then, did he take no delight in it?

He watched her, his lips forming a smirk as she crossed to the door. All the better for her to be more quickly gone.

She reached for the latch but paused.

What now?

"It is not for Ludek that I tend you faithfully," she tossed over her shoulder.

He wished for her eyes upon him once more that he might see the lie there.

Though when she turned, he regretted his wish. For the blue fairly glowed in the bit of light coming through the window. Rather than prove the lie, they appeared sincere.

"It is because the Lord cares and has appointed me to this task."

He wanted to laugh. God? Care about him? But he could do nothing more than stare after her as she slipped from the room.

Had she believed her own words? There was no indication of falsehood in her.

Perhaps she was an adept liar after all.

CHAPTER 9
HANA & RADEK

Radek blinked. Or at least he believed he did. The darkness remained whether his eyes were open or closed. But he was certain he had regained his hold on consciousness, for he felt a chill in the air. And he heard the crackling of the last embers of a fire.

Fire!

He jerked his head in the direction of the gentle popping and could just make out the tiny sparks of glowing orange and red. So, his eyes *were* open, though all that surrounded him was as night.

Something shifted beyond the bed. When had he lain down? He bolted upright, hands searching for a weapon, anything that might defend his person.

"Lord Miklas?" The voice had the sound of youth about it. That eased the tension in his shoulders. Was it a servant?

Radek let out a breath. "What is the hour?"

"My lord, it is the middling of night."

Radek watched the boy rise, his outline discernable now as Radek's eyes homed in on him as they adjusted. "What do you here?"

"I have been charged to rouse the margrave should you wake."

"Even in this depth of night?"

The boy nodded.

Radek heard more than saw it.

The lad must have realized he was nearly invisible in the darkness, for he said, "Yes, my lord. He said no matter the hour."

Radek thought to stop the boy but did not do so as the youth opened the door and slipped beyond.

Now alone, Radek took stock of his person. A deep throbbing from his shoulder, surprised that he had not discerned it before. He fit a hand over the joint but bandaging there kept him from assessing the extent of the damage. Had he been tended by a healer? What had happened?

He lay back against the pillow and, closing his eyes, searched his memory. Only a handful of moments later, it all came back—the attack, the interchange, the arrow. Somehow Ondrej and Father must have gotten Radek back to the castle. Was there anything further to the exchange after he had lost consciousness? No, he distinctly remembered the brigands' retreat. Father was safe. Radek breathed out the remaining tension in his body.

Though...a thought struck him. The men that attacked had not been typical riffraff. They had been skilled at arms, even possessed fine weapons. And something else nagged...

Try as he might, whatever it was did not come forth. Not before a pounding of feet upon the stairs snagged his concentration. A light from somewhere outside the room created a silhouette of the door, the muted brightness seeping in the line between it and its frame. Only a moment later, the door opened, and Father entered, a candle in his hand.

The servant boy crossed at once to the hearth. Perhaps to bring the fire back to life.

"Radek!" His father drew near, his voice betraying his concern. Must everything the man felt or thought be on display for all? Even this young servant?

"Yes, I am awake. And I am well." He lifted to a sitting position. The pain in his shoulder nearly stole his breath.

"Thank heaven!" Father paused to look toward the ceiling as if he spoke to the Almighty.

Radek did not have the time for this. "Father, I do not wish to disturb your sleep."

"Nonsense." The margrave glanced toward the servant. "Fetch the healer."

"That will not be necessary," Radek seethed through clenched teeth as the ache sought once again to rob him of air.

The boy paused, looking between the men. Was he uncertain as to which command to honor?

"You must be assessed." The margrave's features, now illuminated by the fire, gave away his feelings.

It sickened Radek. "I am well enough. Leave the healer to his sleep. It will keep 'til the morrow. Your attentions as well could have been left for daybreak."

Father's eyebrows gathered. Did he detect the less veiled rebuke in Radek's tone? Did Radek care if he did?

"There is naught that can be achieved at this hour," Radek continued. "I wish to see you returned to your wife and your bed."

The margrave turned to the servant and spoke softly. Still, Radek could hear enough to know the boy was being sent for food and water.

Would Father have the entire estate roused? This was nonsense.

Radek waited until the youngster had disappeared down the stairs before he shifted his focus to his father. "This is wholly unnecessary," he ground out. "I assure you I am well enough."

Father's features, clearly visible now in the flickering light of the flames, turned downward. "You cannot know that the injured shoulder is well."

Radek looked to the wall, steeling himself for what he wished to say. Control maintained, he regarded his father once more. Still, he could not hold back. "It makes me seem weak. Do you not understand that? Though you may not care how you are viewed. I do not wish to be made into a whelp."

Father jerked back. And several long moments of silence followed.

Radek waited for regret to sweep over him, but it did not. He had meant what he said.

When the margrave did speak, his words were quieter. Almost too much so for Radek to make them out. "Is that what you think? That concern after my son makes me weak?"

Radek looked away. He could not take back his words and would not deny the truth of them.

Father swallowed. "I see. Then I shall not degrade your image any longer." The man turned, more slowly than Radek liked, and walked out of the room. Was it Radek's imagination, or was there a slight limp to his step?

It mattered not. Soon enough, Father was no longer discernable in the shadows. Only then did the weight in Radek's stomach roll. It did not help the sick feeling from earlier. If anything, it intensified it.

He looked to the ceiling. Was God up there? Listening? Watching? Was he amused?

Radek blew out a breath as he lay back down. If only he hadn't let loose his tongue. Where was he to go from here?

Hana stared across the room at her father's glowering face. The man had not looked so cross since the past spring when she told him of her desire to follow the Hussite army. This would not go well.

Her attention was drawn to the man-at-arms standing beside her. His features were more controlled. But she discerned his ire as well in the lines around his narrowed gaze.

"What are you doing?" Father repeated.

Hana stepped forward, past the knight. "I must speak with you."

"And just how long did you hover beyond that door, listening to what I trusted was a private conversation?" His question was pointed and his tone flat.

She licked her lips. How best to proceed? Should she deny it? She hadn't truly heard anything that mattered. Nothing that meant anything to her anyway. But Father would believe that to be a falsehood regardless.

"I only paused without because I heard voices exchanged within." Taking a breath, she then rushed on, "It was not my intention to overhear, but I couldn't help but—"

Her father's brow furrowed. And he held up a hand. "I wish not to hear excuses for improper behavior."

Was that all it was to him? Improper behavior? Though it rubbed at her, she did not wish to make matters worse by speaking further. So, she only nodded.

"My lord, I will escort Lady Hana to her chambers." The man-at-arms grasped Hana's upper arm. "There is no need for you to be further disrupted..."

She pulled against the man's rather solid grip. Seeking out Father's gaze, she hoped her eyes sufficiently beseeched him to let her remain.

The duke waved a hand in the direction of his guard. "Leave us."

Did she hear correctly? Would he hear her out then?

The man-at-arms continued as if he had not heard, tugging her toward the hall. "Too long has she been indulged—"

"I said, leave us." Her father's voice rose.

The knight stopped, his glare no longer on her face, but directed toward Father. "My lord, I but—"

"Do not make me say it again." A tinge of red touched Father's face.

"Yes, my lord." The man released her and, shooting her a hard look, slipped outside. He closed the door soundly, sealing her in the solar with her father.

She rubbed at her arm, though the injury was imagined. The guard had not gripped her too tightly. "I never thought I would see a day when Sir Nate would behave so."

Father's gaze settled on her. "He's not wrong. You have been allowed much leniency in this castle. You do not understand how you press against boundaries that should not move."

She looked down and swallowed. "Yes, Father."

"Now," he said as he ran a hand over his beard, "What is so important that you must violate the sanctity of my conversations?"

Perhaps she best not continue and risk his refusal. Her mind once again warned that if he denied her request, there would be no further recourse within the bounds of propriety. Should she chance it? How could she bear it if he rejected her heart's desire? Then again, she would be no better off than if she did not seek his permission at all. Yes, she must push into the difficulty of the moment.

"Hana?" His voice was stern.

She lifted her eyes to meet his. "I...apologize once more for the intrusion. Please believe me, it was not my intention."

He waved his hand in a gesture of dismissal. "I do not wish to hear anything further about that. I would know what you seek."

Hana swallowed. Her heart banged against the inside of her chest. Was there any way he would see her predicament as she did? "I..." she started. Then swallowed and tried to put confidence in her words before she continued. "Have you noticed that it has been a fortnight since we have received any word of Lord Miklas?"

"Yes." The word was abrupt, but with a soft edge to it. Did he understand her concern? Did he share it? He dropped into his chair and picked up his quill. "What of it?"

Would he simply move on to his next task? With her heart bleeding out in front of him? She straightened her spine and pressed forth. "I cannot hide that I am...concerned as to how he fares."

Father laid the quill to the side and steepled his fingers in front of his lips. Did he consider her words? How carefully? Dare she continue?

At length, she ventured further. It was the only way. "With the unrest in Bohemia, I find I cannot...bear the lack of knowing."

"Shall I send a couple of my men to Horice? Determine whether he has arrived safely?"

She nodded, releasing a breath. The first hurdle had been crossed, though it was the easier of the two.

Father leaned forward. "That is simple enough."

Hana offered him a slight smile and wondered how she might transition into her true reason for seeking him out this morning.

"You may take your leave," he said, grabbing the quill, dipping it into his inkwell, and then scratching something onto the paper. He continued for a handful of moments.

She remained as she was, telling herself to breathe.

He paused. And without looking up, asked, "Is there something else?"

"Yes." She tested the waters with the one word.

He set the quill down again and leaned back, clasping his hands in front of his chest. It was not an encouraging sign. He appeared rather put out.

It would be best if she abandoned her quest here and now. Let things remain. Leave hope where it may still prevail.

Light from the approaching dawn spilled into the room all the more. It made the lantern unnecessary. Perhaps she could come back when she had more confidence.

Preparing to do so, she opened her mouth.

"You want to go to him, don't you?" Father's face was a mask of indifference. It wasn't the worst thing.

She licked her lips and ventured where she had feared she dare not. "I cannot explain this urge that pushes me to do so. But I admit I must."

His brows rose. "You must?"

She nodded, tempted to look away, but forcing herself to hold his gaze.

"And if I refuse, will you defy me again? Run off on your own?"

How could she explain? Might she respond with the truth? This time she should perhaps be as transparent as possible.

"I do not intend disrespect. And I have no firm plans to go against your wishes. But I fear in my heart, I may lose that battle."

His eyes lingered on her face. He was quiet, solemn. With slow movements, he stood and strode to the window. Why must he draw this out? The silence ate at her. Yet there was naught she could do to force a response.

"I appreciate your forthrightness, Hana." His tone was deep, thoughtful. At least he had not outright rejected the idea.

The seconds ticked by; each feeling as an hour. It reached the point she could no longer hold her tongue. "Father, I—"

"If you consent to do this my way," he said, turning. "I will allow it."

Had she heard correctly?

"You will allow it?" Her voice had not the force she wished it to. The words were all but squeaked out.

"Yes." When he set his gaze upon her this time, she saw a tenderness there that made shame bloom in her core for her defiant flight to Prague those months ago.

She nodded, lowering eyes that could no longer bear it.

A rustle of the rushes told that he moved closer. And then a hand lay upon her shoulder.

"As long as you keep your word, you will have my support in this."

Peering at him, she sniffled. Was she so moved? "I give you my word."

He squeezed her shoulder and turned back to his desk. "I will assemble the knights required for your escort. And you will take Mistress Huddard as your companion."

"Yes—" she started, her voice cracking. Mistress Huddard was strict and dull. This was not a welcome addition to her journey. But this was what he had decided. And she *had* given her word. She swallowed. "Yes, Father."

He waved a hand. "Please, begin your preparations."

She nodded and slipped from the room. But as she stood in the hall, having closed the door, she braced herself against the stone wall and held a hand to her midsection. Her father had given her reprieve. She would go to Radek.

Thank You, Lord. Thank You.

CHAPTER 10
KARIN & PAVEL

T he landscape about Pavel had become increasingly more familiar in the last two hours. He neared home. The hills and valleys were known to him—Tabor. And soon, he would be on Duke Novak's lands.

He had left the ravages of the most recent battle in Nemecky Brod, but would he ever be able to erase them from his mind? There was reason to hope, was there not?

A portion of the Hussites who fought beside him had journeyed with him back to Tabor. Zizka had taken most of the army to Prague. The civil unrest there—politics and some such nonsense—had developed and became out of control. Pavel had only heard bits and pieces as he had not the stomach for it.

As much as Pavel wished he might join General Zizka and assist in sorting out the madness, his longing for Karin was greater. Zizka was a capable man, wise beyond Pavel's years. And so, Pavel had been all too eager in volunteering to deliver these men and women to Tabor. Which he had done with success. Now he moved on to Novak territory.

The duke's castle sat on the horizon ahead. It was grand and well-fortified. Everything it should be. It stood in the distance, situated on a hillside. How long before Pavel could take his family home to Krejik lands? There was much progress made in rebuilding what fire had consumed, a fire that had nearly stolen his wife.

Pavel pushed those thoughts to the side. His father had seen to Karin's survival. And she yet lived.

Perhaps they would soon return to his own castle and truly begin their life together. Although...they would return without an important member of their family—Pavel's father. The realization still pained him deeply. As if no time had passed.

Pavel had first become acquainted with this painful grief when he and Karin lost their first child. He thanked God every day for the birth of their second child. And that Karin had endured through the difficult labor.

Still, despite these wonderful thoughts, something tugged at him. And he wondered...when would he come out from under this shroud and see light? The death, the depth of the abyss the Hussites had traveled to come out on the other side, weighed on him. Would he ever be free?

If such were possible, being with Karin was the first step. Of that, he was certain.

Too long had they been apart. And so soon after Jaromir's entrance into the world.

After these weeks of separation, he pondered how the child fared. Did he grow stronger? Had he gained Karin's eyes? Or Pavel's nose?

Pavel allowed a smile to lift his lips. Jaromir had been a force to be reckoned with from the moment he first breathed. Just like Karin. There was much of her in the infant. Even those months ago as the babe was only newly in the world.

So distracted, Pavel only then realized he approached the great walls of the castle. He prepared for the exchange with the guards on the wall, but it was as if they had expected him. For the drawbridge lowered.

Pavel nodded at those looking down on him from the battlements. Was this the hero's welcome he had feared? He wasn't certain he could withstand such. For he did not feel the champion.

He was welcomed into the inner bailey without pause. And, as he moved farther within, he saw that Duke Novak awaited him. Had something happened with Karin? To Jaromir?

Pavel dismissed such concerns as there was no sense of urgency or distress about the duke. That eased him as he pushed the horse the remaining steps to Duke Novak.

"Dobry vecer," the duke greeted him.

"Dobry vecer." Pavel responded in kind. Was it truly afternoon already? He glanced upward. The sun had indeed made the majority of its journey across the sky. How had he lost his sense of time?

A stable hand neared and took Pavel's horse after he dismounted.

Duke Novak strode forward and clapped him on the back. "A warrior returned! You are most welcomed."

Pavel fought the cringe that threatened and instead nodded. "It is good to be back."

"And how does the army fare?" The duke's eyes held a hint of concern. Did he wish he could join them? Fight alongside his brethren at arms? Pavel did not believe that would be best. For the man's age and health would not go well in battle.

"Victory was ours," Pavel said, but not without regret.

"As I had heard." The creases about Duke Novak's eyes smoothed. Then re-formed. "But you do not seem well with it."

Pavel shook his head. "I am," he lied. "It is only that I tire after so long in the saddle."

The duke studied him. Was the man not ready to take him at his word? Regardless, Pavel was not prepared to offer anything further.

A lightness returned to the duke's features. "And I am certain your wife—"

"Is eager to see her husband," a feminine voice broke into the man's words.

Pavel turned. And there she was—in all her beauty. He drank in her visage as if she were an oasis in the desert. When last he had laid eyes on her, she had been abed, unable to even carry her own weight. And now she stood before him without aid. He breathed in deeply, pleased to see color in her features and strength about her form. Oh, that he might gather her into his arms in that moment. But he did not wish such a display in front of these men. Though he did not stop himself from stepping to her and sweeping up her hands.

"It is..." he breathed, "good to see you up and about."

"Yes, my lord. And I am relieved you are returned." A small smile that appeared forced touched her features.

He nodded. And as he let his eyes delve into hers for a moment, he attempted to gather what he could about her wellbeing.

That well-learned mask her parents had insisted upon was up. Why? Was something amiss?

He did so despise the front she could put up and that she ever felt a need to resurrect it. But it was not something to challenge in this moment. Propriety demanded he leave it for a more private moment.

So, he put forth his arm, which she took, and they followed Duke Novak into the keep. The castle and its inhabitants continued as if there was no war tearing apart Czech lands. He found it comforting and jarring all the same. But there perhaps was no place for judgment. Or should not be. These people only did as they must. Did he?

The duke led them toward the Great Hall, though it was not nearing mealtime. Did Duke Novak have things to discuss with Pavel before he took his leave?

Pavel was determined that he would do his duty to their host with all the grace he could muster.

But they continued to move through the keep, and the duke stopped at the stairs to the upper chambers. "I am certain that you are much in want of quiet and respite. A bath is being drawn forthwith."

Pavel nodded. "I thank you."

Karin tugged him toward the stairs.

He offered a slight bow to the duke before setting eager feet on the proper steps.

Not long after, as he entered their provided bedchamber, he drew Karin to himself, slanting his mouth over hers. Hungrily. As he pulled her impossibly closer, he continued to move his mouth over hers. How had he not felt the ferocity of this before now? It was as if he hadn't had a drink for far too long, and she was the spring from which he would find life-giving sustenance.

He entangled himself in his wife's arms. And, somewhere on the edge of his consciousness, he became aware of another presence. He dragged himself away from Karin, pressing her behind him as he turned, hand on his sword's hilt.

Then he found himself looking into the widened eyes of a maid-servant bearing heated water for his bath. He shook his head at his lack of forethought and eased his features.

"My lord, my lady, I did not mean to..." The servant girl searched for the right word. Had she never seen a man and his wife in an embrace? The servant did appear rather young.

"Bring the water over here." Karin stepped from behind Pavel, her arm outstretched toward the metal tub. He noted a reddening in Karin's cheeks. From their moment or from regret at being caught?

Dare he speak into the tension? What would he say? He watched Karin direct the young girl and decided that his opportunity had passed. Perhaps it was best for all that he had not cluttered the exchange with extraneous words.

Steam rose from the tub. This had not been the first of the water carried up. He stepped closer and noted that the water had reached an appropriate depth. His muscles ached for the relief of the heated water.

The girl left and Karin closed the door.

"Shall I call for a someone to attend you?" Karin shifted toward him, a strange timidness about her.

He drew nearer until there was precious little space between them. "I would have you attend me, dearest wife."

There was that color again. How long had he been distracted with the war and resulting unrest that he had not paid proper mind to his beloved?

He lifted a hand to the side of her face.

Her eyes slid closed as she leaned into his touch.

The kiss he pressed to her lips this time was more tender. It was sweet and full of promise. A promise...he intended to keep.

CHAPTER II
PATRICIE & STEPAN

Of all the men in all the kingdoms, why did she have to tend to this one? Patricie's anger from her exchange with Lord Dvorak on the day past still simmered, but here she was yet again, fighting herself as she approached his room. What was God asking of her? And why?

As she drew closer to the door, a tightness filled her chest. Did she dread these interactions so much? *God, give me strength. Give me the words.* She reached for the latch and thought better of ending her prayer there. *Or the ability to hold my tongue.*

She sucked in a breath and steeled herself before pressing the latch and leaning on the door. It opened without resistance. And there he was, lying across the bed just as he had been every day she came to him. Only this time he did not look at her. Did he know it was she who entered?

Pausing just within, she wished to all heaven she wouldn't have to go farther. But that was for naught. There was much to do in the next hour and no leeway to tarry. Not even for as long as she had. But the way he stared overhead. It was eerie. What was happening in his mind, in his spirit? For sooth there was much. Why else would he be so bitter? And so determined to die.

She stepped into the darkening space. The afternoon sun had accomplished much of its descent from above. It would be best if she lit a candle or two. But as she scanned the few surfaces in the small room, she came up empty—nothing promising with which she might produce flame. Perhaps she could take care of her duties here without needing extra light. After all, waning daylight still seeped in.

Focusing her attention toward the bed once more, she jerked back. Lord Dvorak now stared at her. Though he remained soundless, a blank look stilled his features. His glare was intense.

Her heart thumped hard, and her breaths deepened. Had he so unnerved her? Regardless, her one regret was that her surprise was likely easy to discern. Even were he not examining her as he did.

She attempted to shake off the sensations crawling along her spine. This was nonsense. He sought to intimidate. And she had nearly let him succeed.

Squaring her shoulders, she moved closer. Nothing about her movements registered in his regard. What was in that head of his? She shook herself. That line of thinking would lead nowhere. This much was certain.

"Lord Dvorak." She worked to get out the greeting with as little affect as possible. "I have come to tend your wound."

He remained as he was, the coverlet still over his form.

So that was how it would be. Again.

She could manage.

Blowing at an errant strand of hair that forever fell into her face, she set her things on a nearby table and grabbed for the thin blanket.

His hand shot out and gripped her wrist.

She gasped. Just as before, it was not painful. But it did alarm her all the same. Still, she swallowed the words climbing in her throat to scold him. And she let her care for him, for all of those she tended, reach her eyes.

His glare held a challenge, one she feared she was not ready to take on. The day had been long and her duties many.

"Please." Her voice came out soft and meek even to her ears. Pitiful.

One of his eyebrows rose. What lifted it? Curiosity?

His hold on her slackened, and she slipped free.

Without shifting her focus from his face, she tugged at the coverlet. This time he did not stop her. But the rise and fall of his chest became more pronounced. Or was it that she could now see his torso better? Either way, it caught her attention. And her gaze drifted.

His tunic had been torn at some point in tending him, and the opening widened. She could discern the nuances of his muscular physique though most was still covered by the piece of clothing. Why should she notice such?

Her eyes darted back to his.

The green of his widened eyes flashed brighter despite the lessening sunlight.

Her gaze cut to his leg, still blocked to her vision by the blanket. Had she truly stopped her progress when she caught sight of his...

Stop it! He is nothing more to me than a wounded soldier—a Royalist at that.

Even as her mind scolded her, she worked to even her breathing.

"H-how..." She cleared her throat. Goodness, what a simpleton she was becoming. So she tried again. "How is your pain?"

Removing the cover from his leg, she managed to grab firmly onto the mindset of a healer. The bandaging looked clean enough... no sign of seepage.

She paused. He had not answered. Dare she look to his face again? She would already berate herself later for her lack of composure.

"It is...not as it was," he ground out.

Did he mean that the pain had subsided in some measure or was this his acknowledgement that his once perfect limb had been damaged? Perhaps beyond repair?

She latched her gaze to the bandaging and pushed past the distraction of her thoughts. "If you wish it, I can brew another tea."

He grunted.

Nothing further was forthcoming as she went about removing the bandaging. She would make a more careful examination today if he would continue to behave.

When she stripped the final portion of the linen away, he seethed.

She felt for him. It must burn and ache. My, how quickly she forgave his behavior from her last visits. How was it that she conjured up such kindness? And care? She was indeed hopeless.

But he was her charge, she reminded herself, and she had promised that she would see this through. Best she find some amount of neutral ground from which to do so. Only...the fact that it wasn't simply neutrality that stirred her thought of him in that moment bothered.

She leaned forward and examined the stitches. They held and all seemed as it should. Except...her hand had settled unnecessarily on his knee. His bare knee.

Patricie jerked away, prompting a twinge in his leg.

The desire to look at him and discern his thoughts, if she could, overwhelmed. But she would not allow herself to even peer at his features again. Not until she had time to sort out her own thoughts on this matter.

So, she set her full attention to her work as she cleaned and redressed the healing wound. As much as she wished to make light of it by conversing about something of no consequence, she found herself unable. And unwilling.

She finished soon after. Her swift motions with the bandaging had made her normal attempts at gentleness difficult. Still, he made no further sounds in protest nor any other indication of pain. But she sensed it the moment he looked away. It was as if she could breathe again.

When she finished, she all but tossed the coverlet over him. "I—um—someone will be along shortly with your tea."

He grunted. And she felt the intensity of his gaze on her once more.

She turned and stepped toward the door without further delay. But as she crossed the room, she realized she had left everything on the bed beside him. How thoughtless. Indeed, it must be due to the lack of light and perhaps some fatigue.

Moving back to the bed, she gathered what had been left and then lengthened her stride to more quickly relieve herself of the space. Not that he made any attempt to stop her. What must he think now? She did not wish to consider that.

As she came to the doorway, she nearly collided with Ludek. Her breath caught as his eyes seemed to question her. Unable to stop herself, she threw a glance over her shoulder as she stepped aside for Ludek to pass.

"I only wondered where you were," he said as he regarded her.

"Where I...?" she all but stammered.

He peered into the room. "Did you not light a candle in here? It has become rather dark."

"Yes...I mean..." She looked within once more. "No, I did not. I have finished my work and need to..." What did she need to do again?

Ludek looked to the things she carried. "Of course. Please do."

Letting out a long breath, she brushed past the healer and prayed he would neither follow nor seek her out. For she was quite certain she needed every moment she could garner for herself. And her wayward thoughts.

CHAPTER 12
HANA & RADEK

Hana was worn and ragged. Many hours in the saddle had taken its toll on her. And everything around her looked as it had an hour past...and the hour before that. Was there any way to discern their progress? She would just have to trust that the knights knew the terrain better than she. Were they close? It seemed they should be.

Not that it mattered. Mistress Huddard insisted they stop every few minutes, it seemed, to allow Hana to catch her breath. The older woman maintained that she would not have the lady appear winded and bedraggled upon seeing her betrothed. What nonsense was this? Did the woman not understand what Hana and Radek had been through together? Mistress Huddard would likely faint if she truly knew.

It didn't matter either that Hana requested they keep moving. Mistress Huddard's voice was more shrill and more forceful. The constant stopping not only delayed their arrival but wore on the knights traveling with them. There was naught Hana might do about that, however. So, she complied and kept things as pleasant as possible. That was perhaps the most difficult thing about their journey.

When the tops of a tower peeked over the tree line, Hana's heartbeat picked up its pace. Their steps were numbered. It was all she could do not to put heels to flank and spur her horse to the castle as fast as the mare could go.

Mistress Huddard's voice cut into the moment. Her distress evident.

"Hold," one of the men called as Hana turned.

The older woman's horse stuttered about, behaving as if something had vexed it.

Two of the knights came to both sides of the animal, trying to still it. Would Mistress Huddard be thrown? That could mean disaster!

"Be calm," one of the men said. "Pull hard at the reins."

But the older woman's fear was palpable to Hana, and no doubt to the horse as well. The animal would not be stilled anytime soon.

The knight who had taken the lead time and again latched onto the horse's bit. Finally, the jerking calmed. Though the mare continued to shift this way and that. Even as that continued to distress Mistress Huddard, Hana doubted she was as at great a risk of being thrown.

As the man spoke gently to the horse, he tugged at the bit.

How might Hana aid in their work? Could she ensure Mistress Huddard made it to the ground safely? How so? She leaned to one side, preparing to dismount.

"Do not," another of the knights said with firm voice and set jaw. "Remain astride."

Hana gripped her reins all the tighter.

What had upset Mistress Huddard's struggling mare so? As the animal stilled for the most part, the first knight lifted his arms for Mistress Huddard. It took some doing to bid her release her hold on the pommel and dismount. But, at length, she did drop into the waiting arms.

"Praise the Lord Almighty," she declared as she moved away from the creature who had nearly seen her more swiftly to the ground and most assuredly bruised and broken.

Hana's gaze remained rapt on the situation. Would the men now hurt the horse? What did they intend to do?

"It's thrown a shoe," the first knight muttered. "No sign of it. Must have been farther back."

"'Tis a wonder you weren't thrown, madam," the knight looked to Mistress Huddard.

But she would have none of it. She spun toward Hana. "Get off that beast at once, my lady."

Hana tugged at her mare, urging the animal to move farther away from Mistress Huddard. Might the woman rile another horse with her abrasive behavior?

"I am well enough," Hana assured her.

"My lady, I say it is not so." Mistress Huddard seemed quite out of breath. "Did you not see what that...that *thing* almost did to me?"

"I beg you, see reason. The horse might have become lamed had we persisted. It is not the animal's fault, but ours."

The knights looked to one another. But their expressions remained impassive.

But then Mistress Huddard's glare set upon them. "Speak some sense to her."

The knight who stepped toward Mistress Huddard did so slowly. "She speaks true. The horse may indeed be injured. Perhaps far worse than you understand."

"Why, I *never*...such talk!" Mistress Huddard's face reddened. "I have been given charge over Lady Hana. And I will see her delivered safely."

Hana hung her head. Why did the woman persist so? "What would you have us do? Walk the rest of the way?"

Mistress Huddard looked between the faces of those around her —first to Hana, then to the knights. She appeared rather flustered. "Why...I...no."

Hana breathed relief. She did not think she could bear further delay.

"But I must insist we send one of these men on to the castle and return with a more acceptable, safer means of transporting Lord Miklas's betrothed."

Hana frowned. Send a knight on ahead? Were they then to wait here? Halt all forward progress?

"Mistress Huddard, I implore you—" one of the men started.

"I shall not have it. I will not allow the lady to be endangered." Her words were simple and curt.

The men exchanged looks once more.

"So be it," the knight holding the horse, still stomping, ground out.

"And I demand that one of you help Lady Hana down from that atrocious animal." The woman's shrillness had started to grate.

One of the knights shrugged and moved to assist Hana.

She wanted to resist, but there was no use. Mistress Huddard would have her way. Hana had learned as much. Allowing the knight to assist her down, Hana paused a moment. How to proceed? As she looked at Mistress Huddard, still bumbling about the 'dangerous creatures,' Hana made up her mind and approached the older woman.

"Might I speak with you?"

Mistress Huddard shifted her focus from where the knights had gathered, discussing which of them might ride on and secure the required assistance, and stared at Hana.

"I have said all I wish on this matter," she said with finality.

Of all the self-important, inconsiderate...

Hana forced herself to pause and take a breath. Though she hated to stop now, when they were so close, she didn't want to press the issue either. Such would likely be in vain.

One of the knights stepped to Hana. "We are sending the swiftest rider. All will be well."

Had her inner struggle been so obvious? Her face warmed at that thought.

Another of the knights moved to his horse.

But Hana was helpless to do anything beyond watch him mount and ride off.

As he did so, the clouds grumbled. Hana looked up and noted the darkness hovering on the horizon. This would be a long afternoon.

Radek watched rain falling beyond his small window. The *ping-ping* of droplets against the panes were harsh. As had been his words to his father. But he had already thoroughly berated himself. And that left him in a foul mood. It was fitting, then, that the world became gloomy as well.

Nothing offered him solace. Not even the quiet chambers. It had been some time since the fire was stoked, and the room had chilled. But it mattered not. Too much weighed on his mind. And in his heart.

If only Hana were here. Or perhaps Zdenek. He longed for someone to share with...find some better perspective about the situation. For surely he was not thinking clearly. There would be great comfort in a kindred soul, even if that someone could only tell him that all was not lost.

Hana brought out the softer side of him. Perhaps that was what the situation needed. For as cross as he might be with his father, the words were not untrue. Perhaps, then, he just needed the edges of his ire to be smoothed out. And bless it all, he missed her.

The sound of footfalls in the corridor beyond his chamber drew his focus. Soon enough, the door opened. Slowly. Too slowly. Who would be so unsure? Was such timidity borne of nervousness? Or cowardice?

Though as the intruder stepped through the opening, the swish of skirts was discernable. Skirts? Who would—?

The figure stepped from the shadows. Mother.

What purpose did she have here? Had she come to see to his injury? Scold him for his words? He held his tongue and tried to slow his breathing as he waited for her to state her purpose.

"Are you well?" Her voice came out matter-of-factly, but it wavered. However slightly.

"I am." There was little gain in telling her of the dreadful ache that never eased. But it could have been worse. He'd been much worse.

She looked to the darkened hearth. "I will call for someone to remake this fire."

"My lady," he said, watching as she startled at his address. "Pray do not. I am well with it."

"But it is quite cold. Do you intend to rush off any who would linger?"

That had been a benefit of the cooler room. No one, not even the healer, would stay long. Dare he deny her statement? Still, her words challenged. So, he lifted his chin and met her gaze.

She made a sound that seemed exasperated.

So, he disappointed. She was not pleased with him. How did that differ from their last interaction?

"What do you hope for here?" He ventured the question, attempting to put forth his frustration. Did it ring true in his tone? For he fought a desire to hear that she regretted the hand she had delivered across his face days past.

"I..." she said, pausing. Did she think twice upon her intent? Her throat cleared and her features hardened. "I am to tell you that the carriage has been sent to fetch the woman you shall one day call wife."

What did she speak of? A carriage? Wife?

Hana.

His heart stirred. Was she in need of escort? And he had not been told until *after* it was sent? The dilemma had not been presented to him, and only now he was informed. His hands became fists, but he bit back his words. He did not wish to repeat the mistake made with his father.

"I shall leave you then." She turned.

"Tell me." He ground out. "What tidings are these? My betrothed has been retrieved without my knowledge?"

One of her eyebrows shot up. "One of Duke Novak's knights brought news that she and the remainder of her escort were stranded in the wood and required a means to complete their journey."

He clenched his jaw even harder, so much so that his teeth hurt. "Was an invitation issued from this manor for her to travel?"

Now confusion swept Mother's features. "Not from my lord husband nor myself."

Radek frowned.

"Did you not request her presence?" Mother seemed truly confused.

He shook his head.

Mother frowned. "She is bold."

His head snapped up, and he glared at her. What a thing to say of his beloved. But he could no more deny her assessment than he could his own ill-timed words to Father.

"If you will excuse me, I must make ready a chamber." Mother did not seem eager to do so. But she would.

However, it was likely that Hana's actions would forever mar his mother's good opinion. And once lost, it was difficult indeed to reclaim. Regardless of Hana's station. It would not gain her the approval she might have lost. Mother could be quite set in her mind in this way.

Radek considered Hana's journey. She had proper escort. Did that mean her father had permitted it? For what reason? Or was this a product of Hana's flights of fancy? Her history would support her following her own impulse, regardless of reason or propriety.

A moment passed before Radek realized he was alone. He crossed to the window once more. The rain, once a thing of refreshment upon the earth, now worried him. How far away had Hana been when she sent for help? And why? Had they been set upon by the same brigands that dealt him this injury? If not, would they be?

He hit the window casing. Hard.

There was naught he might do to secure her safe passage. To protect her. All was in the power of others. Others who knew not of the danger lurking.

Lord...

He was still not given to prayer, but in that moment, it seemed his best option.

Keep her safe. Make her way easy and no danger to befall her. May she be close. May she be well. She is my heart.

CHAPTER 13
PATRICIE & STEPAN

"Now where did I put that salve?" Patricie looked in the cabinet, moving vials and pouches of herbs. "It was just here, wasn't it?"

Setting hands to her hips, she tsked. Ludek must have more. It wouldn't do if they were low on something they needed for burns and irritations. Perhaps it was a good thing Ludek had ventured out to collect more medicinal plants and herbs.

She sighed. Mixing another container of the valuable compound was just one more thing she would have to attend to today. That is, provided things remained as calm as they had been. This was the very reason Ludek chose today to spend the afternoon in the forest—things had been rather mundane of late. Their charges were healing well, and everything was as it should be.

Even Lord Dvorak—perhaps the most difficult of their patients—seemed to finally accept their aid and settle within himself that they would do what they had to in order to preserve his life and his limb. An image of him came to the forefront of her mind. It was not welcome. And yet it was. More than she dared admit.

"Nonsense." She shook her head.

Pushing that to the side, she continued cataloguing supplies. Not that it was necessary. Ludek had done so yesterday. Still, she might as well. Nothing else pressed for her attention. And she must pass the time somehow. Perhaps she might check in on their patients with more serious needs. Again, not that it was necessary, but one must find something to do with oneself.

"Now what about the vile of feverfew? I know we have more of that." She peered along the neat rows.

"Patricie?" a familiar voice called from the direction of the stairs.

Before setting eyes on the woman, Patricie knew it was Eva. But why had she come? Did the woman *need* a reason to seek out her sister?

"I am here," Patricie raised her voice as she shut the precious cupboard. She then turned to greet the woman who meant every-thing to her.

Eva rounded the corner. Her eyes lit when she spotted Patricie. "I have been looking for you. I wondered if you might have time to join me. You've been working so diligently and probably have neglected to eat. I am not sure you always take proper care of yourself."

Patricie smiled. Just like Eva...mothering her. When would the woman have children to dote on so she could leave Patricie alone? It wasn't as if Eva needed encouragement. Her sister had confided that giving Zdenek a baby was on her mind nonstop.

Patricie released a breath. Could she sit with her sister and listen to tales of the happiness of married life? It tended to make Patricie's insides feel hollow. There was no mystery about this, however—she wanted what her sister had. So much.

"I only wish I could." Patricie folded her hands in front of her hips. "I have to..." What might she say? Certainly, she could conjure some task, some need, couldn't she? But her mind mutinied—nothing but a blank where her thoughts should be.

"What?" Eva's smile fell. "You have to what?"

Why couldn't Patricie think of something?

Her sister eyed her. "Are you trying to avoid me?"

Patricie swallowed. "Of course not. I only meant that there are many things to do while Ludek is away."

"Where did he go?" Eva's eyes narrowed. Why was she so suspicious?

"He is searching to replenish some of the medicinals. I think in the nearby wooded area."

One of Eva's eyebrows rose. She doubted Patricie...and for good cause. Why couldn't Patricie just be honest about her challenges with Eva's happily ever after? They had always shared everything. Why was her tongue so averse to the truth now?

"Very well." Eva deflated in front of her. Maybe there was something in particular she wished to tell.

Patricie's heart lurched. Was something amiss? "Perhaps I can—"

A door below stairs slammed into the wall with such force the sound reverberated throughout the small building. Had these men no care for those being tended within these rooms? Patricie was of a mind to scold them.

"We need the healer," a voice called, his desperation evident. "I was told he is here."

The innkeeper's voice rumbled, not loud enough for Patricie to discern his words.

Eva's eyes widened as they set on her younger sister. Did she think Patricie in danger? Or not capable without Ludek's guidance?

Patricie preferred not to think on that.

"I am here," she called, realizing the moment the words left her lips that she had not clarified herself. Still, she moved toward the stairs. "What calls for such haste?"

She held her skirts as she descended the narrow stairway. The corridor opened into the room below and she saw a man from the village, his breaths heaving.

"Where is the healer?" the man asked again, this time his words were directed at Patricie.

"He is not here. But I am his apprentice, I am able to care for—"

"Please, come." The man waved and stepped outside. Clearly, he did not have the patience God gave a nit. Else there was great need of her services.

She followed, switching to a sprint when her feet hit the floor. "Has something happened?"

"The miller. And his daughter." The man who hurried her along spoke in fragments. "They were trampled."

Had she heard correctly? Trampled?

"God in heaven." Eva, who somehow remained at Patricie's elbow, slipped into prayer.

Patricie did not tarry. This could be bad. Thankfully, they did not go far from the inn. A gathered crowd at the roadside signaled they neared.

The man held out a hand for her to go on ahead. Though he did not offer any assistance with the throng of onlookers.

She charged into the mass of bodies, trying to press through.

Protests were voiced in anger.

"I am a healer. Let me pass," she demanded.

But as the way opened, and the injured man and girl lay before her, it was all she could do not to press her hand to her mouth.

God in heaven. She prayed her sister's earlier beseeching.

The small girl, no more than eight summers, lay bloodied and broken. The miller lay curled beside her. He reached to gather the child to himself.

"Do not," Patricie commanded. She could not let him move the young girl. Injuries within her body may make matters worse if disturbed.

Patricie knelt next to the man to assess the situation. The miller had a gaping wound in his stomach. It would need to be sutured. But the girl? There was no hint she was conscious. And the damage done to her was much worse.

Patricie pulled at her hem and ripped at the bottom of her chemise. She managed to free a good-sized strip of cloth. Then she leaned over to press it to the man's injury.

"No." He seized her hand. "My daughter. Tend my daughter."

Patricie frowned. How could a father not deny his own healing for the sake of his child? But the girl may already be gone. Still, Patricie let herself be swayed by the man's urgings and moved closer to the child. Patricie looked over the girl to ascertain the situation, then moved tentative hands over her. There was much broken.

If she tended the child whose injuries were greater, the man could bleed out. But if she didn't, the girl would most certainly perish. If that was not already an unavoidable fate. A decision had to be made. She looked once more at the man, who alternated between pleading with God for his daughter's life and pleading with Patricie for her help. There was only one real choice that her heart would allow.

Patricie called to Eva, listing the things needed from the cabinet at the inn. Even as she did so, she pressed the makeshift bandage from her chemise to the child's head wound.

The father's pleas increased as did his words of gratitude.

Eva returned quickly with almost all the things needed.

Patricie worked, only vaguely aware that the man's voice began to fade. How long had she been here? She worked to stem the bleeding and stitch what she could. Her vision blurred a couple of times as frustration claimed her heart, clamping around it like a vise. But even as her back ached from the angle she settled into, and her fingers numbed, she refused to stop.

Patricie had not been home in time to prevent her mother's death. She carried that with her every day since. But she was here now. And she could make a difference. She must do this. She just had to.

"Patricie," a voice called from what seemed far away.

There wasn't time. Patricie had not a moment for distraction. Too much was at stake.

The voice called again, more insistent. "Patricie." Was that Eva?

Patricie shook her head, hoping that would thwart any further effort.

"Patricie, it's over." The voice was calm, but firm.

Patricie would not give in so easily. She must save this child. She must.

Hands settled on her upper arms and jerked her upright. She attempted to pull away from whomever tried to impair her work. But she found herself face-to-face with Ludek.

He knelt then. The image of his crouched figure was hazy as emotion filled Patricie's eyes. But he only lingered for a matter of seconds. And he stood, shaking his head.

The crowd had thinned, but several people still lingered. They stared at her. Why would they not let her alone?

Ignoring them as best she could, she looked to Ludek. "We have to save her."

He set a hand to her shoulder. "There is no one that can do so. She is gone."

"What? No." Patricie's heart squeezed again.

"There was never hope for this girl." Ludek's voice was soft, but pragmatic. "But the father..."

Patricie's core shook. What was he saying? That she had lost the man unnecessarily? That her decision to tend the girl had been futile and had cost the man his life? "But...I couldn't just let her..."

"I understand." Ludek tugged at her, pulling her away from the clustered villagers still looking on. "You have to make these decisions. But not with your heart, with your head." His voice had sharpened—not to the point of being harsh, but plain and straightforward. "The miller might have been saved had he your attention."

"He told me to tend his daughter. He asked me to—"

"*You* must make the decision."

Her eyes met Ludek's. She could not escape his disappointment.

He turned away from her and stepped back to the center of the small crowd, giving orders of what needed to be done with the bodies.

It all happened as if time slowed. She watched as others moved in to follow Ludek's instructions.

Another, smaller hand fell to her forearm. "Let's get you cleaned up."

Patricie jerked from the touch as she spun in that direction. It was Eva.

She wanted to resist her sister's urgings, to naysay her, to push into the situation again, to run, to do *something*. But at length, she let herself be led away. What had she done?

Stepan examined the divots in the wall beside his bed. He had many times counted and re-counted them. But he could not divert his thoughts. Zdenek, his *friend*, had come by earlier that day. And try as Stepan might, he could not convince the man that he cared not to renew any camaraderie from the past. Too much had happened. Too much had been done—to him, and by him. How could any of these Hussites even think to forgive him?

A dull ache, that was ever present but rose to a level beyond annoyance on occasion, snagged at his thoughts. How was he to endure more of this?

It was true that his body healed under the Hussite woman's care. As much as he wanted to rage against that fact, it was true. And he found reason for hope. Enough that he began plotting his escape. He would have to be able to bear his own weight. As it was, his meager recovery had not yet allowed for him to attempt such. Pushing himself, he had been assured, would only erase much of the progress made and may consign him to the certain loss of his limb. That didn't mean he couldn't plan.

Shuffling beyond the door snagged his attention. Was it that time already? The sunlight streaming in the window had dimmed somewhat. This was the time of day the Hussite woman would come and tend him. If it wasn't her, then who? Maybe the healer. That was possible. But he would wager it was the ever-faithful caregiver.

The door creaked as it opened. Indeed, the dark-haired woman slipped in as if she feared he slept. Though as she lifted her face toward him, his eyes caught hers.

"Did I disturb your rest?" She asked this often. Perhaps because he did nothing more than lie in this accursed bed. Did she think him so weak?

He would like to find ire to put behind that thought and make it into words, but the fact that he *was* weakened vexed him even more.

She stepped toward him, and he noticed that certain things were much different about her—her clothes had dried blood upon them, her affect was downcast, and there was evidence of tears upon her face. What had happened?

He caught himself. It wasn't as if he should care. She was no more than a tool and an obstacle. Still, he could not deny the heaviness settling in his chest. Not even as he tried to tell himself it was naught but his inability to properly digest his last meal.

She did not speak further as she came closer. Setting her things to the side, she reached for the coverlet.

He did not know why he would, but he pressed up into a seated position and lowered the blanket for her.

Surprise briefly registered in her eyes. Then it was gone, and her attention returned to his wound.

Never before had she seemed so delicate, so vulnerable. What was this stirring within?

"Are you well?" the words shot from his mouth before he could stop them.

Her gaze found his. "I...am."

How to save the betrayal of his softer emotions toward her? "Because I do not wish to be made sick under your care."

She nodded. But was that moisture in her eyes? "I would not risk your health, Lord Dvorak."

Her ministrations commenced—the unwrapping of his wound,

the herbs and salve. What had happened to deplete that fire, that spirit he had known in her? His curiosity increased the more she worked.

She passed the back of a hand over her forehead. Was she so wearied that she would perspire? But as he watched, he noted that the movement was likely to stem the emotion releasing from her eyes.

He caught her wrist. Not for the first time, he realized. Yet she did not even glance in his direction, only pulled against his hold. Had he been so harsh with her?

Even as she tugged to free herself, he wouldn't relent. That brought her eyes to his.

"Release me." Her words lacked force or conviction.

"What has happened?" Had another patient, or that healer, taken liberties? Something about that thought filled his stomach as if an anchor. His breaths came a hint heavier.

She turned away, her eyes settling on the wall. "It is nothing."

"I daresay it is." Why did he care? Why would he not leave her be, all the sooner to be rid of her?

Now she wiped at the side of her face. Had she lost the war with her own heart? Such that it spilled out of her eyes?

"I...lost a patient," she said more simply than he'd have thought. She closed her eyes. "Two." Was she correcting herself? "Two patients."

This could not be the first, could it? If not, why did this move her to such a display? "It must be something you are trained for."

She nodded, but her features did not convince him.

And something in him softened all the more. "How did you...?" He stopped himself. There was no need for him to know. And no reason he should ask.

"I chose poorly." Her voice was thick, a slight tremble to it.

"Chose poorly?" Had he heard her well enough?

"Two patients. I chose to try to save the one who had no chance. And lost the one that did."

Compassion rose to the surface. Why should it? Was it his own demons? The men he had caused to suffer? Or those for which he had extinguished the flame of their life? Perhaps all played at his heart and mind.

"You are not God." His words were curt.

Whether it was what he said or how he said it that drew her focus to his face, he did not know. But he warmed under her scrutiny.

"People trust me. Ludek trusts me. That man trusted me to save his..." She cut herself off. And hung her head. "I bear the responsibility."

"You cannot believe you can steal from death."

Her eyes widened as they set on him once more. "I would not dare to think that I—"

"You are no more able to pull from the grave than any other mortal."

She watched him. What was in her thoughts? If only he could read them. At least better than he could his own in that moment.

His hand settled on her trapped one. "You must forgive yourself. And see that your only responsibility is to do what you can. No more."

She lowered her regard to his leg once more. The wound had been unwrapped already and, as such, was exposed to his own scrutiny. It was not as it had been. Marred flesh had worked to rejoin.

Then he realized that he held her hand captive still, pressing it tenderly. He let it loose.

She drew it back to her side, her features scrunched, as if she worked to gauge his words. In time, they softened. "Thank you."

Her reply was simple. But he felt as if it reached the very core of him.

CHAPTER 14
KARIN & PAVEL

The sun's warmth filled Karin's face even before she opened her eyes. Yes, she thought as she took in the morning light, the day was indeed welcome to come. At least, in her world. Her husband had returned, and all was well.

But she sensed emptiness beside her. Stretching out an arm, she confirmed it was so. Where had Pavel gone? She strained to discern any sounds in the room. Swishing of the rushes became evident. And then a humming. Masculine humming. Was that her husband?

She turned toward the sound to find that Pavel was not attending to her, but to Jaromir. When had the babe been brought?

Pavel cradled the child close to his body. And looked at his son while he sang so softly it had sounded as a hum. The baritone of his voice warmed the space.

A smile spread across her features. Yes, this was bliss.

As Pavel paced the room with their son, he came near the desk. Had she put her papers away well enough? She didn't wish for him to find them, to know. Not yet. Had she even made a final decision on the matter? Weighed the costs appropriately? She must have for she had started the work again. God's call on her was sure, and it was important to her that there be no barrier between her son and God's Holy Writ.

"Dobry den, my darling." A gentle voice teased her.

She shifted and her gaze landed on the startling blue eyes of her husband. So strong, so sure. Could she ever be so confident? "Dobry den, my love."

His eyes glistened in that moment. Moisture? Would she have noticed if she had not already been so intent on them? What bothered him so?

She slipped from the bed and crossed the room. Looking at her son over Pavel's shoulder, she pressed a kiss to the side of her husband's neck.

Pavel neither moved nor spoke.

"Did you sleep well?" She leaned into him.

He remained silent.

"Pavel?" she entreated, concern edging into her mind.

"I...was not able to rest."

Her heart ached at his words, and she sensed there was more to it. She spoke gently into his ear, "Tell me."

"Hmmm." It was not a question, but a hesitation.

She squeezed his upper arms. "Please."

Nothing.

"This won't do." She kept her voice low and quiet, her urgings tender. "Tell me."

He drew in a breath. "When I look at him, at our son, I wonder..." His words trailed into silence.

"What?" she prompted when he didn't continue.

"What it would be like for him if something happened to me." The words were plain, but he could not keep from her how they affected him.

She pulled back only slightly, wanting to look full in his face. But her desire to comfort him anchored her to her place beside him. Words to negate his fear and a request he not speak so were on the tip of her tongue. But she could not make them come. His worry *was* founded. She carried the same fear with her each day he was away.

"We have to trust God." These words held her in place day after day, perhaps it was what he needed now.

He shifted until he met her gaze. Silence filled the space between them for a moment.

She bit her tongue to keep from breaking into it.

"I trusted God with my father. And now he has passed into eternity."

Her breath stilled. Pain radiated from his eyes. How could she speak to such things? Such heavy things.

"What of that?" His words were not harsh, but tender, sincere.

What could she say? Would the Lord give her the words? And then a thought occurred. "Do you not think the Lord mourns with you?"

Pavel's eyes widened.

"This...separation between us and loved ones passed on was not part of God's plan. His intent has always been for fellowship. Never-ending."

He swallowed, causing his throat to bob.

Dare she continue? Something compelled her to. "This separation is not good. It's not supposed to be good."

He looked back to Jaromir. "Then why does God allow it?"

She wanted so very much to comfort his heart. To make the truth not be what it was. But she couldn't. And he knew as well as she did, the answer to what he asked. "It is a consequence of sin in our world."

His eyes were on hers again. She saw there that he wanted to understand, practically begged her to help him.

And she wanted to. But she had never known what it was to lose a loved parent. All she could do was let the Lord lead her. She slid a hand down his arm and held to his wrist. "But God did not leave us like this—hopeless, helpless. He provided the remedy."

In the next moment, his arm wrapped around her, pulling her to his side. And his face pressed into her shoulder.

Startled, it took a moment for her to register what had happened. Her first thought was of Jaromir's safety. But he remained tucked in close to Pavel's chest, resting.

She looped an arm over Pavel's shoulders and held him to herself as he started to shake. Then she whispered words of grace and of understanding close to his ear. And just let him fall apart. For as long as it took.

Pavel had long been in the saddle the previous days but found himself astride again. His destination—the castle once belonging to his father. The one that had burned. He shuddered again with the memories of his father's death. But he let Karin's words of hope wash over him anew. They softened the sting but could not completely dispel his agony.

He had been hard pressed to leave Karin and Jaromir, but it was past time for him to check on the progress of the rebuild. His mother had been watchful over the work in these last weeks, but what kind of lord would he be if he remained afar whilst everything came together? He prayed that those who relied on the castle and lands, on him, would understand he was needed elsewhere—fighting the Royalist army for their freedom. Yet he wondered how much that affected the daily lives of these who labored to bring his manor back to life. It was best he make an appearance. For their sake as much as his.

He slowed his destrier as they climbed the great hillside. At this rise, he would lay eyes on the place he would bring Karin and his son back to at the proper time. This was where they would make their home. It was a place his father would never see made whole.

Grief sucked Pavel's breath away. Why must he dwell on such things? His father was at peace. That's what he should focus on. The once great warrior had laid down his sword and embraced the ever after with his Holy Father.

Pavel directed his attention to the castle in the distance as he halted his horse. No longer did it seem so vulnerable—charred and vacant. The walls had risen again and appeared every bit as sturdy as they had been before the fire.

Pavel prodded the destrier to speeds he had not yet used on the journey. So eager was he to more closely inspect the demesne and speak with his mother, though the thought did bring a renewed ache in his chest. She had lived out her Christianity ever so faithfully. Her sorrow had not been hidden, nor was it paraded. By all appearances, the woman had come to a place of peace with her Lord as to her husband's absence. Had she truly though?

He neared the structure. It would only be a matter of minutes before he approached the large drawbridge that had been opened to permit his entrance.

Nodding to the men gathered for his arrival, he slowed the horse and settled back into his saddle. The men about were in good form. Pavel could not help but wonder what it would mean for the war effort if these men, and others like them, could be at the front rather than defending the homes of nobles.

Shaking such thoughts free, he released his speculation. It was not for him to determine these things. Didn't his mother and his lands need protection? Especially after...

He squared his shoulders, wishing the memories could fall off as easily as the lingering fatigue in his muscles. This was not a time to dwell on the past, but rather focus on the future—his and his family's.

Drawing his horse to a stop, he dismounted. The men around him—even the one that took hold of the reins to see to his horse—looked familiar. But were they? Or was it wishful thinking?

"My lord," one of the guards stepped forward from the group. "Your mother regrets that she cannot greet you. She is abed."

Pavel felt every crease in his brow at the news. "Abed? What goes?" Even as he questioned the man, Pavel moved forward to the keep.

The knight kept stride with him. "She has fallen ill."

Not Mother, too. The thought came unbidden. And with it, a fear he could almost taste, it was so palpable. He had not yet come to an understanding with God about his father's passing. It was not possible to bear the prospect of losing his mother as well.

Pavel held his breath for a moment as he closed his eyes. This was not the time or the place. He would not take even a moment to bemoan the situation in front of the guards. That would be unseemly. "Take me to her."

"But, my lord, the healer has ordered none to go near but those who see to her comfort."

Was she so ill? Or did the healer only concern himself with containing the sickness?

"I will see her. Now." He put more force into his voice than necessary. Having been an absent lord, he must present himself stronger than he felt necessary if he were ever to earn the respect of those who served him.

"Aye, my lord." The knight dipped his head, then led Pavel across the inner bailey and into the keep.

They moved up the stairs with no further exchange. But at the door to a chamber that had not belonged to his parents, the man hesitated. Was he so fearful of this disease? That did not bode well.

"Fetch the healer. I will hear from him." Pavel excused the man with a wave of his hand.

As the knight turned, Pavel took a moment for himself. He drew in a breath and prayed. Though his anger toward the Almighty was as bile rising in his throat, still he knew the only power over this situation belonged in God's hands. Then he pushed against the door. It gave way under his touch.

Nothing seemed amiss. The room was warm and smelled of herbs.

"Nikola?" His mother's voice, weaker than he cared for, came from the bed.

"No, Mother. I have come."

"Pavel?" Her question hung in the air.

He stepped to the bed. His mother lay under a fine coverlet. As he neared, he discerned weariness about her features.

"My son," she said, before a coughing fit wracked her body.

He held firm to his place and to his impassive expression. "Why did you not send word?"

Her eyes met his. They, too, bore signs of fatigue about them. "I wanted to—prepared the letter even—but I did not wish to alarm you."

His gaze searched her form to gauge how she fared. Impatience for the physician's presence gnawed in his gut. "I should have been summoned."

Her eyes softened. "You have much on you. The war, your wife, Jaromir…" As she spoke the name of her grandson, her lips tilted upward. "I could not bring myself to worry you."

"It should be for me to determine what is to concern me." His chastisement lacked heat. And he found it increasingly more difficult to harden his heart against the possibilities that lay ahead.

She opened her mouth, but the door opening behind him cut off her words.

Pavel turned as the healer came closer. "My lord, I did not know you had arrived until just now. It was my hope to greet you as you—"

Shaking his head against the man's rantings, he pressed out. "I would have more so wanted to be notified when my mother took ill."

The older man looked between the dowager baroness and Pavel. "I…yes, my lord. My apologies."

It did not escape Pavel that his mother likely ordered he not be alerted. But it was the healer's place to know better. He was Pavel's vassal, after all, no longer hers.

Still, Pavel waved a hand. It was nothing to delve into in this moment. "Tell me."

The healer tossed another look at Pavel's mother, licking his lips. Did he not think he could be honest in front of the woman? It was, after all, her wellbeing they discussed. Pavel had no wish to hide it from her.

"Now." As the word shot toward the healer, Pavel sensed his ability to control his frustration giving way. "All of it."

The intensity of his emotion surprised even him. It was not like him to lose control. Perhaps it was the stress of the last several days. Nothing more.

Meeting Pavel's gaze, the healer appeared resigned. "The baroness tempts death's grip."

Choosing to employ strength in that moment, Pavel spoke. "That is a conclusion. I wish to hear what ails my mother."

Out of the corner of his eye, Pavel saw his mother's hand reach for him. Only, the next moment she pulled back from touching him. Did she fear for his wellbeing?

Again, the healer appeared as if he would side-step the truth. "I have seen this before. What she needs is—"

"God's teeth, man. Can you not find your tongue? I wish to know her ailment. In its fullness."

The man closed his eyes and tried again. This time, he spoke plain. "She is fevered, chilled, and struggles to breathe at times. The coughing aids, but only somewhat. And there has been little which will remain in her stomach."

"How long?"

"A sennight." The man turned his regard from Pavel to the floor.

Pavel forced his anger down and drew in a deeper breath. "You said you have seen this illness before. What happened to those under your care?"

"Those who are youngest and those with advanced years suffer the most and slip more assuredly into God's hands."

"And the others?" Why did the man have to dole out information

142

in such a way? Was his mother's situation so dire that the man did not wish to disclose more than he must?

"Most recover."

Ah, there was hope after all. His mother was not so aged. Though she did have more years than he'd like, given this man's experience with the illness.

"She will need to remain abed," the healer continued, "until her breathing is no longer labored. Nourishment has become a priority. If she can hold to anything."

Pavel looked at his mother once more.

Her dark eyes watched him. She seemed apologetic.

Why must he contend with this when still he struggled to accept the losses he had already sustained? There was naught he might do, however, to avoid it.

"Do as you see fit. But keep me informed. I will not abide secrecy any longer."

The man nodded.

Though Pavel wished to speak further with his mother, he doubted his ability to keep his warring emotions in check, so he spun and quit the room.

CHAPTER 15
HANA & RADEK

Hana shivered as she tucked within herself. She was thankful for the dryness of the carriage, but it offered only so much protection from the dreariness. Nothing could be done for the dampness of her clothing, which made the chilled wind sting.

Her ire burned toward Mistress Huddard. She did not wish to be presented to Radek this way, not that he hadn't seen her in all manner of disheveling and mess. Still, she had hoped to have him marvel at how well she appeared and held herself. This was far from it.

Why had Radek not come with his father's men to collect her? Was he so vexed? How would she bear the weight of that in addition to how she presented? If she were but at her finest, she could hold up under his ire better. Now, she lacked hope of a good reception.

If he wasn't angry now, he soon would be. And perhaps ashamed. Oh, how she prayed his parents would not be there to see her arrive! That would not be good at all.

"Something distresses you?" Mistress Huddard spoke at long last.

Hana looked in her direction. She did not have good words, so she held her tongue.

"Perhaps it is because of how long the margrave took in sending aid. Unseemly." The woman gazed out the window.

"I can't imagine he was sitting at the ready, just waiting to send his men out into the storm." She bit her lip. She had said too much, and as Mistress Huddard's surprised expression settled on her, she regretted the harsh edge to her words.

Hana closed her eyes and leaned her head against the back of the bench. She did not want to allow the woman to speak thusly against Margrave Miklas, neither did she wish to make trouble in this enclosed space.

The woman's face colored. It was evident even in the dimness. And Hana regretted her words all the more. It would be best if she had remained silent. No matter how the woman reacted or what she said.

But Mistress Huddard did not speak further. She folded her arms into her torso and watched beyond the window.

It wasn't long before the horses' steps altered. Yet it felt an eternity had passed. Eagerness and dread filled her as the realization of their proximity fell on her. She would see Radek soon. If only she could have a bath and be refreshed first. Still, she could not make herself pray for such. Even as she hated to be in such a state, her desire to see Radek was too great to wish for a delay.

The clomping of hooves changed pitch as they no longer thudded upon earth, but stone. Hana drew in a slow breath. This was it.

Moments later, the carriage halted. The door opened, and a knight reached in to assist her exit. She slid her hand into the proffered one. And was led into a sparse reception of guards. No Radek? Not even his parents? How could this be? As much as she had feared it would be so, the lack of proper welcome stung for what it implied.

Her presence was not welcome. Or appreciated.

The guard hurried her into the Great Hall. And there, she came face-to-face with a woman, finely dressed and aged enough to have birthed Radek. Margravine Miklasova did not look the least bit pleased. Nor did she speak.

But it was improper for Hana to open her mouth until the lady made way for discourse.

The woman studied her with a glare that took her in from head to foot.

"Welcome," the woman said, but her tone betrayed her lack of care for the intrusion. "I am certain you wish to bathe and rest after your journey."

"I—"

"Please, do come this way. I will show you to your chamber."

Hana didn't move. She couldn't. This was even worse than she could have imagined. The woman regarded her as if she were little more than a wet dog trespassing in the fine room. She...a duke's daughter. Though she knew she appeared as anything but.

Perhaps she should inquire after Radek. As much as it hurt that he was not here to receive her, it also gave her cause for concern. "Where is—?"

"Make haste," the margravine commanded. "Before you catch your death of cold."

Yes, Hana had made herself a nuisance. Yet she could not stop herself from becoming more of one. "Might I seek an audience with Lord Miklas?"

The lady turned, brow raised. "With the margrave? In such a state?"

"No, my lady. I seek to speak with Lord Radek Miklas."

The woman put a hand to her heart. "As you are? I should think you would wish to present your best to your betrothed." That last word had an added tone to it.

So, the woman did know who she was. And clearly did not approve.

"Yes, my lady." Hana dipped her head and moved to follow.

"Regardless how she may present," a voice came from farther up the stairs, "I wish it."

Hana lifted her gaze. There he was—Radek—strong and confident. Her eyes drank in the nuances of his features. Was he angry? Was he pleased? It mattered not, she wanted to rush to him and let him shelter her in his embrace.

"My son, you should not have left your chamber." Lady Miklasova's words were short and sharp.

Was something amiss? Only then did Hana let her gaze take in the whole of Radek. That's when she saw it—the bandaging about her beloved's shoulder.

The margravine continued. "You are not well enough to—"

Radek held up a hand. "I will see her."

Even with her limited view at the woman's back, Hana sensed that the lady seethed.

She whirled on Hana, a fire in her eyes. "So be it."

Radek continued down the stairs as his mother gripped her skirts and moved upward.

As they passed each other, there was a pause and a meeting of eyes. As well as a clear dismissal.

Could this be worse? Hana doubted it.

As Margravine Miklasova moved on up the stairs, Radek again descended.

The woman was all but forgotten as Radek drew near, reaching for Hana's hands. She slid them into his waiting ones.

"Hana," he breathed.

She wanted him to take her in his arms and chase away all the uneasiness. But that would not be well with Mistress Huddard. So, she contented herself to let his care for her seep through his gaze.

He tugged her forward, moving a step away from the others. Then he lowered his voice and spoke words that broke her.

"I wish you had not come."

Radek held Hana's elbow and escorted her farther away from his mother's ever-listening ears—the servants. Indeed, he wished he might be truly alone with her. For many reasons. But just now, he wanted to do what he should have already—ease the truth of his feelings about her arrival.

His heart thudded almost painfully, so great was his concern after her and fear for her safety. Not to mention his rather selfish desire to resolve this thing with his parents on his own terms, without her distracting him or interfering, as was one of her gifts.

"My lord!" Her words bounced off the nearby wall as she exclaimed but made no effort to resist.

"Lord Miklas?" the woman who accompanied Hana called out as well, a hint of worry about her voice.

"I only wish to speak with the lady privately," he said over his shoulder. "We will remain in full view, I promise it." The idea that he would endanger Hana's reputation was laughable. His actions of the last year alone had proven him honorable.

Bringing them both to a halt near the far door to the kitchen, he turned to face Hana. "Why have you come?"

Her gaze darted from him to the floor. "I-I was concerned, my lord."

He stepped closer, grazing the side of her face with his fingertips. "There is no need to address me so formally."

She set a hand over his and pressed his fingers to her cheek. "I hardly know what to say." Her words were whispered.

Bold as it was, he stepped closer yet. "Tell me what is on your mind." He let his gaze linger on the lips he longed to claim but dare not in the presence of the older woman. "On your heart."

Moisture brought a sheen to her eyes. Would tears be forthcoming? Best he keep those at bay if possible.

"I am not vexed. Truly. I only..." He looked at the archway to his right. "I do not want harm to come to you. And the road can be treacherous. I was just this week set upon by brigands."

Her brow furrowed. "Are you—?"

"I am not mortally wounded as you see. 'Tis a minor injury."

Her gaze settled on the bandaging about his chest and shoulder. Her hand slipped from his and reached for that place.

He claimed her hand again before she could set fingers upon the injured place. "It is nothing."

Her eyes glistened and they seemed to deepen in that moment as she frowned. She did not seem convinced.

"But that does not mean it is safe for you to have come." He let his worry affect the softness of his voice. Indeed, the entreaty was rather harsh.

She jerked back at his words. Or perhaps his tone. "I did not do so alone. My father saw to my safety with an escort. And to my virtue with Mistress Huddard." There was a hint of something else in her voice. What was it? Frustration?

He couldn't help but admire it. For it was endearing. His Hana became all the more alluring when she was frustrated—her cheeks had more color and her full lips turned into a pout. Those lips drew his regard once more.

"I apologize." He could not keep the smile from his face or out of his voice. "Of course, your father would see to it you were well guarded. In all respects."

She watched him. For what? But her ire settled as she did so. What did she see in him? More than he wanted her to? More than he was?

"You are not cross with me?" Her words lilted as if hope anchored her to the moment.

He considered her. "No."

"And you are glad to see me?"

"Yes." He smiled but allowed the truth to come as well. "And no."

She opened her mouth, but he held up a hand.

"You still have yet to tell me what drew you to defy me and come to Horice."

Her gaze set on his chest. And she was silent so long he feared she hadn't heard him. "It is...difficult to explain."

He rubbed a thumb across her knuckles. "Tell me anyway."

Mistress Huddard made an exasperated noise from across the hall.

He ignored it and kept his gaze on Hana, as if he could encourage the answer to come forth with his eyes.

"I...thought you needed me." Her cheeks flushed a deeper red. "It sounds odd now that I say it, but I—"

"No," he said gently, interjecting into her words, which would likely move toward rambling. "I *do* need you. Never think otherwise." Leaning toward her, he pressed a kiss to her forehead.

Her whole being slackened. Had she been so tense?

Despite his very valid objections to her being here, he was glad she had come. That surprised even him. If she was here, he could keep watch over her and her impulsive ways. And though reluctant to accept it, he knew there was more—much more—about her arrival that gave him peace of mind.

CHAPTER 16
PATRICIE & STEPAN

Patricie considered her sister as she spoke. Adamantly. Eva had much to say. But as much as Patricie tried to concentrate, Eva's words were muted. Even as Patricie watched her sister, an image of Lord Dvorak came into focus.

The man had been unexpectedly kind to her, understanding even. From aggressive and ill-mannered to thoughtful and sympathetic. What a change. Was there more to him, then? How much more?

"Patricie?" Eva's eyebrows rose.

What had she said? Nothing came to mind. Patricie blinked and dropped her gaze. "I'm sorry. I...didn't hear you."

Eva pursed her lips. "What fills your thoughts so? Are you thinking of what happened yesterday?"

"What?" Patricie jerked back. Eva couldn't possibly know of her exchange with Lord Dvorak. Could she?

Eva's eyes softened. "I don't want you to wear this burden. You did everything you could."

Patricie lowered her head. Of course, Eva spoke of the injured man and child. What was wrong with Patricie? How could she have been so mistaken?

"Are you all right?" Eva's words were so tender, it brought regret. Patricie was shamed.

"I am...as well as I can be. All thing considered."

Eva continued to watch her.

Patricie didn't like it when she did that. It was as if she could peer into Patricie's thoughts.

"Or is it something else?" Eva's words were still gentle. "Perhaps someone has caught your eye?"

Eva couldn't mean it. Did she think Patricie's mental distance was because she thought of a man in hopes of ensnaring him? Patricie wanted to balk at that, but she couldn't.

"Come now, Patricie. That is the third time this hour that you have lost where you are. What else could be stealing your thoughts?"

"I...am thinking on a patient." That felt weak. A half-truth. "On what else needs be done today for his comfort."

"His?" Eva's lips spread in a smile. "Do tell."

Patricie rolled her eyes. How could she explain this to her sister? It wasn't like Eva alluded. Lord Dvorak was...and his manner was...it just wasn't possible.

Eva tugged at Patricie's sleeve. "You cannot hide it from me." The smile brightened her eyes that had been sorrowful. "You are smitten."

Patricie met her sister's gaze. Surely, Eva did not see what she thought she did. Or could she know Patricie's heart better than its owner?

No. Not possible. Not in the least.

Patricie leaned against the tree at her back and let the sun shine upon her face. She would need to return soon enough to make afternoon rounds. Besides, she did not wish to speak of this any longer. How could she tell her sister so without rousing more suspicion? And more questions she didn't wish to answer.

Eva tipped her head back as well. "One would doubt winter still clung to the earth with such warmth."

Patricie could breathe easier. Somehow Eva knew and respected her wishes. Her sister wouldn't speak more on the matter. At least... not directly.

"Aye." Patricie released her pent up tension. "Would that I could stay until the evening meal."

Eva looked at her again. "You must go so soon?"

Patricie turned and gave her sister an amused expression. "It is so. But I will see you at supper?"

"As you cannot escape me if you tried, I would say so. And I expect to hear more about this mystery man."

So much for that. Patricie let out a breath and attempted to appear exasperated. Indeed, it was no act. She prayed Eva would leave this conversation to rest. Permanently.

She hugged her sister briefly and waved before turning toward the small village. Soon enough, she was stepping back within the inn. It's dampness and dimmer lighting brought a shade onto her spirit as well.

Where to start with her last round of the evening? Something drew her to begin with Lord Dvorak. Perhaps she might leave him for last. That would give her some space to shake these thoughts free. Then again, did she want Eva to see into her decision to do so? Would her sister suspect more if Patricie had only minutes before been in Lord Dvorak's company?

First, then.

It took a few moments to gather her supplies. Then she moved to Lord Dvorak's room. As she neared, she took a few minutes to pause. Was her hair mussed and tousled by the wind? How did she look?

Putting a hand to her hair, she smoothed the tresses that had escaped. Hopeless. This was hopeless.

Patricie stopped herself. What did it matter anyway? She was a healer doing her work. That was all. Wasn't it?

Determined anew, she pressed through the door and slipped within the room.

There he sat, raised in the bed such that he watched her enter. His eyes were striking and curious as their focus fell to her.

Warmth spread from somewhere between her shoulder blades. This was nonsense. Nothing more than the lingerings of her conversation with Eva.

"Dobry vecer, Lord Dvorak." She kept her tone light, but her words were clipped. Yes, she was here to do a job. That was all.

He nodded. "Is it not early in the day for you to come to me?"

What? Come to him? What could he mean? She shook her head, he merely commented on her appearance at this hour, as she had come to his room first rather than go in her usual order. Surely, she was losing her mind.

"I was concerned after something I spotted this morning," she lied. "And I want to check once more to determine if the healer needs to see you before the day is done."

Lord Dvorak's brows furrowed.

Now she had worried him. She could just sink into the floor. Well, she wished she could at least. Raising concern had not been her intention.

She stepped forward. "Oh, do not be troubled. It is nothing."

"Yet bothersome enough to affect how you carry out your rounds." His features were flat. How was she supposed to discern anything?

Blowing out air that seemed to have collected in her chest did not alleviate the tightness forming there. Could she not bring this situation under control? Why did her tongue insist on causing trouble?

Lord Dvorak stared at her, his features shadowed with worry lines.

She moved to his bedside. "Please, don't give it another thought. It is nothing worth being upset over."

He eased his weight into the pillow, but the edges of his face did not soften.

With careful hands, she removed the coverlet and set to the task of unwrapping his leg. A glance at his face proved a mistake. For he still scrutinized her every movement with trepidation. Oh, that she could take those words back.

Once the wound lay bared before her, she settled her breathing. Cleaning and bandaging did not require her full attention. Not after having done it so often. Dare she engage him in conversation? Of something else other than his injury? But what had they in common to speak of?

"How..." The pause that followed seemed to drag into eternity. Had she not a better idea of where she would go with it? *Think!*

"Yes?" His voice held a hint of levity. Did he find her uneasiness amusing?

She regarded him once more. And saw that a smile touched his mouth. Some of the tension seeped from her shoulders. "How are you today?"

He blinked. Was that too personal? How had she lost all sense of the chasm between the Hussite and the Royalist? "I am well enough."

She cleared her throat. Perhaps she could bring herself back to the healer she was. "Do you have pain?"

"No." His voice was soft. And she sensed that his gaze was intent on her face.

Something fluttered in her stomach. Not unpleasant exactly. "I—"

"Patricie?" another voice spoke from the doorway.

She turned toward the intrusion.

Ludek stood in the opening. "May I speak with you?"

"I have just uncovered Lord Dvorak's wound. Shall I cover it again?"

"That can wait." Ludek's words were spoken with finality.

Could it? That did not seem wise. At the least it made for an uncomfortable wait for Lord Dvorak. Glancing at the viscount's son, she hoped he could sense her unspoken apology.

Then she moved to the door where Ludek remained. He tugged her in the direction of the hall, but she resisted, wishing to remain in visual range of her patient should something unforeseen happen.

She shot Ludek a look as she planted her feet. "What is it?"

He looked over her shoulder at Lord Dvorak, as if deciding how to proceed. Then he lowered his voice. "I wanted to speak with you about what happened yesterday."

Her brows furrowed. She, more than anyone else, did not wish to revisit that. Glancing at the floor, she whispered, "Yes?"

"I..." Ludek said, then paused. He shifted his feet before facing her again. "It was not my intention to be so harsh."

She widened her eyes. How was that? Was this some manner of apology? Wetting her lips with her tongue, she tried to bring words forth.

He set a hand to her arm. "I...had hoped you might forgive my reaction."

What? She had been the one in the wrong. He only did his duty in correcting her. Though, his manner had stung.

"It is difficult..." He shot another glance in Lord Dvorak's direction before he continued. "...to know the boundary between my feelings and my duty."

What did he mean by that? What feelings did he refer to?

Ludek's gaze settled on hers. "Especially when it comes to you."

Stepan glowered at the door. Patricie and the healer had left the room some minutes ago. Their exchange, perhaps just out of sight, was all Stepan could think about. Why? Was it the way the man looked at her? Or the way she pulled back at his effort to apologize and step closer? Stepan had heard their conversation quite well. Until Patricie insisted they step into the hall. Had Stepan's hearing improved? Or had the healer not made any real effort to hide his words?

This was not something that should interest him. Not one bit. Yet, he fumed.

Fumed?

That wasn't right. But it was. He was angry. At what? At that healer making an overture toward Patricie?

His stomach curled uncomfortably. Though...this should not be any of his concern. So, why was it? He couldn't help the pressure between his shoulder blades and how it intensified each time he recalled the look in the healer's eyes.

Had the man made Patricie uncomfortable? When she had looked back toward Stepan, she had seemed distressed. Only, then she set a hand to the healer's arm and stepped beyond Stepan's line of sight.

And here he lay, his leg wound exposed, waiting for her to finish her work. Perhaps that was what bothered him so. Not that grasping, inappropriate knave.

But what if the man made an unwelcomed advance toward Patricie? Shouldn't Stepan bear witness to their continued discussion for good measure? For propriety's sake? Such was not possible from this bed. It occurred that his desire to protect the healer's assistant was beyond what it should be.

He best guard himself against such entanglements. Is that what this was?

Regardless, he moved his legs to the edge of the bed. He cringed against a flare of pain, pulsing from his lower leg. But that would not stop him. He had a job to do—Patricie might need him to defend her honor.

That thought drove him onward. Surely, he could stand and use the opposite wall for support. He had healed more than he'd let on. This task was not insurmountable.

Gritting his teeth, he pushed off the bed and all but fell against the wall.

There, then. He stood. Though it was neither stability nor confidence he exuded.

No matter. He pressed against the wall and moved his upper body in the direction of the door. But if he wished to move farther, he would have to shuffle his legs.

With tentative movements, he tested the injured leg, setting a portion of his weight on that limb. It pained, but he was certain it would hold him.

He leaned on his good leg and, with great care, shuffled the other along the wall. Then, letting the wall bear as much of him as possible, he pressed into the wounded leg that he might scoot the good one forward.

And collapsed.

He wasn't even able to register the sharp ache before he sprawled upon the floor. Seething, he grasped the injury. Which only brought on stabbing pain.

The door opened.

"Lord Dvorak!" Patricie called as her footfalls pattered across the small room.

Stepan could not unclench his shut lids until hands lay upon him. Only, these were not the gentle hands of the healer's assistant. Had Ludek come to help?

"My lord," the healer pressed through gritted teeth, "you cannot."

Stepan jerked free of his hold.

"You must let me get you to the bed." Ludek's words were harsh, as if reprimanding a child.

Stepan felt the child, pushing beyond boundaries that his body now knew. "I can manage."

"Can you?" There was a hint of humor in Ludek's gruff voice. "I daresay you cannot."

"How might I help?" Patricie's words exuded sympathy and care.

It only made Stepan feel more the fool.

Before he could bid her to take leave, Ludek attempted to lift

Stepan's body, grunting. Was the healer not able to raise Stepan from the floor? The weakling.

Other hands—feminine—pulled at the side opposite where Ludek struggled. Did she attempt to aid? How could Stepan recover from such humiliation?

He jerked against her grip, but that only managed to cause further, searing pain to fill him. Must he surrender to this?

Undone, Stepan released the tension in his body. No more childishness.

Ludek and Patricie worked to get him onto the bed.

"Are you hurt?" Patricie's words cut through his awareness as the room swirled.

Why must she? And why must his leg throb so? He brushed her off but couldn't cobble together words.

"I'm going to move your legs to the mattress." Ludek's gaze leveled on Stepan's.

He wished to God Almighty that the healer did not have to— first, because of the pain and, second, for the invalid it made him.

Stepan refused to look at Patricie and bit into the inside of his mouth to keep from crying out when his legs were shifted.

"Ludek," Patricie breathed.

Stepan peered in her direction.

Her eyes were trained on Stepan's leg, a hand on her chest.

What was it? What had happened?

"God's teeth," Ludek sputtered. He leaned over the leg and set to work.

Not that Stepan could feel his ministrations through the blinding pain. But he soon found solace in the dark of unconsciousness.

CHAPTER 17
KARIN & PAVEL

That couldn't be right. Karin stared at the words she had written. No, not right. She sighed as she tore the page she had spent the last half hour on. Leaning forward, she rested on her arms upon the desk. This work was not for the faint of heart.

She'd been bent over, deeply focused, for untold hours. And she had not quite scratched the surface in the task before her. Couldn't she give up? The thought flitted into her mind, and she dismissed it. Her work was for Jaromir and others who would someday be able to read the Scriptures unhindered. She must push through.

Glancing across the room and out the window, she noted the placement of the sun in the sky. She breathed in deeply. Pavel would return soon.

As she stood, her leg muscles protested, reminding her how they, too, had suffered. She strode to the window and gazed over the grounds and hills in the distance. Did she think she could see all the way to Krejik lands? For it would be beyond coincidence to see Pavel ride in as she stood here. Such was nonsense.

Still, she looked as far as her eyes could focus. Hopeful. Eager.

Moments later, she folded her arms against herself to ward off the chill. It may be time to stoke the fire. Wouldn't that be better for her beloved? To return to a warm room and perhaps a tub.

But as she stepped from the window to call for these things to be done, she caught sight of a rider. Farther away. Yet there all the same.

Her heart leapt as if it would beat out of her rib cage. Had it only been a sennight since she had seen her husband? And yet it seemed a lifetime had passed.

She followed the approaching figure with her eyes, her heart calming to a mere fluttering. How was it that his presence still did such to her? Perhaps because she had not known what it was to truly live with him. Their times together had always been shortened, as the army had need of him. And his sense of duty bade him answer.

Didn't she need him too, though? And Jaromir? What of his duty to them?

Pushing down the rising disquiet, guilt poured into her. These were unusual times. This war would not last forever. Then they'd have years to concern themselves over a life together.

Conceding her soul to this truth, she set her eyes once more on rider and horse. And noticed more details of the approaching man. It was not Pavel. Her excitement before made all the more notable by the cavern left. For as the rider came nearer, she could make out the color of his hair and his movements. It couldn't be her beloved.

Had something kept Pavel? Made him send someone ahead of himself? She looked back over the crest of the hills but did not see any other sign of life. What could have prevented him from fulfilling his word and returning this day?

She pressed back against the frustration growing within. No, she would not allow it to take hold. There no reason not to trust him.

Though...Pavel had been somewhat changed since his return to Tabor. His sleep was restless, when he did sleep. And he startled awake often, begging it off as nothing more than a bad dream. As well, he was not himself—troubled, with emotions not as well veiled. Was this, too, the product of his struggle to sleep? Or had the war taken some toll on him beyond what either considered?

The door opened behind her, rousing Karin from her musings. Her nursemaid stepped within, bearing Jaromir in her arms.

"My lady, your son hungers."

Now? She wanted to be available to receive any message Pavel may have sent. Was it wishful thinking that this rider came from Krejik lands?

But as she set eyes upon her stirring son, becoming more distressed with each passing moment, she pushed it all to the side. Her son needed her. And she would not let him down. No matter how she ached within. She had a duty to fulfill.

Pavel wiped his brow. The work to rebuild required much from him. His mother would not like that he labored out here alongside the men under his charge, but how could he not? He may be lord of this manor, but he had also spent many months fighting for the revolution to prove that all had merit and inherent value as God's creation.

And so, the days following his return to his father's—now his—lands found him out in the chilled weather, moving stones and overseeing the reconstruction. He could not have been more pleased to do so. Working with his hands and pushing his muscles to their limits had been oddly soothing. Was that because it distracted him from other things? Or because it offered an outlet for his pent-up energy? He wasn't certain, but he had found the work to be healing in its own way.

A touch on his shoulder disrupted his reverie.

He turned toward the interruption.

It was his ever-present man-at-arms. The man had been his father's right hand. And Pavel had no reason to oust or replace him.

"What goes?" Pavel asked, concern gripping his heart. Did Mother's sickness claim more ground?

"It is only a thought, my lord." The knight's words were sparing and tight. As if he feared speaking up.

"Yes? Tell me."

"The nooning hour nears. Perhaps the men are due a reprieve."

Pavel scanned those about the area. Yes, the men put their backs and full effort into their tasks, but he discerned the truth of the knight's words—the men slowed. Mayhap that reprieve was long overdue.

He nodded at the man-at-arms. "Call for everyone to pause for replenishment."

The knight nodded. Something in his manner spoke of his approval.

Pavel had not realized his need of such, but seeing the older man offer it gave Pavel some measure of peace. As if his own father instead had proclaimed Pavel's decision right and good.

Jerking his head in response, Pavel wiped his hands across his tunic and moved toward the castle. He hadn't the heart to dwell on the need he found within himself. Soon after, he stepped into the Great Hall. As he looked across, at the door to the kitchens, he became tempted to check after the meal preparation. Such was the work of the lady of the manor, but Mother was in no condition to do so. And so, it fell to him. However, as he crossed the space, a voice called to him, announcing that a rider had been spotted.

He turned in the direction of the warning shout. Was someone expected? Who would trespass? With his mother in such a state, the castle was not in a situation that permitted them to receive guests.

Abandoning his desire to set the kitchens to rights, he shifted his focus to the inner bailey. In moments, he drew alongside his guards on the wall.

Only then did the rider come into view—his friend, Zdenek Ambroz.

He gave the command for the drawbridge to be lowered.

Pavel itched to rush to his friend. Did Zdenek bring tidings from Tabor? Word of Karin and Jaromir? Was something amiss? His impatience no doubt displayed on his features as he gave little effort to disguise it.

Soon enough, Zdenek halted his horse and dropped down.

"It is good to see you," Pavel started. "You are welcome to dine with us."

Zdenek's tight features did not slacken. He appeared concerned.

Was there something he did not wish to share with many ears about? What had happened?

Zdenek smiled at last, easing the hard edges of his face but slightly. "I am pleased that mealtime is upon us. I had expected it would have passed."

Oh yes, it was indeed late of hour for the midday meal. Pavel prayed that was all that bothered his friend.

"I must request we speak privately before we take our repast." Zdenek's effort to keep the telling lines around his eyes and mouth neutral was wasted. His emotions were always easy to read.

Pavel nodded. And to the waiting guards, he said, "I will be in my solar. We shall dine within the hour."

He looked once more to Zdenek, then, indicating they move into the keep, led his friend through the now more solid hallways, and up the stairs to his solar. It was still difficult to own the chamber as his. For not too long ago, his father did business here, sat at his desk—now replaced—and went over ledgers. Father made plans here, received guests here, talked of many necessary things.

Pavel pushed that to the side of his mind as far as possible. Such became easier as time passed. Was that a good sign? Or did it evidence he forgot his father?

"What brings you this far outside of Tabor?" Pavel turned to his friend.

Zdenek closed the door. "Though I do enjoy your company, it is not for myself."

Why were Zdenek's words so short? Guarded even? Did he resist speaking true? Zdenek allowed a smile to touch his lips but firmed his stance. There would be no chasing Zdenek's hesitation today. The matter would be out in the open soon.

"General Zizka sent me." Zdenek's features hardened again, his eyes were serious. Something wasn't right.

"What is it?" Pavel tucked away his desire to be done with it and instead pushed the conversation onward.

"There is much unrest in Prague. General Zizka fears the future of our movement may be at risk."

Pavel let down his guard and widened his eyes. "What do you say?"

"One grace given us is that the opinion of the fighting men has been sought before things are done that cannot be undone."

So, the general summoned Zdenek and him to Prague. What would that mean for his mother? Could he leave her in the care of a healer who had already proved reluctant to keep Pavel informed? Dare he risk that in his absence his mother might take a turn for the worse? No, he couldn't think like that. It would not behoove him...or those who needed him, including his mother.

Pavel dropped his regard to his feet. "When are we expected?"

"The day after tomorrow." Zdenek swallowed. Then he continued after a pause. "I cannot tell you the urgency General Zizka expressed in this. And in our presence."

Pavel frowned. "I have no doubt of that. We shall set out at first light on the morrow."

Zdenek's shoulders dropped, and he appeared to settle into himself once more. What had made him so tense? Did he think Pavel would deny the call?

There was more at stake here than his own wishes, or his desire to stay near Tabor. This went beyond him, beyond his mother, even beyond his need to return to Karin and Jaromir. Too much hinged on it.

His general summoned him. And he would go.

CHAPTER 18
PATRICIE & STEPAN

Patricie watched, horrified, as Ludek worked on Lord Dvorak's leg. And she prayed—for him, for his leg to be preserved, for his recovery, even for Ludek's efforts.

"Put pressure here," Ludek all but shouted without a glance in her direction.

Her thoughts scattered.

"Now," he insisted, pushing the words through his teeth.

She moved closer and put a hand over the leg wound. Her wonderings about the likelihood of Lord Dvorak's recovery were on her tongue, but she bit at her lip. Ludek did not need her questions now. He needed to focus.

The healer grunted as he worked.

"Bandages," he demanded.

Should she relieve the pressure she applied and go for more bandages? Or remain as she was?

Then Ludek's gaze was on her, his eyes wild. "I need more bandages."

Nodding, she rushed from the room and to the cabinet. Gathering strips of linen, she then stepped back into the room.

"What is taking so long? Patricie!"

"I am here." Her words sounded timid even to her ears. At least, what of them she could hear. The urge to fling the strips at him nearly overwhelmed. But she held herself in check, and instead walked to Ludek.

"If he loses this leg, it will not be on me." Sweat droplets formed on Ludek's brow.

Patricie resumed pressing on Lord Dvorak's leg and did not comment. Her gaze drifted from Ludek's flustered hands to Stepan's face. Even without benefit of awareness, he appeared distressed. Did he still feel pain? If so, how great? Had he slipped into a depth of sleep from which they could not revive him? Or had his eyes but closed for these moments of greatest pain?

She prayed again, begging that God's hand would see the viscount's son revived.

"Patricie!"

Her head jerked toward the healer's voice.

His eyes were as stone on her. "What do you?"

"I...but pray for Lord Dvor—"

"Enough. I need you to focus."

She nodded, her face burning with shame.

"All right. Now that I have your attention...I need catgut. And a needle."

Her desire to look more closely upon the injured area was great. But she nodded and obeyed, watching as Ludek took up the task of applying pressure for the moment.

Again, she raced to the cabinet for supplies. Her return was only seconds hence. Even before she reached the bed, she caught sounds that were difficult to identify. As she neared, she realized that Lord Dvorak had started making guttural noises and moans.

Ludek took the items from her. "If he wakes, keep him still."

She placed her hand where Ludek's had been on the soaked bandages and then shifted her focus to Stepan's face. Something unpleasant stirred high in her chest. What was it?

As Stepan continued to shift and release pained noises, she placed her other hand on his face. "Lord Dvorak, all is well. We but mend your leg."

"No..." It seemed she caught that word, but was it only another indistinguishable sound?

She slid a hand over his forehead and then let it settle on the side of his face. *Do not take him, Lord. I cannot bear another death.*

Stepan tilted his face into her hand, as if seeking what comfort she offered.

Ludek pushed her hand that had remained on the bandages to the side. A look in that direction told that the healer would start stitching in the next second.

Stepan gasped, jerking as Ludek pierced his skin.

Patricie put both hands on his shoulders, pressing down and leaning over him. "Shhh..."

Green eyes met hers. Had he awakened?

She pushed harder against his torso to keep him from moving. "We do as we must. For your leg."

Recognition flashed in his gaze. Then he groaned loudly.

"Keep him still," Ludek yelled.

She moved her face closer to Stepan's, setting her hand to his cheek again. "All is well."

Stepan gritted his teeth.

She moved fingers over his forehead and brushed back his hair. When her gaze met Stepan's again, his eyes held hers. "Yes, I'm here. Look at me."

He reached shaking, tentative fingers toward her hair.

She found she didn't mind the intimacy. In fact, she welcomed his touch when he made contact.

Pushing out a breath, he seethed and cinched his eyes closed.

"No...me. Look at me," she implored, keeping her words gentle.

He obeyed, opening his lids to display twin emeralds.

She remained as she was, comforting him. It had become her mission, her heart's wish even.

Untold minutes later, the tension in Lord Dvorak's body slackened, if only slightly.

"There," she soothed, "all will be well." And she prayed she spoke true.

A hand pressed to her back, but she did not turn.

"Patricie," the deeper voice of the healer entreated.

Pulling back from her charge, she paused when Stepan's hands gripped her arms.

She leaned over him again. "I must help attend to your wound."

He stared but did not make a move to keep her from rising.

Only then did she face Ludek.

The healer grasped her arm and pulled her to the far side of the room. Stepan looked after her but did not stir further.

Ludek watched Lord Dvorak's form even as he tugged Patricie toward the door.

She put up a hand to halt him before they exited. "How is he?"

Ludek frowned. "It is...even more uncertain that he will keep that leg."

Patricie widened her eyes but bit at her lower lip to prevent interjecting something she wasn't sure she wished to voice.

"I hope we can keep it from turning putrid. But that is all the more difficult now."

"I will do whatever I can."

Ludek's brows dipped. Was he confused by her insistence? Did he think more of her determination than he should? Or did *she* think less than she should? "All we can do is wait."

"And pray," Patricie offered.

Ludek allowed a half smile to crack his features. "Yes. And pray."

Her gaze slanted in the direction of Lord Dvorak again.

Stepan now stared at the ceiling. But she remembered all too well what it had been like to have his eyes delve into hers. A pleasant, warm sensation pooled in her middle despite the worry that filled her. What was this? And more, how unwise was it to allow it?

Stepan struggled to pull himself from the thick mire of unconsciousness. It tugged at him, making it difficult to open his eyes. But struggle he did, until he succeeded. Light pierced through the window—what he could only assume was the sun. It made him want to seal his eyelids once more, but he dared not. His hold on consciousness remained tenuous.

Though light filtered into the room, everything appeared hazy. And a voice surrounded him—a woman. She spoke to him. Or so he thought. Then her presence filled his senses as she leaned over him. Still, it was as if thick liquid separated them. It was rather difficult to hear her or make out any details about her person.

His eyes slid closed. It was too much. In his mind, he remembered bright eyes hovering over him amidst great pain as soothing words flowed from her. Was that...Patricie? Perhaps it was...and her even now, seeking his attention.

He opened his eyes.

The feminine form shifted over him. But her words were clearer... somewhat, though broken.

"...are you...well...Lord Dvorak?" She sounded quite concerned. Was it possible she cared so? Maybe more than she should? Even to the depth he did?

Something in that thought gave him pause. *Did* he care deeply?

Fighting to surface again, he latched onto the hand that lay upon his shoulder. She anchored him and drew him forth. When the darkness became light once more, the blurred things around him took better form. As did the face that still watched him. Her dark hair framed her features, and her warm eyes drew him in.

"Patricie?" Had he spoken? His throat scratched as though he had.

He moved arms that weighed more than he remembered, lifting them toward her. His fingers connected with soft skin. The contact to her face was minimal, but still heaven. Though he couldn't seem to hold his arm up.

She clasped his hand in hers, holding his palm to her cheek. Could anything feel so good?

Pain slammed into his awareness, and he cried out, unable to contain it.

Her other hand pressed against his chest. And she spoke. While he couldn't make out the words, they soothed. Her warm tones and gentleness were what he needed most.

"Stay with me."

Those few words were all he understood from the string of tones that abated his pain. His eyes found hers again. And he determined that he would stay with her...for as long as she would allow it. He wanted to say more, but his throat was raw. The utterances he croaked out were likely not discernable.

Her hands vanished. And she no longer moved over him. Where had she gone?

Soon enough, however, she returned and urged his head up. Why was she so insistent? Didn't she know how he ached?

Something solid touched his lower lip. He opened his mouth to receive her kiss.

But cool liquid slid across his tongue. Water? It assuaged his throat but still, he found reason to be disappointed. For he longed to taste her lips, to find out if she could pull him farther from this place and more into the heaven she had created. Would it never be?

He groaned as frustration poured through him. His eyelids became heavy again and the dark pulled at him with a strength he feared he wouldn't be able to escape.

Yet she continued to speak over him, her voice a melody he wished he could tune to. It was for naught, however, as the night rushed at him, pulling him under once more

CHAPTER 19
HANA & RADEK

Hana frowned as Mistress Huddard fussed over the fine dress. The older woman had once been a lady's maid but not for many years, and she seemed to struggle with her duty tonight. Radek's mother had offered a lady's maid to care for Hana's appearance, but Mistress Huddard insisted she was capable. Now Hana had reason to doubt.

The woman did not seem easy with her work. Her fingers fumbled with nearly everything they touched. This kept Hana standing at the ready for some time. Much longer than she wanted to, at least. Her desire to go below stairs and rejoin Radek pulled at her. Just the thought of being in his company once more made her heart skitter.

"Don't be so downcast, my lady," Mistress Huddard muttered.

"What was that?" Hana looked over her shoulder to where the woman stood at her back. Why she feigned mishearing, she wasn't sure. But something had to give way.

"Don't frown. It is not becoming." Mistress Huddard crossed until she stood in front of Hana.

Trying her best to disguise her exasperation, Hana relented and eased the muscles of her face.

"There. Much better." But the woman narrowed her gaze even as she spoke. What now?

Then Mistress Huddard reached up and pinched Hana's cheeks. A bit too firmly. Hana had to fight the urge to pull away.

"I think that will be enough." She shooed the older hands away.

Mistress Huddard looked as if she wished to challenge such a notion but took a few steps back. "It is as well as it can be."

What did that mean? Did she believe Hana so difficult? Or was it that challenging to bring Hana up to the level expected of a lady? She had never considered this. Then again, her lady's maids had never been very talkative. Certainly not so bold.

Mistress Huddard patted Hana's shoulder as if consoling the ugly duckling.

No. Hana pushed such thoughts from her mind. They would not serve her. Yet as she peered in the mirror, she could not help but study herself. Were there things that made her unbecoming? Turning her face this way and that, she attempted to tell herself it was only an overreaction. After all, she had always been told she was pretty. Maybe not as much as Lady Karin, but Hana had always presented well. Hadn't she?

Curse these doubts! And fie on Mistress Huddard for her words. This would not do. Radek loved her. *He* found her becoming. That was all that mattered.

"What is it?" Mistress Huddard's question hung in the air.

"I but examine your work," Hana lied.

"Did I miss something?"

Father God in heaven, please no more fussing over me!

The older woman stepped toward Hana, hand rising.

Hana deflected the attempt. "All is well." She then moved to the door before Mistress Huddard could stop her.

A sound escaped the woman's lips, but Hana ignored it and slipped into the corridor, determined, and set on the Great Hall.

Mistress Huddard fell into step behind her.

Though as they descended the stairs, Hana struggled to find her confidence. The exchange above stairs had done much to damage that. Still, Hana lifted her chin and pressed every bit of pride she could onto her features. She would playact until it held true to her core.

They entered the Great Hall, and she scanned for her beloved. It wasn't long before she set eyes on him near the hearth, speaking with a man she did not know. Still, she made her way across the large room toward them.

Radek looked in her direction as she drew near. His features did not reflect any discernable amount of pleasure. Was he not eager to see her? Did he disapprove of her appearance?

Mistress Huddard's words came back to her. *It is as well as it can be.*

Hana's steps slowed. Perhaps her and Radek's bond had been born of their extreme circumstances, not from admiration.

As she watched, Radek excused himself from his conversation. Then he stepped forward to intercept her. She straightened her shoulders and put on her best smile.

"How do you find your chambers? Comfortable, were they?" His expression retained some level of indifference.

What she wouldn't give for an upward tilt to his mouth. Or some sign he was happy to see her.

"Hana?" His brow furrowed.

Was he now upset? She shook her head slightly. This would not do. Then she remembered...he had asked her a question, and, in her distraction, she had not answered. What was it he asked again? Oh yes, her chambers.

"All is well. I am happily placed." She pressed what confidence remained, though waning, onto her features.

"I am glad." He reached for her hand, his eyes searching her person.

She prayed he would find it well enough. Could she bear it if he did not give her some sign of encouragement?

"It is good to see you thus improved. I confess, I worried when you arrived soaked and chilled."

That wasn't quite what she hoped for, but there was nothing untoward in his words. Nothing at all. So, she nodded. It was the best she could manage.

He smiled at her then. And the warming of his regard soothed her.

Something caused the hair on the back of her neck to stand. Her gaze wandered to the head table. Radek's mother glared at her. What was in the woman's head? Did she scorn Hana's appearance? Or express a more general dislike?

"Hana?" Radek's gentle voiced urged.

She shifted her focus back to him. "Yes?"

"Is something wrong?" His eyes followed the path hers had taken. His mother no longer watched but spoke with a maidservant.

"It's nothing." Hana gave him her best smile, praying he would dismiss any fall in her countenance.

His hand touched hers. "Shall we find our places?"

Hana nodded and slid a hand onto his arm. She was grateful they were on the opposite side of the table from his mother. Instead, their seats took them closer to the margrave.

She chanced another glance in the margravine's direction. The woman watched her again, but her gaze was fleeting, turning to her companion rather quickly.

Hana's face warmed. What had she done to deserve such censure? How was she to get through this?

Radek stopped at a chair two down from his father. Was she to sit here while he took the seat beside the margrave?

Hana shifted, preparing to sit.

"Father, I would like to introduce you to Lady Hana Novakova, my betrothed."

Hana turned her focus to the margrave, whirling slightly as her body changed direction.

Radek firmed his hold on her. It was perhaps the only thing that kept her upright. His eyebrows meeting on his forehead told of his concern.

She hoped her slight smile would be apology enough. And though she was loathe to face the margrave after her misstep, she did so.

The large man's mouth spread. Was he so pleased to see her? That was refreshing.

"Lady Hana," he said, his eyes gleaming. "It is good to meet the woman who captured my son's heart."

She warmed under his acceptance. And felt her lips widen. "The honor is mine, my lord."

"Sometime," he responded, "you must tell me just how you did so. I would enjoy the tale."

"Of course." Her cheeks flamed. How was it that Radek had not expounded on their meeting and subsequent journey? Had he never a thought of sending for her?

"Shall we?" Radek indicated their seats.

She nodded and turned.

"I will have that story before a fortnight has passed." The margrave's eyes danced with what seemed contained laughter.

"I look forward to it." She offered the older man one more nod before claiming her chair.

Radek slid into his seat beside her. Would he now further engage his father and leave her to fend for herself? But much to her relief, his eyes found hers.

He opened his mouth, but another voice cut through from behind Hana.

"Is this the woman who stole the heart of Lord Miklas?"

Hana jerked her head around and found herself staring at quite easily the most beautiful woman she had ever seen.

Radek's attention homed in on Hana as she turned. What had disturbed her so?

His sister stood over them, staring down at Hana, a determined look on her face. Determined for what purpose? Did she seek to confront Hana? Know her? Dissuade her? It was unclear from where he sat. Perhaps he should intervene. But he paused. Would Hana appreciate that? Or prefer to manage these things on her own? All he could see was the back of her head. His family could be a bit much, both his sister and mother were rather protective.

"Galina," Radek said as he stood. He moved around Hana to embrace the girl three years his junior. "Mother said you had arrived." As he enfolded the slight form of his sister, he attempted to discern Hana's features. It was for naught.

Galina pulled back, forcing him to face off with her. What could she want? There was a heaviness beyond her eyes.

"It is good to see you." Galina's words were for him, but her gaze cut to Hana.

"I don't believe you have met Lady Hana." Radek turned to include his beloved.

She stood, but wavered. As if her legs wouldn't hold her. Was she well?

Radek resisted the urge to reach out to steady her. He did not wish her to appear weak.

Galina regarded Hana with eyebrow raised and full lips thinned. "Lady Hana?"

Hana nodded. "Yes. It is good to meet you."

Galina's eyebrow lifted all the more as she crossed her arms.

Radek watched the scene unfold, wishing to all heaven that he could step in without making the situation worse. But how?

"You are a lucky woman to have captured my brother's regard."

The words were well enough, but the tight press of Galina's lips defied her even tone.

"Oh," Hana laughed a little, but it came out more nervous than Radek thought it would. "I don't know that I would say 'captured.'"

"No?" Galina's eyes narrowed.

Hana licked her lips. Was she as uncomfortable as she seemed? The tension between the women was apparent. Was it time for him to speak up? He thought it best.

"I would say that I gave it quite willingly," he cut in. He sensed Hana's gaze on him. His chest warmed despite the tightness in his muscles.

"Is that so?" Galina challenged. "I had feared your heart was rather out of reach. And that it would take...more to turn it."

"Galina," he pressed out, trying to keep his admonition low. But enough was enough. It was one thing for her to be protective, another entirely to insult his intended.

Galina's stony gaze turned on him. "Pardon. I did not mean to offend."

That was exactly what she'd intended. And it was well felt. He prayed Hana had not been too injured by his over-reaching sister.

Hana's hand lay on his forearm. Her way of delaying his further comments, or did she seek reassurance?

He put his opposite hand over hers. "I think it best we return to our seats. The meal will commence soon."

Galina looked across the room as if bored. "I suppose." Then she gripped the back of the chair beside Hana's.

Dear Lord, no. Radek hoped it was not so.

But indeed, she sat.

Hana's eyes set on his face, her worry naked about her features. Did she dread sitting beside Galina as much as he imagined? It seemed so. But dare he switch seats with her? His father and mother had set the arrangements as such for a reason. Had they a thought that Galina would receive Hana so poorly?

Radek shot a look toward his mother.

Her head jerked away, regarding the woman on her other side. But he knew...she had been watching. This was her doing.

CHAPTER 20
KARIN & PAVEL

So, her husband would not be returning in the near future. Karin sighed and her shoulders somehow felt heavier.

The messenger that came yesterday bore news of Pavel's mother's illness, and bore Karin's frustrations as well. And the messenger that came this morning told of Pavel's summons to Prague. The change of plans had been met with silence from Karin. How long would it be before she and Pavel could truly be together? It seemed a dream that was forever out of reach. She did not want to be selfish, but it was only right for husband and wife to be together. Wasn't it?

She looked at her son, lying on the bed beside her.

Jaromir gurgled and shifted, but his eyes soon closed. He had eaten well and would likely be sleeping soon. What would become of him? Was she consigned to bring him to manhood herself?

Now, that was nonsense. Pavel cared deeply for his son and for her. He would find a way. *They* would find a way. Somehow.

Glancing over the latest missive again, her heart dropped once more, and she set the paper to the side. There was no reason to keep returning to it. No good could come from dwelling on the problem.

Perhaps she might look more to the task that had absorbed her every waking moment—the transcription of the Scriptures.

She had gotten farther with her Psalter, but she would need access to a Holy Writ if she wanted to do this right. But how? Might she inquire after Baron Novak—had he a copy? How would she go about doing so and yet keep him from guessing what she attempted?

Her sigh came heavier than before. It seemed as if the whole of her being released its energy in total. She lay back against the headboard and let her mind wander.

A knock on the door sent her thoughts scattering.

"Come." She shook her head, freeing it from the touch of sleep she had dipped into.

The nursemaid entered, her eyes scanning the room.

"He is here." Karin waved a hand to her side where Jaromir had a firmer hold on sleep.

"Is he—?" the woman started but paused as if unsure what she wished to say.

"Yes, he has nursed and is ready for his bed."

Coming closer, the older servant slid hands beneath Jaromir and lifted him.

His brow furrowed and his lips turned downward. Karin feared he might stir and protest the movement. But as the nursemaid pulled him closer to her chest, he soothed.

After the pair quit the room, Karin wondered if she might venture out into the castle. Yet her body weighed her to the spot. She had pushed herself these last days, fatiguing her mind even as her body still struggled to recover from bringing Jaromir into the world.

How did women do this multiple times? How did they bear it? Perhaps that was a question for another time. For now, she slipped farther down on the bed until her head found the pillow. And she lost her hold on consciousness.

Pavel fought the urge to draw his hands into fists. How long had he and his fellow nobles been at this? The manipulations afoot, the games, the bid for control...it was too much. Was it for this grasping and currying favor he had left his ailing mother? His beloved wife and child? That nagged. For he had not an answer that satisfied.

So many men had fought for this cause, putting their very lives and families in jeopardy. And these politicians sat in Prague, chasing their tails, trying to climb to some level of authority over the others.

It was nonsense. Yet it was happening.

And so, he and these other men of battle, of action, had been called in to manage this. He shot a sideways look at Zdenek beside him. His friend set a hand to his forehead, a look of torture upon his features. Headache? Yes, this whole affair had been one big headache indeed. There was nothing but glorified intentions of greatness here.

General Zizka and his men had met with a great number of men on all sides of the issue. Yet there was little more clarity than before. These avaricious men were certainly of a different ilk than he. They created troubles amongst themselves, comfortable in their places in Prague, while others died in battle for the cause. This did not endear these men to Pavel.

Was the only real solution to relieve themselves, and Prague, of the entire lot? Pavel found that his own opinion aligned with several of the military men. And General Zizka's. Perhaps they, like Pavel, had soured to these men of great words and little action.

"How will we keep them from disrupting the peace should it be found at last?" one of Zizka's captains asked.

The general frowned.

"The solution may be to place the same stake on their lives that we have faced time and again," an Orebite captain said.

It was not a bad idea. If these men of politics had any hint of what their countrymen at war faced, it may wake them up. At least one could hope it would.

"How do you propose we accomplish this?" Zizka turned toward the man.

"Enact punishment by execution for those disturbing the peace." The Orebite captain lifted his chin. His bold support of his suggestion told much.

Pavel certainly understood the desire to be harsh with these covetous men. But would they truly inflict such punishment against their own? There was enough loss of life without them taking each other's.

"Or spreading falsehoods," one of the noblemen among them added.

Pavel agreed that somehow, someway they must bring a stop to all of this. But was this the way?

Opening his mouth, Pavel prepared to press his thoughts out. But as he set eyes upon Zizka, he knew. The great general considered the recommendations. Would he bend to them?

More voices called out in support of these suggestions.

Pavel's heart dropped. It became less and less likely that General Zizka would defy so many of the same mind. Unless he felt strongly otherwise. Though it did not appear so.

Zizka set his jaw and called for the rabble to quiet.

All fell silent and every ear tuned to their leader—first in battle, now in this.

"It shall be so, then. Punishment by death for either offense."

"Must it be death? For any infraction?" Pavel spoke before taking even a moment to consider his words.

A dozen others glared at him.

He would not become timid in light of scrutiny. Too much had happened. They must temper their decision lest the dictates they hand over be no better than what Sigismund would have exacted.

"What say you?" Zizka regarded Pavel.

"It may not be that any and all accusations—founded or not— lead to a loss of life. Perhaps we may soften that blow, if only just." Pavel's words were bolder than he'd expected. But this mattered.

"What challenges you about this? You are not against harsh punishments surely," a man across the small crowd called to him.

Pavel narrowed his gaze, trying to home in on the face. But it was only one among many. He could not find the source. "I tell you; it is not so easy to order our fellow Czechs to their death."

"But it was a simple thing for you to chase after Ulrich of Rosenberg with little forethought?" the man became louder.

Pavel narrowed down the nobleman who addressed him only to a selection of five. But which spoke? Instead, Pavel offered a response. "It was no easy thing."

"Your father's death was reason enough to divert all your attention to avenging him, yet protecting our cause does not warrant such?"

The mention of his father stirred Pavel to launch himself forward. He would not be still while this...this buffoon ran at the mouth about things he could not possibly understand.

Hands pressed at Pavel as he moved to step forward, blocking him. Others surrounding him prevented further progress in the direction of the voice.

There—another of the Orebite captains sneered at Pavel. Was that the man who had challenged him?

"Don't think yourself so unnoticed, or so important," the man continued.

Pavel fought anew against those that restrained him. "You would insult my honor? We shall have at blades, you and I."

"Enough," Zizka's voice boomed. "We will not turn on one another."

Pavel ceased his struggle and looked to his general.

Zizka's regard darted between Pavel and the Orebite captain. "Not here and not for the council."

The words brought some measure of peace to Pavel's conscience.

"What of this?" Zizka proposed. "Immediate re-election of the entire council. Will that do?"

There was a mill of voices.

"But..." Zizka said as he raised an arm to silence the rumbled protests. "None who currently sits on the council may attempt to be re-elected."

The resistance to his suggestion let up. All listened for what he might say further.

"And punishment shall be set upon the shoulders of those who threaten the truce or spread heresy."

Punishment? What did he speak of exactly? Death? Pavel drew in a breath to speak once more.

General Zizka pressed his hand farther forward, calling for the men to maintain their patience and silence. "Punishment may include execution...but not necessarily."

Pavel wasn't entirely easy with this. But it was a compromise. Perhaps the best any of them could hope for.

"Any opposed?" Zizka pushed out in a firm tone.

None responded, but all scanned the room, seeking out any who would defy their general.

"Let it be done then."

"Here, here," many voices called out in agreement.

Pavel's gaze was now set on the Orebite who had accused him. Was he finished with the man? Or would the insult drive him toward another confrontation?

CHAPTER 21
PATRICIE & STEPAN

Patricie moved through the village. Another meal spent with Eva, bemoaning that Zdenek was away in Prague. One would think the woman had never been on her own. Was this what it was to be in love? To always have to be with the other person? To long for their return when one was away?

It did not appeal. Though...

She had to admit that she found herself drawn to Lord Dvorak's room more and more. Perhaps it was simply a desire to tend his wound and fend off infection. Yes, that must be it.

But it nagged at her. There was something more.

Had it been two days since that encounter—the one that had shaken her to her core? He had been in so much pain and delirium. But the way he had looked at her...and responded to her touch. There was something beyond what had been. Or should be. Something she could not shake.

She picked up her pace as she approached the inn and moved through the lower floor to the stairs. Would he be awake? Or still caught in the healing dark of sleep? She could find a reason to visit him first. Mayhap even spend extra time with him...tending his wound, that is. Or such she would tell herself.

Gathering the supplies she would need, she worked to concentrate. It would not do for her to go about, mind set on her dreams and not on her tasks. Still, she could not stop the fluttering in her stomach or the speed of her heartbeat. Those testified to how she both looked forward to and dreaded time with Lord Dvorak. What did she, in truth, hope for? Joining with a Royalist was beyond impossible. How could she want to endear herself to someone who would support and take part in the killing of fellow Czechs?

Regardless of how her body reacted to his presence, she could not.

"You are deep in thought." The voice cut through her musings.

She spun, falling backward toward the cabinet. Something halted her, keeping her from knocking into the precious stores of herbs and vials. Or rather...some*one*.

Lifting her chin, she then stared at Ludek. The lines around his eyes told of his concern, yet a tilt to one side of his mouth betrayed his amusement at her reaction.

"Are you all right?" he asked, clearly fighting his emotions. Was there levity to his voice? Did he find humor in this?

"Quite. Though I admit, you startled me." Now steadier on her feet, she tried to pull free.

His hands did not maintain such a hard grip on her arms, but they remained all the same. "I could not have, had you paid any mind to the things around you."

She dropped her head. He was right, of course. "Yes, I was distracted."

"What so captivated your thoughts?" Was it her imagination or did his thumbs rub over her sleeve?

She ignored the movement, but her face heated at his question. Could she answer? Perhaps, but not truthfully. What was she to say?

"Your face is all the more becoming when there is color about it."

She jerked her attention back to his eyes. Easing of the lines there gave her pause. Despite his jocular tone, no sense of laughter remained about his features. Only intensity. What could that mean?

"I was...focused on my rounds." Again, she pulled at her right arm. And again, he held it fast. Her pulse quickened at his resistance. Surely, he did not intend to hurt her. That seemed counter to what she knew of him.

"Were you?" He leaned nearer, tugging her toward himself as he did so.

"I...yes." She attempted once again to create space, though only her head could now be distanced from his.

"Oh?" His voice deepened.

"I am well enough." She tried to keep her voice even, pushing down the panic rising in her chest. "And I have patients to see."

His eyes widened slightly. "They can wait."

She swallowed. Her options dwindled by the second.

"Turn me loose." Her voice had not the force behind it she would have hoped. Was she so timid in his presence?

He pressed closer until their faces were but an inch separated.

"I..." What could she say? How might she stop this? Had she in some way communicated she desired this? Maybe she had a month ago, but now?

"What?" His voice softened, and his lids lowered as if heavy.

And she knew. He intended to kiss her. How would she keep from injuring his pride and yet still create the much needed distance?

Raising her arms to set hands on his chest did halt his progress. Indeed, his eyes opened again...for a moment. Then a slow smile crept across his face, and he moved toward her lips again.

Pushing against his chest with all she had brought more separation. His hands slipped to her forearms, but his fingers dug into her flesh there.

"What is this?" His voice was full again. And angry.

She struggled until his grip gave way. Then she backed against the cabinet. Some of the vials rattled. "I might ask you the same question."

He pushed out a breath. "Don't pretend you haven't wanted to be near me."

She searched for an answer that was both truthful and yet would discourage further efforts. "I admire you as a healer. And I do wish to learn from you. But I believe you have misunderstood."

He shoved a hand through his hair, then set his gaze on her once more. "*I* have misunderstood?"

She nodded, bringing her arms up to cross in front of her chest. "I admit, I have a care for you. But I do not want this."

"You but tease me, then." His voice was rough.

"No!" She dropped her head into a hand. How to make him understand? Must she bare more of her true feelings to him? "I did not intend to make you think that I..." She paused. Didn't she wish him to admire her? When they worked so closely, when they would talk of other things...before Lord Dvorak...

She halted. So abruptly her thoughts jumbled. It took a moment to sort them.

Lord Dvorak? Had he been the catalyst here? Whereas she once hoped for more with Ludek, now her heart had shifted to Stepan? That did paint her as a tease, did it not?

"What is it?" Ludek's voice was neither gentle nor gruff.

She met his gaze. "I...don't know what to tell you. I am truly sorry for misleading you, but I do not wish to draw your heart in any way."

He smirked. "As if you could involve my heart."

"But you said..."

"Come now, you are no child. Surely you know what affection goes between a man and a woman."

She stepped back but felt the cabinet once more. "You mean that you intended only to—"

"I did not intend to take what would not be offered."

Patricie bit at her lip. How could he insult her so? Did he think her so beneath his station? The truth of it sliced through her, cutting deeply. As far as he was concerned, she was no more than a maiden to be trifled with.

Glaring at him, she lifted her chin and swallowed. She would not let him believe himself so fine, so above what he had thought to do.

"Ah, there is that spirit." His features smoothed and his hands lifted.

"You will keep your distance." She pressed all the ire she could muster into her voice. "And I will fulfill my duty. Nothing more. Nothing less."

"What if I were to decide I no longer need an apprentice?"

"What if I expose to all the kind of man you really are?"

He snorted. "We shall see, little mouse. I don't believe you have it in you."

Stunned at his words, her breaths came in heaves. "I have patients who need me." She grabbed for fresh bandages and picked up the salve she had dropped. Then moved past him. Still, she felt his eyes boring into her until she turned into a room.

Patricie tried to gather her wits about her. It would not do to tend patients with her thoughts caught up in what happened with Ludek. It wouldn't. But how could she put the encounter with Ludek out of mind? It did not seem possible. Her shame, her ire...all of it fell over and surrounded her.

She moved numbly through the hall and entered the next room —Lord Dvorak's room. And toward the encounter she had been delaying. Could she face him right now?

As she stepped within, she knew she had to. Stepan needed her to care for his injury. Now in the confining space, she moved to the bed and peered up.

Stepan slept—evidence of God's mercy. Salvation from yet another strained interaction. Perhaps, if she were careful, she might clean his wound and change his bandage without rousing him. But as she drew closer, the old floorboards creaked.

He stirred and opened his eyes.

Too late for her to make an escape.

He scanned the area, settling his gaze on her.

She cleared her throat. "I am here to check your wound."

He nodded but studied her all the same. What was in his head? She wanted to know. Though it didn't truly matter what he thought. She had a task before her, and she intended to do it.

But his eyes...they never left her face. His attention seemed rather intense.

She unwrapped his lower leg with great care, determined she would not be the cause of further pain. He had been through much. What had he thought that day? What had made him attempt to move beyond the bed? Had he intended to cross the room? For what reason?

There had not been any discussion about his thought process, as to why he risked injuring himself again. Nor did she have the strength for it now.

"Are you well?" His words were quiet. Almost inaudible.

She avoided his gaze. "I should be asking you that, hmm?"

He didn't answer.

It prompted her to look at him. The consideration in his eyes undid something in her.

"I..." She swallowed. What had she started to say? Best to reassure him and then quiet herself. "I am well enough."

"Well enough? Even you don't believe that." Again, his words were every bit as tender as they were firm, as if he could sense how tenuous her hold on her calm demeanor was.

She shrugged and continued her work, though her hands blurred slightly. Would her emotions overcome her ability to contain them?

"What has happened?" His tone had more heaviness to it. Almost as if he could guess what had transpired.

She sighed. "It is nothing."

"No...it bothers you." He swallowed. "Did that healer...?" His voice caught.

Her eyes found his again. How could he know?

"Forgive me." His voice deepened. "It is not my place."

She nodded. "Do not concern yourself so."

"How can I not?"

When she turned to him again, she found him regarding her oddly. As if he hadn't meant to speak so. But he had. Did he care so much? Worry, even?

"Put your mind at ease. Nothing untoward happened." Did she lie to herself or to him? Surely, Ludek would never have—

"Did he...?"

Patricie could not look at him in that moment. Would he continue?

Stepan sucked in a breath. "Was that...man...too forward?"

She stilled her movements as her throat thickened and the blurriness of her vision increased. Still, she repeated her earlier statement. "It was nothing."

His fingers touched her forearm. But he made no move to further the contact. "You don't believe that. So don't try to convince me."

She wiped at her eyes.

"I should have stopped him." His words were ground out.

Her gaze found his. "What?"

"I saw...the way he looked at you. I feared he would..." A muscle twitched in Stepan's now-clamped jaw. He lifted his hand toward her face but let it fall when he couldn't reach her.

"None of this is your doing. Ludek simply..." Why was she telling him this? "...thought something existed between us that does not."

"He did more than that." Stepan's statement was brazen. "He should not have presumed. Especially as you are his apprentice. It is unseemly."

She turned away. Stepan's words bombarded her wounded heart, but his strength offered her a salve. In this moment, with his protective anger, she was cared for. And worth more than she had dared believe since the incident with Ludek.

"Patricie," Stepan said, his words calmer.

She bit at her lip. How was he so kind?

His fingers were on her arm again. "Patricie."

Had anyone ever spoken her name so tenderly? She chanced a glance at him. And found a deep well of emotion in his eyes. Did her situation tear at him so? The urge to look away was great, but she could not make herself turn.

"It is not your doing." His words were a balm.

Moisture escaped her eyes. She brushed it away.

There was a shuffling from the direction of Stepan's upper body. Did he move to sit? She could not drag her gaze up to determine if that was so. It became impossible to tear her gaze from her lap.

His arms came around her, urging her to lean into him.

She resisted for but a moment. Would she cause his leg further injury? Would his arms bring greater injury to her heart?

But at length she relented and fell into him, letting her tears come.

He pressed a hand to her hair and whispered soothing words. She granted herself release of the pent up swirl of emotions as she relaxed into his hold. His arms were warm and strong and everything she could have hoped for. While they secured her, supporting her as she fell apart, they brought a new sensation. She thrilled as a tingle of pleasure curled around her heart.

Patricie remained locked in the comforting circle of his arms longer than she should have allowed. And it was difficult to draw back from him when she finally did.

Only then did she meet his gaze.

His hand settled to the side of her face for a moment before dropping. Was he likewise affected by their exchange?

Every part of her felt alive and longed for more of his touch. But she could not...nor should she have even permitted the embrace. It was time to do what she came to do. And shake free of this...it was, after all, forbidden her. Both because of his station and his situation as a Royalist.

"I...need to finish cleaning your wound."

He nodded. "As you will." Why did his words have to be so gentle? So understanding?

His gaze followed her every movement as she worked.

She breathed relief when, some minutes later, she finished and stood. As much as she wanted for more out of their interaction, she knew it was necessary she remove herself lest she give up all sense. She needed time to think, to consider all that had happened. And what exactly she would do about it.

When she looked at his features again, they melted her. This man...this Royalist soldier...had offered her kindness and strength when she needed it. How could she turn from him without further words and just leave? But she did.

CHAPTER 22
HANA & RADEK

The evening meal had been arduous at best. Hana had worked to avoid Galina as much as she could. That had not been easy. When they did exchange words, Radek's sister had been rather off-putting. How was it possible that, of all the people in Hana's acquaintance, Galina, a lady she so wanted to befriend, would not be moved?

There seemed a hardness to her. At the very least, she did not give any hint that she was open to knowing Hana—only judging her. How was Hana to come out from under that? It was difficult enough that Radek's mother despised her. Must his sister as well?

"Something distracts you." Radek's deep voice scattered Hana's thoughts.

She pressed a smile she didn't feel onto her features. "It is nothing."

His eyes sought the truth in her affect. Dare she share her true thoughts? What good could come from that? "I am only tired."

He did not seem convinced, but he did not push further. "Shall I see you to your chamber then?"

She dipped her head, though she was loathed to bring a close to her evening. If only she could spend more time with Radek. If only she could be stronger. If only...

Hana wearied from the difficult exchanges and her wariness over the meal. And something did not settle well in her stomach—be that from the interactions or from the food, she could not know.

Sliding a hand onto Radek's offered arm, her gaze flitted across the room to where Galina and her mother were engaged in conversation. The two talked adamantly. How was it that, of the two, neither were the least bit receptive to her? Was Hana such a poor choice for Radek? Had that been so obvious? The fact that she was a duke's daughter did not seem to matter. Not that Hana wished to rely on her station. Though it did not appear it had done her any favors here.

She told herself they were only being protective of him. Wouldn't she be in their position?

Galina's gaze turned on her and Hana jerked her regard back to Radek.

His eyebrows gathered, a look of concern about him. Could she reassure him? Indeed, there was much uneasiness in her own stomach. How must he feel?

Still, she put on a smile, as pleasant as she could make it, and tugged him in the direction of the stairs. "Please. I am well enough."

He did not believe her. That was clear. Yet he picked up step beside her and assisted her above stairs. For which she was grateful. With her stomach ailing to some degree, she was uncertain she wished to manage on her own.

They did not speak as they climbed the stone steps. Though her silence was not for lack of care for him. Quite the opposite. Her discomfort with his kin brought about a churning of her insides at the prospect of seeing them on the morrow. Why, again, had she come?

Beyond that, the fatigue of her body was all the more felt. Had the days of travel been so trying? She was surprised to find that a sheen of sweat had broken out about her face and neck. Could it be that she was so bothered by the women in his family that it would affect her physically?

She tried to push the disaster of an evening to the side, but her body's response only intensified. Pausing at the top of the stairs, she put a hand to her middle and gasped. Even assisted, could she go on?

"What is it?" Radek's gaze was on her as he turned her toward himself.

She tried to wave him off. But her legs protested, weakening beneath her as she moved.

Radek leaned her against the stairway wall. "You are *not* well." His voice soothed her worn nerves.

She nodded, putting her other hand to her forehead. The pain in her midsection increased and the whole of her vision danced.

"Hana?" His arms surrounded her. How was he near enough to touch her? Everything in her awareness—including his voice—seemed far away. The floor tilted and the walls spun.

"Hana," Radek's call seemed a great distance away, too far off to intervene.

Then she was carried. When had he lifted her? Nothing was as it should be. The upturning of her insides intensified, and she cried out.

Radek said something, but she could no longer discern his words.

Spindle-like fingers entered her consciousness, and they gripped at her.

"No..." Was the word spoken from her lips? It echoed in her ears as if it had been.

Intrusive darkness pulled at her, and she could find no reason to fight it any longer.

Radek tucked Hana as close to himself as possible as he rushed to her bedchambers. What had happened? There had been little warning before she collapsed. Had some sickness befallen her? Would it continue to intensify?

Mistress Huddard was within Hana's chamber, securing the room.

He moved through to set Hana upon the mattress and commanded the woman, "The healer. Now."

The older woman's shocked face was her only response.

"Now," he insisted once more. If he could have afforded the woman a harsh look, he would have indulged himself. As it was, his every sense was fixed on his beloved.

Mistress Huddard scurried from the room, calling for help as she went down the corridor.

Radek released Hana onto the bed but did not pull back. He leaned over her, pressing a hand to her face. How could one look so devoid of life and yet breathe? The fairness of her skin had been intensified by her pallor. Her lips had likewise paled. She seemed but asleep, though he knew it might well be much more.

"Hana," he breathed. He wanted to plead with her to fight this, to come back to him. But no further words came.

God, please don't let her die. That was the extent of his ability even to pray. So, he remained as he was, stroking the side of her face and repeating his simple but heart-rending request to the Almighty.

Footsteps beyond the door warned that others came.

"Be strong," he whispered. "And stay with me."

The footfalls neared.

"I tell you, I know nothing! Lord Miklas brought her in, and she was lifeless." Mistress Huddard's shrill voice bounced off the walls.

The rustling of fabric told that the women had entered, but it was the healer's movements Radek concerned himself with. He turned in that direction as the healer stepped closer, attempting to shoulder him out of the way.

"Please," the thin woman spat as she moved hands over Hana. "I need to work."

He hated to do so, but he pulled himself away from the one for whom his heart beat furiously.

The healer paid him no more mind as she went about her work.

Then Mistress Huddard tugged at him. "My lord, you must trust that all will be done for the lady. All that can be."

He resisted the older woman's urgings.

"Lord Miklas," the older woman said more loudly. "You must step outside."

That was the last thing he intended to do. But then the healer worked at the laces on Hana's dress, and he realized he must. Only then did he allow Mistress Huddard to direct him out of the room.

He stepped into the hall and when the door shut, creating a very real barrier between him and Hana, his heart sank. What would he do? If Hana did not revive, could he continue? Of one thing he was certain—he would never let his heart be so vulnerable again.

The seconds blended into minutes. How long he paced just beyond the door, waiting, he did not know. At length, he settled on a stair.

"How is she?"

Radek looked toward the owner of the voice. But he didn't need to.

His father stood over him, his eyes deep with sympathy.

"I do not know." Radek didn't believe he could afford any more words and still rein in his emotions.

"Our healer is capable. The best perhaps." Father's words were not the balm he'd probably intended.

Radek nodded but kept his gaze trained on the door.

Father set a hand to Radek's shoulder. "All will be well."

Then he met his father's eyes. "How can you know that?"

"It is no easy thing to say this, but it comes from facing much and finding God is faithful."

Radek turned aside. He didn't feel much like exercising what little faith had begun to spring in him over these last months. It was too great a request. God asked too much of him.

Father's hand lifted. And Radek was surprised that regret filled him. What support had come from that simple contact had eased him to some extent. He was tempted to say as much, but he could not bring himself to admit it. Not with things between them as strained as they were. Yet he turned even that thought over in his head.

As he did so, the door opened.

"Hana? How is she?" Radek all but attacked the healer as she stepped from the room.

The woman startled, but only just. That was encouraging. Shouldn't it be?

"She is well enough," the woman said, peering to where Radek's father stood. "I believe she has expelled much of what ailed her stomach."

"Expelled?" Radek wasn't certain he wanted to understand what had transpired between when he held Hana and this moment.

The healer looked to the margrave and then back to Radek. "I gave her something to assist with that."

Radek's features dug lines in his face as concern filled him anew. "Is she in distress?"

"Only mildly." The healer met Radek's gaze. "As I said, she expelled much. And she rests now."

He let out a breath.

"Thank you," the margrave spoke into the space, "for your efforts."

Radek wanted to balk. After all, the healer had only done her duty. But he could not. For gratitude did indeed swell for what the healer had done to preserve Hana. "Might I see her?"

"For a moment." The healer's eyes were hard, determined. "She needs her rest."

Nodding, Radek stepped forward.

"But I must say," the healer said, her words stilling him. Her pause bothered. "I believe she took in some manner of ill-used herb or poison." The woman's affect testified to her seriousness. Her own

210

concern shone through. "Had we not acted so quickly, this night would have ended differently."

Poison? How could that be? Hana had only just arrived. Who would wish such ill on her?

Radek's mind reeled with a barrage of speculations. Unbidden, the memory of his mother and sister's reception lay just above the surface of those thoughts, though he dismissed it. They may not wish her well, but that didn't mean they planned harm. It couldn't be.

His thoughts spun, but he gained no ground. At length, he nodded to the healer and stepped around her. He needed to see Hana.

CHAPTER 23
PATRICIE & STEPAN

S tepan stared at the ceiling. How long had he done so? Since Patricie left the room earlier in the day? It mattered not what he told himself, he stared and thought.

What did he think? What did he feel? Embracing the healer's assistant had been more than he could have fathomed. Patricie had fit so well in his arms. Those moments of bliss had transported him to somewhere that existed for only them.

Even now his heart stuttered as the memory overwhelmed him. Or was this due to something else? Fear, perhaps? He'd not had such tender feelings toward a woman since...Karin. And that had been devastating. She had not returned his affection. Though...at first it had seemed she did.

He grimaced.

The fact that Karin hid her true feelings from him had been diffi-cult to understand. Still, it had not merited his reaction and the injury he visited upon her. But that seemed a lifetime ago. Things were...different now. The war had shaped him in unexpected ways. Things were not as clear cut as he had once assumed.

If he had the chance to talk to Karin, even for a moment, would he make amends? Or cling to his injured pride and dejected heart?

Perhaps so. Though he wanted to believe otherwise.

Her betrayal still stung. No matter how founded it may have been. No matter what he told himself. But this was not about Karin... it was about Patricie. Did he have reason to believe Patricie had feelings for him? Or would this be another disaster? It was best he shield his heart.

Turning his attention to more pressing matters, he considered his leg. How did he truly fare? Were there things about his condition they did not disclose? Would he walk again? Or be lame for the rest of his life? If only he had heeded the healer's words and remained abed. Still, he could not regret his actions attempting to protect Patricie. Especially as it seemed she had needed someone to intervene. That man—Ludek—it was all *his* fault.

Stephan groaned. What good would stewing do? He must focus on the next course of action. How was he to get out of his predicament? He was not certain what the Hussites would do with him once he healed. Would they ransom him or have him tried? Possibly executed? He let out a low laugh. What good was all this work on their part to see him whole if he was meant for the gallows?

Absurd. Maybe, then, that wasn't what they intended at all.

Still, he could not allow himself to be used against his father or his fellow soldiers. What, if anything, did his father know of his predicament? Did he care?

Stepan closed his eyes against the rush of shame. That proved one way to keep himself from boring a hole into the roof.

In the midst of his pause, he heard steps in the hall. They drew closer. Patricie? Had she come again? It was rather late for another round. But if the moment they shared had meant as much to her as it had to him, perhaps she came to speak with him. What would he say?

He gripped the edges of the mattress and dragged himself into a sitting position. His heart thumped almost painfully.

The footfalls were just outside the room now. And they stopped.

He licked his lips.

The door creaked open.

His pulse thundered in his ears. How was he so affected by the possibility of seeing her again? He was at a loss.

A Hussite soldier stepped within the room, glared at Stepan, and shut the door. What did this man want? Stepan eyed the sword at the man's side. How would he defend himself if this soldier meant him harm? With what? He almost laughed at himself. Even should he have a weapon, it wasn't as if he could jump up and engage the man at blades.

The man glanced about the room as if he had not noticed Stepan. What did he seek? Was he uninterested in the Royalist prisoner confined to the bed?

At length, the soldier set his gaze on Stepan and moved closer.

"Stepan Dvorak?" the man asked, his gaze still darting about into the dark corners of the room.

Should he lie? Of what use would that be? He set his jaw. "Yes."

"Your father sent me. I'm here to get you out."

Darkness had fallen over the small village. And all was quiet throughout the upper level of the inn. Patricie climbed the narrow stairway noting how different things were below stairs during the day and as evening neared. The main room only came to full life in the dark. Lights, joviality, all manner of people moving about...it seemed to exceed the walls that worked to contain it.

As for Patricie, she had no desire to be party to the raucous laughter and drinking. And so, she slipped through the hallway, hoping she would remain largely unnoticed by the rather distracted men who huddled over their pints.

It did give her a moment to catch her breath and question her decision. Why did she make her way to Stepan's room? It wasn't wise...or prudent. Yes, they had shared a tender moment, but that didn't mean she should be drawn back to him, did it?

Though when she stopped to consider this, her footfalls resumed almost without a thought. The warmth and strength she had found in his arms during their earlier exchange drove her onward.

What would she say of her purpose for sneaking into his room? Would he believe she needed to check his bandaging again? Or would he think her a grasping commoner?

That gave her pause once more. What were the chances of that? He was nobility—a viscount's son. Her father was only a merchant. Would he think she only sought to aim higher than she should?

She closed her eyes. This was nonsense. There truly was not a good reason to visit him at this hour.

His door lay just a few feet ahead, and she halted, second guessing herself. What if he did think more of her? Wanted to see her again? Wished to reason out this heat between them as much as she?

Her heart pounded. Could she rest if she didn't go through that door and speak with him?

A couple more steps brought her face on with the wooden barrier.

Then more doubt crept in. Perhaps it would be best to wait for the morrow. What good could be accomplished in the dark? Was it even appropriate for her to be in his room at this hour? Probably not. Her role as caregiver may blur the lines of propriety in many cases, but it would not stretch so far.

She turned but caught the sound of voices within the room. Who was with Stepan? There were two distinct male voices. But their words were lost beyond the thick oak.

Had Ludek decided to speak with Stepan? Perhaps Stepan had challenged Ludek?

The voices quieted.

Her pulse quickened. She would not let Stepan fight her battles. But could she face Ludek?

She had to.

Gritting her teeth, she sucked in a breath and steadied herself for what she might find. She closed her eyes and reached out. Pushing against the latch brought her into the room in one movement.

Then she was pressed against the other side of the door, something sharp pressed against her neck.

"Do not," Stepan yelled.

Was this a blade at her throat? The pressure did not ease.

"What do you want?" a stranger's voice said. Dark eyes glared at her so close to her face she felt the heat of his breath. This man was not discernable as anyone she knew. But the man wore the garb of a Hussite soldier. Had he come to exact some version of justice on Stepan?

Her eyes flicked to Stepan, seated on the edge of the bed.

His widened gaze pinned her.

The soldier slammed her against the door. "What do you seek here?"

Fear seamed her lips.

"She is the healer's apprentice." Stepan's words were only a little softer than before.

The tension in the blade did not alleviate.

"Shall I rid us of her? She is an unnecessary obstacle." The sharp point pushed deeper, biting into her skin and cutting off any response. Would this be her end?

"No! Turn her loose," Stepan demanded.

Her vision swirled and the world started to spin.

The man turned on Stepan. "But she could—"

"Let her loose." The words were forceful.

And then nothing pinned her to the door any longer. She fell, and the floorboards coming up to meet her shook her to awareness. When she peered upward, the man's boots were all she could see.

The air in the room thickened as the men conversed, but her ability to discern anything was hazy at best.

Then, just as suddenly, hands lifted her once more. She worked to put her feet solidly beneath herself.

SARA R. TURNQUIST

"...can't leave her here," the gruff man seethed.

"Must...with us."

She craned her neck to peer over the man's shoulder in time to see Stepan shift as if he would attempt to stand.

"No," she choked out. How was her voice so hoarse? Stepan could fall and damage himself further.

"Quiet," the man grunted.

"Bring her here." Stepan appeared to be in charge. But the Hussite soldier was the one she feared.

Half dragging her, the soldier pulled her to Stepan's side.

"Now loose her," Stepan said, then amended with, "Carefully."

This time, she had more opportunity to find her footing before the larger man released her and stepped back. Patricie had never been so thankful for space to breathe. Her gaze darted to Stepan. What was this about? What did he intend? But none of these questions made it past her lips.

The Hussite soldier ran a finger along his blade. "We don't need complications."

"Perhaps this is not the challenge it seems," Stepan said, his eyes on Patricie.

The man gritted his teeth. "How can this woman—?"

"She might be the key to our escape." Stepan's eyes narrowed.

Escape? How did he think he could leave this place filled with Hussites unscathed? And why did he think she would aid him? A weight settled in her stomach. She had been wrong about him.

Stepan raised a hand in her direction. "Come."

She would not comply. Would not be a part of whatever he planned.

One glance at the soldier unsheathing his dagger once more, however, told that he was well enough prepared, and ready, to finish what he'd threatened.

She stepped to the bedside. Words of accusation to throw at Stepan filled her, but again, nothing came forth. Had she lost her nerve? Or did she still feel some misplaced loyalty to Stepan?

"Help me up." His words were curt.

She opened her mouth to protest. But that, too, would be useless. If he so willed it, he would gain his feet one way or another.

"Do it," the other man commanded, his dagger gleaming in the moonlight.

Gripping Stepan on the side of his injured leg, she tugged him upward. He gained his feet faster than she'd thought possible. Wasn't his injury too severe to have allowed such?

"Hand me that." Stepan indicated the small blade.

The soldier complied.

He jerked Patricie to himself and pressed the short blade to her side. "Now, we go."

CHAPTER 24
KARIN & PAVEL

Karin crept into Duke Novak's library. The man had given her full reign of the room, but she felt the need for secrecy all the same. It wasn't as if she was on an errand to read a book of poetry. She sought the Holy Writ. And as odd as it would be for a woman to be found reading it, it would be all the more so if she were caught transcribing it. Would she be dragged before the priest? The church? What would happen to her? That was not certain. But she would not welcome the censure all the same.

The room was dim. Some light seeped in through the window, but heavy drapes disrupted the flow of sunbeams, blocking them from bathing the space. Shadows about the room added to a sense of intrigue.

Moving farther in, she scanned for where the Holy Writ might be kept. Would it be on a shelf amongst other works? Or did the duke have it prominently displayed? That was the way of it for Baron Krejik. The Holy Writ had been on a pedestal in the library, a place of honor. But that was before the fire. Memories filled her of that night, when everything changed in their lives. Would Pavel's father still be alive if it had not happened?

She shook her head. If she started down that path it would never stop.

Karin resumed her search for the Writ. It did not take long. The precious book sat in a corner on a raised stand. Setting her hands to either side of the book, she touched the pages. The book was amazing in and of itself—the papers within were forever marked with God's words. Having spent hours transcribing her Psalter, she marveled at the workmanship of the copy, with design and art displayed on every page.

She took a moment to acknowledge the hours that went into copying the ancient words so that this noble family had a copy. Not altogether different from what she did, yet it was.

The whole of what she attempted slammed into her. As did the danger. Was this worth her life? Her standing in the world? But an image, a dream, of Czechs having access in their own tongue filled her mind. As well, the sacrifices others made in pursuing God's best flitted across her thoughts. Of most import to her was Tomas. He did not care about the price he might—and did—pay for his disobedience to the Church. Because of his boldness, Karin and others followed God's direction in a war for their kingdom. And prevailed.

What would Tomas think of her now? Could he have imagined she would take on such a task? He would chuckle at her for certain. Then again, he had risked much to bring her the truth. And, in the end, it cost him everything. Tears stung her eyes. How different would her life have been had her childhood friend not shared Hus's writings with her? Or spent countless hours sharing with her the truth he had discovered? She owed him so much. More than she could repay. Even if that were possible.

Yes, the reward far exceeded any risk.

Lifting the sizeable Writ, she moved it to a small table and chair that sat on the opposite side of the room. Then she gathered her yet empty papers, spreading them alongside the book. How long might she work? Could she remain here, undisturbed, for an hour? Two? Would she accomplish enough?

Enough for what? She shook her head. This was a labor of love. It would take however long it took. She silenced her worry and went to her work. Even as she worked, memories of Tomas plagued her.

She was so deep in her thoughts she didn't hear the approaching intrusion until the door opened. Pulling herself from her task in a moment, she shoved at her papers in the far hope that they would not be seen.

"Karin?" The voice came from the doorway. It was familiar.

She looked up and found herself staring into brilliant blue eyes—Pavel's.

What was this? Pavel's gaze settled on his wife. She appeared almost mortified to see him. Why would that be? True, he had come without warning. But should she not be happy to see him?

"Karin?" His words echoed in the space.

She had shoved several papers to the side. Papers she had been writing on. Why? Had she some secret? Something she did not wish him to know? A pang shot through his chest and an anchor filled his gut. Was there more to this? Who was she writing to?

"Pavel," her gasped response hit his ears a bit oddly. She rose and stepped toward him, leaving the discarded papers where she had tucked them.

That did not mollify him, however, it only added to the apprehension welling within.

She moved across the room, abandoning her writings. Did she seek to distract him? As she came closer, her arms lifted and came around his shoulders. "You have returned!"

Stunned by what he could gather of her behavior, he brought his arms around her. Experience told him that his distraction would typically bother her, but she seemed—or rather acted—oblivious to his lack of enthusiasm.

"It is good to have you back...and whole. You cannot know how I fear for you when you are away."

He met her gaze. Was that fear in her eyes? Or a vulnerability? It did nothing to quell his nerves.

She set a hand to the side of his face. "I am certain Duke Novak was pleased to see you." Then her features fell. "What of your mother? How does she fare?"

He searched her features. To seek out a sign of betrayal? Or something else—perhaps reason to hope? Was it his imagination, or did she tremble slightly?

She grabbed for his forearm and stepped toward the door. "Come, see how Jaromir has grown in these few weeks, I—"

He stood his ground and moved his gaze from her to the half-hidden papers and back to her.

"What is this?" His tone was neither harsh nor demanding but bore the weight of his suspicion all the same.

Now both of her hands were on his arm. "It is nothing."

A tremor took hold of her. Or a chill. Though the room was not cold.

He disentangled his arm from her grasp and stepped to the small desk that bore a large book with papers shut into it and shoved beneath.

"Pavel..." came her half-hearted attempt to dissuade him.

Laying a hand upon the book, he noted the cover. It was a Holy Writ. Would she use the precious book to disguise her treacherous papers?

He opened the priceless pages to where she had pressed her writings. His heart nearly stopped as he pulled them out. Should he read them? There was no other way to discover the truth for himself. Yes, he would have to read it and then manage the fallout as best as he could.

But when he looked upon the crumpled pages, he found passages from Exodus scratched out. In Czech.

He regarded her across the room, having wrapped her arms about her torso. Then she did not attempt to hide these because she had been unfaithful, but because she undertook something dangerous.

"Karin?" The question hung between them. Could he voice this new fear which now took hold?

Her shaking worsened. Was she afraid of *him*? Did she not trust him?

"What is this?" He couldn't keep the pain from seeping into his voice.

She lifted her chin. "I do what I must."

He furrowed his brow. What she must? Had she no concept of the position she put herself in? That the church had killed others for attempting such?

Jan Hus himself had worked to finalize a translation of the Writ into Czech. And that, among his other *crimes*, had seen him burned at the stake.

"Do you not know what this...?" he said as he advanced on her, "What could come of this?"

She remained rooted to the spot.

Now he stood directly in front of her. "Why?"

"I want Jaromir to be able to read God's Word without hindrance. And for all children to have access to these Scriptures. Not just those who are taught to read Latin."

"But why you?" Something tore through his core, leaving molten fear in its wake.

Her eyes glistened. "Why not me?"

He enfolded her in his arms. "Because you are dear to me. I cannot—" His words caught in his throat.

She leaned away and set her hands to frame his face. "Bohemia is different now. There is no reason to think mortal punishment would be inflicted."

He watched emotions play across her features. False confidence?

For him? He swallowed. "There is no reason to assume it would not be."

She looked to the ground. "Can you not see? God has called me to this." Her eyes sought his once more.

He fought a tightness in his throat. Could he even speak? As he tried to work out words and failed, he drew her to himself again. What was he to do?

CHAPTER 25
HANA & RADEK

Hana sighed. Her head ached terribly.

Not that it mattered one bit to Mistress Huddard. The older woman yelled into the hall for the healer. Was that truly necessary?

Hana was sore and tired, generally unwell. But that did not mean the woman had to shriek, did it?

"She is awake?" another, masculine, voice called back.

Where did it come from? The hall? It sounded like Radek.

"Yes, my lord," Mistress Huddard said into the corridor, "but I do not know if she is well enough to receive. I..." The woman's protests continued.

Regardless, Radek appeared beside the bed. He was a sight indeed, a welcomed one.

"Hana," he breathed.

Her eyes sought his. They were bright and filled with worry...and hope.

"How are you?" His voice was gentle.

There was little reason to lie. "I ache, but I am better now that you are here." She pulled a hand free of the bedclothes and reached for him.

"I have been so worried." He knelt, taking her hand in both of his. "I have never been so..."

The statement lingered in the air. His mouth closed and he swallowed. What had he almost said?

Radek looked to where Mistress Huddard stood.

For her part, the older woman watched them as if a hawk over a mouse. Was the woman still concerned for Hana's virtue?

Ignoring their chaperone, Hana tugged at Radek's hand, attempting to draw his focus back to her. His gaze was on her in a second.

"I will be myself soon enough." She squeezed his fingers.

"How can you know that?" His darkened, deeply lined features betrayed the depth of his concern.

"Because I have to." She shifted toward him. "For you." A smile touched her lips.

He leaned forward. Would he kiss her in front of Mistress Huddard? Everything in her cried out for the feel of his lips upon hers, but he halted.

She pressed her disappointment out in a sigh.

He brought her hand to his chest. "I will take care to better watch over you, my love." His words were spoken quietly as if he wished to exclude Mistress Huddard.

That did not bother Hana in the least. The woman was too intrusive.

"It is not your fault," Hana insisted. "How could you have foreseen a fainting spell?"

His brows gathered. "No one has told you?"

Her heart hammered within at the seriousness of his gaze. "Told me what?"

"You were..." He paused.

She feared he would not go on, but he did.

"Poisoned." Pain appeared in the lines of his face.

"Poisoned? How is that possible?"

He rubbed her knuckles with a thumb. "Your drink or perhaps your food."

"Who would...?" But she silenced the words as a thought came to mind—the look of vehemence that had been upon his sister's face, and the distaste on his mother's. Why did they despise her so? And to what lengths?

"It is not known. But I assure you, no one will be at rest until answers are found."

Her eyes met his once more and she found there a level of determination she had not seen before.

"Thank goodness you have come." Mistress Huddard's voice broke into their moment.

Hana shifted to peer over Radek's shoulder.

A woman she didn't recognize had entered. Was this yet another sister? She wasn't dressed finely. The woman drew near and Radek stood to make room.

"How do you feel?" As the woman spoke, she looked at Hana's eyes in a strange way. And she felt along Hana's wrist. Was this the healer?

Mistress Huddard crowded the woman from behind. "Tell me, is she well?"

The thin woman turned. "I have not yet discerned her state. Please allow me some room to do my work."

Mistress Huddard frowned and stepped back.

The healer looked to Radek but did not demand he move. For that, Hana was thankful.

"How is your stomach? Your head?" the woman asked.

"I feel as if there has been a great war in me. That my body is at odds with itself."

The woman nodded. "I imagine so. But you are awake." Then she turned to Radek as if she spoke to him more than to Hana. "It is a good sign."

"Is she able to travel?" Mistress Huddard broke in again, this time stepping between the healer and Radek.

"Travel?" Radek's jaw clenched. He released Hana's hand and seemed prepared to square off with the woman. Was that some level of ire in him?

"Yes." Mistress Huddard lifted her chin. "We must return to Tabor where her father can watch over her. Keep her safe."

Radek fairly bristled. "You speak as though I am not capable of caring for the woman I am to wed."

A moment of uncharacteristic quiet fell over Mistress Huddard. For a moment. "I...do not mean to imply such. But surely you see it would be better for all involved if she were to—"

"She is not to be moved." Radek's voice was firm as his arms crossed and features set.

The healer pressed between them. "I must agree with Lord Miklas on this," she said to Mistress Huddard. "The lady is not well enough to take on such a journey."

Why did they discuss her as if she weren't here? Shoving against the bed, Hana struggled to a seated position. As she did so, she found herself gasping for breath. Such a simple thing. And yet it taxed her.

"Hana," Radek said, moving to her once more.

She held up a hand, halting his efforts. "I am well enough." But was she? Her body trembled with the expended effort.

"Of course, dear. It is my job to keep you safe." Mistress Huddard stepped to the bed.

"I think Lady Hana could use some space to breathe." The healer challenged the older woman.

Once again, Hana was grateful for the kind healer. "Yes, I thank you."

Mistress Huddard made a face at Radek but took two steps back.

"I wish to speak for myself," Hana asserted. She couldn't disguise her own frustrations, nor did she try. Surely it came through her voice and in her features.

Radek's jaw muscles moved beneath his stubbled face. So handsome. And all the more with a day's lack of shaving on him.

Focus! She drew in a deep breath and looked at each person by her bed. "I won't be going anywhere. Not until we can determine what has happened and by whose hand. I will *not* tuck my tail and run because of an inconvenience."

Mistress Huddard's voice boomed. "I would not call poisoning an inconvenience, my la—"

"I have spoken." Hana glared at the woman whose antics she had long tired of.

Radek nodded. He made no effort, it seemed, to fight the smile that crept upon his features.

"As you will," the healer said. "Now, I must insist on some peace and quiet for Lady Hana. Her body has been through much."

Mistress Huddard all but stormed across the room.

"You as well, Lord Miklas." The healer held a hand toward the door.

He nodded but took a moment to lean over Hana and press a kiss to her forehead.

She relished the feel of his skin against hers, even if only for a moment.

As he pulled back, he said, "A knight will be posted outside your room. I will not risk you again."

Then he retreated. That, she wasn't so certain she liked. But she did wish to sleep. Already her body slackened against the bed.

"Let me see you settled." The healer assisted Hana's shift onto her back. "There now. Rest well. And send for me if you need anything." Then the kindly woman nodded and slipped from the room.

Hana was once more alone, but the peaceful deep of sleep wooed her. And, as she closed her eyes and gave in, she wondered again at Radek's mother and sister. Was it possible they wished her dead?

It had been a sennight since Hana's poisoning. And the time had passed without incident. There had been little progress, if any, on finding the perpetrator. It burned Radek to no end and filled him with a sense of urgency. But there was nothing more he could do.

Even so, he was immensely grateful that Hana continued to heal and grow stronger. Despite his discomfort with it, she moved about the castle without assistance these days. Which meant the ever-present Mistress Huddard did not always have to be by her side, though she still was. And Radek's father maintained the constant watch of a guard over her well-being. This gave Radek some level of comfort.

And this morning, he wished for nothing more than to pass the time with her, to ensure her safety himself. But instead, he found himself in his father's solar, discussing matters of the village. Planting season was upon them. And while he didn't enjoy such matters of the estate, it was his duty to learn them. Albeit, he had determined that he would never present himself a weak man such as his father no doubt appeared to all who encountered him.

Father's steward ran a finger down the papers on the desk. He droned on about yields and costs.

Radek attempted to keep his focus on all that was discussed, but taking it in challenged him.

The door to the solar clattered open, garnering Radek's full and alert attention as he set a hand to the hilt of his sword.

Ondrej entered. "My lord, forgive the intrusion. There is a...situation that requires your attention."

Father stood and came around the desk. "What is it?"

The knight tilted his head toward the ground for a moment. "It is two of the village men. They seek mediation."

Radek watched his father as he considered the steward. Would Father dismiss him to entertain peasants? That would only make Father appear more accessible. Maybe that is what caused the brigand attack in weeks past—Father's approachability left much room for the wrong kind of advantage.

The margrave nodded. "I will come."

Radek widened his eyes, then narrowed them. His father was an enigma—tender and kind when it came to Hana's attack, but also a bit too vulnerable before his people. Still, Radek picked up step behind his father, and they followed the knight below stairs.

Father paused. "Do not think you must accompany me to see this dispute."

"Nonsense," Radek countered. "I will stay by your side."

The margrave offered a tight smile and continued on his way.

Radek considered his father's back. Yes, he must stay near the aging lord and protect the more vulnerable places. Ondrej had done a fine job of it, but the knight had many years as well. Someone must take up the task anew.

They moved beyond the keep and through the inner bailey where two rather plain men stood, throwing insults at each other.

Father did not hesitate as he neared them but rushed forward and set his hands in the air. Then he stepped farther, as if he would stand between them.

"Father," Radek ground out as he came alongside the margrave.

His sire all but ignored his plea, continuing forward. Was there no end to the recklessness?

Radek held back but kept his hand upon his sword, ready to defend the margrave when it was needed. For there was little question of *if*.

"What seems to be the trouble here?" Father's voice was not as loud as those of the men flinging crass and harsh words.

"He has cheated me," a lanky man with sandy-blond hair and a long nose said.

"That's not true, my lord. He won't listen," the other man, portly and balding, shouted.

Father lowered his arms but did not drop them. The movement seemed to encourage the men to lower their voices.

"I will hear each of you." Father's promise assuaged the men. "But you must go in turn."

Both faces lit up, waiting for their lord to call on them first.

"Geoff," Father said, "Please tell me your way of it."

Geoff? How did Father know the names of these villagers? Was he thusly acquainted with everyone under his protection? Odd indeed.

"This is the whole of it, my lord," the blond-haired man said. "We agreed to share the cost and labor of our fields this season, then split the harvest. However, I find this one," he said, jabbing a finger in the direction of his opponent, "hoarding seed. It seems he either intends to sow another field...or sell it behind my back."

"That is not true," the wider man argued.

Father held a hand up at the balding villager and nodded toward the lankier one. "Please, continue."

"I just can't help but wonder how else he thinks he will rob me. I don't want to share the work or the produce with him. Not now."

Father nodded. Then he turned to the other man. "What say you?"

"My daughter is set to marry in a fortnight. I acquired *extra* seed to help start her and her husband's crop."

"That don't make it well with me. We had a deal," the thinner man shouted.

Father shot him a look. "I listened well enough to you. Let your neighbor speak his piece as well."

The first man sulked, but quieted.

"That's all there is to it, my lord. He wouldn't hear me when I tried to explain," the other man said.

"Because you are a cheat," the first man blurted.

The margrave gave the lanky man a harsher look. One Radek had not known his father to deliver. Was there any weight behind the look? Or did the villagers know, as he did, that Lord Artur Miklas was soft?

Father turned to the first man. "I'm curious about something. How is it you came to find this extra store of seed you believe him to be keeping from you?"

The man paled. "I...I just saw it."

The margrave frowned. "How did you come to see it?"

Shrugging, the blond man shot a glance to his counterpart. "I..."

"Where was this seed kept?" Father shifted his focus to the balding man.

"In my house. In a sack." He glared at the other man.

"How did you come to be in his home?" Father asked, his eyes had no hint of hardness about them. Did he not wish to remind these men in any way of his power over them?

"He...must have invited me in."

The portly man shook his head. "I did not."

Father looked back at the lanky figure. "Did you enter his house without permission?"

The man's shoulders drooped. "No, my lord."

"Then how?" Father's voice didn't sharpen as Radek's would have—an attempt to drive out the truth in fear. But rather it softened, as if coaxing their words out.

"I...my son discovered it when he was invited in."

"Your son?" The second man's face reddened. "That's a lie!"

"No, I speak true," the lanky man turned to his neighbor. "I tried to keep my son away from your daughter, but he believes she has a care for him."

The balding man's face scrunched. "Your son..." he seethed. Surely steam would come from his ears soon.

"Yes. He and your daughter believe they are in love."

"Love? They can't be. My Glenna is to be married...she is...that is, I thought she was...happy."

The lanky man put a hand on the other villager's shoulder. "I know. I should have told you. My boy...he waited too long. But I...he wants to make it right."

Radek watched with increasing curiosity. Was it possible that his father's easy manner and gentle tone disarmed the men? And then opened the way for words that might allow them to see the situation more truthfully?

"I believe," Father said, "we need to shift our discussion."

The men both nodded with some reluctance. But all did seem well with them. No longer were they at each other's throats. Instead, they appeared ready to solve this newly arisen challenge.

Did this way of managing the dependent villagers actually work? Was his father not the crazy man he had assumed?

As Radek watched his father continue the discussion with these men, he began to wonder.

CHAPTER 26
KARIN & PAVEL

P avel moved through the halls of the Novak castle. His conversation with the duke had gone as expected, the man was reluctant but supportive. Still, he did not relish the coming response from Karin. She may not be so quick to agree with his decision. Perhaps he was wrong. Maybe she would be happy, even relieved. That, however, was not certain.

He approached their shared chamber, his steps slowing. As he paused, he drew in a breath and prayed. *Father God, give me the words.*

Then he worked the latch and pressed into the door. It gave way, ushering him into the room. He scanned the enclosed space. But Karin was not within. Where would she have slipped off to? But he knew—her desire to continue her translating work tugged at her. So, he turned and moved on toward Duke Novak's library.

An anchor weighed in his midsection as he walked the last several paces. This was no easy thing he would ask. But it was the right thing.

At last, he stood in the doorway to the library. His wife sat at a desk, leaning over the Holy Writ. What book did she read? Job?

Lamentations? What chapters? Would the Scripture soften her heart to hear him out?

"Pavel?"

Though he had been watching her work, her address startled him. He offered a smile, the best he could conjure.

Her gaze latched onto him. "What are you doing here?"

He stepped into the room. There was a thought to make light conversation, but that did not suit him. It often was best to be forthright. "We need to speak."

Her eyebrows arched. "Oh?"

He nodded and moved toward her.

She rose, setting her things to the side.

Taking her hands in his, he drew her in. "It is time we returned."

Her brow furrowed. "Returned?"

But he sensed that she indeed knew what he meant. Was this but a foreshadowing of her reaction? "To my father's...to *our* castle."

She held his gaze but said nothing.

"My mother regains her health, but it is not her duty to oversee the reconstruction efforts. Nor is she capable. Besides, it is time we were back on Krejik lands. I do not wish to test the boundaries of Duke Novak's kindness."

Karin licked her lips and looked down. But she soon set her green eyes on his again. "What...of the Holy Writ? Did your father's survive the fire?"

Pavel pressed a breath out. This was the place he feared to venture. "No, it did not."

She looked to the desk where Duke Novak's copy lay. "Then... how will I..." She swallowed.

Lifting a hand to her face, he stroked her cheek with his thumb. "I don't know. But I cannot stay. *We* cannot stay."

The area about her eyes betrayed the war within. "What of my... calling?"

He set her hands upon his chest so he could pull her even closer. "I am not certain. I can only speak to what we must do."

She bit at her lower lip, drawing a portion between her teeth as she looked down once more.

"I know this is difficult." Pavel softened his tone. "But I have to do what is right by you and Jaromir and my mother. You are all under my protection. As are those who rely on the providence and security of the castle. We have already lingered here too long. I am needed elsewhere."

"Perhaps Jaromir and I could..." Her eyes met his and a spark of hope shone through. Much to his chagrin.

"I will not leave you or our son behind. It is best we stay together. Haven't we been apart long enough?"

She nodded, but with hesitation. What emotions swirled within her? As if he didn't know.

"All will be well." He attempted to assure her. Or was he trying to assure himself? It wasn't as if he felt as confident as he put forth. No, there was a war in him, too. "I—"

Voices in the hall, at first distant, quickly grew louder. At least two others came this way.

Karin's gaze darted to her work.

Pavel gave her a slight nod before loosening his hold and turning toward the door. If need be, he would create a visual barrier as she retrieved her things.

The rustling of papers behind told that she moved with haste.

"I don't understand. How can it be that..." It was Duke Novak's voice. But who was his companion?

In only a few moments, the duke entered. Alongside him paced Father Dominik.

Duke Novak paused as he entered. Had Pavel's presence disrupted him?

"Lord Krejik," the duke offered. "I expected you would be well into preparations."

"As I will be soon, my lord." He wanted to glance back over his shoulder and see if Karin had finished. But he dared not.

As it was, a stolen look was not necessary. Karin touched his elbow and then slid a hand onto his arm. "Duke Novak, Father Dominik, how do you fare this fine day?"

Pavel cringed. Her pleasantries and upward lilting of her tone were a bit too put on.

The duke blinked. Was he, likewise, thrown off by her overt display? "I am well enough. As I was at the morning meal."

Father Dominik glared and stepped closer. "Lady Karin, I have not seen you since our conversation of weeks past."

"Why, yes, I believe that's so." Her words still dripped far too much sweetness.

"I do hope you heeded my words." His gaze darted between husband and wife.

"As much as possible." Her answer was a dodge and, from the look on the priest's face, he knew it too.

Awkward silence fell over the group.

"If I may, we have many things to attend to." Pavel tugged at Karin as he stepped toward the door.

"Has my Holy Writ been of good use to you?" the duke asked as they passed.

Pavel shot a glance at Father Dominik, whose features became more deeply lined.

"I..." Karin started, but stuttered, seeming to choke on her words.

"We found the passages we sought." Pavel moved closer to Karin, as if he could shield her from the priest's suspicions. Gripping her arm, he pulled her onward.

"Lady Karin." The priest's retort was sharp.

She halted, as did Pavel. He would not leave her to face this man alone.

"Father," Pavel said, making only a slight turn in the man's direction. "My wife is much needed elsewhere. Whatever you wish to discuss, perhaps it can wait."

The priest stared openly, his eyebrows lowering and pinching together.

"Come." Pavel urged Karin to keep step with him.

"I *shall* find a moment of your time," the priest said with finality.

Pavel paused only briefly. He prayed it was indiscernible. But he quickly picked up step again, bringing Karin with him to the safety that lay in the recesses of the corridor and beyond. Their exodus just became all the more imperative. He must be certain Karin did not find herself alone and at the mercy of Father Dominik's questions.

Karin allowed Pavel to lead her, weaving through the corridor and down the stairs. What had just happened? Did the priest suspect that she...?

She shook her head. How could he not?

This was a predicament indeed. Though, as she stole a glance at her husband's determined face, the churning in her midsection calmed. He would protect her. But at what cost to himself?

Would he lie? He had already stretched the truth nearly to its breaking point. She frowned. Her strong Pavel was capable. But this was not a war of arms, but a battle of words and wits.

Knowing that they prepared to leave gave her some comfort. But then, what would become of her calling? Of what God had pressed into her heart? Must she abandon it?

There was reason to remember that the very Scripture she so longed for, and had spent hours with, directed her to submit to her husband's decision in such things. And she did trust that his actions were honorable and good. Though...did he realize he was asking her to die to herself?

They approached their chamber. He opened the door and ushered her inside faster than she'd imagined possible. One moment, they were in the hall, and the next they were within.

Pavel gathered her in his arms. Only then did she feel the thundering of his heart under her ear. Had he, too, been afraid? He had not seemed so. But as he pulled her ever closer, she knew it was so.

"Are you all right?" came his hoarse whisper.

She nodded against him, not trusting her own voice.

A knock sounded on the door. Had Father Dominik opted to follow them and press the issue now?

Pavel jerked his head in that direction, preparing to face off with whomever might intrude on their privacy. "Who goes?"

How was his voice, just a moment ago so uneasy, now steady and firm?

"I have her ladyship's son, my lord." It was the nursemaid.

Karin released a ragged breath.

Pavel strode to the door and released the latch.

The woman stepped into the chamber, bouncing the child in her arms. Jaromir fussed quietly. Though it was only a matter of time before he would let loose with everything his lungs had.

"I'll take him." Pavel held out his arms.

The woman looked to Karin only briefly before surrendering the bundle.

Jaromir was not the least bit cajoled by the movement. Soon enough, despite being in his father's capable arms, his cries intensified.

"I will send for you," Karin told the kind woman.

The nursemaid nodded and, with hesitation in her movements, quit the room.

"What is the matter?" Pavel's gaze was on his son.

"He hungers." Karin could not help the twinge of a smile that tempted her lips.

"Ah." Pavel held the child close to himself, but it would not suit. Jaromir was angry.

Karin moved to the bed.

"What do you?" Pavel's words were strained.

"Bring him." She ignored his question and prepared herself to feed her son.

Pavel crossed the space between them, and realization lit his features. He handed the baby to Karin and turned his back to her as she settled their child. Her husband had spent little time with them these last weeks and had always seemed to be asleep or out of the room when it was time to nurse the babe.

"Does it bother you?" She kept her tone gentle. There was no need to accuse him. It wasn't as if he had been a father before.

"It...does not."

"Then why do you look away?" Her voice broke. And she wondered if his actions bothered *her* so. This was his son. And his wife. Doing as God intended for them in order to sustain the babe.

"I...only mean not to intrude." His words were measured.

"You do not." Her heart warmed at Pavel's intent.

He turned.

She watched as his gaze took in her and Jaromir.

"It is a wonder."

"What?" She could not stop the slight laugh that wove into her response.

"What you are doing." His eyes met hers, the blue as brilliant as she'd ever seen it.

She smiled and looked down at their son, rubbing his soft cheek. Then she turned her regard back to her husband, holding out a hand. "Come."

He took a few steps and gripped her fingers.

She tugged at him until he settled on the bed beside her.

He reached tentative fingers toward Jaromir, touching the wisps of hair before laying a hand on the child's head.

Karin watched her beloved through this exchange, her heart moved by his reverence and awed at how he marveled so over the simple thing. She leaned into him, resting her head on his shoulder.

How could she doubt this man? He *did* care for her mission, for what God asked of her. She knew he did. But he also held close his responsibility for their safety as well as that of many others. She couldn't ask him to remain torn between the Krejik lands and these.

Yes, she would go and trust that God was bigger than her assumptions.

Pavel pressed a kiss to the top of her head.

And all was right in that moment. Even if it was only for a moment.

CHAPTER 27
PATRICIE & STEPAN

Stepan moved with Patricie, leaning on her more than he liked. But it couldn't be helped. Yes, he had disguised just how healed he was. Hid it from Patricie and Ludek for his own benefit. Though the fall he took significantly damaged his plans. Now it mattered not, as his father's man was here to assist.

He considered, however, that what he had done and was doing to Patricie tore at him.

Yet he *had* saved her, hadn't he? This soldier would have ended her life in a second if Stepan hadn't intervened. He was the hero here, right?

As much as he told himself this, he could not make himself believe it. For he knew he drew her toward an even greater danger— his father. Perhaps he could find a way to release her once they were clear of the village.

Patricie stumbled, and he with her. Nearly losing all sense of balance, he gripped her all the more.

"Do not," the large man warned. "If he can't run you through, I will."

Patricie tucked herself closer into Stepan. Did she even realize she did so? Perhaps instinct or some reliance on their shared encounters spoke louder than his current actions. Indeed, she *was* safe with him. He would do all he could to ensure she wasn't harmed.

"Lead the way," Stepan gasped. When had he become so weak of breath?

This escape had already taken more effort than he'd accounted for. If he had known, he would have been working to regain strength in his legs sooner. As it was, he was more unsteady than he'd like. The stairs, just conquered, had nearly been his undoing. But Patricie assisted more than she needed to, as if she still cared for his well-being. And he hated that he took advantage of every inch of that consideration.

"Move," the gruff voice of his father's knight growled from behind.

Patricie obeyed. Was she worried after her own life? Or had she been so easily swayed because of something she felt for him?

That thought pained. But he couldn't think of that in this moment. His father had sent for him. Soon enough, he would be free and safe from these Hussites. Why, then, did that thought bring with it a sinking feeling in his gut?

He pushed it to the side. It was time to pay attention, to watch, to wait.

They had made it to the stables just beyond the inn. Not that any of the merrymaking drunks in the inn detected anything amiss. For that, he was thankful. The less they involved—and endangered—others, the better.

As he searched the area now, he was dismayed to see a stable hand step out of the shadows. The man had a strange look on his face.

Coming toward them, the man called, "Do you need help? Shall I fetch the healer?"

Were his words directed to Patricie? Or Stepan?

"There is no need," Stepan responded, halting the forward movement of the mercenary. Stepan prayed he would not have this young stable hand's blood on his hands. If only his father's man would calm himself.

The stable hand lifted a brow.

"We are only about to exercise this man's leg," Patricie cut in. Did she fear for the stable hand as well?

The younger man nodded and moved back toward the paddocks.

Dare Stepan release the tension that had built up in him? The prospect of what this man—who perhaps cared only for the money due him—was capable of filled Stepan with doubt. He did not wish to see any more death. Certainly not for his sake.

"Thank you," Stepan whispered as they continued their slow progress.

"I did not do it for you." Her reply was all but hissed.

That was where they stood, then. Did she hate him now? It would only be fitting.

After an eternity of hobbling, the pain in his leg increasing all the more, they arrived at the forest's edge.

The mercenary led them to the left and into a clearing.

Three horses stood at the ready, and another taller man with dark red hair came around, pointing at Patricie. "Who is this girl?"

"It is no matter," the one garbed in Hussite colors said. "We can finish her h—"

"She is coming with us," Stepan broke in.

"But, my lord, you must see that—"

"I have said what I will on the matter." He stood as straight as possible. It would be best if he presented a strong front.

The men exchanged a look. Would they decide to do as they pleased and ask forgiveness later? After all, their payment would be tied to his safe arrival. And likely naught else.

Stepan eased his hold on Patricie, preparing to step in front of her and act as a shield if need be.

The man guarding the horses held up his hands. "As you will."

"She will ride with me," the first, bulky man said.

"No," Stepan insisted, pressing out the words as harshly as possible. "She will ride with *me*." Even as he spoke, he tried not to pant. His pain was great, and his exertion likely showed.

The men again looked at one another.

Stepan grabbed for Patricie and moved to one of the horses. He stepped to the side of the animal. How did he plan to mount the horse? He had few options. And of them, the most likely was with the aid of one of these men. But he must keep this air of power about himself if he intended to keep Patricie alive.

He turned and glared at the heavier man. "If you will assist me..."

The man grumbled, tossed yet another glare at the other mercenary, and stepped forward. Soon enough, he hoisted Stepan into the saddle. And though he did not appear pleased with the prospect, he handed Patricie up.

She fought against the harsh grip. Or was it more than that? Perhaps she detested being settled in front of Stepan. Though once she was astride, she calmed. And even leaned into him. Perhaps nothing more than fatigue. Either way, he must build a better barrier around his heart. He could not feel for her as he did. Not anymore.

It seemed as if hours had gone by. How much farther into the night would they press? Stepan's leg throbbed, driving him quite mad to distraction. This could not be good for the barely healed limb. In truth, his vision became rather hazy, and he gripped even harder to stay aloft.

That was met with shifting from Patricie, who sat in before him in the saddle. How did she fare? Was she likewise tired? Or only stirring? There was little doubt she felt nothing beyond contempt for him at this point. And that pained him perhaps more than it should. Had he truly had hopes otherwise? False hopes. They had always been and would always be false hopes. For how could there be a future for a noble Royalist and a Hussite, a person of common birth additionally?

But he could not paint her in such a light, even in his mind. She was perhaps more noble than he—the way she had cared for him diligently these last weeks.

His head drooped. What a mess he'd made of things! He wouldn't blame her if she never looked upon him with any semblance of kindness again.

"He can't go on like this." Patricie's voice surprised him.

Did she make demands on his part? Why would she do so if she didn't care? Something sparked within him. But he pushed it to the side. As much as he could.

The viscount's hired men ignored her.

"I need to see if he bleeds," she insisted.

The taller man turned toward them. "Cease! Shut your mouth or I will shut it for you."

Stepan grimaced. Must they address her so harshly? He wanted to speak up, but the pain shooting through him left him biting his lower lip in order to seal it against his cries.

"He could bleed out. Then where would you be?" she challenged.

The other man shifted his focus to Stepan. It would be best if he could meet the knight's gaze and assure him, but that was for naught. Stepan struggled to even lift his head.

Words shot between the two guards—a discussion about whether or not to stop. The prospect of their payment ran among their exchange. They *were* mercenaries, then. With such skewed loyalty, how far could he trust them?

Patricie grabbed at the horse's reins and pulled, halting the animal.

The two men spun on her, urging their mounts closer.

"Do not," one man seethed as he turned and dropped out of the saddle.

Did he think Patricie attempted escape? That would be awkward and clumsy.

Stepan had no second thought about it—he knew she worried

255

after his well-being. The warmth that had budded within grew anew.

"Help me," Patricie glared at the man whose face read contempt.

The hired men exchanged a look and the other shrugged and dismounted.

"I can manage," Stepan muttered. But could he? He lifted his damaged leg to prove he could find his own way to the ground.

Patricie set a hand to the thigh of his good leg. "No."

He watched her but could no longer hide that his light-headedness intensified.

One of the men grabbed at Patricie and hauled her out of the saddle.

She let out a startled cry.

Stepan leveled his gaze on the man. "You will not harm her."

The man scoffed but turned her loose.

As the larger of the two men assisted Stepan down, he maintained his attentive watch on the other knight standing near Patricie.

Stepan's foot touched the ground and he held to the saddle to keep from crumpling completely. How was it that this weeks-old wound could pain him so? It wasn't as if he had been walking these last couple of hours.

Patricie was at his side in a moment. "Help me get him against that tree." She pointed to a sturdy oak.

The men only looked on as Patricie pushed out a frustrated cry and stood by Stepan's injured side.

Stepan wanted to command that they obey, but he was too consumed with the pain and the trial of staying upright.

Patricie maneuvered him to the trunk's base. It wasn't easy and it was far from a smooth transition. But she managed. How, he did not know.

He heaved once he was settled. This night had taken more out of him than he'd wagered. As his vision cleared, he saw more than felt Patricie working at his wound.

She made a grunting sound as she ripped open the bandaging. Then gasped.

"What is it?" Stepan spat out.

Patricie's eyes were on his then. "You will not live if you continue this fool's errand."

One guard stepped forward. "She only means to delay us, to hope that we will be found out. Surely, we are soon pursued, if not already. We must—"

Stepan held up a hand. "She does not lie. We must remain...only as long as it takes for her to do her work. Then we go."

The men shook their heads and turned their attention to the horses.

Patricie's eyes hardened. "Go? We can't. You could die."

Stepan shrugged. "So be it."

Her features contorted into a cringe. For a moment only. Then all about her was calmness and determination. "I will not allow it."

There was that stirring in his chest again. Were her words because she would not lose another patient? Or because she refused to lose *him*?

She shook her head as she applied pressure against the wound. "I need something to make a..."

Make a what? He watched her and could not quite discern what she needed.

She scanned the immediate area and then the two men farther away. What did she intend?

Stepan leaned forward, preparing to grab for her if she tried to run. That would be suicide with these men so close and so lacking in conscience.

She pulled at her skirts and then ripped the hem of her chemise. It was not for the first time, he noted, as he spotted that the bottom of the thin fabric had already been torn. Then she wrapped the long strip around the bandaging that had been in place. When she tied off the strip, it was tight. Painfully so.

Stepan could not stop the sound that escaped. But he promptly bit at his lip once more. That would not happen again.

She stood and approached the men.

Stepan wished he could stop her. How fool-headed was she?

He could not make out her words, but the men shook their heads. She continued to speak, her movements and words becoming bigger and louder.

The bulkier guard grabbed at her arm and all but dragged her back to where Stepan still leaned against the tree. Then the man thrust her down next to him.

She cried out as she hit the ground.

"What do you?" Stepan called out.

The man's face tinged red. Was he angry? "If she wishes to keep you well, she should tend to your wound and spend less time pressing her thoughts into words."

Stepan burned. Such treatment of Patricie dug at him. "You will not lay hands on her again."

The man gave Stepan a long look. "Yes, my lord."

And Stepan wondered if he had just erred. Did the man now believe Stepan had a care for Patricie? What would the guard say to the viscount?

Patricie rose.

The man pointed at her. "Make him ready to travel."

She stared back. Would she defy the man again? Would Stepan be able to protect her if she further provoked the dangerous mercenaries?

"I will be ready." Stepan lifted his chin, hoping he appeared more confident than he felt.

The men took the horses and moved off through the trees. Stepan wondered at their actions. But then he heard moving water. Yes, it would behoove them to refresh the animals while stopped.

Patricie leaned over Stepan's leg once more.

Stepan watched her. The desire to say something grew, but he could not make the words come out. What would they be if he could?

Patricie's shoulders shook. Was she trembling? Or crying?

"Patricie," he started.

She shot him a hard look. Her eyes glistened as if moisture waited to make trails upon her face, but her features belied that it was so.

He spoke. "I will do what I can to keep you safe." What was he saying? How could he guarantee such...especially once they reached his father? Could he possibly keep that word?

She looked away and rubbed at her cheek. Were the tears making their way even then? That stabbed at him deeper than the pain of his injury.

He didn't realize he had reached out to her until his fingers made contact.

She jerked away.

That stung. Though, he couldn't find it in himself to blame her for her reaction. She had been wronged—taken and manhandled. It wasn't right. She should be treated with kindness and tenderness. That's what he longed to do—reach out and touch her face, tilt it toward himself, and wipe away her tears. But he dared not.

"Please, do what you can," he whispered and indicated his leg.

She nodded and turned her attention back to his wound.

And though her touch was for the purpose of his preservation, he imagined she didn't hate it so. He set his head against the tree and remembered holding her. Her touch then had sought comfort and offered something more than he could have hoped for. And so, he watched her work and let himself dream that she did not despise him.

CHAPTER 28
HANA & RADEK

Mid-morning spread a blanket of fog over the land. Radek watched from the outer bailey, studying the landscape without allowing it to be beautiful. Nothing could ease his restlessness...except perhaps to find the person behind Hana's poisoning.

It had been a month yet since the attempt on her life, and Radek was no closer to discovering the one responsible than when it had first occurred. He couldn't bring himself to tell Hana how he had failed. That had led to more than a few awkward silences amidst otherwise pleasant conversation.

As he observed the castle grounds, he pondered the matter as if for the first time. It may help to come at it with fresh eyes. And so, he considered what questions remained, though there were many. Who would have such malice? Or something to gain from Hana's death? She had only just arrived when it happened. Nothing about it made sense.

"I thought I might find you out here." The melodic voice did not disrupt as much as it should. For he knew its owner—Hana. And he wasn't certain he wished to have this conversation here and now. But what could be done to escape it?

She came closer to his position on the wall. By the sound of her movements, he would guess her but an arm's length away. After all, he couldn't avoid her forever. Perhaps not any longer.

"Yes, you have discovered me," he muttered, yet maintained his regard over the hills beyond.

"Are you...avoiding me?" Her words were timid, almost fearful.

"I am not." He turned. And found it a mistake. For her eyes glistened with emotion. Would she let it loose?

She looked to the side and nodded—a swift, light movement.

He stepped closer and reached out to touch her face, directing it toward himself. "Why would you think such a thing?"

"You have been...more difficult to find of late. And our conversations seem to be simple and short before you must away."

He looked down, not wanting her to see his regret. Yes, she was right. He had done those things. "I only wish to discover the truth behind...what happened to you." Shifting his focus, he watched her again.

Her features scrunched. "What happened to me? Do you make progress?"

Again, he had the urge to look away and he denied it. It was time to face her, to speak with her in earnest. "No. I...haven't even found a place to begin."

She sighed and her body eased. That seemed odd. Perhaps she had been truly concerned he did not wish to be with her. When she gazed at him again, there was indeed relief in her eyes. It was almost tangible.

"Does that not challenge you? How can I protect you if I cannot find your attacker—someone who wished you harmed, perhaps even dead?" His voice became louder.

Her eyes widened. "There are more important things."

"How is that?" Her conclusion was unimaginable. What could be more important than her well-being?

She moved forward, closing the distance between them. Her hand rested over his heart. "Like this."

He opened his mouth, but the words he wished for would not come. Setting a hand over hers, he rubbed at her fingers.

"And this." Her other hand waved between them. "What is happening here matters so much more to me. Can you not see that?"

He looked down at the small space that separated them and let out a breath. "I need to know that I can keep you safe."

Her other hand lifted to touch the side of his face. "Perhaps we can work this out together."

Was that best? How might she be able to assist him and stay out of harm's way? "I don't think that is the right course. You should stay as far from this as possible."

When he allowed his gaze to meet hers again, that strange, pleasant warmth filled him and intensified his concern. She was in danger. He could feel it. "Whoever made this attempt will try again. I will not risk you."

"Have you traced the actions of your...?" Her voice trailed off.

"My what?" His heart sped. Was she about to say what he thought? His mother and sister?

"It is nothing." She started to pull away.

He held her one hand fast and used his other to grip her arm and keep her in place. "No. What did you intend to say?"

Her eyes again betrayed her. She was as if a deer that discovered itself to be targeted. "Do not think on it any longer. I'm not even certain what I thought."

That was a lie. She knew quite well. And how did he know? Because he had already had—and dismissed—the same thoughts. To his chagrin, he had considered the women of his family. They did not deserve such.

But he refused to release Hana or give her room to distract from her statement. "You were about to accuse my mother or sister, weren't you?"

She tugged at her hand again, trying to create more space between them.

He would not allow it.

"I..." She dropped her head. "Yes."

He loosed her and stepped back.

Pulling her hands to her chest, she pleaded with him, "Radek, I am sorry. It was wrong of me."

He turned his regard once more to the horizon, leaning on the battlements.

Her hands did not follow him, rather she kept her distance. "Believe me."

He wanted to believe her. Wanted to extend her the same grace he had given himself for his thoughts about his kin. But how much longer would he excuse her actions and words? She was to be his wife. Though she only did as she pleased. First, she had disregarded her father's wishes and rushed off to Prague for the sake of the Hussite cause. Now she had left her Father's protected castle and journeyed through war-torn lands to come to him. All because she wished it. Was there any ability in her to control impulse?

"Radek, talk to me." Her hand landed on his shoulder.

He jerked away. "Perhaps it is best you leave me be. I...need space to think."

She drew her hands back to her chest. "Don't send me away."

Did she mean right now? Or did she fear he would send her back to Novak lands? That was where she belonged.

"I can't do this right now," he said, wishing he didn't feel a weight in his stomach.

She sniffled. Those wild emotions of hers.

"Leave me," he said with finality.

Her response was muffled by something. Perhaps her hand?

"I said leave me be." He turned on her. And immediately regretted it.

Her eyes were red and her tears evident.

"Please. Just go." He looked away.

The swish of skirts warned that she obeyed. At least this once she did. But what might he do with a wife that did as she saw best? With little trust in the opinions of those she should heed?

It may be that he had tested the thought of his mother or sister's guilt, but something beyond Hana's reluctant accusation nagged at Radek. But was it his own inability to completely dismiss the possibility of their involvement?

Hana's vision blurred as she made her way to her chamber. What did this mean? Would Radek push her away? Or...perhaps worse...send her back to her father? She had sought him out this evening in hopes of discovering what weighed on his heart. But this?

It couldn't be. He couldn't have meant what he said.

Hana pressed into the privacy of the small room and flung herself on the bed. Moments passed, but nothing improved her situation. These tears were not helpful in the least.

Leaning up on her hip, she wiped at her eyes. Oh, if only she weren't subject to these feelings. She did love Radek...so much. Maybe she felt more than she should for a man who was not yet her husband and she not yet secure in his affections.

She swallowed against a thickness in her throat. All of this was for naught. It would be better if she focused on how to overcome this. Perhaps his ire had been borne of his concern for her. Wouldn't that then mean that his feelings for her ran deep? For his anger had seemed rather full.

Knock.

It was a gentle sound on her door. Had Radek followed her? Mayhap regretted that he turned her aside?

She straightened her skirt as she rose. Then, drawing in a breath, she stepped to the door. There was no reason to let him see how this affected her. No, she best hold as much as she could under the surface.

"Come," she said, her voice wavering. Fine thing, that. She was hopeless.

The door opened and revealed a maidservant on the other side.

She had no doubt her disappointment was displayed on her features. For it cut through her and she did nothing to hide it.

He had not come after her.

The servant held up a sealed envelope. "A missive, my lady."

Hana stepped forward and plucked the letter out of the woman's hands. She turned it over and noted her family seal. Had father need of her? Perhaps he regretted sending her. But as she flipped the missive once more, she noticed that her name had been written in her mother's hand.

The servant shifted her weight.

Hana had not dismissed her. So, the girl stood at the ready, awaiting instruction.

Waving a hand in her direction, Hana said, "That is all for now."

The young woman nodded and walked off down the corridor.

Hana shut her door and brought the letter to the lone chair in the room. What could mother need to share? Had something happened?

She ripped open the seal and delved into her mother's words.

Hana,

By now you have likely heard of the election of the Polish Vytautas as Bohemia's king. Your father is pleased that our country now has proper leadership. However, it has become clear that General Zizka remains uncertain. So much distrust rises in Tabor. I fear there will be civil war before this is over.

Hana frowned. That was the last thing the Czech people needed— in-fighting. They must be united. They must fight for a common cause if they were to retain their freedom from Sigismund. An uneasiness settled in Hana's stomach. This would not bode well.

And I wonder if you should request an escort and return home, daughter. I would feel more at rest knowing you are safe and protected within these walls. Especially after reading your last letter. I do worry after your safety. Your betrothed is kind and capable indeed, but can he guard against a villain within the walls of the castle? I am less certain.

How would Hana respond to that? It was true that Radek had made no headway in discovering who wished harm upon her. But could she tell her mother that? Or should she speak to his efforts in her response? Maybe it would be best to not address it at all. Would her mother see through that?

My daughter, I must ask for wisdom and prudence on your part. Consider this situation with your head and not with your heart. I believe you will find that I am not wrong in this.

The weight in Hana's gut tightened its hold. Her mother was not a forceful woman, but her words were insistent. It may be that Hana needed to think more on them.

She folded the paper, unable to read anything further at this moment. She would return to the missive perhaps tomorrow, but these things were much. Big decisions needed to be made. At the very least, she was thankful that nothing from her father had come. For if he decided she needed to return, there would be little she might do to thwart him.

Sighing, she set the letter on the bed table. What could she do? Did she need to distance herself from Radek? From this place and whomever wished her dead? She thought on her recent conversation with Radek again and felt sick. Was there any right answer?

CHAPTER 29
PATRICIE & STEPAN

Patricie caught herself before she fell forward, nearly toppling off the horse. The jerking movement startled her, and she opened her eyes. When had she closed them? How long would they push on? How far could they be from their destination?

Stepan shifted behind her. Was he concerned after her? How was that possible?

She was in this predicament, after all, because of him. If he truly cared, he would not have forced this situation and had her at the mercy of these men. But had he really put her here? It was she who had gone into his room, she who had resisted the men. Would she not have become victim to the mercenary's blade had Stepan not intervened? That did not mean there was no place for her to be angry.

Beyond that, this unsteadiness in her body would not do. The little sleep these hired swords afforded her the previous night had not sufficed. Especially as it had been restless, what little there was. Had she worried over her virtue? Or perhaps she had been more disturbed by Stepan's closeness. It was difficult to discern her own heart on this matter.

She glanced around. The terrain had become mountainous. Were they headed for the border? Would these men take her into the Kingdom of Hungary? Or worse—the Holy Roman Empire? That would not be a safe place for a known Hussite.

Yet she had not seen the Botic River. And they had certainly not crossed it. Perhaps not to the Holy Roman Empire then. But if they passed into Hungary, her chance of rescue—and survival—diminished greatly. Not that her life was worth much even now.

The men turned and pushed their horses out of the forested area which, until now, had offered cover. A small village lay situated just to the side of the next mountain. Might she slip the guards and find protection there? Maybe a place to hide herself?

Stepan tightened his hold around her waist. Could he read her thoughts?

She grimaced and slackened her body.

He did not relax his.

How had she been so wrong about him? Even cared for him? There was no use berating herself now. She must stay alert, watchful for any opportunity to evade her captors.

The mercenaries directed the horses into the village. This had to be their intended destination. Would they make life difficult for the villagers? Insist on provisions and rooms? The thought of these men taking advantage of those too weak to fight back bothered her. Yet there was naught she might do to stop it. Being so, how could Patricie use this to *her* advantage?

Only a few moments passed before they were surrounded by the collection of small buildings. She scanned for the villagers. Seeking to...what? Warn them? Plead for help?

But she found the hamlet rather quiet. Oddly so. Why were there not people going about their business? While she hadn't anticipated the dirt roads to be filled, they should be far from empty.

The men guarding her showed not so much as a flinch at the

barren houses. It seemed, rather, that they expected nothing else. How was that possible?

Stepan remained tense at her back. Perhaps he was no more knowledgeable than she. Was his arm about her firmer out of concern then? What would he do if these men threatened her? What could he do?

Without warning, the two guards halted. As did the animal beneath her. Was this it? Her chance? Or a fate she did not wish?

One of the men looked back at Stepan. "This is it."

A shiver shook Patricie unbidden as she pictured just what these men might mean.

The mercenaries dropped out of their saddles. One took the horses' reins. The other moved toward Stepan and lifted his arms.

Would Stepan hand her over to this unscrupulous mercenary? Did he trust these men?

His hold remained.

A glimmer of hope—not more than the tiniest seed—birthed anew in her. She longed to turn and meet his eyes, to see that there was a care found in those depths, but she dared not. No, she couldn't hope there. The best that could happen would be his aid in escape. Delusions about his feelings for her must not cloud her judgment or her need to get away.

"My lord?" The man's gaze hardened even as it questioned.

"I will assist her." Stepan's tone was resolute.

She bit at her lip. Might she press the horse as Stepan dismounted? Find her freedom in the dense forest they had passed through? Everything in her came to life—every nerve-ending, every sense—as Stepan twisted his torso and brought his leg over.

Would he be injured if she spurred the horse forward as suddenly as she must? Dare she wait until he alighted to firm ground?

Her heart tore at her better judgment. She would leave him in a precarious position. Even to the point of risking him being trampled. Could she?

He grunted as he worked his way out of the saddle, bringing his good leg around.

Now. She must do it now.

No.

What? Why would she let her best chance elude her?

Hands gripped her leg before she could answer herself. She kicked out in that direction, her foot landing on something solid. An answering *ooff* gave her some satisfaction.

She pulled at the reins and pressed her heels to the animal's flank.

The horse reared up. And the guard pushed Stepan away as he grasped for something, anything...some chance to regain control.

And as the animal continued to rear and buck, she fought to keep her own hold and her position in the saddle. Both challenged her limited skill.

But in the next moment, the horse took off. She was free!

Leaning over the great neck, she did what she could to encourage speed. Where the animal headed mattered not to her—only escape.

The thunder of hoofbeats sounded behind her. Closer than they should be. The urge to look was compelling, but she forced her gaze forward.

Her heartbeat raced, pounding within her so loud it nearly covered all else. How close was her pursuer? Did both guards follow? What of Stepan? Shoving that thought down, she continued to beg more and more from the horse. But it, too, breathed heavily. The animal had carried two, and for many miles. How much could it be pushed?

Not as much as she needed it to be.

A hand shot toward her, knocking her off balance. Did her captor intend to smack her off the horse?

Soon enough, the large fist covered the reins and pulled.

The horse halted immediately, unsteadying her tentative balance all the more. And she fell.

Earth met her. Hard. Punishing.

One glance at the looming horses, and she attempted to tuck herself into a tight ball. Until she was jerked upward, an iron grip on her arm.

She cried out before she could stop herself.

Jerked to a stone chest, she felt the mercenary's hot breath as he swore in German.

Refusing to give in, she fought—clawing at his face and kicking at him.

That only caused him to grip her more tightly and continue his string of German curses.

She then found herself staring into eyes that were just as cold as she'd imagined.

"Do not think I won't kill you right here." Metal scraped metal and a blade stung her midsection.

Her struggles were for naught. They only drove the point closer to her skin.

"Cease!" The man spat as he commanded.

She stilled.

This may be the end of her escape. This time.

And she would relent...to prepare for the next opportunity.

She glared into gray eyes that seemed they would welcome her death and determined that the next time she would die trying.

Why had she done it? Stepan closed his eyes against renewed pain that coursed through him from his leg. Did Patricie not think he would protect her? That he would not do whatever it took to ensure her well-being?

He grimaced. Why should she believe any of that?

A shriek brought his attention to the top of the hill. The knight all but dragged her along.

She stumbled as they walked. Was she injured?

His heart fell as he could only look on as the man jerked her up and continued. Dare he speak out against such treatment? Everything in him pressed the words against his lips, but he must not. He had already pushed any acceptable boundaries. Anything more would only endanger her further. There was no way to know if these guards would abide his interference again.

As he watched, his chest tearing and his gut sinking, he assured himself that she had not been damaged. Her protests and fight brought about much of what he did see.

She and the guard drew near, and Stepan sucked in a breath, straightening his shoulders. He would hold his own and do what he could for her.

The guard beside him snickered and swore. Something about how feisty she was.

Indeed, she was. She clearly wasn't about to give in without a fight. Despite the direness of their circumstances, admiration for her tenacity swelled his chest. But reality caught him. That wouldn't bode well for her. Not here. Not now.

Moments that stretched into eternity passed before the greatly angered knight and Patricie rejoined them. Though Stepan's gaze latched to her, she kept her regard to the ground. Was she avoiding him? To what end?

The guard controlling Patricie huffed. "Now?"

A laugh came from the other mercenary.

It was silenced with a stern glare from the out of breath man.

Then their attention fell on Stepan.

"The viscount waits," the taller guard said.

Father? He was here? Stepan lost his breath for a moment. Fear for Patricie replaced every bit of the admiration that had earlier warmed him.

The first guard half-dragged the still resisting Patricie toward the door of a nearby structure.

Stepan glanced at the taller mercenary and moved to follow, wishing that his limp was not so bad.

Without warning, the man that brought Patricie turned on her, hissed something in German that Stepan couldn't discern, and back-handed her.

Stepan opened his mouth to protest, but the taller guard glared at him. In this, Stepan had to remember, no matter how his heart burned, her best chances were for him to remain in the good graces of their captors.

Patricie whirled and would have fallen had the man not a firm grip on her arm. Instead, she scrambled to follow.

Stepan hated himself for his silence, for not coming to her aid. But he had to feign some amount of coldness regardless of how it pained him.

They moved into the building that Stepan decided was some sort of inn. But where were the patrons? The innkeepers? Had his father run the villagers from their homes?

One of his father's knights met them among the tables and chairs. "His lordship has run short with his patience."

The mercenaries looked to one another.

"We were...unavoidably detained," one said with a side look at Patricie, who seemed rather unsteady on her feet.

"The viscount's son had an injury. It slowed our progress," the other said in a gruff voice.

His father's man glared over the group. "Why did you not rid yourself of this one?" He nodded at Patricie.

The taller guard jerked his head toward Stepan. "He had other thoughts."

Although more familiar to Stepan, the knight's presence did not bring any semblance of comfort. He set his hard gaze on Stepan and scoffed. He then turned and said, "This way."

Stepan heated. How dare this man not show him more respect. He was the son of a viscount, and this man was nothing more than a hired sword. But Stepan also knew he walked a precarious line where Patricie was concerned.

They were led up the stairs, which did little to help Stepan's pride as he worked his way upward. Though he had strengthened his upper body in the time he had been under Ludek and Patricie's care, pain rushed through him as he advanced, making him light-headed. They stopped at the first room. The man at arms knocked lightly.

A muffled voice bade them enter.

Stepan couldn't help but hold his breath as he prepared to come face to face with the man whose good thought meant much to him.

They stepped into the room, and Stepan spotted his father. He stood across the small chambers, perhaps having been interrupted.

"Stepan," the viscount boomed as he stepped nearer and set a hand on Stepan's shoulder. "When I heard that you had been captured, I feared the worst."

Stepan nodded. "As did I."

"And I—" His father peered over Stepan's shoulder to where Patricie stood. "What is this?"

The mercenaries shifted.

"I did not tell you to grab some Hussite girl and drag her along." His voice was stern.

To their credit, the guards did not run at the mouth, instead the taller one deferred to the other.

"It was unavoidable, my lord."

"I expect you to get rid of her." Father's command was spoken with finality.

Stepan's heart stopped.

Father narrowed his gaze. "Now."

CHAPTER 30
KARIN & PAVEL

K arin watched the mountainous landscape as they moved through it. But the view brought no comfort for her this day. For they journeyed from the place she had lived for much of the last year. They left the place where God had brought her son into the world and delivered her from death. No, leaving had not been easy.

Beyond these things, she struggled with putting aside her mission. Why would God call her to such a task and then not make a way for her to see it through? Perhaps she was only meant to transcribe a portion. Mayhap she missed God's direction entirely.

Pavel called out for the wagon to stop. Was something amiss?

She glanced at Jaromir, still asleep in the nursemaid's arms. The halting of the carriage stirred the woman from a doze. Her gaze darted about as if assessing the situation as well.

Pavel pulled up alongside the window.

"What goes?" Karin tried to keep her worry from mixing into her words.

"It is time to refresh the horses. As well, I thought you might like a moment." His regard, too, moved to Jaromir and then back to Karin.

"Aye, I would much like the opportunity to stretch my legs."

Pavel smiled. But something about it remained tight. Because he was still on guard against possible dangers about the roads? Or due to their last exchange?

Did he think her likely to hold to some malice against him? True, he had forced the issue, and against her desires. But this was the way of things. He had been charged with their safety and well-being. And so, she must submit to his course in this.

That didn't mean she did so with her whole heart, however. For she could not deny that there was indeed a seed of discontent within her. *Oh, Lord, what have You wrought here?*

She refused to let this small thing shine through in her countenance or bearing. There would not be anything for her husband to read as malcontent in her. Of this, she was determined.

Karin smiled softly at Pavel. Would that encourage him to loosen his guard with her? Indeed, as her mouth spread, she noted an easing about the tension in his shoulders. Almost imperceptible, but there all the same.

He dismounted and reached for the latch on the door. Once it was open, he lifted a hand to her.

She slipped her fingers to his palm, and he helped her step down.

There was an uncertainty about his features, not in a hard way, but it seemed as if he warred with drawing her close or maintaining some distance between them.

She held her breath, wishing he would pull her in for an embrace.

But he turned and led her away from the carriage. "My ladywife and I will not be far," he called to the knights that accompanied them.

A general assent was the only response. Who would deny their lord a stroll with his wife?

Pavel moved in the opposite direction of the stream. Did he have something to speak with her about? Or did he only wish to enjoy her company without audience?

She decided the latter as they walked in silence. Might she break it? With what entreaty?

"How much longer until we are within Krejik lands?"

He glanced at her then directed his attention once more to where they stepped. "Perhaps an hour more."

"And until we reach the castle?" She felt the urge to keep the conversation going.

"A half hour hence."

His short answers weren't making it easy for her to keep him engaged.

She scanned the area and noted the distance created between them and the rest of their traveling party.

Pavel turned her to himself. His gaze worked over the area. Did he attempt to discern the level of their privacy? Then he grabbed for her free hand, bringing both to his lips.

"What bothers so?" she asked, worry creeping into the edges of her mind.

He was silent for a moment, staring at her captured hands as he rubbed his thumbs over her knuckles.

She gave him space to speak, though it seemed much time had passed.

Then he met her gaze. "I struggle."

Struggle? With what? Her heartbeat quickened.

"I know I do what is right by those who rely on me. And by my mother. Even by you and Jaromir. Yet, I cannot escape this thing I have asked of you."

She watched him and hated this strife within him.

"I wish that I were able to support you better in this." His words were firm, yet hesitant.

Sucking in a breath, Karin moved a step closer. "I know you seek only what is best."

He watched her.

"And truly, it is not you that I wrestle with. But God."

His eyes widened. "With God?"

"Yes," she said, then licked her lips. Would that she could just let it be that, and not have to venture further into this uncomfortable place. "He put this desire in me...only to take away all hope that I might continue. That does not feel loving or good."

Pavel frowned. "But it is I who pull you away."

"Not truly. I trust that you only follow that which God has directed you."

He looked down and nodded. "Yes."

"And I see how difficult it is for you. That only deepens my resolve that you but listen for His guidance."

"Is there hope that you can continue your work in time?" His words lilted upward, as if he embodied that very hope.

"That is what I seek. Yet I cannot quell this urgency in me." She chewed at her lower lip. "Though perhaps that is only my flesh."

"I promise you, Karin, I will do what I can to secure what you need to continue...in time."

Her heart ached at his words, yet he had bared himself and his guilt. He did not shy away from the blame that he felt should be his. Nor did she wish for him to carry remorse for a thing in which there was no sin, but rather was right and good.

She pulled her hands free and leaned into him, encircling his waist with her arms.

He gathered her to himself and pressed a kiss to the top of her head.

A shout from the distance found her set apart from Pavel as he turned in that direction. He glanced back at her with a wariness in his eyes. "Stay behind me."

Why would she do otherwise?

More shouts came from where they had left the carriage.

Then she was struck by awareness—Jaromir! They had left him with the nursemaid. Karin's knees weakened and the whole of her insides seemed to pitch downward.

284

Pavel drew his sword. Everything in him wanted to run back to the carriage for the sake of his son. But he was challenged to stay with Karin; he would not leave her unprotected. What had befallen the group? Were they under attack?

"Jaromir!" Karin started to move around him.

He struck out his arm to hold her back. "Stay behind me."

She pushed against his arm but obeyed, though there was a tensing of her muscles that she must be fighting.

He had to think. Should they run back or go slowly and take in the situation before nearing? He did trust his men. They were well trained and capable. But nothing could keep him—or Karin—from seeing that their son remained safe.

Scanning the tree line, he watched for an attack. None came. "We will go. You *must* stay behind me."

Her breaths came in gasps, but she nodded.

He moved forward, as quickly as he could and still remain cautious. There was no sound of metal clashing. Either his men were dead, captured, or there was naught to fear. No matter which, he would not risk his beloved wife out of a desire to rush in.

As they continued to move onward, his senses on alert, he became more certain he heard voices. He paused, his sword at the ready.

Karin seethed. She did well to hold her words in, which must be a battle.

He could not afford her a glance, however, as his awareness was homed toward the space on the other side of the trees where they had left the rest of the group.

Waving a hand, he indicated to Karin that they would commence their progress. Still, his movements were slow, measured. They reached the point at which the trees thinned. Pavel crouched, pulling Karin down with him. Pressing his hand in a downward direction, he indicated she should stay.

Her eyes pled that he not make her keep her position, and her lower lip tucked between her teeth. To hold her words back?

Regardless of her plea, he hardened his gaze and pointed down. She was not to follow him. Not yet.

He regarded the surrounding area again. The voices were louder now. And though he could not pick up the words, there was no distress about their tones. Creeping forward, he left Karin farther at his back. The temptation to peer back and ensure she remained was great, but he did not sense movement behind him.

Still, his slow and cautious progress pulled at him. What of his son? What dangers may be ahead? If brigands had overcome his men, how would he fight the many it would have taken to do so? He shook his head. Now was not the time for such concern. His son needed him. His men needed him.

Approaching the tree line, he kept behind a large trunk. And stilled his own breath for the better to hear. His knights' voices were clearer. As was his right-hand man. No longer were they loud. Nor was there a sense of fear. He did pick out the presence of a man unfamiliar to him. Though the knowledge that his men were well and unharmed allowed much relief to flow through him. He eased tight muscles and stood.

When he chanced a look around the tree offering him shield, he saw better what must be. There was indeed a strange horse. And, as he scanned, he spotted a man, perhaps ten years more aged. The man held no threat about himself, and the men-at-arms had no aggression about them. But Pavel needed to see Jaromir and know that he was well.

The nursemaid stood off to the far side, lightly bouncing the child who grabbed for her bound hair.

Pavel released a long breath, letting loose the final bits of tension. He looked to where he had left Karin.

It seemed as if she would faint so much of her color had drained.

He moved back to her and helped her stand. "All is well. I have seen Jaromir and the nursemaid. They but play."

Her eyes closed and she breathed a prayer.

"My men have intercepted another traveler, who is alone as it seems. There is no immediate sense of danger."

She opened her eyes and nodded.

But, with senses heightened in preparation for battle, he worried after her state.

"Shall we go then?" she asked, her features an easy read of how worried she continued to be.

"Aye. Though I would have you take some deep breaths. You do not seem well." He laid a hand on her shoulder.

Her brows furrowed, but she obeyed, pulling in air and pressing it out several times. He noted that the pallor about her reassumed more color.

"Now?" The word was pushed at him. Her concern still tangible.

Though he wished she were not in such a state, he doubted anything but holding their son would alleviate the apprehension that lingered.

Taking her hand, he stepped closer and then led her beyond the trees and into the open. At first, he did not see Jaromir and the nurse-maid where they had been. Did the woman take him back to the carriage? Scouring the area, he then spotted the servant coming around the backside of the wagon.

Karin let out a whimper on a breath and rushed forward.

The nursemaid's eyes widened as Karin approached with speed and grabbed for Jaromir. "My lady!"

Ignoring the woman, Pavel watched his wife gather their son close to her chest. The young child squirmed and let out frustrated sounds, but Karin would not relent.

With that reunion in place, Pavel directed his focus to his knights and the stranger among them. What did the man want? Was there any potential danger there? There was but one way to find out.

CHAPTER 31
HANA & RADEK

H ana stepped out of her room. The silence had become deafening. How long had she holed up here trying to avoid everything and everyone? Had it been days? A fortnight yet? Still, as much as she wished to retain her solace, she could not manage another minute of the intense quiet.

But where should she venture? The inner bailey for a stroll? There she might come across Radek. And she wasn't certain she was ready to see him. She doubted that he cared about her isolation. He hadn't tried to discover the reasons for it at least.

Perhaps moving among the serving staff in the Great Hall would be sufficient. That would provide much interaction should she wish it, or none if she only intended to be out among people. Yes, the Great Hall it was.

Hana moved below stairs, questioning her decision the whole of the short journey. What if Radek were within? Perhaps she would cross paths with Mistress Huddard. She cringed. The woman had been difficult these last days, trying to convince Hana once more that returning to Novak lands would be best for her. The truth was that

Hana found it harder and harder to convince herself that Mistress Huddard was wrong.

The thought of returning to her own home appealed. It would certainly please her mother. Father had yet to write, but Mother's missive had weighed on Hana. Mayhap that was the best course. It would provide space between her and Radek. Though that thought brought a heaviness with it. Could she leave Radek? With so much between them unsettled?

And again, she was not certain of anything.

She alighted from the last step and glanced around the Great Hall. A few servants milled about. They began preparations for the nooning meal as it seemed. As Hana's gaze skirted the whole of the room, she spotted Margravine Miklasova and Lady Galina near the hearth with their sewing.

No. She couldn't do this. Her heart was too fragile and her status too uncertain.

But as she turned to climb the stairs once more, Lady Galina called. "Lady Hana, there you are. I was beginning to think you had disappeared entirely."

Hana drew in a long breath. Did she have to face them? Could she escape without an affront to Radek's female relatives? She turned.

Both women watched her.

She swallowed. "I have...not felt well these last days."

"Oh?" the margravine said, a tightness in her words. "Shall we send for the healer?"

Hana shook her head as she stepped forward. "I am well enough now."

"Are you certain?" Margravine Miklasova eyed her. It was not, however, with an encouraging regard. Rather, it seemed more inter-rogative.

"I do wonder," Lady Galina said, setting her stitching to her lap, "why you never join us. Does something offend?"

"I..." How was she to speak of her discomfort with the two women?

"Please," the margravine said, "If you are well enough, join us now."

Hana hesitated but decided to seek the best in their intentions. Moving to the fire, she sat in an empty chair near the matriarch.

Radek's mother laid a hand to Hana's arm. "Truly, it pains me that you do not feel at home here." Her words were thick and overly sweet.

"I...do not feel unwelcome," Hana told a half truth. "I appreciate your hospitality."

Margravine Miklasova looked at her daughter. Their tight-lipped expressions told that Hana's response was expected.

"I understand that Radek has not been very...attentive...these last few days. Is that because you have been ill? It does seem he has busied himself elsewhere rather intentionally." Lady Galina peered down at her work as she spoke.

Did she intend to insult Hana? Or was that just her way?

"Perhaps it is nothing more than it seems," the margravine added.

And what did she think it seemed? That Radek had lost hold of his tender emotions for Hana? That he cared not to see her? Hana steadied her breathing. There was no need to let these women know how they injured her.

"It is a wonder," Lady Galina said, looking to Hana. "I have not known Radek to be so interested in Father's work. Mayhap it is nothing more than a needed distraction."

Hana rose, knocking against the chair with the back of her legs.

The women did not so much as glance her way as they continued their work. What was this?

"I...have a...that is, my headache has returned."

"Has it?" Margravine Miklasova peered at her. "Shall I send for the healer now? Or perhaps something about this place is not fit for a duke's daughter."

Hana's mouth dropped open. She shut it with firmness, the

clashing of her teeth giving her pause. "I...cannot know what you mean."

"Perhaps Radek's mood and lack of presence about the place is a reflection of his change of heart," Lady Galina challenged.

How was it that this woman could fit a barb for Hana's heart so well? It wasn't right.

Hana cleared her throat and started, "I don't believe—"

Lady Galina's eyes sparked as she cut in. "I would not be surprised if Radek sends you away."

Could that be? Would he do so? Hana had held to hope as he had not done so yet. But perhaps he only tarried over his decision.

Hana's knees felt weak. She gripped to the back of the chair she had vacated. "I...think I need to lie down."

But as she turned, she found Radek standing in the center of the Great Hall. What had he heard?

The Great Hall fell quiet. Had Radek heard correctly? How could his mother and sister say such things? It was obvious they had not realized any more than Hana that he stood nearby.

He flexed his arm muscles. The ache to pull Hana to himself and console her overwhelmed him. Or did he more wish to let loose his ire on his mother and Galina? The way his pulse sped and his whole body flushed, he knew it was more due to the latter.

"Lady Hana," he managed to press out as he stepped closer, "I must speak with you."

Hana turned her head to the side. Not so much that she looked back on those at the hearth, but as if she avoided his gaze. "I...confess a headache. I must excuse myself."

She strode forward, her steps directed toward the stairs as if she wished to move past him.

His hand shot out and grasped her arm.

She startled.

He forced his fingers to not flex so tightly. It had not been his intention to work his emotion on her. But he could not let her slip by and walk away. Too much was at stake.

"I would have you speak with me before you retire."

Her eyes were downcast, but she gave a hesitant nod.

Radek shifted to hold her elbow with his other hand. Then he moved her toward the stairs. He caught her intake of breath as he did so. Did she fear being alone with him? Perhaps taking her to her chamber was not the best decision. Where, then, might they have the privacy he needed, but keep her at ease? The garden.

Shifting his step, he moved past the steps and farther into the castle. The walk to the courtyard seemed quite lengthy, but it could only have been a matter of seconds. Still, as they stepped outside into the light, she pulled free of his grip.

Having lost contact with her, the swell of apprehension and the thought of what it might be to lose her filled him. How was he to go about this? Everything was magnified—the thoughts and emotions coursing through him as well.

She stepped forward, her back to him, and brought her arms to cross. Though with the air of spring about them, it could not be due to a chill. Everything had warmed, preparing to greet the fresh flowers that even then reached at him with their fragrance.

He drew in breath and pressed it out. How was he to contain himself? The fear of losing her escalated. There was naught for it...he had to speak, had to make her see...

"What is it you need of me?" Hana's voice seemed so small.

Though he tried, he could not gain control of his emotions. Not even to answer her question. So, he remained as he was, focused on his breathing.

She shifted her weight to her other foot and dropped her head, her cinnamon-colored tresses falling behind her in waves.

He sucked in one more long breath, but when he opened his mouth, his words were tight. "Do you plan to return to your father?"

She spun to face him, though her gaze did not hold on him but sought the ground once more. She did not answer.

Radek wanted for the possibility to erase his words. This was not the right way to do this.

He stepped toward her.

She flinched. Had she become so uncertain in his presence? That injured.

"Hana," he said, pushing his own emotions down that he might speak plainly, "I would know if you intend to leave."

Her eyes met his—again, only for a moment before she focused elsewhere. "I...don't know."

He could have taken a blade to his skin better than how he received her statement. Indeed, it was as if he were cut the way he took a step back, the way everything in him suddenly tightened. And he remembered his sister's words.

"Do you..." he started, then cleared his throat and tried again. "Do you believe that is what I wish?"

Her intake of breath was long and pained. "I do not know."

The urge to gather her to himself overwhelmed again. But how would she receive that? He forced himself to keep his feet planted. What was best? To address her fear or give it greater depths? After some moments of indecision, he said, "I do not."

She pressed her lips together and tugged her arms closer to herself, rubbing along her sleeves.

"I would have you remain. And I," he paused as he drew in a breath, "would have us understand each other."

Her brow furrowed. "Do I misunderstand?"

"Aye. It is not as my mother and sister would have you believe. I do not intend to send you away. Far from it." He licked his lips. "In fact, when I discovered you had reason to leave, I realized I had let you think less of my affection for you. And my desire to keep you safe."

She shook her head. "I do not doubt your desire for my well-being."

"But what of the other?"

"I...was given much space to question your affection. Between our last encounter and the long days of silence thereafter, I no longer know what to think." Hana lifted her chin and let her gaze meet his. There was so much uncertainty in her eyes that he cursed his poor judgment.

"I did seek distance to work out my own thoughts as to your... tendency to assert your own wishes."

"My what?" She appeared stricken.

"You cannot deny, Hana, that you have, at times, proven impulsive, and acted as though the only outcome that mattered was your way of things. Even were they against the advice of your father...or me." Radek attempted to keep his voice calm, but there was an edge that crept into his tone. Even he could hear it.

"But I..." she started, but soon quieted, swallowing, as if she considered his words. Then she looked to the ground. Was she repentant?

"That was not all I claimed time for. I also wanted to work alongside my father. To try and understand him. And his ways."

Silence fell between them. And Radek's heart thumped hard. He cared too much for her. Would it one day be to his detriment?

He used a finger to tip her chin upward, raising her gaze to his. "That is all, Hana. My regard for you has not changed. Nor have my intentions...my wish to marry you."

Her gaze held his, and her eyes glistened. There was indeed much emotion in this exchange. Much that needed to be said. That must be worked out.

She looked away again and bit at her lip. Then she paused. "Why...why would you think I was to leave?"

His heart beat harder. There was no cause to keep his actions from her. He should not. "I read the missive from your mother. I was—"

"You read my letter?" She dropped her arms, an eyebrow piqued.

He fought down the urge to defend himself. The truth was best.

295

"I went to your room...to speak with you. But you were not within. However, Mistress Huddard was and bearing the missive. She told of your mother's entreaty. When I questioned her as to the veracity of such, she handed me the letter."

Hana's features tightened. "You would read the private things my mother writes to me?"

He pushed out a breath. "I know that it was untoward of me to do so."

She nodded and rubbed at her face, looking off in the distance again.

Radek moved closer. Would she move away? Or might she receive him? "I am sorry that I did so. This...distance between us has dragged at me. Though I know I am most to blame."

She watched him but did not move—either to back away or close the remaining space.

"And I would have you know that I regret that, too." He stepped forward again; he was but an arm's length away now. Lifting a hand, he traced fingers along her cheek. "Do you not know the depth of my affection? Of how I ached for your presence when we we're apart?"

She gasped.

"I do not think I can...manage it were you to part from me again."

A tear slid down the side of her face.

He took one more step, closing much of the distance between them. "I love you, Hana."

She fell against his chest, clinging to his tunic, and released a great sigh. "Good, because I am lost to you."

And he felt more whole than he had in weeks.

CHAPTER 32
KARIN & PAVEL

Pavel wished he could let the soothing sound of the nearby stream flow over him. But that could not be. Not just now. For he faced down the stranger among them who might yet represent a threat. Were there others? Did he seek ill, so close to Krejik lands? What might this mean? Regardless of the situation, Pavel determined that this man would not be a threat to Karin or Jaromir. That was what mattered.

He set his gaze on the man, who appeared innocent enough. And Pavel strode toward Sir Marek, close at hand.

The knight spoke as he neared. "The man calls himself Martin of Pisek. He seems to be lost, but he claims to seek the Baroness Krejikova."

Pavel looked to Sir Marek. "My mother? For what purpose?"

"He will not say. There is some reason he feels bound to keep that to himself."

"What did you share with him?" Pavel examined the knight's face, seeking out any hint that the man spoke less than the full truth.

"Only that we journey as well. And that you would like to speak with him." Sir Marek was nothing less than forthcoming.

Pavel had no reason not to believe him, so he shifted his focus back to the stranger among them. "Aye, that I would."

He continued to watch the bumbling man as he wondered at this new information. Martin of Pisek was nearer his intended destination than he realized. Was he sent only to speak with the baroness? Or did he mean to work harm upon her?

Waving Sir Marek to the side, Pavel stepped forward and called out to the stranger among them, "I would speak with you." As he stepped closer, he could make out the man with greater clarity.

Pavel was satisfied that the man did not appear alarming or suspicious. Martin of Pisek was no man of war. Rather his girth spoke to an ease of life. His garments told that he was neither a poor villager nor nobility, but more of a merchant in some respect. He did not challenge Pavel or his knights in stature but fell a full foot shorter than most.

"Yes, my lord?" Martin stared up at Pavel. He seemed rather unsettled by the encounter.

"What is the reason for your presence here?"

Martin looked about, maneuvering his jaw as he sought...what? Assistance? Help from somewhere beyond Pavel's men?

To their credit, the knights kept their eyes to their surroundings and their hands near their sword hilts.

"I...am at a disadvantage. You know my purpose, but I have yet to even learn your name." There was a boldness in the man's eyes that belied his position.

"I do *not* know your purpose," Pavel challenged. "I only know that you seek the Lady Krejikova." Something about speaking the name that his mother and his wife shared gave him a slight pause. Perhaps no one noticed. "I do not yet know what you intend."

Martin set his wandering gaze on Pavel. "My lord, I beg you...my task is my own. I am not at liberty to divulge it."

Pavel ground his teeth. Would the man not yield to good sense? This...merchant was surrounded by men of the sword under Pavel's command. Did that not intimidate him in the least? "Perhaps I am not at liberty to permit you to continue your journey. For on my honor, I will not let you bring harm to the baroness."

The man's eyes widened, then narrowed slightly. "I am a simple man with a task that I have been trusted to keep. Admittedly, I am at odds with the prospect that, dare I keep this confidence, you will prevent me from completing my errand."

"Then we are at an impasse, hmm?" Pavel hardened his gaze on the man.

"Will you not satisfy my lord husband's need to know you seek no ill?" a voice said from just behind and to the left—Karin.

Pavel glared in her direction as he held up a hand to halt her progress. The man could very well be concealing a weapon still. He might be cut down in doing so, but he could still work harm upon Pavel's wife. A flash of heat coursed through him. What did Karin intend to do? Ease this situation? Did she not trust Pavel to do as he should?

Her green eyes pleaded with him. For what? To relent? He would not sacrifice her or his mother.

He waved at Sir Marek to draw closer to Karin. Whichever knight should have remained with her and kept her a safe distance from the exchange would be punished.

Then he turned to the merchant once more, struggling to press his anger down. Only, his ire was not for the stranger, but for his wife's interference.

"Martin of Pisek." Pavel firmed his voice as he spoke. "I beseech you to state your purpose before I am forced to have your person and your wagon thoroughly searched and then you bound and held until you will reveal it."

The man's features fell. Yes, he knew he was out of options.

"Lord husband, perhaps—"

"My lady!" he cut her off. There would be no further engagement on her part. He would know this man's reason for seeking the baroness.

She paused and her face flushed. Indeed, the shock upon her features would not have been greater had he slapped her.

Pavel ached for it, but he would have this done with. Shifting his regard to the man, he pushed one word out through clenched teeth. "Now."

Martin looked to the ground and back at Pavel. Did he consider this a bluff? He would learn otherwise.

Pavel motioned for the knight nearest the merchant to seize him.

The man did not so much as struggle.

Until another of Pavel's men approached the wagon.

"Do not," Martin called, turning his gaze on Pavel. "I will tell all you wish to know."

Was there something in that wagon he wanted to keep secret? Something that might endanger Pavel's wife and son? Or his men?

"Bring him closer," Pavel said, not taking his eyes from the man. His desire to separate the merchant from any potential weapons urged Pavel toward rashness. He prayed it was unfounded.

The knight brought Martin of Pisek nearer.

"My patience has worn thin," Pavel said. "No more of this. Tell me what I wish to know."

The man hung his head. "I come at Baroness Krejikova's request."

"Why would she seek you out?"

"'Tis not me. But what I carry."

This did nothing to ease Pavel's mind. "Stop these riddles. What have you?"

Martin let out a breath. "As God Almighty watches, I pray do not harm me. For I bear a Holy Writ."

Karin's knees felt as if made of weaker substance or that they may not hold her up. Her breaths came quicker. *A Holy Writ.* How was this possible? Was this God's answer to her prayers?

She glanced at her husband. Pavel did not betray any emotion in word or movement. From her vantage point, all she could discern was that he continued to stare at the man. Thick tension hung in the air. Why? This man couldn't seem a threat. Not after this new information. Martin of Pisek was no less than a godsend—a messenger straight from the Almighty.

All was quiet but for the deep breaths taken by the knight at her right.

Someone needed to break this stalemate. Perhaps it should be her. She stepped forward, opening her mouth to speak sense to the men still poised for a heated exchange.

Sir Marek shot an arm out in front of her, effectively halting her movements.

Dare she skirt around him? Defy her husband and his man? If only Pavel would look at her. If only his eyes would soften. Then she would know that all was well between them. That her earlier actions had not damaged his good opinion of her. But had they? For he would not so much as glance in her direction.

She bit her lip to keep from calling out to him, her heart aching for the separation created by her actions. And his.

Yes, he had been harsh. Had it been truly necessary? Or was he so different, changed by the hardness of war, that he no longer regarded her as tenderly as he always had?

It was true that he wished to protect her and their son above all else. Had her forwardness been an affront to that end?

"You bear a Holy Writ?" Pavel's strong baritone filled the space.

The man nodded, eyeing the knights closer to him.

"For the Baroness Krejikova?"

Martin of Pisek again nodded. "It is requested."

Did Pavel share Karin's work with his mother? Was nothing kept between them? Should she give in to the relief that a Writ would be accessible? Or disheartened that her husband had not kept her secret safe?

Silence fell over the group once more. All Karin could see was Pavel's back. And there was little she could read beyond the tightness in his muscles.

"We shall see you to Krejik lands," Pavel announced, his words exact and rather curt.

Martin's eyes widened. Had he hoped to be free of the entourage? That was not to be.

Pavel looked toward the knight at his side. "See this man to his wagon and keep close to him."

So, her husband did not trust Martin of Pisek. That was bothersome. Had he lost his faith in men? Perhaps that was what brought about his reaction to her—he no longer trusted her.

Pavel turned then to where she and Sir Marek stood, all but dismissing Martin. Or was it that he believed his words would be carefully followed? Either way, he strode toward her now. His bearing was still tense and his emotions well concealed.

As he neared, he said to Sir Marek, "See that we are ready to depart."

"Aye, my lord." The knight moved into action, calling out orders.

Pavel took her by the elbow. But it was not the touch she was accustomed to from him, rather it was firm, though not pained. He then moved her toward the carriage.

Karin rushed to keep in step with him.

The nursemaid, with Jaromir, was being loaded even then.

Should she take advantage of this moment to speak with her husband? Whether or not it was wise, she could no longer hold her tongue. "Pavel, I did not—"

"This is not the time." His reply seemed forced through teeth. The words were every bit as commanding as those he had spoken to his men. Is that what she was to him? Someone to control?

She told herself this was not how he dealt with her. Not usually. But the sting of his words drove in further than her self-assurances.

Pavel stopped at the door to the carriage and urged her within.

She paused, meeting his hard gaze. "I—"

He frowned. "Watch over my son. And yourself." His words had not a hint of tenderness, only brusqueness.

Karin allowed him to help her into the confined space. But before she was quite settled, he shut the door and walked away.

CHAPTER 33
PATRICIE & STEPAN

Patricie couldn't breathe. Her life was left to just moments. Terrified moments.

A dagger was unsheathed behind her. She tried to jerk away, her only recourse. The mercenary beside her firmed his grip on her arm.

Her back then hit the firm wall of the guard's chest. And though she fought against his hold, she found even those movements restricted. There was no way out!

The viscount's eyes were hard and his air dismissive. How could he care so little for life?

Stepan moved forward. "You cannot."

Would he truly speak for her? Would it matter?

"What say you?" the viscount's expression did not change. It seemed as if Stepan's words only served to amuse him.

"I...sustained injury from the battle. As you see." Why was his voice so timid?

It was not possible that Stepan's lack of confidence would sway his father. Her heartbeat raced and she felt light-headed. Her limbs were shaky and seemed as if they were not her own.

The urge to cry out against it all overwhelmed her, but she gulped down her words. If this was the end, she would not betray her fear. She would not let this man know his power over her was so complete.

An image of the dagger against her skin, spilling her life, flashed through her mind. And she tasted bile. But she refused to give in to it and held to herself with all she had.

"You will be well enough," the viscount stated flatly.

"But—" Stepan tried again.

His father waved a hand.

The cool metal of the dagger pressed against her neck. This was it. She would be with her mother soon.

Stepan side-stepped in that direction, dragging his wounded leg, as if he would stop this from happening. Though she knew that was impossible.

Patricie closed her eyes. She would not give them the satisfaction.

A loud thump broke into the still moment.

Dare she look?

"Stop!" It was the viscount who called out.

And the weapon let up its cutting press. Was it over? Was she dead? But she still felt the hands of the guard upon her as sounds of movement surrounded her. Fearing the worst, but unable to shut it out any longer, she opened her eyes.

Stepan was on the floor. Had someone cut him down? It couldn't be!

But two men had rushed to his side.

"He breathes," one of them said to the viscount, who had stepped forward. And the relief upon his aging face was evident.

"What goes with my son?" Viscount Dvorak demanded.

Was he speaking to her? He seemed to be eyeing her.

The viscount moved forward a couple more steps. "I said—what goes with my son, Hussite?"

Patricie worked to find her voice. And when it came, it was rather strained. "His leg is damaged. And though I told your men, they would not slow. The journey has seen him much deprived of rest and his wound has reopened and started to seep."

The viscount's eyes narrowed. "Tend him."

Arms that held her now shoved her to the floor. She fell a few feet shy of Stepan's position.

He was so still. Too still. But the man had said he breathed. Was that true?

Crawling to him, she laid a hand on his shoulder. "Help me turn him."

No one moved.

"Do as she says." It was the viscount's insistent voice.

The two guards on either side of Stepan shifted him.

"Careful!" she demanded. It wouldn't do for them to injure him further.

Now that he was on his back, she leaned over his upper body, pressing a hand to his neck and face.

"He has fever," she announced. "His wound may be putrid."

"You are not able to save him?" The viscount's words were measured, but the emotion underneath came through. He was concerned about his son.

"I do not know. But I do not believe all hope is lost."

The viscount's lips thinned. "You will save my son."

Patricie met his gaze. Not that she needed to. The hard edge was back in his voice.

She nodded. Her life was now tied to Stepan's. For if she could not bring him back from the edge of the abyss he now walked, her own life was forfeit.

Stepan did not think the world had ever seemed so at odds. His mind felt as if it fought deep waters. Had he drowned? Was he dead? He moved his head. Or what seemed movement. The whole thing made him rather nauseated. Where was he?

Fingers skimmed over his leg. Gentle fingers. Who?

Though the touches were tender, so was his flesh. His leg ached. Sharply. He bit the inside of his lip to keep from crying out.

"Be still," the voice beseeched him through a thick haze.

Should he obey or fight to sit up and determine what his circumstances were?

The fingers probed with more force. Pain coursed through him in a heavy wave. He tried to rise and get free of the encroaching presence. But his body wouldn't concede his efforts.

The movements over his wound continued. Whoever leaned over him gasped and grunted.

Yes, he was wounded. The battle, the healer, the escape...all of it came rushing back.

Was Patricie dead? Had his father seen to her end after Stepan blacked out? Or was this her even now, working to sustain him though it pained? The world cleared somewhat. He came to see that it was dark. A few candles alone lit the room. Where was the light of the moon? Had that, too, abandoned him?

A small hand landed on his knee and the digging around his wound subsided. For the one who worked to catch his or her breath? Or for a stretch?

He homed in on the figure that leaned over.

A dark braid fell over the visible shoulder. Could it be...Patricie?

His heart lightened. Prayer moved into the small opening created by his observation. Had she somehow survived? The image of his father's determined features pressed into his mind. Yes, Father had been set on her end. And Stepan's plea had fallen to deaf ears. What happened to change that?

As Stepan shifted, the figure peered at him. Though loosened tendrils fell over her face, he did recognize the bright eyes—Patricie. He wanted with all he was to collect her in his arms and promise that he would protect her no matter what came. But he lacked the strength to rise. And her expression, though it read concern, was hard.

His memory continued to clear. He had wronged her. Had angered her. But she was whole and well. That meant something. He could lean on that.

"Be still," she admonished once more, laying a hand on his chest, and applying the lightest pressure. The words were firm but had a softer sound about them than before. She must care.

And as the dark surrounded him, closing in from the edges of his mind, he knew hope.

CHAPTER 34
HANA & RADEK

Radek dropped out of his saddle. The horse had worked well for him. Though the ride had not lasted long enough to quell his anger. His mother and sister's words to Hana still rang in his ears. What was he to do? Could he turn a blind eye to their behavior? Such as his father did when his mother slapped him upon his return? And perhaps it would be more fitting for him to let his father handle the situation, but he had no confidence it would be any different. Just brushed to the side.

He would not do that to Hana. If there were any chance for things to go well with her and his family, he needed to speak with his mother and sister. Together? Or would that be too much? As it was, the thought of addressing either of them gave him tremors. But it must be done. He would not shirk his responsibility in this.

A new-found respect for his father had started to grow weeks ago, but Radek did not wish to have it dashed by the same nonchalance the man exhibited before.

Radek rubbed the horse's neck down. Yes, the animal had given him some space to consider his options and think on the next course of action he must take. For that, he was grateful.

The destrier tugged against the bit. Was he eager to return to his stall and fresh hay? Radek would ensure the horse got his due. Moving farther into the enclosed area, he searched out the stable-master. Or at least a stable hand. Was there no one to assist with his horse? Had something happened? Shrugging off the sense of fore-boding that never eased completely, he went about removing the animal's restraints himself.

It wasn't often he enjoyed the smells of the stables, but this day, he embraced it. The hay, the scent of the other animals moving within, even the evidence of his own horse's hard work. They grounded him.

He had just closed the destrier in his stall when a younger lad rushed up to him. "My lord, let me get fresh hay for your horse."

"And he needs a brush down," Radek said as he eyed the youngster.

The boy turned, but Radek called him back.

"Where is your master?"

The lad seemed hesitant. Would he answer truthfully?

"You will not be punished. Speak true."

"I don't know, my lord." The boy shrugged. "I actually expected him to thrash me for wandering off."

Radek nodded. This did nothing to abate his concern, but he believed the boy spoke honestly. He watched as the lad turned back toward the horse. But Radek only lingered for a few moments longer.

Then he made his way into the inner bailey. Several others milled about, more and more so as he approached the donjon. But his thoughts were on the coming confrontation. What would he say? His mother and sister were important to him, but so was Hana. And it had become clear to him that the animosity toward her was wholly one-sided.

Radek's shoulder slammed into something. Or someone.

"Watch where you're going," a man's deep voice muttered.

"What say you?" Radek narrowed his gaze on the man who had stumbled into him.

The man's eyes went wide. "No, my lord, I would never presume to speak to you in such a way. This miscreant nearly knocked me over. I had no idea you were…"

Radek scanned the area. And indeed, there was another man moving away with hurried step. He was garbed in Miklas colors.

The strange man looked back as he continued to move away at a rapid pace. Something about the man struck him. Had he seen this knight before? Radek searched his memory. And felt it was there, just out of reach. Enough so that he found himself following after the guard.

The man dodged people and his path jerked about. It became difficult to keep step with him, but Radek managed and still maintained a distance. With any luck, the knight wouldn't know he was being followed. He turned a couple more times and scanned the area.

Radek was thankful he had chosen to remain as concealed as possible. For the man did not seem to notice him. Though the more Radek watched his movements, he was certain he had seen him before. But why should that bother? He had chanced upon many of his father's men and not been so troubled. Yet when he caught glimpses of this man's face, heat poured into his awareness. Something about him felt dangerous. And Radek would not abide such among his father's guards.

The man moved farther away from the castle, and it became more difficult to remain hidden as he followed. However, it mattered less as the man seemed more intent on where he went rather than what may be behind.

At length, the knight slipped across an open area and into the nearby forest.

Should Radek follow? He would have to make himself more visible—and vulnerable—before slipping into the cover of the trees. He watched only a few breaths more…and, keeping low, rushed across the space. Then he was among the trees. Where had the man gone? Had Radek lost him?

Closing his eyes, he listened for the rustle of undergrowth and any hint of movement. There, the man moved not twenty paces ahead and to the right. Shifting his weight, Radek then stepped out from behind the trunk he had used for shield.

And a weight came down upon his back.

He tasted dirt as his body slammed against the earth.

Then his vision blurred and went dark. Though he heard voices. Were they as far away as they seemed? Only snatches of the words were clear.

"Why did you...him?" one voice said gruffly.

"He...followed you," another challenged. "I can't...have him... discover..."

"Is he dead?" Those words were clearer and closer. Did someone lean over him?

"He will be."

Metal whispered against metal.

"Not that way. Give me his sword."

There was heat to his side as someone fumbled for the hilt of his sword.

"What was that?"

"Move! Someone...coming..."

Boots stomped through the brush.

And Radek lost his hold on consciousness.

Hana paced the Great Hall. She thought over Radek's last words to her. They had both soothed and reassured. As had their embrace. He did love her. He did.

And he would be by her side the next time she would have to face his mother or sister. That gave her great comfort. Though...either of them was likely to come below stairs at any moment. Hadn't Radek promised to meet her by now? Here? And yet nothing.

Had he changed his mind about her? About them?

No, she told herself. She would not believe that. Not after what they had said to one another. At some point, she would have to start trusting in him. And that time was now.

She held her head up and glanced around the room.

Servants milled about, preparing the space for the evening meal. Their presence was good for her. Those coming and going from the room offered a fine distraction from her harried thoughts and heart. But that could not satisfy.

"You will wear holes in your slippers," a distinctly feminine voice said from the stairway.

Hana turned to see who might be disturbing her.

Lady Galina.

Hana swallowed. She didn't have the courage for another confrontation right now. Not when Radek...

"Why do you look so lost?" Lady Galina moved toward Hana.

Dare she speak to the question? Or would that only give Radek's sister more weapons for her words?

"Have you lost your tongue?" Lady Galina stopped a few feet away.

"No...that is, I am quite distracted." Hana shifted her weight.

"Oh? What is it that has driven you to such...distraction?" The words were fine, but the tone in which they were delivered baited Hana. Did Lady Galina enjoy their clashes? It seemed as if she did.

Hana shook her head. She should not engage with the woman, but how to politely ignore her? Was that even possible?

"I understand that my brother went for a long ride. Perhaps he is working out how best to eliminate his...distractions."

Hana clenched her teeth. There would be no benefit in biting back. The woman couldn't understand what went or how she had angered Radek. Though...were Galina's words unfounded? They didn't possess the weight the lady thought they would, but was there a bit of truth to them?

Lady Galina folded her arms. "Have you gone mute?"

"I don't wish to—"

A disturbance rippled through the Great Hall. Hana turned toward the corridor. What was this?

Several guards appeared, bearing a weight.

Hana's stomach lurched. Something was very wrong. No matter how she angled her neck, she could not determine what they carried.

Lady Galina moved into action. "Bring him."

To Hana's surprise, the lady shifted into an air of authority and grace. Gone was the woman that was little more than a thorn in Hana's side.

Radek's sister led the men farther into the Great Hall, but Hana remained rooted to the spot. What might she do to assist? Or would she be in the way?

But as the men passed her, she saw Radek.

They carried Radek. And he bled.

"Radek!" Hana's heart pounded as she rushed to follow.

There was no indication that he heard her.

Lady Galina shouted orders, which the servants and men obeyed without question. But when Radek was laid upon the table, Hana could not stay herself. She rushed to his side, grabbing for his hand.

She felt more than saw Lady Galina's scornful expression on her, but naught was said or done to remove Hana.

"Is he alive?" Hana watched Radek's chest for evidence he still breathed.

Lady Galina moved hands over her brother. "I believe so."

The men backed away.

"What happened?" Lady Galina's sharp words were on someone other than Hana now. But her tone was assured and commanding, not harsh.

One of the knights spoke up. "I discovered him in the forest while on patrol. Like this."

Lady Galina frowned. "You saw naught else?"

The knight shook his head.

Hana could not contain the moisture building behind her eyes, though she fought it. She brought Radek's hand to her face. There was the subtle movement of his chest. And that's what she held fast to. He was alive. That was enough. Wasn't it?

CHAPTER 35
KARIN & PAVEL

The castle had long since appeared in the distance. Now they closed in upon the portcullis. In a matter of moments, they would be within. Karin could almost taste the viands. They had not paused to eat, as Pavel had wished to be at the castle before dark settled upon the land. A messenger had been sent to request the dowager baroness hold the evening meal until their arrival.

Karin was weary of the rocking and bumping of the road. Time to settle into a chair, a bath, a bed—something steadier.

The carriage halted. And, moments later, Sir Marek reached in to assist Karin. She worked to hide her surprise. Why did Pavel not do so? But she consoled herself. His priority was Martin of Pisek. He had to make sure the man was watched and settled appropriately.

Stepping down, Karin scanned the area. Could she spot her husband?

He was not in the vicinity it seemed. Perhaps he had ushered Martin of Pisek into the gatehouse. She couldn't be certain.

Sir Marek turned to her after the nursemaid was out of the carriage. "Baron Krejik wishes for everyone to make their way into the Great Hall. Lady Krejikova will have the evening meal served shortly."

Karin nodded. There was naught else to do but obey. She did not want to put off her mother-in-law.

She made her way through the inner bailey and toward the donjon. The nursemaid broke off from the group as they entered the Great Hall and took Jaromir above stairs.

Karin nearly called her back. Should she go after and ensure that Jaromir was fed and sated for sleep? Still, she thought it best to be where her husband expected. There was already too much tension between them.

Dowager Baroness Krejikova greeted her at the doorway. "Lady Karin, you are a sight for sore eyes indeed!" The woman embraced her, though her arms did not tighten. Was she still weak from her ailment? She seemed well enough, even if a little wane.

"It is good to be back." Karin pulled away and drank in her mother-in-law's kindness.

"It has been too long." The words were gentle and hesitant, as if the woman struggled with emotion. "But it is good to see you are well. Much better than last I laid eyes on you."

Karin nodded. Pavel's mother had quit Duke Novak's castle before Karin was able to leave her own sickbed. "Yes. I am blessed that God has shown me favor."

Lady Krejikova nodded. "That he has." There was something more meaningful in her regard.

Was it because of Karin's work to transcribe the Holy Writ? She remembered that Pavel had shared the secret with his mother. "I...do what I can."

Lady Krejikova's brow furrowed. "What you can?"

Now Karin was confused.

The woman's features eased. "I suppose that is all one can do."

That did not ease Karin's discomfort.

"Come, daughter," Lady Krejikova said as she ushered Karin forward. "Let us take our places."

"Actually," Pavel's familiar voice said from behind, "I need to speak with my ladywife."

Karin tried to hide how unsettled she was as she looked to her husband.

His mother appeared as if she would question him in this. But her only words were, "Shall I hold the meal another hour?"

"No. That is not necessary." Pavel stepped forward. "My men are hungry and require refreshment. We shall join you in a few moments."

A tingle went up Karin's spine. What might he wish to say to her? Would he chastise her for her actions? There was little doubt of that.

Pavel held out his arm in her direction.

She hesitated but briefly and then set a hand upon it as she tossed her mother-in-law an apologetic smile. It was the best she could manage.

By then the din of voices in the Great Hall had grown. Though they quieted again as Pavel escorted her up the stairs.

How could she prepare herself for this encounter? She reran the last hours in her head, both her words and his. Indeed, this was best —a talk. Getting everything out. But at what cost? Then she did the best thing she could think to do—she prayed.

Their walk to the solar was not as lengthened as she wished it, nor did she want to prolong her agony. She barely noticed the work done to rebuild before Pavel opened the door and indicated she should go ahead of him.

She swallowed and stepped within, but before she had a chance to turn toward him, he started speaking.

"That will not be the way of it."

Karin spun. What to say? To assent or share her heart? She had never felt the need to hide anything from him. Until now.

He stared at her, his gaze neither hard nor softening. It just was.

"I...regret my actions." In truth she did. Though she did not understand his hardness in that moment, she should not have questioned him in front of his men.

He studied her. "You do not seem as if you believe your own words."

"I..." Now was the moment. Would she embrace who she was, who she needed him to see...or what might prove to be the easier path?

"Yes?" He stepped closer.

"I only wanted to ease the tension of that moment. I did not wish for you to spill blood."

One of his eyebrows arched. "Oh?" Again, his speech was simple and not complicated by emotion.

"It was not my intention to make it seem as if I..." She caught herself. What had it seemed?

"As if you had no respect for my ability to manage the situation?" His tone took on an edge.

She pinched her lips. Why couldn't she relax and let the worry seep out of her? "You know that is not how I feel."

"Do I?" The response was fairly growled, his voice full of tension.

"I only wished to help." Moving toward him slowly, she lifted her eyes to his. She needed him to understand, to know what went on in her mind when she had spoken out. "I don't see how that can be so wrong."

He pressed out a breath.

She paused her forward movement.

His glare was filled with heavy emotions. And his posture was rigid. "Do you have any idea what could have happened had you approached him, and he have a weapon concealed?"

She turned away. That thought had not occurred. "No, I—"

"What would I do if...?" he broke in. "How could I go on?"

The blue in his eyes had deepened in color and they were alive with the stirrings of his heart.

"Oh, Pavel," she said as she stepped toward him again. "I didn't think..."

"I know." He watched as she neared.

In but a few paces, she would be able to touch his arm. Might he gather her in his embrace? And everything would be well with them?

But as she reached out for him, he jerked away. "And that's the problem. You didn't think."

She recoiled as if stung. His words had been harsher than expected. Did the well of his anger run to such depth?

He turned and crossed to the door. "I must join the others. I will have some viands sent up for you. And water for a bath if you wish it."

Was she not to join the others? What did he mean by this?

She struggled to find her voice, but at length she did. "I...thank you. I would like that."

He pulled the door open and paused. Without looking back, he said, "I...don't know that you can understand what that did to me."

With that, he passed into the corridor and shut the door behind himself.

And she was alone.

Pavel grumbled. He ran a hand over the back of his neck. The muscles there were sore...as seemed the whole of him. Sleeping in a chair had not been the most comfortable thing. Though he could not find it in himself to face off with Karin again.

But his decision had perhaps not behooved him. Mayhap was not fitting for the lord of the castle to avoid his wife due to emotional discomfort. Although his frustration still burned, so did his love for her...and his desire to set things aright.

He stretched his arms once more as he climbed the stairs to the solar. He would speak with Karin and be done with this nonsense. For he knew the wound he had dealt her. And also knew it was not likely she had forgotten. Still, he must. He could not go on with this thing between them. She was his comfort, his strength, his gift. This had to end. Now.

Now at the landing, he approached the door to the solar. Leaning in, he listened for sounds of his wife moving within. But there were none. Was she still abed? The day was well upon them.

Easing the door open, he pressed it until it swung wide. He found an empty room.

"Karin?" he called, though he did not expect an answer.

Where had she gone? Perhaps to care for Jaromir? Or seek out solace in the chapel? As much as he wanted to slip into the room and wait for her return, his heart would not let him delay the exchange that was due him. But where might he find her? There were many places within the newly restored walls that she might venture. Though the chapel was the most likely, and that is where he must go.

Moments later, he came up empty yet again. His frustration grew. Not for her actions this time, but for his inability to locate her.

He moved back toward the donjon and caught her voice on a breeze. Turning in that direction, he spotted a flash of red hair atop the wall. Was she out for a stroll? With his insides tied in knots, was she able to move about without a worry?

The stairs that would take him to her lay on the left. Did he wish to nurse his wounded pride or seek out the resolution that may find all well again? As much as he wished to stew, he knew the latter would provide more peace. It only required risk—for him to bare himself to his wife and admit he may have been wrong. At least in his manner.

Up the steps he went until he found himself just paces away from his beloved. Her back was to him as she strode alongside the battlements. And something else. She carried Jaromir. How had he not noticed before? Truly this heaviness in his stomach and in his heart had compromised him.

"Karin," he spoke her name with tenderness.

She turned, her singing halted. Her eyes widened as they set upon on him. Was that a good sign?

"Pavel," she breathed, the word so quiet he barely made it out.

But what was that look about her? Fear? Trepidation? What had he wrought?

He closed the distance between them. And of a sudden, he was unable to find his words, so he set a hand upon Jaromir's back.

The babe had become livelier in the last month. He preferred to be upright. And he grabbed for most anything in sight. Even then, he claimed Pavel's finger.

Pavel couldn't help but smile at his son. When he looked up, he saw that Karin watched him. He shook his finger in a game of cat and mouse with Jaromir but kept his gaze on his wife.

She remained as she was, only glancing down at the little one in her arms for a moment here and there. At length, she pressed a kiss to the babe's brow.

Pavel ached. There was reason enough to keep his family safe, but there was much to be said about how he went about it. "Karin, I—"

His words were drowned out by the call to readiness.

He shifted his focus outward and spotted riders coming in. Setting his regard to Karin again, he wanted to command her below to the courtyard where it was safer, or to the donjon where it would be safest. However, he need not speak further.

She nodded and moved around him toward the stairs.

His gaze once again went to the horizon, trusting that she would make herself and their son secure. Calling orders to his knights, he watched. The riders wore Hussite colors. And there was a woman among them. Was that...could it be...Zdenek and Eva? What news might they bear?

CHAPTER 36
HANA & RADEK

Hana paced in the corridor while the healer was with Radek. What would happen? Would he recover? The healer had offered no such assurances. But she couldn't lose hope.

Lady Galina sighed from off to the left.

Hana glanced in her direction. There was something different in her affect. Something had changed between them, if only slightly, as they had labored alongside one another. It had almost seemed as if they might be able to move past any misgivings that lay between them.

Lady Galina's gaze flitted toward Hana, but her mouth turned downward, and she made an exasperated sound.

Would they lose what camaraderie had been erected in the last hour?

Hana opened her mouth to speak into the space, but the rush of slippered feet and the swish of skirts drew her attention.

Margravine Miklasova appeared at the top of the stairs. She glanced between Hana and her daughter, all but dismissing Hana in the next moment.

"How is he?" The words pressed out as if she had held them long captive.

Hana swallowed her trepidation. "The healer is with him now—"

"Not you." The margravine whirled on Hana, a red tint to her face —from her hurried flight up the stairs or something more...disconcerting?

Hana took a step back.

Lady Galina's stunned expression brought some comfort to Hana. Perhaps she, too, was unsure of her mother's reaction. But she soon furrowed her brow and flattened her lips. There would be little help there.

"Haven't you done enough?" Margravine Miklasova choked out. "Isn't it time you scurried back to your father?"

Hana searched for words to offer kindness, for the woman's heart must certainly struggle with her son's life in the balance. But there were none. Nothing that would allow softer feelings to come forth. She was too hurt and much to weary of these attacks.

"What have I done, Margravine?" Hana pushed out with some amount of hesitation. But she could not let the woman treat her thusly. After all, her beloved may well be on the brink of life and death. It was not a moment to be timid. "Why do you detest me so?"

Hana wanted to soften her words and speak of her genuine care for Radek, but she had reached the end of her ability to press into the tension.

"Ha." The margravine's exhale almost sounded a laugh. But was it more of an attempt to quell her ire?

Hana prayed she wouldn't speak further. For the margravine's feelings were easy to discern from her right, yet pained expression.

"You speak as if you do not already know." The woman advanced on Hana.

Taking another step back, Hana hit the wall with her back. Did she truly fear the woman? Would the margravine strike her?

"Mother," Lady Galina started. "It is not necessary to—"

Margravine Miklasova held up a hand to silence her daughter. It was effective.

"I pray, tell me. For I swear I do not understand your animosity." Hana swallowed against a suddenly dry mouth.

The margravine's eyes narrowed. "How can you not know?"

"I...don't know, my lady. But I don't."

Lady Miklasova scoffed. Then looked to her daughter again. But Lady Galina seemed as much at a loss as Hana.

Then the margravine glared at Hana once more. "How can you claim innocence? For certain, you are your mother's daughter."

Hana doubted she had ever been so confused in her life. It was true that the nobility of Bohemia were aware of others of that rank...at least to some extent. Had Hana's mother done something so egregious to bring out such hate in the margravine? What could it be?

"Do you claim to have no knowledge of your father's betrothal to *me*?" Margravine Miklasova shot the statement as if she wished it were an arrow, aimed for Hana's heart.

Hana's mind whirled. Radek's mother had been betrothed to Duke Novak? It couldn't be.

"Ah, I see we shall continue with the innocent act," the margravine sneered. "You might pretend, but that does not change that your mother manipulated Duke Novak to set me aside."

"Lady Miklasova, I did not know."

The margravine crossed her arms. "I was fortunate indeed to endear myself to a margrave or I might have found myself at the mercy of my brother's wife. For who wants a woman that has been set aside?"

Hana's eyes widened. Did her mother somehow bring this about? Or was this an unfortunate circumstance for the margravine that had the appearance of something more? "Lady, I cannot attest to any such knowledge. I did not know."

The woman glared at her as if she might make Hana disappear simply with her own will. But it would not be. Hana was here. And no one, not even Radek's mother, would remove her from him. Not while she still had breath.

"Mother," Lady Galina started again, coming to lay a hand on the margravine's arm. "Come, let me take you somewhere you might sit. You are greatly disturbed."

The margravine resisted for a moment, her gaze piercing into Hana. But at length, she allowed her daughter to take her down the stairs.

As Lady Galina passed, she offered Hana an apologetic look. It seemed as if even she had not known these things that plagued the margravine. What would this mean for Hana's future interactions with her? What would happen when Radek was told of this connection?

Hana closed her eyes and whispered a prayer for strength and for her beloved's recovery. For all would be for naught should Radek slip into eternity.

CHAPTER 37

PATRICIE & STEPAN

S tepan had cheated death once more. He could not believe he yet breathed. But he did. And, more than that, he recovered. It was not on his own merit, however, for Patricie had labored over him. Struggled alongside him. Prayed for him.

How long had they been in this place? The stench from the lack of cleaning and the men that moved about the halls became more than he could stomach. Though the herbs Patricie brewed helped alleviate it somewhat.

He stared at the roof and waited for her to return as he did every morning. Her presence and the occasional visit from his father were the only things that broke up his day. She had been a constant—no matter the depth of the pain or how tenuous his hold on consciousness, she was there.

All the while, he couldn't bear the thought of what may become of her when Father deemed her no longer necessary. Stepan worried after her quite constantly. He was glad she had not stopped sleeping across the room. The small pallet wasn't much, but it eased his concern after her virtue.

The clang of chains told that she returned from whatever errand she had ventured on. Gathering herbs perhaps? She had not been gone long. Perhaps she had stayed close to the inn.

Her chains kept him apprised of her movements, but every *chink* tore into his heart. Must she be kept in this way? With such restriction? Though he knew it to be a compromise, an allowance to permit her better movement throughout the inn.

The door opened, and Stepan drank in the sight of her.

Patricie appeared weary and harried. Having been confined to this place without benefit of tub or basin, her face was streaked, as were her clothes, with his blood and the filth that surrounded this place. Although she had replaited her hair often, it seemed ever in a state of disarray. None of that made her any less in his mind. She was a breath of fresh air and a comfort in his darkness. What had he allowed to happen in his heart? Wasn't he supposed to guard it better?

She neared, setting a tankard on his side table.

He didn't have to ask. It was his tea. Not only did she bring him herbs each day, the pleasant aroma cut through all else.

Patricie heaved a sigh. Was she despondent? Or perhaps it was her work that labored her so? Mayhap even caring for him dragged at her.

"What bothers you?" he ventured but wished he hadn't. Not only because he didn't want her to know he concerned himself with her well-being. But when her eyes set upon him, he noted how they had dulled. Had she given up? Lost all hope?

She did not answer, only shook her head.

That pained him. Her spirit, once so fiery and set at him, now seemed but a faint glimmer. This was damage his father had wrought, and he bore the blame.

Over and over, he considered what had gone from the moment she came upon his escape and was dragged into it. He still believed she would be dead had he not engaged her in the attempt, but he had reason to doubt.

She bent over his leg and checked his bandaging for the hundredth time this week.

"Please," his words were soft out of necessity, for a guard stood watch in the doorway.

She stilled and sat on the edge of his thin mattress and said, "The danger is passed."

Why did that not ease his mind as it should have? He feared she placed herself in a dire situation by making such a pronouncement within earshot of the guard. "And will I keep my leg?"

Shaking her head, she looked to the floor. "There is little more I can do. And no way to determine the extent until you start using it."

He swallowed. How could he admit that he had tried to stand and even put some weight upon it? Would that be a death knell for her? Stepan glanced at the guard in the doorway.

The man glowered at them.

"Leave us," Stepan demanded.

Even as the man shifted his footing, he did nothing to distance himself. Was Stepan not to be heeded? On whose authority? He grimaced—it had to be his father's doing. Did Father suspect he was not to be trusted? Should Father not trust him?

For the tender pull in his heart toward this woman, he knew his father was discerning in his lack of faith. For if it were in his power, Stepan would see Patricie freed.

"Is there anything I can do to make you more comfortable?" Patricie did not look at him.

He set a hand on hers. "Patricie," he breathed.

She only let her hand linger for a moment before she pulled it away.

If she were to assist him, could he overpower the guard? But that would put him at odds with his father...the one person whose good opinion meant everything to him. Could he do that? As he watched her features, pale and marred, he knew he was in danger of doing just that.

Solid footfalls on the stairs brought him back to reality. Someone ventured to the upper level. Who might it be at this hour except his father? His earlier thoughts left him with a heavy feeling of guilt. His father cared for him and had done so much for him. How could he defy the man?

"What goes with my son?" the booming voice entered the room before the viscount became visible.

Patricie stood and dropped her gaze. Was she so beaten down?

The larger man stepped within the space and eyed the occupants. "I asked you a question, healer."

"He continues to improve." Her words were simple and quiet.

Father glanced between Patricie and the guard. "Leave us."

With those words, the guard stepped forward and gripped Patricie's arm, tugging her to the door.

Everything in Stepan cried out against it, but he did not utter a word. Would it do anything after all? Other than paint him a traitor?

As the sound of the chain faded and ceased, Stepan focused on his father and worked to calm the pounding of his heart. "What do you have need of, Father?"

"Spare me," the viscount thundered. "I have seen what I care not to."

What did he say? What had he seen? But Stepan remained silent. It would be best to let his father work out his anger as he intended. Speaking to it never made it better.

"I have seen how it is between you and that...Hussite." Father glared at him, raising a finger and pointing to him. "I won't have it. I cannot imagine how you thought it would end, but she will be eliminated as soon as she outlives her usefulness. This you know. This you pretend not to know."

Stepan firmed his jaw. "Father, I do not think that—"

"Stop!" Father said, throwing his hands up. "You are meant for more than this—a warrior, a nobleman, my *son*. I will not see you throw your life away on a peasant, one whose days are very short at that."

Stepan looked to the wall. He wanted to side with his father, but he feared the emotions coursing through him would be too easily seen in his eyes.

"Be done with this now." Father turned toward the door. "Or you may find your own end soon after she has met hers." Then the viscount walked out.

Could his father mean that? Would he see his own son—his only son, his heir—run through? By his own men? It didn't seem possible. But Stepan knew better than to underestimate his father.

Patricie sat as still as possible where the guard had shoved her onto a bench just outside the inn. What did the viscount want to speak to Stepan about? She found that she had cause to worry after him. But why?

Stepan had reached out to her more than once. Still, she could not overcome her disparagement or her anger at him. Had he not forced her to come with them, she would be with her people, with the Hussite camp, safe and secure.

As many times as she told herself this, she knew it wasn't true. He had done what he could to preserve her life. Or prolong it, as it were. For the moment she stepped into his room back in Nemecky Brod, her life was forfeit. She must accept that.

It wasn't long before the door opened, and Viscount Dvorak stepped out. Then, as he took in the scene, he whirled on Patricie. "You will see my son is walking within two days."

"My lord, I cannot possibly speed the healing of—"

"I said you have two days." The man's face reddened. "It is beyond time we left this godforsaken place and returned to the Empire."

Patricie looked to the ground. "I will do what I can."

The viscount let out a *hrumph* and moved off.

What was she to do? Stepan was more than capable by now of

standing and perhaps even walking. But that would spell certain death for her.

She hadn't much time to consider it before the guard gripped her upper arm and half dragged her up the stairs. He thrust her into the room and sneered. "You heard him."

Stepan drew in a breath as she hit the floor. But when she looked at him, his expression was placid and hard. What had happened between him and his father?

Patricie lifted herself with effort, working with the chain had not become easier. Still, it hindered her movements. That was its purpose, after all. She stepped to the bed and looked at Stepan. "Can you lift yourself up?"

He glanced at the guard and then back at her. "I will."

Using his arms, he pressed up into a sitting position. He then swung his legs over the side of the bed and winced.

"You must take your time," she admonished. It wouldn't do to reopen the wound. Would that see her spared for another fortnight, or would the viscount give up on her abilities? And possibly his son?

She couldn't allow that. For as much as she angered, as much as she regretted some things, she still had a care for him. One that she could disguise but not extinguish completely.

"Let us try." She set an arm under his right side and pulled upward as he tugged at her. Then he was on his feet. And more stable than she'd have thought. It pleased her in an odd way. For first and foremost, she was a healer and her patient had made progress.

Creaking of the floorboards told that the guard moved.

She glanced up to see him step into the corridor, but she knew he would remain just outside. From time to time, he seemed to bore of these interactions and give himself some distance.

When she looked back at Stepan, she noted that his gaze had followed hers.

But she turned to the side and said, "Let us take a few steps. Lean on me if you must."

He nodded.

She slid her foot forward as he shuffled his right leg alongside hers. But when he leaned against that leg, it gave way, and his weight was on her shoulder.

Holding firmly to him, she pressed against his side to offer more stability.

He cursed under his breath. Because of his inability to walk? Or because of the situation and all it contained?

"Again," she commanded. If nothing else, she would see this through. Even though it would likely be the last thing she did.

Pressing against his good leg again, he forced his weaker leg forward. Then, as he stepped onto that leg, he trusted her more and the step was more secure.

"No more," he said.

She wondered at that. Was he not eager to move about on his own again, or was it something else? "For now."

He all but fell back onto the bed after she helped him hobble back.

She drew the blanket over him. As she leaned down, he grasped her hand.

"Do you..." he heaved as he spoke, "remember what you told? That you cared because God Himself cared for me?"

She wanted to look away from the intensity of his eyes. She wanted to lie and say she did not. But she nodded.

"Is that still true?"

Her heart ached for the vacancy in his stare. Was there no life left in him? She grazed his brow with her free hand. Then pulled it to herself. Why had she done that?

"No." The word was choked out, and she bit her lip to stop furthering her confession. Would she be undone if she admitted that she had become more involved than just that? She cared more deeply than she had any sense to?

He released her. "As I thought."

She stood and backed away as he shifted to face opposite.

A part of her wondered at the danger of letting him see her heart, but another part did not wish to bear his scorn, regardless of how many days she had remaining to her life. So, she slipped back and, with nothing else to do with herself, slid onto her pallet. She was sure to face the wall and keep her tears silent.

CHAPTER 38
KARIN & PAVEL

P avel ushered Zdenek into his solar. He was pleased to see his friend, but not as much as he could be. The moment he needed with Karin had been disrupted and then dismissed. It would be all right, he assured himself. He would find her after his talk with Zdenek and they would set things in place. They always did. There was something in that he could trust.

But for now, he turned his attention to his friend. Something about Zdenek's manner told that this was no social call. So as soon as they were within the solar and the door was secured, Pavel said, "I am pleased you have come, but let's not make the waters murky. What have you come to tell me?"

"I have news of Stepan."

What might he mean? Had death claimed their former friend?

"He has disappeared," Zdenek's words were spoken in a matter-of-fact way. "All signs point to an escape."

"Oh?" Pavel quirked an eyebrow. It didn't catch him so off-guard. It was only a matter of time before Stepan's desire to be rid of the Hussite camp and the Viscount's plethora of resources made it possible.

But that wasn't all. Zdenek's features turned, a darkness had shrouded his manner.

"What else?"

"He took Eva's sister with him."

"The healer's apprentice? He would risk the woman who but attempted to save his life and limb?" This, too, unfortunately did not surprise. Stepan's depravity these last few years of war did not allow for it.

Zdenek nodded. "Eva is quite...out of sorts. That is one of the reasons I brought her. I hoped Lady Karin might alleviate some of her sadness. If possible."

"How long will you linger?" Pavel asked, sensing there was yet more Zdenek did not say.

Zdenek let out a breath. "It cannot be as long as I wish." He paused, then, as if gathering himself to push on, he continued, "You know that General Zizka has returned to Tabor?"

"Yes, I have understood that to be the case." Pavel had known of this. And that Prince Korybut of Poland, Vytautas's nephew and regent, had been at work, bringing all things in the Czech lands into order and under his authority. This had given Zizka a reprieve and he had made his way back to Tabor to do what he did best—recruit and train men for the battles they may face.

"What of it?" Pavel asked as he sat.

"The people in Tabor tempt the idea of insurrection. But General Zizka seems to think he owes Prince Korybut his allegiance." Zdenek spoke of things that were, as well, known. To what end?

"Aye." Pavel held to what patience remained in him.

"There is word of Sigismund's work to organize another crusade into Bohemia."

Pavel's eyebrows arched. "Oh?" Had the man no sense of when it was time to give up? Two crusades into Bohemia, two terrible losses on the part of the Royalists loyal to him.

"There is an edict going out to the princes and cities in the Holy Roman Empire."

"Yes?" Why must Zdenek dole out information as if it must be savored?

"Every unit of the empire must provide cavalry and infantry to the effort."

Pavel's eyes widened. This could not have come at a worse time. All of Bohemia filled with strife and dissension. Would the people be able to rally an opposing force while there was inner fighting?

But this was not all. It couldn't be. Zdenek must have another reason in coming. All of this could have been delivered through a trusted messenger.

"And you have been sent to bring me back to Tabor." It was a statement.

Zdenek studied his friend, but at length he assented. "Aye."

Pavel stood and moved to the window. Could he leave his family once more? Could he sit by and not answer his general's summons?

"It is not my intention to push you," Zdenek said, rising. "But the need is great."

Pavel nodded even as he held up a hand to halt his friend. Then he turned to look upon the man who had known him better than most.

Zdenek was the picture of determination.

Strange how a man drafted into the war effort had become so set on the Hussite cause. It was indeed just one more miracle to come from this conflict. His friend had found a place, and a purpose.

Pavel walked to Zdenek. "My general calls." He held out his arm. "I will answer it."

Zdenek slid his hand to clasp Pavel's forearm as Pavel gripped his. They were in this...together. Czechs united. Pavel prayed all would heed the same call and fight with their countrymen for what was right and good and true.

Karin settled into a chair by the fire. And she watched as Eva took the seat opposite. All was well, and all had calmed after the arrival of her and Pavel's dear friends. Except with Eva. She seemed distracted at best, distraught in truth.

"Has something happened?" Karin's words were tentative, seeking.

Eva shook her head and looked down. Would she not speak of it?

Karin leaned forward and set a hand to Eva's arm. "I can see you are worried with something."

Was it to do with whatever had brought her and Zdenek to Krejik castle?

Eva's gaze met Karin's. "It is my sister."

"Your sister? Is she in danger?"

Eva sniffled and nodded. "She has been taken."

Was this what Zdenek came to ask Pavel—to assist in recovering the woman? "How long?"

"Some weeks. The viscount's son, Lord Stepan Dvorak, escaped at the same time. She was seen leaving with him."

Eva's sister was at the mercy of Viscount Dvorak? Karin fought the urge to shudder. The man had not seemed dangerous, until she had crossed his family.

"I will pray." It was what Karin could offer.

There was a gleam in Eva's eyes as she met Karin's gaze, but her focus soon shifted to Jaromir, in Karin's arms.

Karin wondered, not for the first time, if Eva bore a secret in her womb.

"Your son is handsome indeed," Eva said, only glancing at Karin briefly before watching the child once more.

Karin joined her in admiring Jaromir. "That he is. And so lively."

When Karin met Eva's gaze again, something passed through her friend's eyes. She could not miss it, no matter how she wished not to see it, not to understand. But there it was, plain and evident—Eva longed for a baby. Still, there was more than that—a deep sorrow was easy to see.

Karin reached between them and grasped Eva's hand once more. "You think of your sister?"

Eva looked to the fire and did nothing to wipe at the moisture collecting in her eyes.

"Is something amiss with you and Zdenek?" Though she asked, Karin knew the challenge Eva faced was deeper.

Eva shook her head. "He is wonderful. I am truly happy. More so than I have ever been."

"Then what is it?"

The dark-haired woman met Karin's concern with tears. "I fear I will never hold a babe of my own."

Eva's pain stabbed at Karin's heart as well. She could have guessed it but never would have wanted to suspect such. "What makes you feel that is true?"

Shaking her head, Eva looked to their clasped hands. "Zdenek and I have not yet a sign of a babe, and much time has passed."

"Do you have reason to think you won't ever—"

Finally wiping at the tears, Eva chewed at her lower lip. "I have seen a midwife and a healer. There is no reason I have not borne Zdenek a child."

"That is hopeful," Karin said, but she didn't get the sense that it was.

"Though there is no answer as to why not. There remains little to be done, and little hope that it will be."

"Oh, Eva, you can't think like that." Karin found herself fighting her own tears.

"Nor can I continue to hope in vain."

Karin had no words. But she held her friend's hand and let her release her sadness.

Movement across the Great Hall drew her attention.

The dowager baroness had come down the stairs. As she saw Karin, she smiled. "I wondered if you were about."

Was that a reference to her disappearance last eve? Had Pavel made excuses for her? Or shared with his mother what truly went between them?

"Yes. Lady Eva was telling me how handsome your grandson is."

Karin noted how Eva tensed at her raised volume. It was such a habit for sake of the dowager baroness's difficulty hearing, she had not even realized she yelled.

"He is indeed." Pavel's mother strode across the room. "May I join you?"

Karin looked to Eva.

"Please do so, Lady," Eva said, straightening her posture.

Any reluctance or feeling she needed to present a certain way to the dowager baroness was wholly unnecessary. Pavel's mother was truly one of the kindest women she knew.

The older woman hid her confusion over Eva's gently spoken response. Another learned behavior, and she sat before holding out her arms toward her grandson.

Karin handed over the bundle of wiggling limbs.

Then Karin's mother-in-law tucked Jaromir to her chest and sighed.

Karin only then thought about what else occurred last night beyond the meal she had missed. "Whatever became of Martin of Pisek?"

"Who?" Lady Krejikova asked. "Oh, the man with the Writ."

Karin nodded, hoping her interest wasn't too noticeable.

"He delivered the Scriptures and departed this morning to journey to his next appointment."

His next appointment?

Lady Krejikova must have noted her confusion, for the woman continued, "He is a book seller."

"Ah." She nodded. "And you saw need to acquire a Holy Writ?"

"Of course."

Here it was. Pavel had told her and now the woman would announce Karin's secret in the Great Hall for anyone to hear. Karin opened her mouth to distract from the topic, but her mother-in-law spoke in haste.

"We have a priest coming to Krejik castle and so we have need for a Writ in our library. As you could have guessed, my lord husband's copy was destroyed in the fire."

Had Pavel not, then, told his mother of Karin's secret work? Was this truly happenstance, or rather the workings of the Almighty, bringing all these things to pass in good order?

Karin sighed and leaned back.

"Are you tired, Lady Karin?" Eva's concern was plain on her face.

"No. All is well," Karin assured her. "All is well indeed."

CHAPTER 39
HANA & RADEK

Hana sat with Radek throughout the night. Much to the dismay of Mistress Huddard, her very vocal dismay. But Hana would not hear it. Radek might need her, and she would be here.

If she didn't know otherwise, she would believe he only lay sleeping. His wounds had been cleaned and bandaged, the bleeding ceased, and all was as it should be. The healer did not know when he would waken but was confident he would.

That was well enough with Hana. Still, she waited. And pondered the earlier interaction with the margravine.

Despite their differences, Lady Galina had impressed today, and there seemed to be somewhat of a truce between them. They had worked side by side and tended Radek without a cross word. And she had perhaps softened to Hana's situation after the confrontation hours past.

Margravine Miklasova was another story. She had disappeared altogether. As much as the woman had wounded Hana, she still hoped that someone had kept her informed of Radek's injuries. And that he yet lay unconscious.

Hana would wager that that to be true. Though the margravine had not been to her son's bedside at any time. Was she so averse to Hana that she would not sit in the same room any longer?

It mattered not, Hana decided as she looked at the face of her beloved. The fact that she was here and would not leave his side was of utmost importance. For Radek should not wake to an empty room. And he wouldn't.

The door creaked.

Hana turned.

The healer stepped within. "How does he fare?"

"The same." Hana tried to keep her disappointment from her voice.

The healer moved closer to the bed, watching her lord's son. "He will waken, but he is due his rest."

Hana nodded. The healer was right, of course. It was true that Hana's desire for Radek to waken may be a selfish one. His rest was merited and deserved.

As the healer set the back of her fingers to Radek's forehead, Hana grabbed for his hand, as if he needed reassurance that all was well.

Pressing her hand also to the side of his face, the healer then said, "He does not burn with any hint of fever. I believe he will arise soon enough."

Hana pressed Radek's hand.

He tightened his fingers around hers.

"He squeezed my hand," Hana exclaimed.

The healer glanced at Hana with a curious look upon her face, then she reached for his other hand. As Hana watched, she pressed his hand as well.

Then her face lit. "He tries to wake. It won't be long now."

Hana's gaze drifted to Radek's face. His mouth twisted. Was he becoming aware of his pain?

"I will brew a tea for him," the healer said before moving off.

Hana nodded absently. Her whole world was focused on Radek

and the movements he now made, subtle at first but becoming bigger by the second.

She leaned over him, running a hand down the side of his face. "Radek," she whispered.

He groaned. Did he ache?

"Radek, I am here." She let her fingers dip into the smoothness of his hair.

He shifted his head toward her, as if drawn to her touch.

"Come back to me." The words were broken as emotion overwhelmed her. She needed him to be all right. Her very heartbeat depended on it.

Then his eyes slid open.

She brought his hand to her lips but could not form words.

He closed his eyes and grimaced. How badly did he ache? Then he turned his head and set eyes upon her.

"Yes, I am here." She stroked his hair again. "And I'm not leaving."

The corner of his mouth twitched as if it would lift. "What..." he croaked, but tried again, "Where am I?"

"You are in your chamber. You are injured."

His opposite hand moved toward his head.

She halted its progress. "Yes. It is the back of your head. It is bandaged and needs not be touched."

He threaded his fingers with hers. "Was there an attack?"

"It is not clear what befell you, but all else is well here."

That seemed to give him some manner of relief. "And you?"

A tear trailed down her face. "As you see, I am well enough."

He closed his eyes again and seemed to find rest in that knowledge.

"Please don't rush. The healer brews a pain tea even now. Are you in pain?"

"I...some. But it is not bad." He met her gaze, this time the lightness about his features was more evident.

She leaned in and pressed a kiss to his lips. "I am glad to hear it."

Dare she speak to her fears? Tell him of the way the whole incident had affected her? Or of the earlier conflict—and ensuing revelation—with his mother? In the end, Hana decided it was not important in this moment. He was awake and well. She would be thankful in that.

Radek gingerly touched the back of his head. He had healed much in the last week and was glad for it. How he loathed being abed and being forced to rest. It was not in his nature to be still. Even now, he descended the stairs, intent on rejoining the living.

His mother's outburst and accusation of Hana had been told. But not by Hana, by Galina. She had been striken indeed to find that the woman who had been a constant in their life had harbored such a secret from them. And such anger.

No sooner did Radek reach the Great Hall when Hana was at his side. Her hands came around his arm and she beamed. "How are you this evening?"

"As well as I was last eve." His words brought a smile to her face.

"I am glad."

He resisted the urge to taste her lips. She had proven herself capable and true these last days. Anything he needed, she saw to its doing. And somehow, she had made headway with healing the rift between herself and his sister.

"Lady Galina's betrothed is here," Hana said as she looped an arm through his.

He had understood that the knight would return this day, though he had anticipated that someone would inform him upon the man's arrival. Still, he nodded to Hana and led her toward the gathering crowd.

Radek scanned the group for his sister. Surely, she would be with the man, or perhaps his father might monopolize him. Father had told that the knight was a fine man, the second son of a duke, and had distinguished himself enough to gain the hand of a wealthy margrave's daughter.

There, near the hearth, Galina stood on the arm of a sturdy figure. He appeared every bit as Radek had anticipated. His dark hair matched Galina's, and he stood with some bulk about him. Even then, Father spoke with the man.

"Shall we make our way over?" Hana asked, seeking Radek's regard.

He smiled at her. "Perhaps in a minute. I would have a turn about the room with you."

Her lips widened, and she tightened her hold on his arm. "As you will, my lord."

They moved through what space there was around the people gathered in the Great Hall. Radek nodded to those who greeted them, but he wanted to just enjoy the feel of Hana next to him, of the goodwill that surrounded them.

There had been little headway made concerning the identity of his attackers nor on Hana's poisoning. It frustrated, but after his close encounter with his own end, he wished to take hold of these pleasing things and savor them. As they neared the hearth, he found reason to pause.

"Will you speak with your sister? Let her introduce you to her knight?" Hana seemed quite eager herself to make the man's acquaintance.

There was little reason, if any, to put it off any longer. He turned them that way and approached the small group.

"Radek," Galina called. "Come!"

He paused some feet away from his parents and Galina.

"This is Sir Filip, the champion who won your sister's hand," Radek's father said as Radek came to a stop. "And no small task that."

"Oh, fie!" Galina frowned.

"It is good to finally make your acquaintance." Sir Filip bowed slightly. His voice was deeper than Radek expected, but it was familiar. Had they met? The man was not as aged as Radek would have expected. He couldn't be more than five years Galina's senior.

"The pleasure is mine." How was Radek to tell the knight he had not heard much about him? Galina had perhaps been too distracted making life harder for Hana than informing her brother about her betrothed. "Tell me, how long have you served my father?"

"Two years." The man swept his gaze over the gathering. "I have enjoyed little more than learning under your father's leadership."

Strange thing, that. Radek considered the man. For the margrave's ways were rather unconventional. But he had to admit, they were effective. Perhaps the knight spoke true.

"You seem familiar. Have we crossed paths?"

"I fear not, my lord. I have been away these past months since your arrival." The man shifted and placed a hand over Galina's on his arm.

That was odd indeed. Radek was more and more certain he knew this man.

"Shall we get settled for the meal?" Radek's father broke into the moment.

The others nodded and made their way to their seats. Radek was positioned between his father and Hana. Sir Filip was settled on the other side of Father and a couple of seats away. Radek continued to puzzle after the man. How had he been in contact with this man who had just earlier today returned from a long absence?

Hana engaged the woman to her other side in conversation.

Radek attempted to attend to his father's comments, but he was quite distracted. It was probably nothing, he decided. Still, his mind worked.

As the meal commenced, Father spoke with Sir Filip, leaving Radek to his thoughts.

"What of this amassing of forces beyond the border?" the margrave said as he turned his attention to his trencher. Was that for Radek? Or Sir Filip?

The knight answered. "It is curious. And concerning. With much of General Zizka's forces depleted, there is reason to question if the man will enjoy more victories."

"He has proven himself quite capable. I am certain his efforts to train and prepare men for battle will be fruitful." The margrave tested the venison.

"And what of Prince Korybut? He will become engaged as well, shall he not?" Sir Filip certainly had much to say.

"The Czech people do not seem to agree on his regency. Will he have the manpower he needs? Will he be able to garner their support at large?"

"I daresay he may not be ready at present," Sir Filip said, leaning forward, "But he will be."

The words struck him. He had heard them. From this man.

Radek's mind shifted to another place—the forest. He lay on the ground, and this very voice spoke above him. Was Sir Filip the culprit? Was that possible?

CHAPTER 40
PATRICIE & STEPAN

Patricie's shoulders ached from effort. She had been working with Stepan for the last two hours. His steps improved much, but they were still far too uneven. They'd been at it most of the day, as the viscount had insisted he be on his feet and steady by the morrow.

She could not help what the closeness did to her. Though she knew not why she permitted such thoughts and feelings. Even were he not noble and she a merchant's daughter, even if he were not set on destroying the Hussite cause, still his father would never let her live. That made any future, much less one with Stepan, as impossible as it could be.

But how to stop her body from flushing? Her heart from racing when he looked at her? Whatever had begun in that inn in Nemecky Brod had taken hold of her.

"Let's pause," Stepan's words broke into her thoughts.

She started to move him back to the bed, but he held fast. "Are you well?"

"Aye. Just a bit...spent."

"Then we must get you to the bed."

His eyes searched hers.

How was she to shy away from such intensity?

"I remember well," he said before licking his lips.

What did that mean? What did he refer to?

"Those days," he continued, but stopped.

Was he, too, reminiscing about the times spent at that inn? The day he comforted and embraced her? This seemed a far cry from that. But was it?

"You cannot know how I..." He paused, seeming to consider his next words. "How I wish things were different."

Yes, she wished it, too.

A rush of realization filled her. She may well be set to meet God by this time tomorrow. It was clear that Stepan did not need her assistance as much as he seemed to. There was little reason for the viscount to keep her alive. Still, she fought giving in to despair, for that would do nothing.

"Patricie," he said, his entreaty drawing her attention. "I cannot let my father..."

There was no need to finish. She knew. But it bothered all the same. Her regard fell to the floor.

"I cannot," he insisted.

Patricie nodded. She refused to let the emotion overcome her. She would be strong. She would.

He lowered his voice. "And I will help you."

She jerked her head and set eyes on his once more. "Help me?" The words were but a breath. What could he mean? He wasn't strong enough to fight off so many. Even if he would be able to defy his father, something she doubted possible.

"I would see you freed." His eyes were sorrowful. Because of what he suggested? Was he prepared to die to see this happen?

She shook her head. The journey to his wholeness had been long and fraught with challenges. They had seen them through. She did not wish to sacrifice him now, but she could not press down the part of her that wanted to live. "How?" she mouthed, glancing at the door where the guard had stepped out.

"Put me abed and call for the guard." His tone had become more confident, more set.

She weighed the likely outcome with the chance for freedom. If he would help her, it may be worth the risk.

Nodding, she assisted as he half limped half dragged himself to the bed. Settling him upon the thin mattress, she leaned over to cover him.

He caught her hand. A long look passed between them—and it was filled with the tension they had always had between what they were and what they wished to be.

Lifting his hand, he cupped the side of her face. "Know that I have...come to admire you greatly."

She knew as much. Though she had cause to question it. His words, rather than assuage her heart, gave way to a deep ache.

"And I..." she started but caught herself.

He traced her lips with the pad of his thumb.

She fought the swell of emotion.

"Aye," he whispered. And, leaning up, claimed her mouth.

It was bliss and it was brief. Then he lay back and closed his eyes. "Call for him."

A moment passed before she was able to pull herself from their moment and into this one. And she understood. He intended to eliminate their biggest obstacle. This was it.

"Help," she called as she backed away slightly. "Guard, help!"

The footfalls that drew near would either signal their doom...or a hope to come.

Stepan lay as still as possible as Patricie called. He pressed his feelings to the side and prepared himself for action. He was thankful he had healed well, but he wished for a dagger. He would have to take the guard's weapon and dispose of him—a much bigger task, what infirmity remained about him notwithstanding.

The clomping of boots upon the floor drew near.

"What is amiss?" the man grumbled.

"It is Lord Dvorak," she whimpered, her skills of deception largely underestimated by the sound of it. "He struggles to breathe."

Nothing.

"Help me move him!"

Footsteps came closer. Stepan strained his muscles to keep still and remain at the ready.

A presence leaned over him. He prayed it was the guard. Did the man hold his sword? Or was it still sheathed? He would bet his life that it was. And he did place such a wager.

"He breathes," the man said. "What do you—?"

Stepan struck. He rose up, throwing his fist at the man's face. In the same second, he grasped for the man's weapon.

The guard made a noise but was soon silenced. Had he struck the man so hard? Indeed, the man lay upon the floor, blood spurting from his nose.

Patricie dropped beside him, moving hands over his neck. Then she looked up. "He lives."

Stepan nodded as he sat upright. That had been accomplished without much effort. He prayed the remainder of their attempt would be likewise. Only, he realized he was not in possession of the man's weapon.

Sliding legs from under the blanket, he then stood. Dare he try to kneel and collect the sword? Would he be able to get back on his feet?

"His dagger and his sword," Stepan said to Patricie. "Give them to me."

She did not appear eager to collect them, but she obeyed. He was amazed at how aptly she found and relieved the man of those things.

"Now we must bind him. Is there anything we might..."

"I have bandages." She moved to her pallet and brought back strips of cloth that could only have come from her skirts.

He glanced down and spotted more of her ankles than he should. "Aye. Now secure his hands and feet." It would be better perhaps for him to add his effort to hers, but he needed to preserve what strength he had.

She made quick work of tying his wrists and ankles together.

"Now his mouth."

Her movements stilled. Was she less sure about doing so?

"We must," Stepan encouraged her. "And if there are more strips, we should tie him to something in the room.

She nodded, then pressed the cloth between the man's teeth and knotted it behind his head.

Stepan did not miss that she took a moment to ensure he could still breathe. Such was his kind healer. Though the guard would have felled her with but a word from Stepan's father, she did not wish death upon him.

Patricie went back to her pallet but soon returned. "I have nothing else."

His eyes flitted to her hem.

She bent and, lifting her skirt to her knees, tore at her chemise.

Stepan looked away as she did so.

As she stepped toward the guard once more, Stepan moved alongside her. "Secure it to his bindings and hand the other end to me."

She obeyed.

He took the opposite side of the cloth and tied it to the bed post. It was not the best, but it would have to hold until he and Patricie created some distance between them and this place.

Turning back to her, he said, "Now the keys."

"Keys?" She didn't seem to understand.

He pointed down to the chain between her feet. That rattling would give them away and the confinement would slow their escape. "Does the guard have the key?"

365

She dropped to her knees and ran hands over the man's pockets. After moments that seemed to drag on, she pulled the brass piece free. Then she worked the lock and was soon unencumbered.

He reached for Patricie's hand and, clinging to the stolen sword, moved toward the door.

CHAPTER 41
KARIN & PAVEL

Karin leaned over a parchment. She had been up in the early hours of the day, working. And she neared the end of the book of Jeremiah. How had she accomplished so much in so little time? A miracle to be sure. For certain, God enabled her to do this.

The rustle of movement beyond the library gave her pause. Should she hide her things? But the person whose footsteps she heard emerged from the dark corridor before she could make a move to do so.

Pavel.

They had not been in company much since their return to Krejik lands, and there seemed more to say, but she waited for him to finish what he had started. Should she not? Perhaps she might try put herself forth and attempt to ease the tension.

He relaxed into his stance and offered a slight smile. Did the situation merit that? Was this a peace offering?

She set her things to the side and stood, facing her husband, and let the edges of her lips lift in response.

"I have wronged you." Pavel's voice seemed as if pleading.

369

"No. It was I who—"

"I do not admit wrongdoing in my actions, but in my manner. It was harsher than necessary, and I know I injured you." He took a step closer.

She nodded, a stinging in her eyes. Tears would come should she not stop them. "I thank you, husband. I also need your pardon, for I trespassed into a moment that did not need it."

He dipped his head but did not take his eyes off her.

"Then all is well. Is it not?" She stepped to him, closing the distance. Her hands outstretched, she wondered why he did not reach for her. Should he not be embracing her now? A sense of foreboding overcame her.

"It is." He hesitated. "But there is more."

"More?" What else was there to work out?

"I must take my leave." His words were solid and sure then.

"What?" She furrowed her brow. He would leave? Why?

"Sigismund gathers an effort to invade Bohemia once more. General Zizka is in need of fighting men, and I must answer." He put his hands out, grasping for hers.

She pulled back. "You must? I don't understand. Why *must* you?"

"You know why I must." He stepped closer, taking her hands in his. "The general relies on me. And I believe in our cause. How can I turn away?"

A part of her wondered at her resistance to this summons. How did she not understand yet? He would not abandon his men or their efforts. But the larger portion of her ached. How could she endure another battle? Another separation?

"I fear I cannot watch you ride off again." There was a catch in her voice.

"Don't you believe in our freedom from tyranny? Freedom to worship God and seek Him as His word teaches?"

"I...do," she admitted.

"Then?" His eyes were seeking and his gaze tender.

She fell against his chest, wrapping arms around him and burying her face. And she let her tears come.

He pressed a kiss to the top of her head. "I know, my love. I know."

She shook her head against him. How could he understand the torture she went through in his absence? The not knowing?

"But I cannot shirk my calling. I will not." He leaned back and tipped her chin up so that she looked into his eyes. "No more than you could."

Yes, she conceded. That was the way of it. Had God let her experience the journey with no hope of completing her mission so that she would have such understanding in this moment?

It was good and it was right, but it wasn't fair. Nothing about this was fair. Had she not sacrificed enough? She reminded herself that God did not want any less than all of her. This was His call upon their family. Had she herself not risked them with her actions to follow God's direction?

She leaned into him once more. "Aye."

Though no more words were spoken, they were covered with a grace that went beyond anything they could say.

Pavel rode on. The journey had already been longer than he'd have wished it. And they had left not two hours ago. But saying farewell to Karin, Jaromir, and his mother had been difficult. More so than he ever remembered. And though they had not been on horseback for long, there would be a place for them to pause and refresh the horses just as they passed out of Krejik lands. Might he take a moment there?

He glanced to his side at Zdenek. The man was ever the faithful friend and a good man at that, but he'd had his own troubles upon leaving. Lady Eva was, as Karin, clearly not pleased to be left behind. What might their interactions the eve before have been? Probably much like his and Karin's. There was nothing for it. Leaving a loving wife behind was heart-wrenching.

Pavel trusted Sir Marek with his family's safety. None were more capable. But would the knight care for them as if they were his own? Though the thought dragged at Pavel, he knew it to be true. The man was honorable. He would defend his charges with his life if necessary.

They neared the place where the stream passed off to the right.

"Hold," Pavel called. "Let us give the horses respite."

He maneuvered his destrier in the direction of where he knew the stream to be. Zdenek followed closely, as well as the other two knights that traveled along. In a matter of moments, the horses were drinking and grazing. The men had seen to their own relief and gathered to recheck their saddles.

Zdenek had been rather quiet, so unlike him. Where were the days with no care about them? Those days they hunted at the chateau? It had been a simpler time. Pavel let his mind wander back to those early days of his friendship with Karin—which was never just a friendship.

How he longed for that freedom they knew. All had changed. He and his friends had weathered many storms and had known war. Would they ever return to those days when all they worried about was how to pass their time and how best to woo their ladies? Not that he would change the victories or the trials—for they made his marriage what it was, and he cherished that.

The reason for Zdenek's silence may echo his own...thoughts of times long past.

Pavel prepared to bid the small party back to horseback when thundering upon the earth halted him. He looked to the horizon—at least as far as he could see—in the direction of the sound as best as he could determine.

There, cresting the hill, were mounted men, and they made straight for Krejik lands.

What of his family? Would he and these knights become a line of defense for the castle?

"On your guard!" Pavel called as he hoisted himself into the saddle.

But then sense took hold—how were they to fight off so many? There must be at least thirty in the swarming pack. No matter, they had to defend these lands and their loved ones.

The men with Pavel pulled into their saddles and drew their swords. He knew that they, too, were prepared to sacrifice themselves for sake of those but a short distance away.

Pavel watched as the horde came. Who were they? What was their purpose?

"Now," he commanded.

The knights with him moved into action, urging their horses onward and toward the coming threat. But as they neared, the mass broke into two lines and encircled them. There was naught Pavel and his men could do about it. Was it not, then, the intention to fight but to capture? For sooth, it seemed so. Who would want to take Pavel and his men prisoner? And for what reason?

"Stand down," Pavel shouted. If any of his knights rushed forward, it would not be sacrifice, but suicide.

A larger man came from off to the left. He had the bearings of nobility. Did he lead these men? Pavel could do naught but wait for the situation to unfold.

The line broke for their commander and lord to come through. And he did, stopping just short of where Pavel's horse stood.

"What do you seek?" Pavel demanded.

The man set his steely gaze on Pavel. "You."

"And just what can you possibly want with me?" Pavel narrowed his eyes and searched the face he was certain he did not recognize.

"You do not know who I am?" the man's deep voice boomed.

Pavel was uncertain how to answer, so he seamed his lips.

The man laughed. "I am Ulrich of Rosenburg."

It took everything in Pavel to not launch himself forward. This was his father's murderer.

CHAPTER 42
HANA & RADEK

Radek stared at Sir Filip. But when the man's eyes met his, he looked away. How to keep the villain in his sights but not give away that he did? For Radek did not want to tip his hand too soon. He had to get Hana and his family to safety. And quickly.

The expression on Sir Filip's face betrayed that something more rippled under the surface.

Radek turned to Hana. "I need you to get my father, mother, and sister to safety.

"What goes?" she whispered, leaning close.

"There is no time. Trust me." He met Hana's gaze and grabbed for her hand, squeezing it, then releasing her as he set a hand to his sword hilt under the table.

"Margrave Miklas," Hana said as she rose, "Might I trouble you for a moment?"

"What is it, Lady Hana?" Father turned toward her.

"I must speak with you in private," she entreated. Although her features were set in a pleasant way, there was a slight tremor in her voice.

Radek risked a glance at Sir Filip, who watched on with bated breath.

Father moved to rise, but mother placed a hand on his arm. "You most certainly will not leave in the midst of a meal. It is unseemly." Her gaze flitted to Hana, a look of scorn about her. "I should think a duke's daughter would know this at the very least."

The margrave appeared torn. As if he did not wish to defy his wife. Would he not press into his own desires? But Radek knew better. His father was not a man of action or of harsh words.

Sir Filip glanced about the members of the small family. Did he calculate his next move?

Radek must seize this opportunity. He thrust upward from his seat, pulling his sword in the same moment, then leapt across the table and was in Sir Filip's face in a moment.

The knave had only time to rise and reach for his own sword, but he had only started to pull it from its sheath when Radek's blade met his shoulder.

"Do not," Radek demanded.

He noted in his periphery that Hana tugged his sister and mother to her side of the great table.

Sir Filip looked about him. Did he seek salvation from some-where? From one of the men who had sworn fealty to Radek's father?

Radek prayed none would be so vile as to betray their lord. What was there to gain? "I know what you have done."

"What I have...what?" Sir Filip stammered, shooting a glance at Galina and then the margrave. "I think your son's brain has become addled, my lord. He speaks nonsense."

"No," Radek cut him off. "It was you. The attack on my person and likely the attempt on my betrothed."

Sir Filip glared at Radek, his eyes growing dark.

"Why? Did you think to have Galina inherit all should I perish?"

The man sneered. "Do not think that I wasted all this time endearing myself to your father to have him give everything to you.

Why would I? You are a whelp like your father. Neither of you are strong enough to hold these lands."

Why did the man not seem fearful? He was surrounded.

Movement off to the left threatened to distract. Hana gasped and Mother screamed.

Radek held fast to his position but dared a glance.

One of the margrave's knights had grabbed Hana from behind and held a blade to her throat.

No!

Sir Filip launched himself at Radek in his moment of surprise.

Radek jumped to the side and slid downward, dragging his sword across Sir Filip's shoulder.

The man cried out and grabbed for his wound.

"Guards," the margrave called.

"No!" Sir Filip shouted, holding out his uninjured arm in Hana's direction. "Not if you care for the lady to live."

Indeed, the man holding Hana tightened his grip.

Radek backed away a step, but only just.

"This is madness!" the margrave declared, his shock evident in the slight tremble of his voice.

Radek only then had the chance to look upon the man who held Hana. There was something about him. And then Radek knew...this was the man Radek had followed the day he was attacked. But what had drawn Radek so about this nondescript guard?

Images of another battle filled his mind—fighting against the brigands who sought to kill his father. They were not common thieves at all, but trained knights. That's why they seemed so strange to him. Were they not, then, after father, but after Radek?

All of this...was to finish Radek. Not Father. Probably not even Hana. The blade that day, the food the following week...all had been meant for him.

"Give up," Radek held his position, his sword hand firm and unwavering. "There is no chance you will escape this place. Not with your life."

"Kill her," Sir Filip commanded.

Hana's sharp intake of breath and the crimson upon her neck drew Radek's gaze. They would spill her life!

"Pray do not!" Radek called. His tone was no longer as even as he wished it.

"I think there may be hope yet," Sir Filip snarled. He moved away from Radek, crossing to the would-be brigand.

"No," Radek seethed, wanting to thrust his sword into the one who lacked honor, but he stayed his hand.

"Do not follow, or her body is all that will be left." Sir Filip walked past the knight and Hana. Then he leaned toward the man and said, "Come, he's just as weak as his father. There is naught to fear."

Dragging Hana along, they moved across the Great Hall and disappeared.

Hana kicked at her assailant. How was she to free herself? She refused to be used in this manner. Now that they did not threaten Radek directly, perhaps they would falter. She might find a way to escape. She only had to watch and wait.

Sir Filip cursed as he led the other knight down a corridor. Where did it lead?

They soon ducked into a narrower passageway. How did they know it was there? But her question was easily answered. Hadn't these men been here for a number of years? Befriended the servants and even the family? Of course, they would know every secret within the castle.

She only need bide her time until she could get to the dagger Radek had given her. When he insisted she carry it after the poisoning, she had thought it an unnecessary worry. But she was beyond thankful in this moment.

Down, down, down, the darkened space that seemed to close in all the more on them. Were they underground? Where would they emerge?

A sound from behind caused the man to jerk her arms painfully.

Sir Filip seethed. "They dare."

"It is not difficult." The knight holding her sneered. "Any fool would know that we intend to kill the duke's daughter anyway. Let us be done with it. Mayhap her body will delay them."

"We need her," Sir Filip grumbled. "We will not bleed her until we are away from this place."

The other man harrumphed. They were not of the same mind. What else might they be in disagreement about? How might that work to her advantage?

Think, Hana, think!

She couldn't put her thoughts together well enough. Perhaps it was for naught.

Pray.

And she did so until Sir Filip moved the barrier at the end of the tunnel, and they stepped out into a forested area. Her heart beat harder. Would they now finish her and be on their way?

"The stables," Sir Filip muttered.

"Why can we not away now?" the other argued.

"On foot? What madness do you speak? We would be dead before we are through the thicket. No, we must secure horses."

The knight tightened his grip and shifted to follow Sir Filip.

Now that her vision had adjusted to the brightness, she saw that they were indeed on the edge of the wood near the stables. These men couldn't get away! She had to stop them.

Sounds of clothes rustling and footfalls came from the enclosure they had just exited. Radek! He came for her. And he would find her. It took all within her not to call out to him. But pride swelled in her chest. Almost enough so that she forgot where she was.

"They are nearly upon us," the man who half dragged her shouted.

"Come, then," Sir Filip called from some paces ahead.

Hana inched her fingers along her skirt. Could she get her dagger in hand? Would she be able to defend herself with it? She had better do so or more than just she could be at risk.

As she worked her hand to pull up her skirt, she looked back.

Radek and several men emerged. Would it be enough to stop these men and save her? Or did this spell certain doom?

Focusing, she took hold of her dagger and brought it close to her body.

"What do you?" the man huffed. "Trying to slip free?"

Then he looked back and noticed how close Radek and his men were. "We are lost!" He stopped and held fast to Hana then called to Sir Filip.

Hana had but a moment to decide how best to use her dagger. She closed her eyes, gritted her teeth, and stabbed at the man's hand.

He howled and released her.

She fell, hitting the ground hard. But she was free. Hana scurried and crawled in an attempt to regain her feet. Only she slammed back to the ground, the man's weight atop her.

"I will take you with me if it's the last thing I do," he seethed in her ear.

She struggled beneath him but could not free herself.

He lifted his knife and prepared to bring it down into her heart.

She grunted and wiggled, but to no avail.

"Now," the man said with a crazed expression about him.

"No," Radek yelled from a distance too great to do anything.

Then the man screeched as a bolt went through his hand and the knife fell harmlessly near Hana's shoulder.

Radek pulled the man off her, and another knight tugged her to safety.

She watched the man who had just held her captive as he rolled and fought, but Radek had the upper hand. Would he work his revenge on the man?

But as Radek subdued him, he called for two others to come and take him to the dungeon. Then he looked to her.

Who had shot the bolt—the one that saved her? She glanced toward the stables and saw the margrave, a crossbow trained on Sir Filip. It was over.

She rushed to Radek, relieved when he swept her into his arms. He pressed kisses to her face, her neck, and then to her mouth. "I have you," he breathed. "I have you."

She embraced him, tucking her head under his chin. "You promise?"

He nodded against her hair. "For now. And always."

CHAPTER 43
PATRICIE & STEPAN

Patricie's heart raced. Stepan had disabled the one guard. And it hadn't been so difficult after all. Would Stepan see this through? Could they actually escape? She had reason to doubt, but there was also every reason to hope.

"What do we do now?" she said low.

He tugged her to himself and flattened against the inner wall. "Shhh!"

What did he listen for? Did he hope to discover where the other mercenaries might be? Generally, they were with the viscount or spread throughout the abandoned village.

The question always in the back of her mind had been about that very thing. Was it emptied of its inhabitants already when the viscount came upon it? Or after?

She strained to hear what Stepan might be homing in on and failed. Her senses were not as trained. For her part, she could only hear her own breathing. Must it come so rapidly? And with such vigor? Was she so troubled by what they had done?

Without warning, Stepan tipped her chin up to look into his eyes. He held a finger over his lips, then moved his mouth to her ear and whispered. "At least two guards down the hall and perhaps two below."

Her eyes closed of their own accord. Was it the warmth of his breath on her ear? Or his closeness? She did not know. But suddenly, their escape became a little less important.

Then he pulled back. When she opened her eyes, he peered at her curiously.

Her face warmed. How could she be distracted at a moment like this? Their lives depended on her ability to assist him. She opened her mouth to apologize, but he shook his head. It would have to wait.

"Stay behind me," he mouthed.

She nodded.

He turned and stuck his head into the corridor.

She took several stabilizing breaths while she waited.

A handful of seconds later, he waved her closer then stepped into the hall.

Sucking in a final breath, she followed.

The sounds of men milling about were only somewhat louder out here. If he hadn't told her where they were, she doubted she could have isolated their direction. Voices told that the men on this level were farther down, opposite of the stairs, and she only heard snatches from those below.

Stepan pointed to the stairway.

She watched and copied his every movement as he led her, keeping his body as much to the wall as possible. As she took up step behind him, she prayed she would be able to stifle any sound, that she wouldn't be the one that gave them away.

How were his footfalls so soundless? Especially considering his limp. Yet they were. Her slippers aided her own silence as she walked. The tension in her wound tight. There was only a passing thought of how wonderful being free of the chain was.

As they descended the stairs, Stepan was careful to put weight only on the far side of the stair nearest the wall. Still, she winced when the wood creaked. Each time, they would pause and listen.

How much longer could she sustain this intensity? But she must —for both their lives. She ran through her head the potential next moves. If they could disable the two or more guards in the large space below, they would then have to get to the stable. And it always had no less than three of the viscount's knights guarding it.

The task truly seemed overwhelming. But she didn't need to overcome it all. Just this next thing—the men in the main room.

They neared the base of the stairway. Stepan readied the stolen sword, preparing for the coming confrontation. This was it.

He led her toward a side wall and motioned for her to stay put.

Patricie gripped his hand. Didn't he know she could help?

But his lips thinned, and his gaze hardened.

She was to stay put. Leaning into the corner just off the bottom stair, she crouched.

Stepan moved beyond.

She peered around the wall, keeping low and watched as he approached one of the men from behind.

A muffled *thunk*, followed by a *thud* told that he hit the man with his sword—likely the hilt—and he fell. Boots scurried upon the wooden floor.

She peeked again to see two men rushing toward Stepan. But he now blocked their access to the exit and to the hope of reinforcements. What were the chances that those above would come to their aid? The longer the struggle continued, the more likely they would.

Patricie scanned the area. Did anything present a good option for her to aid? For she could not just sit and wait for death to come to her.

The counter held a collection of pots. She scooted in that direction while the men were engaged at swords. If only she weren't so worried after Stepan. There might have been the chance she would have stayed put, but not with him unevenly matched. It appeared his skill bested either of the two but not the two combined.

She neared the counter and grabbed the handle of a copper pan. Dragging it with her, she dropped to the floor once again.

This was it. She had to strike and quickly.

Patricie lifted her head again and saw that both men came at Stepan. Which was a good target for her? Perhaps the one closest to her. She skittered across the floor, keeping low. Silence was not as paramount with the clashing of metal ringing throughout the room.

When she was within a yard of the men, she rose. And, lifting the pan over her head, she prepared to strike. One solid hit on the back of the head should do it. But could she?

Stepan growled as he was forced back against a wall.

She had to.

Rushing forward, she slammed the pan against the dark hair of the man to the right of Stepan.

The man dropped to his knees but didn't fall completely. He seemed but dazed.

Must she strike him again? She did. Twice.

Then he landed face down on the floor.

Stunned at what she had done, she neglected that a sword battle continued.

"Patricie," Stepan said in a hiss. "Get down."

Without another thought, she fell to her knees by the man she had clonked on the head. There was a tug within to ensure the man still lived, but she couldn't bring herself to touch him for fear he would come to.

The remaining man was no match for Stepan's skill at arms, even with his damaged leg. And the man was soon a victim of Stepan's blade.

Patricie tensed as she watched Stepan run him through. The image sickened her, but Stepan was by her side in a moment, gripping her arm, dragging her up. "We go. Now!"

Only then did she hear the heavy fall of boots from above. What had alerted the men at last? Her work with the pan? Her victim who had landed so solidly? Or the clashing of the swords?

It mattered not. Stepan rushed her outside. How was he able to move so quickly on his leg? Perhaps it was the same rush that she felt which drove him onward.

Once in the open, Stepan hesitated, but for a moment. Would they take their chances at the stable? Or on foot? She doubted he could go much farther on his leg.

He turned left and moved forward.

But men rushed from the area of the stables, around the building, closing them in.

Stepan dragged her back toward the inn, but the soldiers had rushed down the stairs and hemmed the two of them from behind. They were stuck.

Stepan pulled Patricie tightly to his side. This was what he feared. This was what he knew to be inevitable. Their escape had been a gamble, and they just lost.

Surrounded by mercenaries, he backed up to the outer wall of the inn, fending them off with a threat of his blade. An empty threat. But he would cling to it and sacrifice himself for any opportunity for Patricie's freedom. Though, that too, was unlikely.

"What is this?" the deep voice of his father thundered through the small inn.

Stepan's heart dropped. Did he have to face his father one last time? Could he not let these soldiers kill him where he stood? One swipe of his sword, one lunge into the group of them and it could be over.

But he would then leave Patricie helpless. And that, he would not do. Not while he had breath in his body.

The soldiers at the doorway to the inn moved and allowed space for the viscount to come through. His eyes were wide and his jaw set. It was a wild look about him.

"Stepan, what is this?" But even as the man asked, there was a knowing look in his eyes. Had he suspected Stepan might risk all to free Patricie? Why, then, had he left them vulnerable?

Stepan held his ground. "I do what I must."

"Oh?" He shook his head. "And I suppose then that I will do what *I* must." The viscount signaled to the soldiers behind him. "Take her."

The men rushed in, relieving Stepan of his sword and tearing Patricie away from him.

"What will you do with her?" Stepan demanded, his eyes following the movements of those who held Patricie captive.

"What needs done," the viscount said as if he cared little for it. "What should have been done."

"Father, I—" Stepan protested.

He was cut off as the viscount came closer, staring him down. "I will not lose my son to some Hussite peasant. You will learn your place." Father spun and walked on.

"And what if I won't?" He shocked himself with the words. All he ever wanted was his father's approval, his father's good opinion. Not only had he risked his life, he prepared to also give up on all hope of that. For her.

His father turned. "What say you?"

"I am not like you. I never have been. And I never will be."

Father's brow furrowed.

"So, if you need that of me, you might as well run me through. Right now. As I stand."

The man seemed to consider Stepan's words. Would he truly see his son dead? He walked to the knight who held the sword recently removed from Stepan. Would he do the deed himself?

Viscount Dvorak stepped up to his son, sword at the ready. "If this is truly your choice, then you are no longer my son. You are my enemy."

Stepan's frown deepened. But he puffed his chest out, ready for the death blow.

The viscount threw the sword to the ground in front of Stepan. "We leave this place," he announced. "Tonight."

Then he walked back toward the inn.

The men surrounding them did not appear as if they knew any more than Stepan what this meant.

"Now," the viscount shouted. "There is much to do."

"What of these two?" one of the men nearest the viscount asked.

"They are no concern of ours. Not anymore."

"Shall we finish them then?" the man looked to Stepan as he spoke.

The viscount met Stepan's gaze once more, and then shook his head before stepping within. "I expect to leave within the hour," he called.

Patricie fell. Had she been released?

Indeed, the men attending to them, one by one, moved off after some task unbeknownst to Stepan.

Was it over? Would father leave Stepan and Patricie...alive?

As more and more of the mercenaries left the vicinity, Stepan dropped to his knees by Patricie.

She straightened and grabbed onto him. "Are we truly free?"

He nodded. The sting of his father's rejection still clung to him.

Patricie leaned back and set a hand to the side of his face. "I... don't know what to think."

"Nor I." He gathered her in his embrace once more. "Nor do I."

There was little chance the viscount—for that was what he was now, no longer father—would leave them with a horse. But if the worst of their problems was having to find a way back, he would take it. For they would be alive and together.

CHAPTER 44
THE END

Radek prepared himself for what the day would bring. Had it finally come? Pulling on his best tunic, he thought of his Hana. How was it with her? His sister had taken on the task of getting her ready. Though he did not worry after Hana. For Galina had become more a friend, her animosity put to the side. He only wished he could say the same for his mother.

The door behind him opened. But he didn't need to turn to sense that it was his father. Heavy footfalls revealed that the man drew closer.

"What do you think?" Radek turned to greet the margrave.

Father set a hand to his shoulder. "I have never been prouder."

Nor had Radek. His father had proven to be a strong and very capable leader. It just took time and open eyes to see it. The man's ways were not what was usual, that was true, but that did not make them less.

"Will you rejoin the Hussite effort?" his father asked. A strange question for his wedding day.

"I do not know." He didn't want to decide at all, but certainly not this day.

"General Zizka and his men have run Sigismund out of Bohemia once again. For all the effort the vile man put into it. Apparently gold coin spoke to him more than he realized."

Indeed, Sigismund had allowed his subjects to pay rather than send soldiers to the crusade into the Czech lands. And, in the end, he had no army to speak of. Another well-deserved victory for the Hussites.

But something else weighed on Radek in that moment. He looked to his father. "It seems I owe you not only my gratitude, but my sincere apology."

"Nonsense. I only did my duty."

"No, I do not speak only of your effort to save Lady Hana. Though I am grateful you rescued her from the clutches of those men. I apologize as I am guilty of thinking less of you."

"Oh?" Father eyebrows came together, creasing the skin around them.

"Yes. I said things...and did things that spoke to my dismissal of your ways. Of you. And I regret it."

Father nodded. His features deepened as he smiled. "I understand." The man's large hand landed on Radek's shoulder again.

Radek released a breath that held what remained of his tension.

"Shall we go get your bride?"

Radek nodded and let the margrave lead the way.

Patricie could hardly believe it when she spotted Nemecky Brod in the distance. How long had they traveled? They were weary and worn, but they had arrived.

Stepan had made it. There were times on the journey she had cause to doubt it. But they had.

His arm came around her. "A sight indeed."

She leaned into him. "Yes, it is."

He rubbed stubble against her forehead as he pressed a kiss to her hair.

She sighed. "I could not have imagined a week ago that we would be here, well and whole."

"I know." He continued to press kisses to her hairline.

"What will it be for us when we are in the Hussite camp again?"

He pulled back to look at her. "It will be as it is now."

"But I am a Hussite and you are..."

He touched his finger to her lips. "No. We are the same."

She frowned. He had been disowned. Would the guilt always weigh on her?

"And I could not be happier that we are." His eyes were clear, hopeful.

She arched her brows. "Oh?" Did he speak true?

"I love you, Patricie. And I have never wanted anything more than I want you."

Wrapping her arms around him, she clung to him for a long, beautiful moment.

"Is that a 'yes'?" he asked, a hint of a smile in his words.

"To what?" She settled her head on his shoulder.

"To marrying me." His chuckle warmed her within.

She met his gaze. "Truly?"

He touched her chin, angling her face toward his. "Yes. A thousand times yes."

Rising onto her toes, she pressed her lips to his. When they parted, she set a hand on his face. "Good. Because I do not wish to be parted, Lord Dvorak."

"Never again. And to you, I am just...Stepan."

She melted into him as they faced the last stretch of their journey back—their journey to each other—together.

A servant rushed through the corridor. Karin looked up from her work. Who would disturb her? And why come with such haste?

"My lady," the woman called.

"In here," Karin said, closing the Holy Writ. Her work was nearly ready to pass on.

"A knight has come to see you. He says he bears news of Lord Krejik."

Karin rose and, lifting her skirts, crossed the room. News of Pavel? So soon? "Take me to him."

She followed the younger woman through the corridor and to the Great Hall. Why were there not others milling about, preparing the space for the next meal? For all she saw was a lone man across the room from the stairs, with Sir Marek beside him.

It was no matter. She strode through the space, moving to intercept the man. She inhaled deeply and disguised her breathiness with strong words. "I am Baroness Krejikova. I understand you have news of my husband."

He turned and examined her features. His intensity bothered, but she did not feel unsafe.

"What news have you?" she beseeched him as she glanced at Sir Marek.

"Your lord husband has been captured," the knight said.

Sir Marek gripped the man's arm.

Her hand flew to her chest. "Captured?"

Karin's knees went weak, and she was grateful for the nearby chair upon which she sank. This news seemed strange. The fighting had ended and the crusade in its beginning was naught of which to speak. Was there even a battle? Or did Sigismund and the Royalists' just tuck their tails and retreat?

"Yes. Many days ago, on the edge of Krejik lands." The man did not seem a normal messenger. He delivered the news as if he had a personal stake. What was it? Did he intend to use the news to get close to her? Did he seek to harm her? Perhaps this was a demand for ransom.

"So many days ago? How do you know that?" She narrowed her gaze upon him. "Who are you?"

"Do you not recognize me, Karin?"

Who would address her so informally? It was improper for him to speak to her so.

She stood, lifting her chin and shoulders to tell Sir Marek to see this man to the dungeons. But when she looked closer, beyond the beard and into his eyes, something deep within her crumpled.

Tomas.

Keep reading for a preview of the next book in The Lady of Bohemia Series!

Thank you, dear reader, for reading along with me! If you enjoyed this story, I would sincerely appreciate if you would submit a review. It would mean so much to me!

To read more about these characters, follow along with The Lady of Bohemia Series. Find it at:

https://saraturnquist.com/lady-bornekova-series/

AUTHOR'S NOTE

Hello, Readers! I managed to create another book chronicling the journeys of my fictional characters in this very real place and time.

For those not familiar with Czech history, the Hussite Wars were sparked by the martyr of Jan Hus. Hus opposed some of the practices of the Catholic Church in his day. I generally tell people to think of Marin Luther, but before Martin Luther. In fact, Huss's ideas and writings inspired Luther. Though, Hus himself was inspired by John Wycliff. The Hussite Wars, if I could boil them down, were religious civil wars between the Hussites (followers of Hus's teachings, opposing the Catholic Church in a sense) and the Catholic Church. This conflict lasted fifteen years.

In the background of this book, we see the Hussite Wars progress to face the 2nd Anti-Hussite Crusade and allude to the 3rd Anti-Hussite Crusade. These crusades were blessed by the pope and led by the power-hungry Sigismund, who already ruled much of the Holy Roman Empire. But he was not able to break the hold General Zizka and the Hussites had on Bohemia.

Pavel glared about the forest surrounding him. He had managed to keep himself awake through the night. The eyes of the knight stationed to watch him hovered. Would there be respite? The camp proved more guarded and provisioned than he would have guessed for a man on the run. What, after all, did Ulrich of Rosemberg want? Why had he taken Pavel prisoner?

Would these next hours be Pavel's last? He well knew how little regard Ulrich had for life as the man had snuffed out those of Pavel's men. And now he was here, alone, facing this foe with his unknown, but no doubt nefarious intentions.

Of what value could Pavel possibly be? Why, then, had he been kept alive?

His head bobbed, but he jerked upright. He refused to lose his hold on consciousness. He determined he would not. For should an opportunity present itself, he must be ready.

"If you will not sleep, perhaps we might continue."

The deep voice grated on Pavel's every nerve ending. He cringed and met Ulrich's gaze. "What is it to you?"

"I cannot have you bedraggled. And unfit for travel. My men far too are taxed with your care as it is."

"Pity." Pavel looked to the ground. How could the man think Pavel had a care for those guarding him? In fact, he hoped, watching for a weak spot in the line of guards taking turns.

"Come now, Lord Krejik, it is not so bad. If I thought you would accept my hospitality, I might offer you better accommodations. For what there is to be had, at least."

Pavel fought a sneer. For he did not wish the man to be able to read his every thought. "What is it you want?"

He had asked this question a number of times in the last few days. Each time to no avail, but he could still hope...

"All in good time, Baron. All in good time. There is, however, a bit of a loose end."

Pavel jerked his regard toward the man, but kept his lips sealed.

Ulrich waved a hand and one of his mercenaries dragged another man into the light.

It was one of the knights from Krejik Castle. Did this mean Ulrich had somehow penetrated the walls and worked harm upon his family? Pavel pulled against his bindings.

"There now, Lord Krejik, no need to upset yourself."

Pavel narrowed his gaze and glared at the monster of a man, barely able to choke out the words. "What did you do?"

Ulrich chuckled.

The guard released Pavel's man and he fell to the ground in a heap, clearly having suffered much at the hands of these men who were no better than common brigands.

"'Tis no matter." Ulrich gritted his own teeth. "I will have my due."

What was he saying? His due? Had Pavel or the Krejik family somehow wronged him? Is that what brought the man's ire against him now? And against his father in the year past? Had the man seen to it that Pavel's...that his son had met with a swift end? And what of Karin? Pavel couldn't bear it. He leaned against the oak that had become his prison, his breaths coming fast and hard.

Ulrich smirked, then unsheathed his sword and put a swift end to the already wounded knight.

Pavel wanted to balk at the barbarism, but he was far too stricken after fear over the possible fate of his family. The death of the men with him had been difficult enough to watch, this made just one more tally mark against the hulk of a man before him.

"Nothing? Not so much as a grimace for your knight?"

Pavel would not give him the satisfaction.

"Hm, perhaps you have more mettle about you than I thought."

Pavel clamped his teeth together as he met the man's steely gaze. He would not betray his emotions, would not plead for his life, would not even allow that he died inside at the thought of what Ulrich had done or may yet do to his beloved wife and child.

"So be it." Ulrich spun and tossed toward the guard, "Wake me if he but utters a word."

The mercenary nodded and settled eyes devoid of emotion on Pavel. "Aye, my lord."

Pavel shifted farther away...as much as he could. And worked to shove his pain, his heartbreak, and his fear far within himself. Or he might as well give up right now.

To read more, find The Lady of Bohemia Series here:

https://saraturnquist.com/lady-bornekova-series/

The Lady Bornekova (Book 1)

The red-headed Karin is strong-willed and determined, she tries to keep her true nature a secret to avoid being deemed a traitor by those loyal to the king.

Karin and her father butt heads over her duty to her family and the Czech Crown. However, her heart soon becomes entangled though her father intends to wed her to another.

The turmoil inside Karin deepens and reflects the turmoil of her homeland, on the brink of the Hussite Wars.

The Lady & the Hussites (Book 2)

Karin and Pavel have found their way safely to his parents home, but things are not as well as they seem. There are secrets between them. A wall goes up. And then Pavel is called into battle.

Radek and Zdenek find themselves pulled into the conflict despite their best efforts to remain neutral, while Stepan finds himself ready for bloodshed.

With tensions mounting within their circle and throughout their country, what will become of Pavel and Karin? Can they find their way back to each other?

The Lady & Her Champion (Book 3)

She needs someone to fight for her. He needs to be rescued.

Karin and Pavel have become separated by war and the destruction of his family's home. When Pavel hears of Karin's predicament, he rushes to his beloved. But what will he find?

Will the pull to remain by her side be stronger than the tug to return to the front lines?

While the Hussites maintain a tenuous hold on their lands, will internal conflict prove their undoing?

The Lady & Her Secret (Book 4)

She seeks the forbidden. He struggles to find peace.

Karin and Pavel are at last reunited. But her desire to take on a task long prohibited has Pavel worried for her safety and that of his new family. She strives to keep her work a secret while he faces his own fight-one of a warrior weary of battle.

While the Hussites wrestle with internal conflict, will the enemy take advantage of their vulnerability...and overtake them?

The Lady & Her Mission (Book 5)

COMING SOON

ACKNOWLEDGMENTS

I always want to take a moment to thank those who have been a part of this book's creation. There are many who have asked after my progress and even talked about it with me. I so appreciate my family and friends who let me gush about my characters!

I want to thank Word Weavers Page 32. This group of wonderful people listen to and read my work each month, giving me valuable feedback that shapes the scenes and hones my skills. The encouragement and camaraderie are a bonus!

My craft partner, Kelly Hollman, you are such a gift! Letting me plot and work out the twists and turns...and pouring into my work... can it really be measured? Thank you for your insight and honest thoughts.

Cindy Smith, your feedback has been more valuable than I can say. Thanks for the plotting sessions and all the support you give so tirelessly.

My editor, Julie Sherwood—I can't say how much you enhance my work through your efforts. You have a gift for kicking my butt.

Cora Graphics, you did it again—another amazing cover. Getting a new cover from you never gets old.

VerBull Photography, thanks for getting my "good side" :-)

My husband and number one fan, thanks for all you do that makes my work possible. Thanks for helping my dreams come true more and more every day.

For my sister, you make me want to be better. For my dad, you make me feel so good to have achieved this dream of writing. For my mom, I will love you forever. And for my kids, you give me every reason to smile.

Last, but certainly not least, my readers, you give me a reason to keep writing.

ABOUT THE AUTHOR

Sara is a coffee lovin', word slinging, Historical Romance author whose super power is converting caffeine into novels. She loves those odd little tidbits of history that are stranger than fiction. That's what inspires her. Well, that and a good love story.

But of all the love stories she knows, hers is her favorite. She lives happily with her own Prince Charming and their gaggle of minions. Three to be exact. They sure know how to distract a writer! But, alas, the stories must be written, even if it must happen in the wee hours of the morning.

Sara is an avid reader and enjoys reading and writing clean Historical Romance when she's not traveling.

Please follow along with her journey through her newsletter at: http://saraturnquist.com/list

Happy Reading!

SARA R. TURNQUIST
Author
Editor
Speaker

facebook.com/AuthorSaraRTurnquist

instagram.com/sararturnquist

x.com/sararturnquist

youtube.com/@SaraRTurnquist

pinterest.com/sararturnquist

ALSO BY SARA R. TURNQUIST

CONVENIENT RISK SERIES

A Convenient Risk

An Inconvenient Christmas

A Less Convenient Path

A Convenient Escape

An Inconvenient Acquaintance

These Golden Years

A Less Convenient Arrangement

Ranch Hands Collection (ebook only)

CRIPPLE CREEK SERIES

Hope in Cripple Creek

Christmas in Cripple Creek

Faith in Cripple Creek

Love in Cripple Creek

- Prequels -

Leaving Waverly

Leaving Stoneybrook

RAILWAY ROMANCE SERIES

Laura, The Tycoon's Daughter

ACROSS THE YEARS SERIES

Among the Pages

Between the Lines

STANDALONE NOVELS

The General's Wife

Trail of Fears

Off to War